D1606209

By the same author

ALEC (Alexander Trilogy, Book I)
ALEXANDER (Alexander Trilogy, Book II)
SACHA—The Way Back (Alexander Trilogy, Book III)
YESHUA—Personal Memoir of the Missing Years of Jesus
PETER AND PAUL (An intuitive sequel to Yeshûa)
MARVIN CLARK—In Search of Freedom
ONE JUST MAN (Winston Trilogy Book I)
ELOHIM—Masters & Minions (Winston Trilogy Book II)
WINSTON'S KINGDOM (Winston Trilogy Book III)
THE AVATAR SYNDROME (Prequel to Headless World)
HEADLESS WORLD—The Vatican Incident
(Sequel to *The Avatar Syndrome*)
THE PRINCESS
NOW—Being and Becoming
GIFT OF GAMMAN
ENIGMA of the Second Coming
WALL—Love, Sex, and Immortality (Aquarius Trilogy Book I)
PLUTO EFECT (Aquarius Trilogy Book II)
OF GODS AND MEN (Aquarius Trilogy Book III)
(coming soon)

Short stories

THE JEWEL & OTHER STORIES
CATS AND DOGS
Sci-Fi Series 1
Sci-Fi Series 2

Non-fiction eBooks by Stanislaw Kapuscinski

VISUALIZATION—Creating Your Own Universe
KEY TO IMMORTALITY
[Commentary on the Gospel of Thomas]
BEYOND RELIGION: Volumes I, II and III
[Collections of essays on perception of Reality]
DICTIONARY OF BIBLICAL SYMBOLISM
DELUSIONS—Pragmatic Realism

Poetry in Polish

[with illustrations by Bozena Happach]
KILKA SŁÓW I TROCHĘ GLINY
WIĘCEJ SŁÓW I WIĘCEJ GLINY

INHOUSEPRESS, MONTREAL, CANADA
http://inhousepress.ca

The Gate

Things my Mother told me

A novel by

Stan I.S. Law

INHOUSEPRESS, MONTREAL, CANADA

Cover design and layout by
Bozena Happach

This book is a work of fiction.
Names, characters, titles, places and incidents are either the products of the author's imagination or are used fictitiously.

Library and Archives Canada Cataloguing in Publication

Law, Stan I. S.
The Gate : Things my Mother told me : a novel by Stan I.S. Law.

ISBN 978-0-9780267-0-7

I. Title.

PS8623.A92G38 2007 C813'.6 C2007-906354-3

Published by
INHOUSEPRESS

http://www.inhousepress.ca

Mother

Sculpture by Bozena Happach

Just yesterday he was here. I looked into his eyes.
He was a man now, even as once a child that suckled
at my breast. I continue to see him. Constantly,
by my side. Or could it be just my longing?
Surely he can't be here.
How come I am granted such wondrous illusions?
Shadows of memories of such joyful past?
But surely he is here. And he'll never leave me.
I feel his gentle touch, passing over my brow. . .
No matter how spent, I shall always see him,
Hiding behind my eyelids, days, nights, even now...

From a collection Więcej Słów i Więcej Gliny by Stanisław Kapuściński

The Pale Horse

The Red Horse

The Black Horse

The White Horse

The Pale Horse

"...and name that sat on him was Death,
and Hell followed with him."

The Revelation
of Saint John the Divine

1

The Institute

He sat so well in the saddle, as though he'd been born to ride a horse. Perfectly erect, heels pushed well down, arms relaxed, yet, I knew, he held the steed in a grip of iron. He'd spent a good part of his life looking down at us, mere mortals, so to speak. He'd joined the cavalry at sixteen and stayed faithful to his original 15th Regiment of the Poznań Lancers all his life, even though he later became equally as committed to other Regiments to which he had been transferred all over Poland. He was in active duty until taken prisoner in 1940. By then he was the Commanding Officer on horseback. A sabre poised against the German tanks.

I'm so very tired....

In spite of Jan seeing action on three fronts, the pictures hanging on the wall were only of the intermittent days of peacetime. He represented Poland, ever seated in his hand-made saddle, throughout Europe: from Nice to Stockholm, from Brussels to the Olympic Trials in Berlin. Before the last war, the World War, his study had been replete with gleaming Silver Cups, gigantic Plates and Commemorative Plaques with his name etched in words of glory. He was that good. At various times he'd won all the riding disciplines. From Dressage through Show-jumping to the Cross-country events. He loved them all. But his particular passion was for Show-jumping. Those were the photos he'd kept. Until now. Until today.

I must get some sleep. I am beginning to smell the horses, feel the wind in my hair . . . I must get some rest...

He was a true horseman. A cavalry man. People actually said he was born in the saddle. Whatever that meant. My mother had laughed. "Most uncomfortable," she'd said. This was in the early 1920s. She was a Grand Old Lady. She rode till she was sixty-five herself.

I particularly like the photograph he nailed to the wall over his desk in our bedroom. Yes, nailed. Ten nails along the top, ten – the bottom, six on each side. All meticulously spaced out, to the millimetre. Perhaps he was making sure it wouldn't fall down. I hope that Steve or Bart will be able to pry it off without too much damage. To the photo, never mind the wall. We will never see that wall again. Never.

I mustn't let him see me like this.

The face I scrutinize in the mirror is drawn; the eyes seem to have retreated deeper into their sockets. They look slightly blood-shot, a dull grey, matching my hair which is uncharacteristically dishevelled. Whatever happened to the cornflower blue he loved so much? I've hardly had time to take care of my appearance lately. What with this and that, all to do with his condition, I've had neither the will nor inclination to make myself presentable. Not that I ever took much care about my face. At least no one could ever accuse me of my hair not being orderly. I held it in a tight little bun, keeping it well off my forehead. My relatively rich dark brown hair. Dark-brown went well with the cornflower blue.... He always liked my hair this way. "I'm an old-fashioned man," he always said, "and I like an old-fashioned girl."

He always called me that. Still does. His girl. Or Mimi. Even after I turned eighty. He was ninety then, some three years ago. I can still hear his whisper.

Mimi, my Mimi....

The intercom just chirped at the front door. Steve mustn't see me like this. It will take him about three minutes to catch the elevator and walk down the long corridor. I take a deep breath. The cavalry has arrived.

I press the intercom buzzer.

"Steve?"

"Hi, Mama!" He always calls me Mama. A sort of Polish mommy. The Italians also call their mothers Mama. Perhaps Queen Bona brought the diminutive with her. In 1994 we celebrated the 500th anniversary of her birth. There were some articles in the Polish press. Bona Sforza, the duchess of Milan, married the Polish king Zygmund Stary, that's Sigismundus the Old (...poor girl), in the early 16th century, around the time Copernicus was working on his *De revolutionibus orbium coelestium.* She was credited with having brought in to Poland a number of Italian vegetables. Tomatoes, onions . . . and such like. And probably also the diminutive 'Mama' among other Italian expressions.

Why do I go on like this?

I comb my hair, dab some rouge on my sallow cheeks, and just a smidgen of lipstick to make me look alive. Jan wouldn't like more than a smidgen. He still thinks that I carry the colours of the girl he met sixty-odd years ago.

I open the door just as Steve's hand is rising to ring. He kisses me of each cheek and walks past me without another word. Halfway into the room he turns.

"Dad...?"

"Sleeping. He takes a nap after each meal. He'll be up shortly."

He nods. Bless him. Who else would give up his own marital bed to spend his nights on a settee? Particularly on a settee that's a foot too short for him. Still, he insisted. "You must get a proper night's sleep," he told me. That is why he is here. So that I can get some sleep.

Steven knows his way around. He makes straight for the bar, pours himself a good portion of Scotch. He is about to sit down when he sees me standing, seemingly at a loss of what to do next. He turns again to the bar and pours me a shot of my favourite sherry. Bristol Cream. Jan and I used to sit for hours sipping the rich nectar, playing with the long, winding stems of the crystal glasses Steve gave us for our anniversary some years ago. We always began by drinking to his health.

Today, it is Steve and I who are sharing the sherry. Short, wispy snorts reach us from the bedroom. He always wakes up like that. A few little snorts and he's wide-awake. I down the sherry in a single gulp and get up to help Jan.

"Stop, Mama! That's what I'm here for."

Of course. Force of habit.

Steve is already halfway to the bedroom. It isn't far. These last few years Jan and I have enjoyed a one-bedroom apartment in the middle of Westmount. Close to two parks. To get to *Parc Westmount*, the one closer to our apartment, we walk past the little, meticulously maintained front gardens of the row and semi-detached houses. On good days, when we feel up to it, we venture along Rue Mt. Stephen all the way up to *Parc King George*. It's quite a climb for us, but the view from up there is great. Once we cross Sherbrooke Street, we go past impressive residences, each basking in their own verdant glory. Higher up, only Summit Circle remains – the enclave of the Bronfmans and Molsons. Too high for us, in more ways than one. That's what's so good about Westmount. The trees and the front gardens. They always reminded Dad and me of our own large backyard in London. Before we came to Canada. To be with Steven and Bart. They were all we had. Seems like ages ago.

I hear Dad's voice from the bedroom. "*Das ist nicht gut....*"

These last few months, now and then, Dad's been slipping into German, his memory jumping back some fifty years, all the way to the time he spent as a prisoner of War. The Second World War. The Big One. The one after which Poland lost her freedom. Again.

"They sold us in Yalta," Dad always said. Perhaps he was right. But surely, after fifty years it's time to let it go.

"We wouldn't be here, if they hadn't betrayed us...."

He meant we would still be in Poland, living comfortably on a retired Colonel's pension. Nice if you can get it. We didn't. Spilled milk.

On occasion Dad would also shout some orders in his sleep. At the *Oflag*, the prisoners-of-war camp, he was the high-ranking officer responsible for the morale of younger men. He also had to face the German *Hauptman* when negotiations were needed. It was lucky Dad spoke German. The Gerries needed him as much as his own people did. If it hadn't been for the former, he wouldn't be alive today.

Here he is, emerging from the bedroom. Still erect, still an officer, through and through. His ascot tied to perfection, his trousers pressed to sharp edges. He still irons them himself. He insists on doing that. Only two pairs remain. He's scorched the others.

He comes to me and kisses me on both cheeks then on the lips, as though returning from a long trip. He always greets me this way. Every morning. Now, also after each nap. Or after he's stepped out for a ten-minute walk. Always. For sixty years.

We all sit around the coffee table. Jan fills his pipe. Suddenly, now that Steve's taken over, the weariness catches up with me. Steve half carries me to the bedroom. Within minutes I'm asleep. Fully dressed. I wake up an hour later, undress, go to the bathroom and return to my bed.

I don't envy Steven. For the next three nights he'll sit with Dad for three, four hours. Then he'll help him undress, put on his pyjamas, take him to the bathroom, put toothpaste on his toothbrush, run the warm water for him, hand him the towel, make sure the toilet is flushed. There are days when Dad can do all that on his own. There are other days when he doesn't. You never know. You have to be there. Just in case. All the time. All the time....

I slept like a log, or a baby. Your choice. I'm about to jump up then I remember Steve is here. I linger in bed a little longer. First time in years.

For some reason I feel guilty. Here I am, relatively sound in limb and spirit, and there's nothing more I can do for him. We learn throughout our lives how to cope with adversities, only to become, once again, helpless.

Somehow, this gate is harder to cross than many others. Even before the War, since my early childhood, circumstances caused me to move from place to place, every few years. Then came the War, and between 1939 and 1946 we moved four times. Next came our escape from Poland. Steven and I crossed the border illegally into the now defunct Czechoslovakia, then we travelled on to the ruins of Frankfurt. A sort of resettlement camp, only not under tents but in a half-bombed out building. The allies did a good job in allowing half of it to remain standing. It gave us a roof over our heads, even if we had to sleep on the landing of an escape stair that my thirteen-year-old Steve discovered. The stairs leading up to it were missing, but you could reach it by climbing along the still standing stringer, while holding on to the wobbly handrail. All the rest of the floor space was spoken for by other refugees. Lots and lots of them. A mere month later, the Polish, and probably all the other Socialist Republics' borders were shut tight. We were the last to escape with relative impunity.

A week after we arrived, an army transport of canvas-covered trucks, lorries they called them, took us north to Meppen, close to the Dutch border, where we waited for another transport to take us to Italy. From Meppen, an army convoy of khaki trucks, loaded to overflowing with our meagre possessions, rambled us down through Holland, Belgium, France, then through the tunnel under Mont Blanc, to Torino.

There I met my husband, and Steve, his father – the father he hardly knew. Bart wasn't born yet. He came later. A sort of consolation for the years Jan and I had been apart. By the time we met, Jan had already been commissioned in the Second Corps under General Anders. He, Dad that is, had been assigned to the Regiment of Carpathian Lancers. Always lancers. There wasn't a horse to be found in their vicinity, but the sentiment was there.

In Italy we travelled, in the relative comfort of an aging army Humber, to Milan, and through Bologna, to Ancona and along the Adriatic coast. There, our holidays really started. For the first time in many years I bathed in the sea. A warm sea. In the Adriatic, as blue as the sky above. Porto Civitanova, Roma, Napoli touching on Capri and Pompeii, and finally back to Porto Civitanova, all were but a blur of pleasure, a euphoria of fulfilling a storehouse of repressed feelings. Dad and I hadn't seen each other for over five years. Finally we flew to England. All within a year. In England we moved six times before settling down. For a while. We lived in Bruntingthorpe, Cleethorpes, Grimsby, the resettlement camp in Delamere, then Ruislip on the west of London, and finally we settled in the north of London, a district called Muswell Hill. There we bought a house. A tiny duplex, with us taking possession of the upper level. Our co-owner was also a Colonel, the pre-war *attaché militaire* for Poland in Berlin. I still recall many of his stories sounding like spy novels. Then, at long last, we bought another house, this time on our own. Actually, Steve bought it. We couldn't qualify for the mortgage. But in all but name, it was our house. We became the kings of our own castle. A three-story house on a busy street. Noisy, old, decrepit but our own. We thought that we'd reached our final destination. Not so. Thirty years later we landed in Canada. By then we carried British passports. Both our boys were already there. Or here, really. And in Canada our apartment in Westmount was our third address. Very likely, the last. Or so I thought.

For two more nights I sleep well. I feel almost human. Dear Steve.

My younger son, Bart, has come to help us move. He and his wife, Zina, live well outside Montreal, and so coming to help is an extra effort for both of them. Bart and Steve have gone on ahead to install the carpet in our room. Shortly Annette and Zina would be following them, with us in the back seat, in Steve's old car, which suffers from intermittent hiccups and unpredictable, loud belching. After each mechanical burp, Jan keeps touching my elbow asking if I'm feeling OK.

The carpeting has to be laid on the sly. We asked if we could furnish our room at the Institute, at least partially, with our own furniture, and got permission but they don't know about the carpeting. By the time management sees the carpet, the two hospital-type beds, the desk, a cabinet with eight drawers, two armchairs and some other bits and pieces are already pinning it down. It's also glued to the terrazzo floor. I imagine that for years to come, our room will be the only one with wall to wall carpet.

"But it's unhygienic!" Sister in charge declares.

"But it makes them happy!" my boys counter unanimously.

"But it just isn't done at the Institute!" she insists.

"But we just did it," they state the obvious.

"But...."

Bart and Steve decide that the Senior Sister of the Order of the Immaculate Heart of Mary should have the last word, which they promptly ignore. The damage is already done, and Jan and I will be happy. As for the Sister? Well, she came three times that first day to gaze at the carpet, waved her head from side to side, as though not believing her own eyes. The Sister obviously considers it her duty to make sure that everyone live as long as humanly possible, in dull, sterile, hygienically exemplary conditions, no matter how miserable it makes them.

I try to explain it to her.

"We have no desire to live long, Sister. We have the desire to live happy."

"But...."

The sister is very good at 'buts'. But what about cleaning? But what about the bugs? But what about the extra dust? But what if you spill something? But what will other people say? But... Had I not been brought up right, I would suggest that the good Sister's a pain in the butt. Or buts, in her case. No wonder Sister finds it such an innovation. Nuns don't have carpets in their cells.

Thanks to our boys, our room is definitely a pleasant one. Large enough. The boys have arranged the beds in an L shape, dissipating the feeling that we live in a bedroom. The teak furniture we've brought with us also adds to a lived-in feeling. As do the soft armchairs. Even more importantly, we have our own powder room, which I treasure above all. Having to get up in the middle of the night to attend to one's bladder is one thing. Meeting a stranger in no man's land is another. Sharing the toilet with one's neighbour is not on my priority list.

Steve and Bart have even put up four of our favourite pictures. Three of them were framed by Jan, back in the days when whatever he did was done with meticulous care. He's always been very precise. The pictures look good on the wall. A radio and TV complement the lived-in atmosphere. I must ask for some vases. I need fresh flowers. I've always loved them. They are so alive. It sounds almost like an oxymoron. I still wonder why we have to live so long. Flowers don't, and they are so much more beautiful than we are.

Consider the lilies of the field, how they grow; they toil not, neither do they spin...

It's all right for them. They die in a day or two. They don't have to toil or spin. Here – we have to toil. And move to the Institute.

After the boys leave, we both feel very alone. Dad doesn't say anything, he seldom does, but I can see it in his face. He keeps glancing at me as though searching for reassurance. I just smile back. Then I get up, go over to him and gently stroke his clean-shaven head. It seems to relax him, as it does me. He's shaved his head ever since the First World War when he returned from one mission during which he couldn't remove his helmet for nearly four weeks. His platoon had been under constant enemy fire for twenty-six days. When he did finally take his helmet off, his hair came off with it. Particularly those on the top. The man I'd fallen in love with was stark bald. And now, as over the years, I stroke this smooth, shining dome I love so much. Just to relax him.

The next big event of the first day is our first meal, a supper, at the restaurant. It is really a cafeteria but, thanks to the efforts of a group of volunteers, it is intimate enough to be called a restaurant. Each table has a little vase of fresh flowers. Actually a single flower per table but the idea and the heart are there. We have a solitaire red carnation with a frond of fern. Other tables enjoy an aster, or a tulip. The tables against the far wall all have a single rose. All the flowers look really fresh. There must be some really nice people around.

We've been assigned our own table. One slightly to the side, allowing us a little privacy. Not that we dislike people, but have you ever watched old people eat? The diminution of our senses, both eyes and ears, proves an unexpected blessing. The avid dedication with which most residents attack their food is fantastic. Often frantic. Either praiseworthy or disgusting, depending on your point of view. Apparently, for many of our *comi-voyageurs*, food is the only remaining interest in life.

Although Jan's hearing is shot, his vision remains quite acute.

"Look! Look, Mimi! Look!" He stabs the air with his crooked, arthritic finger in different directions, admiring the inordinate animus with which a number of residents are tackling their generous plates.

"Look, Mimi, she swallowed the spoon!" *"Zjadła łyżkę!"* he repeats in Polish.

This time his voice carries right across the room. In both languages. There is neither animosity nor sarcasm in his voice. Just something halfway between disbelief and admiration.

I can't get the couplet out of my head: *I knew an old lady who swallowed a spider that wriggled and wriggled and wriggled inside her*. By the end of the main course, a spoon displaced the spider.

I know an old lady who swallowed a spoon,
She'll die very soon, very soon, very soon....

Lucky lady. Here, people die every day. This isn't going to be easy. Not dying. Living.

Food, as such, isn't that bad. Not unless you suffer from some disease that puts you on a special diet – like our neighbour on the left.

"They took away all the good stuff," she complained twice, probably glad to find someone who had not yet heard about her plight. "Like salt, or pepper, or anything remotely connected with enhancing the taste."

I nod my sympathy. It can't be easy for her. Her food, like the walls, like the overall colour scheme, must be bland. She still has the solitaire flower. So fresh, so short lived.

"You must keep your strength up, Mister Somebody," I heard a nurse telling someone. Not that there were many misters. Mostly women. Women outlive men by a margin of five to one. At least here. At the Institute.

I don't know any of the names yet. Mr. Somebody had just finished a pile of mashed potatoes soaked in brown gravy. Two chicken legs had already gone down the hatch. How on earth can they do it, I wonder?

For Jan and me, there was soup, a main course of chicken, potatoes and carrots, a side dish of salad. All this was followed by a *créme caramel* with a good measure of sticky, golden syrup. At home we would have shared a single portion between us. Not just the *créme caramel.* The whole meal. Here, we ate it all. Since the war, we both found it difficult to leave anything on our plates. Funny that. The war has been over for fifty years – the habits drag on. They definitely gave us too much food. I suppose food is a substitute for the growing void in their lives. Their past may be rich, but their future is a dark, or grey, insipid void. All the faces I glanced at in the restaurant looked bored. Indifferent and bored. Or maybe just resigned?

Jan is ninety-three and doesn't carry an ounce of fat on him. I wish I could say the same about myself.

"Don't worry," the doctor told me at my last visit. "You are within acceptable boundaries. And you'll lose it later on. We all do...."

At the time I didn't know if I had to die first to lose it. But Jan doesn't complain so I don't worry too much. But the doc was wrong, anyway. There are a number of people here, not just fat but obese. Like rotund barrels on stumpy legs, just rolling along from one meal to another.

"How are you, Mrs. Kordos," Sister asked as we stepped out of the elevator. "Did you enjoy your dinner?" She knew dad couldn't hear her.

"Too much," I said. I was too tired to indulge in a long conversation on the relative merits of dying from overeating or from boredom.

"Must keep your strength up," Sister replied.

"Why?" I asked.

"Oh, Mrs. Kordos, we mustn't talk like that, must we?" she admonished.

"Why?" I repeated.

The Sister was already gone. She was just being polite.

Finally we are back in our room. I need a door to separate me from the rest of the world. I need my own space. Our room looks almost inviting. Either that or we are both really tired. I'm not sure if Dad's noticed that we aren't back home in Westmount. It's been a long day for him. And for me. The goodbyes to the apartment we spent our last ten years in, the journey here, the newness of the place. Even eating in a crowd of people taxed my nerves. I like people one or two at a time. Three at most. Not a whole cafeteria of them. Not when they are forced upon me.

I switch on the TV. The weather forecast for the foreseeable future is bleak. That's roughly how I feel. Goodbye, Westmount, I whisper. I never realized I'd gotten so used to it. It was small, cozy, and all ours. I never thought we would ever move again. Not under our own steam. Perhaps in a wooden box? There have been too many changes in my life. Too often. This time Dad's the only reason. Can't expect Steve to stay with us forever. What an absurd idea! And I just couldn't cope any more. Not on my own. Not with him becoming so unpredictable.

There are just too many Gates.

He is lucky. He's already sleeping in the armchair. His head tilted slightly back, his face relaxed, his arms resting easily on the armrests. I put a large pillow under his feet. He'll be happy like that until he moves to bed. To sleep some more? To sleep: perchance to dream? I used to like Shakespeare. In another lifetime. Now I don't understand too much of his genius, but like him anyway. Back home, before the War, I taught English. The problem will be with the bathroom. My mind wanders so.... Or maybe he'll celebrate the first night here by being well behaved. Like a little child. We are all becoming like little children. We all need more and more help. I wonder how long fate will keep us here.

I still feel so very tired.

Dad opens one eye. "When are we going home, Mimi?" he asks.

***

2

Alzheimer's

There are many names for growing old. There are symptoms and groups of symptoms, to which the mentally overtaxed physicians like to refer as syndromes. What these group names really imply is that the illustrious doctors, who make a very good living from our impending demise, have absolutely no idea what's wrong with us. Or no more so than you or I could observe.

"Really, Mrs. Kordos, we all must grow old, you know?"

"What do you mean, doctor? I came to you with a stiff back. My son it twenty-five years my junior. He's got a stiff back. Are you telling me that his stiffness is caused by old age?"

"Well, really, Mrs. Kordos...."

"Do you or don't you know what causes my stiffness?"

"I would have to use very technical terms, Mrs...."

"Try me, doctor. If you can't cure me, at least humour me. After all, I'm paying you to do so."

"My services are absolutely free, Mrs. Kordos!"

Ah, the glory of Medicare! "No, young man," I put him in his place. "My sons are paying exorbitant taxes so that you can wallow in your ignorance."

I don't know what got into me. Probably, it was looking after Dad. It took a lot out of me.

I recalled watching a snippet of a Sunday preacher on TV. 'Life's not fair,' the plump Baptist asserted, 'but God loves you.'

Well, bully for me, I thought. I don't know why this pearl of wisdom caught up with me at that particular moment. Perhaps life isn't fair, except to the physicians. And Politicians. And, the so-called, academics. Ignorant or not, they seemed happy. Usually at our expense? Bully for them, too.

"Idioci!" I whispered in exasperation. I shall not translate this word. It is the plural of *Idiota*. Anyway, after that little exchange, I thought it best to change physicians.

I told myself that henceforth I shall be nice to people. Only my back had been hurting now for I don't know how long. Cumulatively, it gets on your nerves. And this so-called physician was the third in a row who had dismissed my ongoing pain as a normal part of aging. They were beginning to disgust me. If they don't know, why don't they admit it? There is no shame in truth. There is in taking money under false pretences. They did. All of them, so far. Over these many years, the brightest in a long line of GPs who looked after my husband and me once told me that medicine is not a science but an art. Well, he did not paint a pretty picture.

After all that, I'd clean forgotten that I wanted to ask Dr. What's-his-name about Dad. Dad had been snoring really loud lately and I wondered if something could be done about it or for it. I would probably be told that it was due to old age. Well, my husband is pretty old. And pretty sick. Anyone who knew him before, even six months earlier, could testify to that.

Steve was right. You are not punished for your sins, but by your sins. I wonder where he got that. Or maybe, just maybe, he was getting smart in *his* old age. I was twenty-five when I had him. Now I am eighty-three. I've got to work it out someday.

Senility, dementia, sclerosis of the brain, amnesia, are all their favourite terms. There is also Alzheimer's. It affects over four and a half million people in North America. It is said to be as hard on the sufferer as on the one looking after him or her. It is completely unforgiving. There are no known cases of remissions.

Alzheimer's is a sneaky disease. It creeps up on you. Quietly. Often slowly. In fact, the later it gets you, the slower it creeps along your individual neurons. It also gets the soma – the cell body, axons – the output connections, dendrites – the trees of incoming connections, and synapses – the regions connecting axons and dendrites. But they don't really know what's going on. Really, Alzheimer's is just another big word.

Steven got angry at me last week about being frustrated with doctors and medicine in general.

"Mother! With an estimated 10^{10} neurons, that's ten followed by ten zeroes, or ten billion, and over 10^{14} connections, and a reset time of say five milliseconds . . . that comes to about 10^{16} synaptic transactions per second. That's ten thousand million million transactions per second, Mother. Or ten quadrillion, if you prefer. I don't think any doctor, or neurologist for that matter, no matter how smart, can possibly claim to know what is really going on in our brain!"

Gobbligook to the power of sixteen is still gobbligook, by any other name.

Perhaps the slowness of deterioration is a good thing. If you contract something incurable, wouldn't it be better to.... The Sisters keep telling me I mustn't even think like that. 'Life is a gift', they insist. Again and again. *Ad nauseam.* Some gift if you have Alzheimer's.

The changes in the brain may begin some ten or even twenty years before any visible signs or symptoms appear. There may be some early memory loss, due mostly to brain shrinkage, but most of us put it to... you've guessed it, to old age. We have been trained like monkeys to blame old age for virtually everything. When my legs got tired twenty years ago – that was because I'd walked too far. When it happens now, it's because of old age. I think all the physicians' brains have shrunk!

(No. I won't say the *'I'* word. I shall be nice and forgiving.)

But Alzheimer's is a different story. Its early symptoms really do sneak up on you quite slowly. You experience a bit of confusion, your short memory fails you now and then, you experience some problems with spatial orientation.

You can't find your glasses, the book you're reading, the front door of your son's apartment. Little things.

Then, still in early stages, it begins to affect your personality. Always gentle, always balanced, Jan began to exhibit mood swings, especially when he experienced language difficulties. He seemed unable to say exactly what it was that he wanted. Even as I watched him, he, a Colonel in the army, a man used to giving orders, began losing faith in himself. In his ability to make decisions, to try anything new. Then came other symptoms, even more insidious. The so-called stage two of the disease. I recall Dad insisting on going for a walk.

"Where shall we go, darling?" I asked.

We had at least three favourite routes. Along Sainte Catherine to the Park, along de Maisonneuve to another park located higher up on the slopes of Westmount, and in the opposite direction, also along de Maisonneuve but towards Green Avenue, to peek at antique shops, art galleries and other boutiques along its length. We would stop at the display windows and pretend to try and make up our minds which item to buy. We would have quite heated arguments about our choices. Not that we ever bought anything. Most items were well above our means.

He looked at me completely stunned.

"I don't know," he said, looking both lost and angry. He stood helpless, his hands hanging at his sides, his eyes searching the walls for an invisible answer. When he became more aware of his inability to make the decision, he grew moody, then depressed. All within minutes. Yet he wouldn't openly admit to his new limitations.

"*Choćmy, choćmy,*" he repeated. When flustered, he would slip into Polish. "Let's go, let's go."

He looked and sounded restless. This too was just another symptom. Irritability and restlessness.

It was towards the end of the first phase of his disease that I'd decided to move to a place where he could get professional help. I could no longer leave him at home for any length of time. Had he left the apartment in my absence, he might not have been able to find his way back. It was three days before leaving for the Institute that Steve came to stay with us. Nights only – he still had to work. By then I needed a rest as never before. It wasn't just a question of sleep depravation. My nerves were pretty exhausted in their own right. I no longer knew what to expect. Jan remained kind to me, he hadn't ever raised his voice, not even once, but he was becoming quite unpredictable.

Like that time when he decided to repair the door to the bathroom. It needed a little glue and duct-tape to let the glue set. He used a dozen screws to reattach about a foot of 1/8" plywood to its frame. Perhaps he was expecting a force-eight earthquake.

"Why did you use all those screws?" I'd asked. He used to be a real handyman around the house back in London.

"There was no other way to do it properly," he replied. His face registered surprise as to why I bothered to ask him such an obvious question.

Luckily, I am told, phase three of Alzheimer's will only manifest itself some years into the unknown future. I'll tell you when it happens. Providing I'm still around, of course. We already had difficulties with the Director of Admissions to get us both in together. Paradoxically, thanks to the last few months in Westmount I was in such a state of physical, mental and emotional exhaustion, that they ignored the fact that I was perfectly capable of looking after myself and assigned us a double room when we got to the Institute. This was particularly important to me as, with the exception of the World War II, we had never been apart. But even more important to me was the fact that Jan was fast losing his ability to understand English. Or French. We'd left Poland some fifty years ago, yet his native tongue returned with a force that would not be denied. He insisted that we speak only Polish to him. Although he still read only English newspapers, read both, French and English books, listened with interest to TV in both official languages of Canada, henceforth Polish was to be the only tongue to which he would respond.

Assuming he'd heard you.

That was the other problem. Being completely deaf in one ear, and 80% deaf in the other, I seemed to be the only one to whom he reacted. In any language.

On the third of October, we moved to the Institute of the Immaculate Heart of Mary. And not a moment too soon.

Phase two of the guileful disease manifested its array of new symptoms almost at once. Within weeks the very essence of his personality began vanishing. He became taciturn and stubborn. He refused to acknowledge anyone's instructions but mine. Only Raphael managed to get through his defences, but he and I were the only two people with whom he ever attempted to communicate.

Later he began losing his ability to chew and swallow. His memory, already poor, was now insignificant. He never lost the ability to recognize me, but even his own children he often mistook for complete strangers.

It was about the time when Jan's symptoms multiplied that I began to have dark thoughts. Euthanasia, suicide, either assisted or otherwise, kept knocking at the back of my mind. Of course, I couldn't take my own life as long as Dad remained alive and, I've been told, that the later Alzheimer's attacks, the slower it moves. I've already said that. I must be getting tired. Again. I probably have too much time on my hands. I must try to keep busy. I write little articles to the local in-house monthly publication. I visit those worse off than myself. Yet the thoughts of suicide keep coming back. If only as a problem to be resolved.

I began examining the conundrum from different angles. Although a Catholic, I've read the whole of the Bible. I say 'although' because in my experience Catholics usually don't. They prefer to rely on priests to feed them the juicy tidbit of information. It's just easier that way and the priests don't seem to mind; it keeps the Catholics obedient. Obedient if ignorant. Anyway, the word suicide is not mentioned in all the volumes of the Bible. Who made up the rules then? The Church? When, or more importantly why?

If life is such an incredible gift from God, as the Sisters of the Order of the Immaculate etc., etc. hold, then why do we insist on maintaining it when most if not all aspects that make it so incredible are withdrawn? Presumably by the same God? Has He changed his mind?

I can hear Him saying it loud and clear. "I DON'T THINK I'LL BE NEEDING YOU ANY MORE."

So often, to so many people, right here. At the Institute. Somehow, no one seems to listen. It is almost like a sign of rebellion against His will. 'None are so deaf as those who have ears yet will not listen'. Or something like that.

"Don't tell me when to die! You gave me a gift and now it is mine to keep!"

"PLEASE YOURSELF!"

I could again hear the sonorous answer. He could as well have added: but you're on your own. Something to do with free will? Do we really have free will? Can we die when we want to?

In many cases I've observed, all aspects that anyone could possibly define as life, as a gift, were gone. I mean human life. Imbued with intelligence. Daily I observe people lying on their beds in their own excrement, being spoon-fed, and when that fails, they're put on an IV, like monkeys in a lab. Poor monkeys, we often thought. How come no one ever says "poor people"? Don't we, humans, deserve as much compassion as our cousins, the monkeys? What is this 'life' they're so adamant about maintaining?

Dad is sleeping. His kindly face completely relaxed. He doesn't have any more problems to solve. There is even a suggestion of a smile on his face. He always liked to smile. At least, he kept this little memento.

My thoughts drift back to suicide. Am I sinning just by thinking about it? And then I sit up, as if facing an interlocutor.

In my mind's eye I see an old man with a long grey beard. A man we all admire. Socrates. When faced with the alternative of compromising his beliefs, Socrates unflinchingly drank poison hemlock. Did the fact that he was condemned to death absolve his action?

Then I see another ancient.

Buddha ate tainted rice, fully aware of the ensuing consequences. He knew he would die. The kamikaze pilots are believed to rise directly to paradise. The Moslems and the Christians also reserve this reward, paradise, each for their own martyrs. Even for the premeditated, fully-aware-of-the-consequences-of-their-actions martyrs who die fighting, killing, murdering . . . on the opposite sides of a theological argument. For the countless martyrs of the 'Holy' Crusades, the Jihäds. Martyr-knights, their hands covered with blood to their noble elbows, serving *their* respective gods.

I AM THAT I AM. I am a jealous God. Allah is One God. Presumably so is Krishna. And Vishnu and Brahma and...

I have said, Ye are gods; and all of you are children of the most High.

I pick up a book and try to read. It's no good. My thoughts won't let go of the subject. Again, I see Socrates sitting among his friends, relaxed, fully aware of his impending departure. A sweet breeze is gently billowing their flowing togas. Even as the tulle curtains on my window. I glance at Dad. Are we masters of our bodies? Are we the sole owners of the biological constructs through which we find our expression? Most of us agree that once we come of age, we are, or should be, responsible for the maintenance of our anatomy, for keeping it in a good working order.

Again I turn toward Dad. Till a month before leaving Westmount he exercised daily. He never ate too much. Every day, regardless of weather he took a walk. He stopped smoking some years ago. He exercised not only his body but his mind. He read more than most people. According to the medical profession, he lived the way a man is supposed to live.

He got Alzheimer's.

This alone lead me to question whether we *are* our bodies, our senses, minds, emotions, or are the bodies merely temporary receptacles for our immortal selves. Once again I returned to the most fundamental question of my existence: who am I?

"We are the children of the most High" I hear my confessor repeating the psalmist. I can detect an ill-concealed smirk on his face.

"By we, do you mean our bodies?" I'd never asked him that question. How stupid of me. I wonder what his answer would have been.

If we identify with our physical bodies then our answer is clear. Anyone who witnessed, even on film, a humpback whale feed on whole schools of fish; who saw salmon fight its way up river to spawn – only to be shredded by bears readying for idle hibernation; who saw Alaskan wolves tear apart live caribou... Anyone who heard of masses of lemmings plunging headlong off a cliff, into the sea... who observes the world as it is – can have little doubt about nature's attitude towards killing. If we identify with nature, then we have a right to kill and be killed, by others or by our own hand.

And yet.... What of *Thou shalt not kill*?

Surely, whenever we kill we commit murder. Regardless of circumstances. To protect our wives, our offspring, or even in self-defence. Murder is murder. When we kill we act like animals. Pure and simple. It is not necessary to justify our acts. Hitler never justified his murders. Nor did Stalin. Some tried, after dropping A-bombs over Hiroshima and Nagasaki. They failed. The carnivores live according to the dictum: kill or be killed. Like the wild beast of Africa, Alaska, or the Middle East.

But what if we are not *just* animals?

There is a knock on the door. Raphael puts his head in through the crack to ask if the Colonel needed help with getting to bed. I almost said no, of course not. I'll manage. And then I remembered why we moved here.

"You are so kind...." I say instead.

Raphael is definitely not *just* an animal. What of the rest of us, I wonder? What of me?

He undresses him, takes him to the bathroom, makes sure Jan washed the essentials and then leads him to bed. There was a time when Jan was pedantic about personal hygiene. Even at times when there was no hot water, he would wash himself from head to toe. Literally. Lately, he's relaxed. He's become just one of us.

I watch Raphael lead my husband to bed. A sportsman of international repute being led by the hand. On the other hand, not even a cane is necessary. Raphael's strong arm does the trick. He then raises the metal bars to make sure Dad won't fall out from his bed, unwittingly, during the night. Finally the big man smiles, bows slightly, and quietly closes the door behind him. Raphael did it all without uttering a word. Perhaps he'd communicated with Dad in some other way.

No. Raphael is definitely not just an animal. Yet I return to the unanswered question: what of the rest of us?

Perhaps, some of us have reached a transitional stage. Steve told me that there were religions averring that we were intelligent beings capable of supporting higher states of consciousness. That they professed that we, through no will of our own, are hosts to our souls.

Soul? This concept had never been defined to my satisfaction.

No matter, even if we belong to this group, unfortunately, little changes. Surely we have a right, as hosts, to expel our guests on our own terms. Why should we wait until the visitors vacate our bodies voluntarily? When they do, we surely die, yet they don't ask our permission before taking their leave. We can get it even by committing suicide. We can tell them when to get out! Are we not masters in our own house? Perhaps this is why most major religions justify murder with convoluted arguments which would make Machiavelli proud. Many religions preach that we are hosts to 'our' souls...

My first reaction is: balderdash. A good expression that.

Alas, murder is murder by any other name...

My eyes are beginning to close. I'm holding the little recording machine Steve gave me at arm's length, but my hand is getting tired. I get up, change into my nightgown, go to the bathroom and soon stretch out on my bed. It isn't bad. Not too soft, yet comfortable enough. I can adjust the height of both, my upper body or my legs at will. Tonight I don't. I fall asleep within minutes. When I wake up it's just after dawn. I feel rested. The recorder is lying on my pillow. I don't remember switching it off. Not once had Jan woken me. Not once. I still had so much to be grateful for.

I get dressed and check Dad. He is still sound asleep. As usual, I go to Mass, leaving the door ajar. Nurses will know that I am out, the Colonel in. I'll be back soon. He'll be safe.

I sit staring at the altar. Steve told me that lots of people have, what he called, 'experiences'. At least those who faithfully practiced their religion. I did my best. At least, that's what my confessor, my spiritual director, seemed to have implied. How come I just sit here, pray the prescribed prayers, yet remain detached? Detached from what? God?

I prayed that God would explain to me the problem of suicide. I promised to abide by whatever I'm told. Didn't I always? That's what being a Catholic is all about. You listen, you obey. There is no free will. You had it, of course, you were just not supposed to use it. So what was the point?

When I got back, breakfast had already been served. That was rather nice. We went down to the cafeteria for other meals, but breakfast was always brought to our rooms. It was much bigger than anything we'd ever had in Westmount. Or anywhere. Some kind of oatmeal, scrambled eggs, bread, butter, a slice of cheese and a plastic package of jam. Like they serve on airplanes. One would think that we were in training for the Olympic Games. They sure looked after our bodies here. Body was all important.

Jan ate well. Slowly, methodically and well. He was always like that. Methodical. Even then, when he'd hammered those nails into the head of the door, in Westmount, the nails, or screws, were spaced precisely, exactly equidistant from each other. He was like that. Perhaps you must be to get anywhere in life.

Sitting back, watching Dad, I realized how lucky I was. There were people who struggled with their mate's disease for years. For some reason they couldn't or wouldn't go into an Institute such as this. Later I realized that such institutions didn't usually take in Alzheimer's patients. At least, not once the sufferers reached phase three. Dad was still, what they called, semi-autonomous. He could, with a little assistance, dress himself, eat on his own, walk around. He was ambulatory.

The Institute defined the window of opportunity for entry by the number of nursing hours a resident needed per week. Under four hours, you didn't qualify. Over six hours or so, and you were a candidate for a hospital bed. If you could get one. Between those two you were welcome, space permitting. There was a long waiting list. However, once you were in, you could spend the rest of your days in the Institute, no matter what your condition. And in the case of Alzheimer's, it was always a one-way trip.

Alzheimer's is a progressive, irreversible brain disorder. There are no known causes, no known cures. It reeks havoc with the concept of free will. Alzheimer's is the most common form of irreversible dementia. So much for the concept of hope.

In fact, Alzheimer's seemed purpose-made for curing you of any form of religion. You could hold no faith in ever recovering, you could not be supported by any hope, and you could do nothing to heal yourself. Miracles? I am yet to hear of a miraculous cure of someone suffering from Alzheimer's. I've never heard of anyone with Alzheimer's going to Lourdes and coming back healthy. God knows I searched. I scanned the Church circulars, pamphlets, publications. I looked everywhere. I asked priests.

"Such is the will of God," they told me with a suitably compassionate expression on their faces.

What about *my* will? What about the will of my husband? Does our free will count for nothing? Nothing at all?

WHAT ABOUT MY FREE WILL?

My thoughts began gravitating towards another concept that, of late, invaded my mind with growing regularity. I had to solve it before it would be too late. Before I too would lose any illusion of being endowed with free will. The concept of suicide.

***

3

Father Mulligan

Even in halls crowded with elderly residents hungry for anything to break the monotony of the autumn days, he always stood apart, apparently in a self-imposed seclusion. I'd spoken to him only twice, so far. He was polite, a quizzical smile barely widening his slightly overripe cheeks. They looked plump and rosy, in contrast to the pallor of the rest of his face. Even his eyes, protected by thick glasses, seemed pale, perhaps even vapid, devoid of any distinct colour. The best that one could say of him was that he was round. Round cheeks, round stomach, round from whichever direction one approached him. I suspected that having deprived himself of the joys of matrimony, he had compensated with a little too much food. He left every plate clean. I know, I watched him in the cafeteria, many a time. After all, how often does one eat in the same room as a priest?

He walks to his table slowly, favouring his left leg, putting a lot of his weight on an elaborate cane, probably a gift from one of his ex-parishioners. A short man, considerably overweight, grey wisps of hair on his shining pate, he doesn't – probably never did – have much personality to impose on other people. In the Institute, he's mostly ignored. In the past, the black cassock and the white collar must have given him an air of importance. I imagine that the regalia of his office were very precious to him. Now, for some reason, he shed his outer skin. After so many years, he must have been torn between figuratively towering over others, and the desire to lose himself within a crowd. If he wanted anonymity, he pretty much got it. Most residents didn't know he was a priest, perhaps an ex-priest, although I'm not sure that one loses one's empowerments on retirement. I always thought they were like riding a bicycle. Once learned, they stayed with you for life.

Nevertheless, each time he goes past my table, I say, "Good morning, Father." Or "Good afternoon, Father," or "Good evening, Father."

He always gives me the same reserved smile, a little nod, but doesn't say anything. He sits alone at his own tiny table, as though reticent to share with others his acquired wisdom. I imagine he has wisdom. For a priest to retire he would have to be on the wrong side of seventy if not eighty. For some reason I suspected that there was something very wrong with his peace of mind. He did not give an impression of being happy. 'I bring you tidings of great joy....' I recall St. Luke. Well, the tidings were missing from Father Mulligan's eyes. Or his face. Not even a little joy. I wondered what went wrong with his life.

Then, one day, Sister Angelica enlightened me. She came into my room, closed the door, and stood looking at her feet.

"Yes, Sister?" I encouraged.

Throughout my life many people had chosen to use me as their sounding board. During the last World War, dozens of people lined up for me to write them letters to the Gestapo headquarters, in German of course, in the hope of gaining release for a dear one, a husband or a brother. Women too were arrested, almost as often. My letters? Sometimes they worked. At other times....

God, how my mind wonders....

"I think he's lost his faith," the Sister said, her eyes still riveted to her sandals. She spoke quietly not to wake my husband. Luckily, he slept for hours during the day as well as the whole night. Except when he decided to go for a walk in the eerie hours along the sterile corridors.

"Who, Sister?"

"I saw you watching him. The Father," she said.

There was only one Father at the Institute. At least only one resident Father. The others came and went to administer the Last Rites and, of course, to celebrate the Holy Mass. They left as soon as possible after performing their duty. They weren't too comfortable here. It was too close. Too close to the door to the Other Side. Perhaps their consciences were more exacting than those of average men and women.

"Father Mulligan?"

"Yes, Mrs. Kordos. Father Mulligan...." She looked as though she wanted to say more but wasn't sure if she ought to. Hearsay was not encouraged by her Order.

"You must have reasons for saying so, Sister?" I prodded again.

"He told me," Sister Angelica said simply. "He was crying. He said that all his life he was a good priest, he did his duty, he gave up all to gain his peace of mind but that now it eludes him more than ever."

"He told you all that?" Such soul baring wouldn't have come to Father Mulligan easily. Nor to any priest, I imagine. "But why?" I asked trying to read the expression on Sister Angelica's face.

"I don't know. He'd asked me why I am always smiling," she said, her tone embarrassed even as she smiled.

That could explain the flood of words that apparently spewed out from Father Mulligan. His smiles were only perfunctory, sparse and never without a specific reason. It was fairly obvious that he was not a happy man. He must have found Sister Angelica's constant smile, day and night, no matter how tired she must have been on occasion, profoundly disturbing.

"What did you tell him?" I asked.

"I told him I would pray for him."

Of course. "And?"

"He just laughed."

For the first time since she came into my room Sister Angelica raised her eyes from the floor. She stood, still just inside the door, in an attentive posture of concern. And now she took a whole step forward as though to accentuate her next observation.

"I'd never heard him laugh before," she said. The next moment her eyes found her shoes again. "It wasn't a happy laugh, Mrs. Kordos."

I didn't say anything. For a while the silence stretched. I had time. That was what you had a great deal of at the Institute. Time. It seemed to follow its own rules, here. Usually, it slowed to fill the long gaps between meals.

"So why are you telling me all this, Sister?"

"I thought you might help," she answered simply.

"Why me?"

"People say that you help everybody learn to smile."

In part this was true. I liked to walk the corridors, on rainy days, and ask people funny questions. About anything. Some stupid questions, also. When I see someone looking particularly miserable I ask him or her things like 'did you break a leg lately?' And then I tell them that if not then they had a great reason to be happy. It worked on some people. Most of them. Although it could be just the fact that someone took the trouble to speak to them. They were lonely. Imprisoned in their own misery – self-centred, introverted. They really were sad. Like little children. Perhaps we all do make a full circle.

"I'll try," I said, although I had absolutely no idea what I might do. I'd never consoled, let alone counselled, a priest; nor an ex-priest, for that matter.

As for the elderly being like children, I was wrong. Children may need a mother, but they were fighting to get out of their cosmic eggs. They were on the way out. Expanding. The elderly were inching themselves more and more inwards. Trying to get back the security of the womb they'd left behind so long ago. Only, they didn't even know that that was what they were doing. Still, their private universes seemed to be shrinking at an alarming rate. Like the Big Crunch which must unavoidably follow the Big Bang. One day they would wake up and not be there at all.

It was time to take Dad for a walk. Raphael just peeked in, as he usually did about this time in the afternoon, and asked if the Colonel felt like taking a stroll. The only problem Jan had was with getting up. The rest was easy. There are days when Dad uses his cane only to point out the various flowers as we stroll around the block. On other days, with just a little more cloud cover, he hardly moves. Something to do with the atmospheric pressure? Yet it was always he who insisted on walking. I've never seen a man so determined to remain ambulatory, almost agile, regardless of any pain or discomfort that it might cause him.

"In Murnau, we walked in the dead of winter," he would say now and then. "And we had no coats," he would add knowingly.

I've heard that story a thousand times. Murnau was the Oflag 7A where dad was held prisoner during the last four years of the five-year war. Yes, the Second World War. The prison camp was located in the Bavarian Alps. The winter must have been severe there. His memories seemed to retreat to stages in his life which were etched deepest in his psyche. What a pity, I thought, that it had to be a war. Normally, he wouldn't mention it at all. In fact, only during the last couple of months, his powers of recall had decided to deal with that period. I wonder why. I've managed to dismiss the 1939 to 1945 years completely from my own mind. At least, so far. Who knows what will happen later? After all, Jan is ten years older than I. He has more memories to process.

Raphael helped Jan dress, lace up his shoes, tie his ascot and stepped back to examine his handiwork. In the beginning Dad always wore shoes. He thought that slippers were for old people.

"As good as new," Raphael announced. Then he gave me a little bow and withdrew before I had a chance to thank him.

Soon we were strolling along the corridor. Jan holding my right elbow, just as he always had, these last sixty years. This left his own right arm free to return salutes given him by lower-ranking officers. And the non-commissioned men and women, of course. Now he still held on to my arm on the pretext of looking after me, and his right arm wielded a cane. Lately, the roles had reversed, although he'd never admit it. On occasion, when he missed his footing, I needed all my strength to hold him up. Moments later his sole concern was to make sure that I was not hurt.

As we neared the elevator, we saw Father Mulligan sitting alone on a bench nearby, as though waiting for Godot. He sat there often. No one ever came to see him. One of the Sisters was looking down at him, concern in her eyes. What could she do? Priests counselled nuns, not the other way round. As she looked up at us, her smile returned.

"It's raining, Mrs. Kordos, I wouldn't go outside," she advised.

We hadn't even checked the weather, let alone taken our umbrellas. I too was getting forgetful.

With the drizzle outside, we decided to pace the corridors. Four times one way and four times the other. Then a short sit down, and another tour of four plus four. When we went outside we would stop to admire the beautiful tree at the entrance to the Institute or our nice front garden. Then the other trees, and anything green or blooming in the vicinity. Here we watched people. I recalled our very first walk. After we'd walked for a little while Dad tugged on my sleeve.

"Do you know, Mother," he said confidentially, "this place is full of *old* people!" He pointed with his cane at different shufflers with whom we shared the corridors.

"Look!" He prodded the air missing a man about his age by an inch. "Him, and him and that lady over there. *Sami starzy ludzie!* They're all old!" His voice carried along the length of the corridor. Deaf people often tend to talk too loud. Dad was no exception.

No one appeared to have heard him. I covered my grin with my free hand. I don't think they were all as deaf as he was. They just didn't listen. They probably reserved their attention for the sound of a cuckoo clock that announced their meals. The rest was unimportant.

Soon enough it was time to return to our room. We were getting used to it. We were also getting used to the invasion of the old men and women, mostly women, into our private world. Our private reality. To this day, Jan hasn't accepted it. Daily he would ask me when we were going to go back home to Westmount. Then, he forgot where Westmount was.

As we passed the elevator for the last time, Father Mulligan was still sitting at his self-appointed exile, close to the elevator. Perhaps he was guarding the third floor? Perhaps he inherited some spiritual powers to keep us all safe. Or, perhaps he was hoping that, if he sat there long enough, one day the elevator door would open and someone would emerge to visit him. A member of his family, an ex-parishioner.... but just for him.

As Dad closed his eyes for another nap, my thoughts return to the disconsolate ex-clergyman. What could have made him so sorrowful, I wonder? If Sister Angelica was right, then he'd had a decent life. He may not have become a bishop or a cardinal, but few of us become CEOs or Prime Ministers either. This alone was no reason to be miserable. In fact, according to Steve, it is something to be proud of.

"Power is the very opposite of love," he told me on one of his visits. He likes mulling over such things. Sometimes he writes essays and things and shares them with me. Some of his points are valid.

"The politicians choose to tell us how to live. They do not propose, they impose. I would hate to inherit their karma," he asserted with conviction.

Until he started writing I'd never even heard the word karma. In the Catholic Church we don't get reincarnated. We die and spend our eternity in hell or in heaven. Maybe that was Father Mulligan's problem. Maybe he didn't like either alternative.

Further down the corridor there was a commotion. Two nurses, a male nurse's helper and a Sister seemed to be banging on the door that appeared blocked or barred from the inside. None of us had keys to our rooms, although officially they were permitted to residents who were still in a decent condition of mind and body, and didn't need nurses to look in on them every now and then.

As we got closer, the quartet of staff saw us approaching, straightened up and seemed to concentrate their attention on the ceiling tiles, as though there lay the sole area of their combined acute interest. I pretended not to notice but Jan decided to display, once again, his unimpaired sense of observation.

"Look, Mimi, they are breaking into Mrs. Whatshername's room!"

Mimi was a name he used as a term of affection that belonged only to Puccini and himself. The fact that Mimi, the soprano, did not survive the opera was of no consequence.

As I led Dad into our room and closed the door, the near hysterical banging resumed. I wondered what might have been the problem. I soon learned.

"It's Mrs. Merryweather, Mrs. Kordos," Sister Angelica said closing the door behind her. She must have thought that we, or at least I, deserved some explanation for the bedlam taking place but three doors down the corridor.

"Is she all right?"

The Sister smiled. Didn't she always? This time there was a surreptitious twinkle in her eyes. I didn't push, but with the tedium that filled our days, anything as loud as what was taking place was a welcome change. Don't ever believe that Senior Citizens want peace and quiet. Most of us are bored stiff. Give us hell anytime!

"It's the second time, Mrs. Kordos. Mrs. Merryweather has barricaded herself in her room."

"Is that dangerous? She seems to be in a half-decent state of health...."

"It's not dangerous for her...."

This time Sister Angelica began to titter. Her titters were replaced by chortles and soon matured to a distinct protracted giggle. I was about to point out to her that nuns don't usually giggle when I remembered the admonition I'd received at my last confession about judging others. My restraint was richly rewarded.

"Shall I tell you the whole story, Mrs. Kordos?" The nun sounded as if she needed permission to do so.

"Sit down, Sister," I pointed to the armchair. As usual, not that she did so that often, she sat at the very edge. As our chairs were on tiny wheels, I was afraid that one day the chair would slip backwards from under her. However, in expectation of a possible new diversion, and feeling just a little guilty, I said nothing.

"You must promise me that you will not repeat this to anyone, Mrs. Kordos."

This, I knew from past experience, meant that everyone already knew about it. I nodded.

"Mister and Mrs. Merryweather had a double room here, at the Institute, until just last year. Rather unfortunately, last December, Mr. Merryweather died."

"Yes? That's what we all come here for," I prompted, "the sooner the better," I added to state the obvious.

"I wish you wouldn't talk like that, Mrs. Kordos. You know how much we would all miss you...."

"Get on with the story, Sister."

"Well, Mr. Merryweather died out of turn. You see, he was about eight years younger than his wife. And he died of a heart attack."

"So?" Every next day someone died at the Institute. This was, after all, an Old People's Home. By any other name, people died. Often.

"He died with a woman in his bed," the Sister concluded looking down at her toes.

"Poor Mrs. Merryweather," I commented in an appropriately sorrowful tone.

The Sister said nothing. As the silence stretched, I began to wonder if there was more to this story. I had time. I could wait. I felt sure the Sister would get on with it in her own good time. I got up and covered Jan, sitting on the other armchair, with a blanket. He seemed to be drifting off. I knew he couldn't hear any of this.

"But . . . it wasn't Mrs. Merryweather," the Sister said at long last.

"Mrs. Merryweather wasn't in his...." And then it hit me.

"How old was he, Mr. Merryweather, anyway?"

"He was eighty-two when he died," the Sister said softly. "It was the third time."

"Third time he..."

"The third time he got caught, Mrs. Kordos." Sister Angelica's voice was barely above a whisper. And then she added so quietly I had to lean forward to hear her. "With a different woman."

"Wow!" That would be what my son would have said. How appropriate, I thought. "Wow," I repeated. I was at a loss for any other words. "Wow...." I repeated, one for each *inflagrante delicto*.

"You promise you won't repeat this to anyone, Mrs. Kordos? You did promise."

I don't think the good Sister was worried about the moral fibre of the residents as much as for her own reputation. Gossip, and all that. I crossed my fingers and held them up above my head. This seemed to have reassured her. She got up to leave.

"Sister Angelica," I waved her down. "Mr. Merryweather is dead. What is Mrs. Merryweather doing barricading herself in her room?"

"She's not alone in there, Mrs. Kordos."

"Not alone?" I must have had a stupid expression on my face.

"Ever since Mr. Merryweather died, Mrs. Merryweather is trying to get back at him. As sort of posthumous revenge."

"I don't understand...." I confessed.

The Sister looked distinctly uncomfortable. She looked over her shoulder making sure the door was still shut. Suddenly it seemed very quiet. Even the noise outside had subsided.

"She is attempting to seduce any man she can, Mrs. Kordos." She glanced at my husband. "I thought perhaps you should know."

"Any man..."

For a moment I didn't put two and two together. Then I couldn't help laughing. I just couldn't imagine Jan with another woman, never mind Mrs. Merryweather. And then it struck me. By that time I knew most men on my floor by sight if not by name.

"And who is the lucky guy this time, Sister Angelica?" I asked still laughing.

"It's Father Mulligan, Mrs. Kordos. It's poor Father Mulligan...." And Sister Angelica, suddenly in great distress, left my room. I wasn't sure if it was sinful that I couldn't help laughing.

***

4

Sister Angelica

"Curitiba is to Rio de Janeiro what Richmond is to New York. Nothing much, not really, only, well . . . in reverse, and only in terms of climate." She seemed a little at a loss for words in her desire to share her memories. After studiously looking at her shoes, she looked up at me, then took another deep breath. "Curitiba is as much cooler than Rio as New York is in relation to Richmond," she explained triumphantly. And then she added, "I've visited all four. I know."

I nodded wondering where it was all leading. She seemed reassured.

"Founded in the 17th century as a gold-mining camp," she continued, "Curitiba became the capital of the State of Parna in 1854, and grew rapidly after 1940 when the Second World War provided immigrants willing to rough it out. Its population grew to over 1.7 million and was made up of several mostly European cultures that originally arrived in the late 19th and early 20th centuries."

For the first time Sister Angelica left the edge of my armchair and began pacing the room. Four paces toward the window, four paces back to the chair. It was more than evident that she was proud of the research she'd done about her place of origin. At least, I suppose, that's how she knew so much.

"Apart from its magnificent Metropolitan Cathedral erected in 1894, Curitiba's other claim to fame consists mostly of its twenty-six parks of well-preserved flora with richly diversified fauna. Among the latter, capivara, the world's largest rodent, stands supreme."

She must have learned those lines by heart. Her grammar was perfect. This time her smile got broader. She evidently thought the extra-large rats, for surely that's what capivaras must have been, were a point of pride.

"In the *Sector Historico de Curitiba* there are countless churches, mostly crowning the many hills which undulate like a mighty ocean swell throughout the city. The churches attest to the powerful influence the Roman Catholic Church had on the city and its people."

I became sure that, for some reason of her own, she'd learned to recite these facts about Curitiba. This wasn't the way she talked normally. This time she also looked up daring me to deny her observations. I had no intention of doing any such thing. In fact, I had no idea why Sister Angelica chose this moment, a good six months after Jan and I moved to the Institute, to share her memories with me. In fact, what she told me sounded more like a lecture than memories. The truth came slowly, as if torn out of her innards at some considerable discomfort.

"It must be a beautiful city," I put in just to register my interest. Sister Angelica's smile broadened. Evidently she thought so too. Then why leave it, I wondered?

To cut the story short, Curitiba, it transpired, was the city to which Sister Angelica escaped after fleeing the Convent of the Franciscan Nuns in Paranague, wherein, after more than seven years of dutiful obedience, she hadn't spent more than a day at a time outside the basement laundry. Originally she had escaped from her home. Being the youngest of fourteen children, she was practically ignored by her parents, who could never afford to educate both girls and boys. The boys won. They had to, to earn money for their own families. Her escape had been motivated by a strong desire to learn to read and write. Not literary works, but street signs. And the inscriptions in the church. Or anywhere. After seven years at the Convent the most they had taught her was to read the labels on the lingerie, habits, bed-sheets and such like that she washed by hand, the old-fashioned way, for the nuns and sisters who seemed to have spent their time mostly in prayer.

There was one other reason, she confessed. "I swore to myself that I would never again be hungry," she said looking me in the eyes.

"And you chose a Convent?" I asked in disbelief.

"Have you ever seen a skinny nun?" she asked before biting her lip. "I mean..."

This was unfair. In spite of her nondescript age, Sister Angelica would, I felt sure, look good in a bikini. Not that I was ever likely to find out. Or want to. Although Jan might still.... Jan was an expert on horses' and women's ankles alike.

"Give me a good ankle, and I'll give you a good leg," he'd announced about sixty years ago and at least sixty times since. To his detriment, the only good leg he ever saw in close-up was mine. At least he got both my legs, not to mention....

I glanced at my husband, fully clothed, stretched out on the bed. Right now he was exploring the never-never land.

Sister Angelica told me her story with a lingering, somewhat distant smile, dry eyes, but with a look that was close to despair. Strange about her eyes. Their blue suggested the serenity of a summer's sky, yet there was a veil implicit in the way she tended to look at her feet.

"You wouldn't believe it, Mrs. Kordos, after seven years I couldn't even write a letter to my mother. And they wouldn't even let me go to my father's funeral." This time a solitary tear did find its way down her cheek. She didn't bother to wipe it. She must have been used to weeping, alone, in her cell, assuming she had her own cell to cry in. A sort of solitary confinement.

"Perhaps they didn't know about your father's death?" I tried.

"Perhaps. Not that it would have made any difference. The Lord giveth, the Lord taketh away, they would have said. Ours is not to reason why.... It was all about God's mysterious ways. They said things like that. They shared them with me after a twelve-hour day I'd spent in the laundry. It didn't do much for my aching back."

There was no animosity in her voice. Even when an unwitting tear appeared, the gentle smile never left her lips. Only her eyes told a different story. I knew that, at the time, she must have been a deeply broken woman. She may well have lost her faith – for a time.

"On the seventh anniversary of my incarceration I ran away. I walked for eighteen hours, along a hilly road to Curitiba. You won't believe what a beautiful walk it was. Roadside flowers, long vistas. No walls. No steam or hot water. The air was so pure. I didn't know what to do with my hands. I waved them all around me. I felt free."

I asked how come Sister Angelica had so much time to spend with me. She confessed that it was her day off. This was how she spent her free time. She visited people at the Institute. Mostly those who never had any visitors. I must have been an exception.

"It's the only time I don't have to rush off on some errand," she explained.

Why me, I wondered. I had two boys visiting me regularly and the company of my husband. Not that Dad provided any intellectual companionship anymore. She must have read my thoughts.

"You are the only person who understands what I am talking about, Mrs. Kordos. The other residents...."

I understood more than her words. People who are lonely, like these residents, want to talk about themselves; they have no interest in other people's problems. The problem was, they had nothing to say. They were already suspended in a limbo of no-mans' land. A mental vacuum. It was a lonely place.

"I really don't know what I would do without you, Mrs. Kordos. You are the only woman I can talk to. The other nuns, well, they are nuns. They've all led such sheltered lives. They'd never run away. From anywhere. Or anything. Do you think I was a coward, Mrs. Kordos?"

Rather than answer her, I got up, walked to my wardrobe where I kept, hidden from prying eyes, a half-full bottle of Bristol Cream Sherry. Sister's question about cowardice reminded me of the proverbial Dutch courage. I looked at my husband. He was still in his private realm, regular breathing spoke of a deep sleep. I poured out two glasses and handed one to Sister Angelica.

"What's that, Mrs. Kordos? It's not alcohol, is it?"

"It's Dutch Courage, Sister. Try it."

She did. Her eyes widened in surprise. She liked it.

"We had something similar in Curitiba," she said.

"We?" I prompted.

All of a sudden Sister Angelica looked flustered. She measured me with her eyes, evidently torn between a desire to share her memories and her need for them to remain her own. I waited. For a little while we sat quietly; I on a straight-backed chair at my little desk, the Sister on the very edge of our only remaining armchair. The other one was full of pillows we used to prop Jan up when he woke up and wanted to watch TV. That's in addition to the bed being adjustable.

Sister Angelica was a small woman. She must have been in her middle fifties. No more than sixty-two or three. Nuns, for some reason, always seem to have good complexions that make their age misleading. And I couldn't tell what colour her hair was as her wimple covered it completely. The white, flowing habit gave her a peculiar grace. Both, when sitting and standing. There is a lot to be said for sacerdotal garments. They certainly enhance the wearer.

Her smile, I already knew, never left her face, and yet it seemed genuine. It wasn't put on for the benefit of others. She really seemed to enjoy her life here, at the Institute. She was both popular and respected, which could not have been said for all the nuns. Some appeared to be holier-than-thou. For the most part, the nurses avoided them. But when they were in trouble, or something really had to be done, they would all run to Sister Angelica. She seemed to be a messenger of wisdom and common sense. She also got things done.

"My husband," she said after a longish pause.

I topped up her little glass. I suspected that she was going to need it.

"When I said we, I meant me and my husband," Sister Angelica explained.

"Oh," was all I could comment – only it came out like an "Oooh?" with a big question mark.

"I married a priest," she said, driving the nail into the coffin.

I refilled my glass. It was time to look at my own feet and wait for her to continue. For a moment I was worried that I might not have enough Sherry for the whole story.

"We met in Curitiba. Frank, named after St. Francis of Assisi, had a small parish, on the outskirts of town. He also looked after a primary school. Later on, I would take the boys and girls out to show them their hometown. That's why I learned so much about Curitiba's history."

Again, I detected a note of pride in her voice. Or it could have been her love for the days gone by. I nodded. Somehow she must have learned to read and write.

"As fate would have it," her eyes drifted away to those forgotten days, "he found me crouching against the church wall, after my eighteen-hour jaunt from Paranagua. I must have been near invisible. A white bundle against a white, stuccoed wall. I still had my one and only habit on. I'd fallen asleep when I felt a hand on my shoulder. He took me in, fed me, and allowed me to sleep on an upholstered church pew. I'll never forget waking up in the church the next morning. I was sure I'd died and found myself in heaven."

There was another pause. We both sipped the Sherry. It wasn't the question of alcohol, but to me, Bristol Cream gave a sense of well-being. Of being pampered. I used it sparingly lest it lose its magic power.

"I had nowhere to go. I couldn't return home. With father dead, and most of my siblings married and busy raising their own families . . . I was the only failure. Remember, I still couldn't read or write. I just couldn't face them. Another escape, I suppose..."

"I am sure Father Francis didn't blame you for staying a while," I opined trying to put myself in his shoes.

"He didn't. He had no housekeeper. Couldn't afford one, I suppose. He did everything himself. It was a small parish. Small and poor, even by Brazilian standards."

I've never been to Brazil, but I've read about the *favelas*. The slums scaling the hills of Rio were reputed to be among the poorest districts in the world, matching those of Culcutta. Brazil was still essentially a two-class society. There was no middle class to speak of.

"I began doing odd things for him. Repairing a tear in his trousers, darning his socks, sweeping his room, then the whole church. I also began learning how to cook. He kept telling me I didn't have to do any of that. Finally we struck a bargain. I would, at least for a while, do his domestic chores, while he would teach me to read and write. At long last, I would become the only literate female member of my family."

I could picture the two lonesome souls sitting on a church bench trying to read a psalmist or some other prayer book. I doubted that the priest could afford any educational textbooks for tuition. He must have been pleased with such a willing pupil. Then I remembered she'd mentioned a primary school. There must have been primers. God works in mysterious ways, I thought.

"How old were you then?"

"I was twenty-three, Mrs. Kordos. I was twenty-three and a half when I lost my virginity."

I kept quiet.

"No one knew. We continued, each with our duties, until my contours became hard to conceal. I was nearly eight months pregnant when Frank first wrote to the bishop asking to be relieved from his parish. By then, neither of us could imagine being away from each other."

"You'd both tasted the forbidden fruit," I murmured.

"Yes, Mrs. Kordos." She'd heard me. "We'd both tasted the forbidden fruit. We'd both tasted the wonder of human love."

I took a deep breath. For some reason Sister Angelica did not look very happy.

"He was refused," Mrs. Kordos. "The bishop told Frank that accidents happen and His Excellency was willing to put me into a home for wayward women. No questions asked."

"How kind," I let it slip out. She ignored me.

"The correspondence with the bishop continued until I got pregnant the second time. Julio was already eighteen months. He was such a beautiful boy. Still is. He works in São Paulo as a computer engineer. He has two girls of his own.... Both girls are going to school," she added proudly.

"So what happened?"

"I gave birth to a beautiful girl. Frank baptized her Juanita. She's in Europe now. I might never see her again. She's a Catholic," she concluded ominously as if it was some sort of sacrilege. "The Catholics are not very forgiving," she tried to explain.

I let that pass. Sister Angelica's concept of Catholicism must have undergone many metamorphoses. "And what did His Eminence have to say about it all?"

"Nothing changed. I remained wayward, Frank would be given all the assistance necessary to extricate himself from his peccadilloes. That's what the bishop called them in his letters."

"And...?" This was becoming fascinating.

"Frank was of Polish origin, even as I am. He'd written to the Pope, who, at the time was also Polish. Karol Wojtyła. Frank had written in Polish throwing himself on the Pope's mercy." A slightly naughty smile began to play about Sister Angelica's lips. "The Pope referred Frank to the bishop's offer, and pointed out that Frank had been granted total absolution. He was offered a new parish, a larger one, far enough away from the people who might have accused him of past malfeasance. I had to look up that word. I never thought of myself as malfeasance."

I knew something else was coming.

"Well, Frank wrote back to thank the Holy Father. He asked, in all humility, if the Holy Father would be so kind as to make sure that the new parish would be big enough to support both his children."

I gasped. "He said that to the Holy Father?"

"Within weeks Frank got his dissolution of sacerdotal vows. Apparently, almost fifty percent of priests in Brazil suffer from the same problem," she added knowingly.

"Problem?"

"Malfeasance," she explained.

"Oh," was all I could muster. "Ohhhh...." I emptied my lungs of air as quietly as I knew how.

We'd run out of Sherry. It must have been a coincidence but the Sister got up to leave. "I mustn't go on like this," she said glancing at her watch. "My goodness, I promised to drop in on Mrs. Merryweather."

That reminded me. "How is Father Mulligan?" I had to ask.

"He'll live." Sister Angelica smiled her most radiant smile. "There was no malfeasance," she said as she closed the door quietly behind her.

But there had been consequences. The whole staff had been told to always keep a keen eye on both, Mrs. Merryweather and, in a protective way, Father Mulligan. He needed protection. He didn't seem attuned to the secular behaviour of the residents of the Institute of the Immaculate Heart of Mary. Some hearts appeared to be more immaculate than others.

Sister Angelica took particular interest in protecting Father Mulligan. She had more experience in clerical weaknesses than anyone at the Institute. She knew how very delicate the celibate condition was. Imagination is a two-edged sword. No matter what their age, the priests were apt to imagine more about their sacrifice than others, the non-celibates, could possibly imagine.

Usually, by the time a boy reaches, say, twenty or twenty-five years, he is well aware that sex is not all it was purported to be. That, more often than not, the expectation is greater than the fulfillment. When young, we all seem to be so much more physical. The mind, even the emotions, seem to take second place. Unless we come down from the Pale Horse, we get nowhere. We die having left nothing behind. Like animals. Except progeny. But doesn't every animal do that? The rest of his life, unless a man is desperate to build up his fragile ego, he tends to sate his desires in slightly more dispassionate ways. Or perhaps the ways are more passionate but not in the physical sense. Unless he truly loves a particular woman. Then we learn to give, rather than take. Then sex is just part of that which unites us. Someone said that in marriage, if sex is good, it is no more than ten percent of the marital equation. When it's bad, then it leaves a gaping hole in their search for each other.

Sister Angelica knew all that. She knew it from her own experience and from having a keen eye. She knew how much help Father Mulligan might need. She also knew that Mrs. Merryweather's appetite had nothing to do with sex. It was all about getting even. It was purely emotional. *La vendetta*, they would say in Curitiba. How she must have loved that town.

I never imagined that, approaching my ninetieth year, I would learn so much about sex. And that, from a Catholic nun.

***

5

The Messenger

For once, the Romans and the Greeks were in agreement. *Archangelus*, in Latin and *Archangelos*, in Greek meant the same thing. The words were identical but for one letter. English was close enough too. And Archangel, meaning Chief Messenger, testified to his function in all three languages. I like that. It gives it substance. Makes it real.

To tell the truth, I think that all of us are messengers. Perhaps not chief, like Michael or Gabriel or Raphael, but messengers nevertheless. We all deliver things to others, other people, that are not really ours to start with. We give presents at Christmas, presents produced or manufactured by other people. We offer 'our' advice, that is usually someone else's wisdom that we overheard or read about. My son gives me flowers, weekly, just to make my room, sorry *our* room – though father is mostly asleep – more joyful. Yet, Steven doesn't make those flowers. They flow from the abundance of nature.

Perhaps Steven's wife is different. Not quite a messenger. What she brings with her is a smile, a ray of sunshine that originates within her. You cannot buy it, steal it, acquire it by hard work or by disorderly means. It flows out of her heart, or what some call, her soul. Though with Steven around, even soul is a questionable concept. My son has conducted some deep studies in the field of the esoteric. Actually I usually call it metaphysics. He calls it reality. Just reality.

"My soul, mother," he told me, "is little more than my subconscious. The sum total of acquired knowledge since I was an amoeba. Whereas Soul, with a capital S, is not mine. It is a quality, not a thing. It is the attribute of the Infinite that enables It to individualize Itself."

Steven is like that. He always veers into some uncharted waters, some arcane subjects, whether prompted by everyday events or simply, out of the blue.

"That's where my ideas come from, Mother, out of the blue," he told me, a far-away look creeping in his eyes.

Once again I've written 'mother', but actually he invariably called me Mama. A Polish affectation. *Mama i Tata* – Mom and Dad. The rest of his postulations were usually in English. When I make notes after the fact, or record our conversations, the two often get mixed up. This is why, now and then, my times get mixed up. When I feel very strongly about something, when I still feel it deeply, I seem to recall it in the present tense. In the now. When I recount things from the perspective of time. I drift into past tense. Somehow it makes sense to me.

Steve is a happy man. He believes that everything that happens, no matter what it might be, is a good omen. Good for himself and the world at large. He believes in the Benign, the intrinsically Benevolent. Whatever It might be.

"There is some good in everything, even as there is no such good that doesn't hold a smidgen of evil. We live in a world of contrasts," he often repeats. "We learn by observing the opposites." He must have read all that somewhere. Since childhood, he's been an avid reader.

I wish there were some opposites in *my* immediate environment. There is instead an all-pervasive sameness. The same drab walls with pale, pastel colours, the same terrazzo flooring looking like a milky way, only with stars being black instead of white. Dying stars? Little dark spots receding into the distance. Forever?

A mere hundred paces seem like forever lately.

Steven is a messenger of stimulation. Not so much physical, we have our daily exercise programs, but mental. After he leaves, I often spend hours thinking about some things he's said. Like this stuff about soul, with a little s. Is it all we are? The sum total of memories spanning millions of years into the past? Are we just mobile robots, designed to enable our genes to seek food in different locations?

"We are all messengers," he had been the first to say it. "We are instruments for the Infinite to deliver Its messages to the world. We don't matter much. The message is all important."

He would express such sentiments in an offhanded way, take his wife by the elbow, and leave without another word. She would take care of the pleasantries.

"Bye, Mama. Say bye to Dad. We'll see you real soon..." Her smile lingered behind. Dad was asleep already.

She also called me Mama. I liked that. I never had a daughter of my own. At least, not for any length of time. My own girl died when she was only eleven months old. I told you about her. In those days we didn't have the benefit of antibiotics. Children died a lot more often than now. So did old people. In fact, most of them had been much younger than I am now, when they crossed the Gate. The Pearly Gates – if they were lucky.

Perhaps Annette is a messenger after all. A messenger of joy. Perhaps she draws upon the inexhaustible source and spreads it freely, generously, wherever she goes. Someone once said that joy is an amalgam of love and life. If you mix the two in just the right proportions, you get joy. Annette is a very good mixer.

There is one other messenger who often holds my attention. His name, coincidentally, is Raphael. He is not even a nurse, but a nurse's helper. He continues to lift people by hand, physically, even though they installed hoists to protect the staff's fragile backs. Many residents need lifting. In and out of beds, transfers to wheelchairs or even just to cleanse them from their incontinence. Sometimes he, Raphael, even apologizes for doing his chores, as if we could cope without him.

Raphael's head fits just below the top of the door, where he would stop before entering, as though asking for permission. He never came in without being invited. Unless he comes in when we're sleeping, of course, to check on us, but how would I know? When sleeping?

The first few months, he'd only come to help father out of his bed. Once up, Dad could make do on his own quite well. He would shuffle to his armchair, or pick up his walker and accompany me along the corridor. We called it the morning, or the afternoon shuffle. In the early days, we would also take the elevator together to the cafeteria, or even go out on a short saunter around the block. After the first winter, his mobility suffered a setback. He broke his hip. Six weeks later he was back in our room, but they decided to keep the rails up on his bed. That was when Raphael came into his own. He would help Dad in such a way that Dad imagined that he'd done the getting up all on his own.

But what really caught my attention about Raphael was the air he exuded. There was an undefined serenity about him that must have veiled his true feelings. He acted as though cleaning the incontinent, dealing with the aggressive Alzheimer's patients, doing the most unpleasant chores imaginable, were all his favourite hobbies. I didn't mention it before, but father's Alzheimer's had changed the most gentle of men into a fairly difficult one. Without any apparent reason he would turn on people, he would raise his voice, refuse to cooperate. All this without any warning. One minute he was a gentle, smiling old man, a perfect 'officer and gentlemen', the next he could shout at you. In German, of all languages. When he was well, some years ago, he could speak four languages fluently. To me he spoke mainly in Polish. German he used only for shouting. I imagined that neither Ghoete, Schiller, nor Thomas Mann would like that at all.

Only, Dad never raised his voice to Raphael. Nor did he to me or Steven; but after all, we were family. But Raphael? Other nurses got an earful on many occasions – but never Raphael. Just the opposite. It seemed that with him, father really tried hard to cooperate. As best he could – which wasn't much lately. Nevertheless, with Raphael, he always tried.

He was a strange messenger, our Raphael. If angels were messengers, then Raphael, as messenger, would qualify to the highest rank. The Archangel Raphael. I don't know if angels are large, but if they are, then Raphael also qualifies on that score. He's huge.

Today Jan wasn't feeling well. Raphael asked me if I would like him to take Dad down to the chapel in a wheelchair. I asked, in turn, if he, Raphael, was going to Mass himself. I didn't want to trouble him unnecessarily. In a pinch, I could push Dad's chair myself. Raphael gave me a strange answer.

"I do not feel the need, Madam," he often used the French form of address.

"No need to go to church?" I was surprised. He seemed to be such a, well . . . such a spiritually minded man.

"The need for religion, Mrs. Kordos."

I must have been staring at him with wide eyes, perhaps filled with surprise and disbelief. He smiled gently. There was no condescension in his look nor in the words he said next.

"The term religion, Mrs. Kordos," he smiled again as though apologizing for stating the obvious, "comes from the Latin *religare*, meaning to bind back. I never suffered the sense of separation and thus never felt the need to be bound back."

"Thus no re-ligion?" I still prodded. I pronounced it with a hyphen, as in re-joining. I never imagined Raphael to be a scholar of anything other than lifting people. He was so very good at that.

"Not in the accepted sense of the word, Madam."

"Then in what sense?" I was going to add, 'if any', but bit my lip.

"I find it necessary to have faith," he replied simply.

"In what, then?"

"That doesn't really matter. In infinite possibilities, I suppose. What matters is that we believe. Without faith there would be chaos."

"As in disorder?" He was leaving me behind in his thinking.

"As in universal chaos. A state of infinite potential but without manifestation."

"I'm afraid I don't follow you, Raphael."

"Without faith there would be no universe. No stars, no planets. No human beings. No beings unto the image and likeness of that infinite potential."

"You mean that we create the reality in which we have our being?"

"Who else?" he answered with a question.

"But . . . but what about . . . about God?" I was fairly stunned.

"I'll answer that with the words of Saint John of the Cross. A lamp am I, he said, to those who seek me, a mirror to those who know me. Shall I take the Colonel to the chapel?"

I was too disturbed by his words to get back to the reality of today. Of the here and now. I'd been brought up in the Roman Catholic tradition, where we were not encouraged to question the accepted mores. I waved my head, dismissing his offer. By then Jan was asleep again. We probably wouldn't make it in time to the chapel anyway. In time for Mass.

"I'll take him tomorrow, thank you Raphael," I told him. I wanted to sit back and give his words some thought. He left with a slight bow.

A nurse's helper, I mused. A nurse's helper. Will wonders never cease?

I haven't found dissecting Raphael's concepts easy. My son, Steven, often talks in a similar vain, but he is still at the searching stage. Anyway, one doesn't take one's son too seriously. He'd once laughed quoting the Bible to me.

"No man is a prophet in his own village," he'd said. "And I am not even a prophet," he added laughing aloud. He was right. He wasn't even a prophet.

Raphael appeared to have his views, or beliefs – faith at any rate – well established. He didn't wonder. He knew.

For some reason, I'm reminded of a sermon our visiting priest delivered some time ago on the theme of 'One Shepherd and but one Flock of Sheep'. Later, on that same day, Steven had brought me an essay he'd written. I must confess that I do not remember the essay itself, but just the observation he'd added at the end of it. He attributed it to Einstein. Apparently the physicist had said that in order to be an immaculate member of a flock of sheep, one must above all be a sheep oneself. I recall that I hadn't liked the quotation at all.

After speaking to Raphael, I liked it even less.

As usual on Sundays, I took a cab to Steven and Annette's condo. It was much more than an original lunch for me. A lunch where the menu was not dictated, imposed, made necessarily by what is the least dangerous to 'people my age', only by what might give us the most pleasure. Without being silly, of course. But, to my knowledge, a smoked salmon served with finely chopped marinated onion and capers, washed down with a thimble or two or even three of *cytrynówka*, a lemon vodka my son had 'elaborated' himself with great care, never sent anyone over the edge.

Three thimbles, not bottles as it used to be when Jan was young. In those days, his uniformed colleagues, young officers, believed that a drop of vodka left in a bottle was a drop wasted.

Father could never come with me. In fact it was only the availability of constant supervision that the Institute afforded that enabled me to go out 'on my own' at all. It helped me to retain the remnants of my sanity. Steve saw to this with vigour. Every time, every Sunday, he would place before me a new essay, which he'd wrenched out from his entrails with unprecedented vehemence. I never knew him like this. I even suspected that he'd written those essays just to force me to cross new ground. To keep going.

"Once you stop, you retreat," he told me. "The world refuses to wait for anyone."

It was supposed to make sense to me. Nevertheless, after the delightful lunch, sometimes a little walk, then within the voluptuous embrace of their oversized settees, I always succumbed to his prodding.

Once again Annette served coffee and chocolate. The dark one, my favourite. It was the sign that Steve's tirade was about to begin. He didn't disappoint me.

"Mozart is dead," Steve announced out of the blue.

I didn't think I was required to comment on this profound revelation. I continued to sip my black coffee. Espresso. So black and so strong that at the Institute, Annette would have been instantly arrested for attempted murder.

"So is Beethoven, Schubert, Chopin. So are Socrates, Plato, Dante and Shakespeare. So is Krishna, Moses, Lao Tsu, Buddha, Zoroaster and Jesus of Nazareth. They are all dead."

I nodded in total agreement. He, as usual, continued undeterred.

"Their Messages – live on," Steve announced.

It was time for me to look up.

"Therein the true immortality of the messengers. Therein their glory. Therein their perpetual gifts to humanity. It is for their Messages that we offer them honour. Our admiration. Our love."

I was beginning to get the drift of his soliloquy. He was telling me, or rather us, that the message is of importance rather than the messenger. But by now, Steven was riding a cloud of thought that required my full attention. He lowered his voice, making it sound as if he was sharing with us something very confidential and of great value yet. He picked up a sheet of paper and read from it. I knew it was his latest.

"There is an Ocean of Infinite Potential. A priceless Source, an inexhaustible Spring of Life, of Truth, of Beauty, ready to be discovered, ready to be brought out into the open. It is there, waiting, eternally available to share Its bounty. Within Its realm await the Messages. The priceless gifts. We, you and I, need the messengers to bring them to us. We need the great messengers to open their hearts, their eyes, their ears. We, at our stage of evolution, don't as yet know how to listen, to see. We often think we know, but this presumption is little more than an illusion fostered by our pride. It is this illusion which also stops us from searching for the Truth. We still need the messengers."

"It seems that you don't want us to confuse the letter with the postmen?" I risked an interruption.

He used the break to fill his mouth with chocolate. Within seconds he continued. Inside my handbag, I had my little recorder going. It helped me later to organize my thoughts.

"The Infinite Source, God if you like, has no desire to remain hidden. No scriptures ever claimed that. All Messages are available to all who would listen. What gets in the way is our conditioning. The knowledge we have already acquired. It refuses to be pushed aside to make room for the new. We tend to get caught in our little ruts. Our mores and morals weigh us down; as do our precious customs and traditions, and all that which keeps us apart – like culture, education, heritage. We are set in our petty ways."

I couldn't argue with that. The residents of the Institute were ample evidence of that. That didn't surprise me. What bothered me a lot more, I realized, was that the staff, the nurses and the Sisters, suffered from the same shortcoming. Assuming it was a shortcoming.

"Are you saying that all traditions are wrong?"

"Most certainly not. I got used to breathing as a baby and made it a hobby for a lifetime. No, Mother. Only those traditions that hold us back are wrong."

"But they all do, almost by definition. Traditions tie us to the past, don't they?"

Steven looked at me with a quizzical, lopsided grin, while Annette was all smiles, presumably proud of my contribution to the philosophical standing of the female branch of the family. The next time Steve spoke he veered on a different tack.

"I heard it said," he continued, "that no mathematical discovery has ever been made by anyone over the age of twenty-six. Apparently there are neuroconnectors which, through non-use, atrophy."

"Don't use it – lose it," Annette nodded in agreement.

"It also applies to *our* brains," again he was on a roll. "The wisdom of the years helps us to interpret what is, not to introduce and accept new concepts. For the *new* we need youth. Not necessarily 'youth' in biological terms, but a youthful state of consciousness. New concepts call on us to wipe the slate clean. Hence the expression to be born anew. Paul, the apostle, a messenger, said that he died daily. Daily! He died to all his accumulated knowledge in order to make room for the new. To become rejuvenated. To delve deeper into the Ocean of Truth. Paul found it necessary."

Steve stopped and began sipping coffee in tiny sips, the way his father drank cognac. Mostly absorbing the aroma and reinforcing it by wetting his lips.

I run his last words through my mind. Do we find it necessary to give up our past to make room for the new? Do we even want to? Or would we rather die of boredom than risk losing what is safe, comfortable? It seems that it is not the Truth that we love, but the emotional security which our acquired beliefs provide. I wondered if such safety wasn't an illusion. It seemed brittle. Deceiving.

Steve put down his cup and saucer and looked through the window facing their tiny terrace. The cedar hedge would stay green in all seasons. But the snow would soon cover the decorative paving. There was a dreamy smile tugging at the corners of his mouth. A mouth exactly like that of his grandfather.

"Freedom comes when the mind experiences without tradition," he said finally. "I learned this from Krishnamurti, a recent messenger. It really doesn't matter if we don't know who Krishnamurti is. But can we recognize his Message?"

I didn't.

They both drove me back to the Institute. They always did. Steve wanted to look in on Dad, and Annette came for the ride. She is such a good girl. She told me that she thinks Steve likes to have company for the return trip. She is like that.

As usual, Dad was still asleep. When Steve leaned over him, Jan opened one eye, appeared to wink, and returned to wherever he was before the interruption. For some reason I was convinced that wherever he was, he was happy. He invariably woke up in good humour. He must have really enjoyed his frequent trips to never-never land.

The moment the children had left, Raphael knocked on the door.

"A little exercise?" he asked.

Fifteen minutes later Dad and I were making our rounds along the corridor. As we passed Raphael, I caught him looking at us. It was as if he sensed that I was thinking about him. I was. I was thinking what sort of messenger he was. But more importantly, thanks to Steve's latest literary efforts, I was wondering what sort of message he was trying to deliver. He certainly did so by action and demeanour. I wondered if he also had things to say. Like Steve, only from within himself. I wondered if Raphael had found freedom by his mind experiencing without tradition. He was performing the most menial tasks imaginable. Wouldn't that alone leave his mind free?

We walked to the end of the corridor and turned back towards our room. Dad felt a little tired. His strength was leaving him fast, yet it was he who insisted on the walks. We didn't talk. By now Dad needed to watch my face to understand what I was trying to tell him. Even then he didn't always understand. Poor Jan.

My mind returned to the Messenger.

I am going to ask him, I promised myself. Judging by what he'd already told me, he might well prove to be a font of knowledge. New knowledge. The sort unmarred by tradition. I was becoming exited.

The next time I glanced at the Archangel, he was smiling at me. I could have sworn that he nodded in agreement.

***

6

Blessing

We sat side by side, in our coasterred armchairs, a cup of afternoon tea at our elbows. A rainy day was purpose-made for some reruns of Star Trek. "Live long and prosper," Mr. Spok said splitting his fingers into a strong V sign.

Live long and prosper. Why long? We are born after a mere nine months, and then we are supposed to drag out the rest of our stay in this valley of tears as long as we possibly can. What is there that is to be cherished in the extreme duration of our stay here? Isn't quality more important, *much* more important? I know there are Stephen Hawkings lightly peppered around the world but, surely, aren't they the exceptions? Perhaps Lou Gehrig's disease traps a man in time – you stay so immersed in your work you are unaware of its passage. Would you really like to live tied to a wheelchair, with a sensitizer in lieu of your vocal chords.

Well? Would you?

"It's a gift from God," Sister Cecilia assured me. How many times have I heard that trite assurance? On and on and on.... At one time or another I've raised the identical question with every single Sister, every nun and every priest. I've invariably received the standard answer. It is a gift from God. That's it.

It's all right for them to talk. They are all twenty years my junior. Or more.

Twenty years ago Jan and I took long trips to Virginia Waters, in England, inhaled the fragrance of a flamboyant mix of flowers as only English people can provide, and then stretched out on the grass to watch the clouds scooting haphazardly across the wide, limitless blue. Today, if I tried lying down on the grass, it would take two strong men to pick me up.

"Yes, Sister," I replied. "I wonder how old God is."

She gave me a dirty look dressed in a benevolent smile. Michaelangelo gave Him a great grey beard in the Sistine Chapel, but, other than that, I don't think God has any idea what it's like to be old. Old and frail. Old, frail and sick. Old, stiff, hard of hearing, hurting and . . . just OLD.

Last week Steve was expostulating on the subject of life. He is a bit of a cynic. I recorded most of our conversation. Actually, of his monologue. It was much easier to swallow with vodka and kippers and onions marinated in oil. I wonder who taught him to prepare such delicious things. I know I didn't, and Annette certainly didn't claim authorship.

"When one human sperm out of half-a-billion is allowed through the egg membrane, an animal with a potential is conceived." He stressed the word *animal.* "There is no human intervention." This time he stressed *human.* "The cells know what to do. They divide. A blastula is formed: several layers of cells around a central cavity continue to divide automatically."

Just how many times have you been pregnant, I wanted to ask him. I didn't. The *cytrynówka* was just too good.

And now, even as I sit alone, making notes on Steve's dissertation, my mind drifts back. I see Jan looking at me. We are about to finish a grand slam in hearts. Since I couldn't dance any more, we played bridge. My head is woozy. I think it's time, I say, smiling as if nothing is wrong. Jan jumps to his feet. An hour later little Steve is born. I can smell the roses in my room. Dozens and dozens of them. The next day I'm back home. The nanny looks after Steve well. I must recover quickly. We are in the middle of the carnival that stretches from New Year's Eve all the way to Ash Wednesday. Steve's arrival is rather inconvenient. No matter. Within a week I am back on the floor doing the latest shimmy that the Western wind blew in. We have such elegant Polish dances, but . . . we seem to like all things Western. From Western Europe.

I hadn't been quite ready to be a mother. Perhaps that was why my daughter died just a few months after she was born. Perhaps she too had been inconvenient?

By the time Jan left for the German front, I was heavy with our third, Janek – Polish version of 'Little John'. We'd named him before he was born. A year later we were scraping hoar-frost from the walls of the single room where eleven of us were living. Also, there was not much food and no medical help at all. In the middle of the winter of 1941, Janek died of pneumonia, hardly a year old. There were no nannies to look after him. I had to work.

When Bart was born I was ready. Ready and able to cope with the exigencies of motherhood. I tried to make up for my past shortcomings. I smile a little sadly. Was Bart the compensation for the errors of my past? Or was it just fate?

As I shake my head, the images resolve into a haze of yesteryear. I pick up my pen. Again I can hear Steve talking. "Go on," I said munching on another tidbit.

"Well, after three months it becomes a foetus...."

"What? Only after three months?" This was Annette and me together. Steve ignored us both.

"...a name given to an animal embryo, including human, in its later phase of gestation. At this stage a human embryo has fewer brains cells than a monkey."

I didn't like that at all. I like monkeys, but I didn't like them being that much smarter than I, whatever my stage of development. According to the Church, my life started at conception. It wasn't nice to learn that I wasn't as smart as our simian friends.

"Are you sure?" I had to ask.

"Don't worry, Mother," he tried to reassure me, "the automatic cell division continues. In human foetuses for another six months, in elephants for a total of two years."

"Still an animal?"

"It has done nothing, so far, to differentiate it from an animal. Surely, Mama, we must earn the privilege to be called human?"

I preferred not to answer. By such a standard, few people appear to have met the criteria of being called human. Surely, he was right. I decided to ask the ex-priest. Apparently, at that stage, we were still blessings in the making. Or still to become blessings.

"Anyway, the cells continue to divide. The baby grows. Ultimately it becomes man. I use the term generically," he hastened to assure us when Annette opened her mouth in protest. "He eats, defecates, sleeps, procreates, works, fights to protect and squirrel his savings, fights to feed his offspring. Often just fights."

"His children!" Annette corrected. "Fights to protect and feed his *children*."

Steve smiled. This wasn't their first discussion on the subject. "If you like, darling. Children. At any rate, the man thinks, schemes, suffers, experiences pleasure. He grows old. The cells are programmed to slow down. He deteriorates. He dies. Can you tell me at which stage he became human, and why?"

Annette and I looked at each other for mutual support. For some reason, neither of us came up with a ready answer.

"During his life," Steve continued, "he's done nothing to differentiate himself from an animal. He may have operated more complex machinery, he may have learned to add and subtract better than a monkey."

"He was a very smart monkey?" Annette suggested.

"Perhaps. He was a clever ape. He was nice, responsible, loving, as we said, he looked after his children. So does an ape, a monkey, a fish or a bird. Yet this nice, responsible, loving man, according to Jesus, was never born. Not spiritually. Not into real life."

I recalled the phrase he was referring to somewhere in St. Matthew. When a man wanted Jesus to wait for him while he buried the body of his father, Jesus told him: Follow me, and let the dead bury the dead. I made a mental note to reread Matthew once again. And there was also that . . . except a man be born again, he cannot see the kingdom of God. No. This one's all right. You only go to the Kingdom after death, if you're lucky. But there was also something about being born of flesh and being born of the spirit. I've read my Bible, but I never really studied those things. They just sounded nice. Sort of....

"He remained one of the dead burying the dead," Steve drove the point home.

I felt lost. All that I've been taught, throughout my life, didn't make much sense. Are we really just animals with inflated egos?

Surely there must be more to our lives than that. An ape never composed the Fifth Symphony, or the Requiem, or a violin concerto or Aida... There has to be more. I began to suspect that Steve would harp on such subjects until I, on my own, began to question the very essence of the Church's teaching. Was he worried about my soul? It was as if he wanted me to break away from the mould in which Rome kept its lieges. Steve was definitely a rebel. Until very recently, I was as orthodox as a fundamentalist, as an obedient sheep. In my traditional milieu one left matters of faith to the priests and Sunday sermons. Was Steve worried about me?

"We must earn the privilege of being human," Steve's eyes drifted in that familiar habit of his, to the square of blue, framed by their terrace window. "We must meet our potential. At least in part. No matter how minute, but we cannot just 'live', as if the privilege had been given us unconditionally."

What if he's right? Just how many humans had I met in my life?

"It's all a question of consciousness. A human entity that becomes aware of its Higher Self, does not die. Remember? Though he be dead, he shall live again.... Gradually that entity learns to identify with those aspects of life that are immortal. In time . . . in time we shall discard our service accoutrements, our redundant paraphernalia. We shall free ourselves from appurtenances that an animal needs at various stages of its journey towards enlightenment."

The silence stretched for a little while.

"So it is true that the human, ah . . . animal alone manifests such a potential?" Annette put in. Her tone was as much a question as a statement of her beliefs.

"For good and for evil," Steven said wistfully. "For spiritual growth and for material decadence."

"And for eventual immortality," I sighed. "Barring accidents the human animal shall find it. It is only a question of time. It could happen in a few billion years. Or tomorrow." Was I beginning to think like Steven?

"Cheers!" Steve said raising his glass of *cytrynówka*. And then, as if reading my thoughts he added, "until that time, I shall remain a confirmed hedonist. I might as well enjoy the trip!"

For the next three nights I had dreams of giving birth to cute little, hairy monkeys. They popped out without any involvement on my part. One moment I was alone in bed, the next a bunch of them were gallivanting up and down the springs, telling me in monkeyese what a wonderful gift life was. After a while, the monkeys assumed flowing white robes. They looked amazingly like habits with oversized wimples that quickly grew into coronets and then into oversized head gear such as worn by Sally Fields in her role as the Flying Nun. During the third night, three of the monkeys floated around my room, gently flapping their head gear while furiously typing on tiny typewriters with all twenty fingers.

"Not so fast," I told my hairy children.

"We must hurry," they replied in perfect unison. "We have all the works of Shakespeare to type before we grow up."

When I woke up a steady tapping on the door drowned the noise of typing. I'd overslept. Raphael wanted to know if I needed help with Dad. For once, I wasn't pleased to see him. I wanted to find out how soon my children would finish typing the complete works of Shakespeare. I'd read somewhere that it was only a question of time. Now, I would never know.

So life is a blessing. I wondered if the sages of old had been referring specifically to physical life. It was obvious that Jesus didn't. He definitely had a different sort of life in mind. Perhaps other sages, the prophets of old, also had some other sort of existence in mind? We are born, we grow up, we change. As did the prophets. Our concepts evolve. I, for one, had a very different idea of life as a child. I'd been carefree, happy, irresponsible. Perhaps we should try to recover that sort of attitude. Maybe that sort of life really is a blessing. Without responsibility. I don't mean to live irresponsibly but not to assume responsibility for mores imposed on us by others. To be more free. To live and let live.

What else is a blessing? Is food a blessing? Judging from how the Sisters of the Immaculate Heart insist on pumping us with three enormous meals a day – it must be. For crying out loud! How were we supposed to burn off those calories? Most of us could hardly move, and not just from overeating.

The pills were a blessing. Pills and all sort of chemicals. Pills of all colours, for all purposes, whatever they might be. Why couldn't they invent an all-purpose pill and be done with it? Not enough money for the Chemical Conglomerates, I suppose. To them the multitude of pills was definitely a blessing. They were a veritable boon.

Jesus didn't recognize life as an infestation of our physical bodies. Didn't He say that His kingdom is not of this world? Is this why nobody believes Him? Isn't He supposed to be God? The Sisters think so. I am sure the ex-priest will once he recovers his faith. But no one acts as if they believe him. Are we men and women occasionally grasping for a spiritual experience? Or are we spiritual beings meant to enjoy the transient experience of becoming. Here. On earth. Before we return to His, to *our* kingdom.

Must idiots, excuse me, must the mentally challenged in the psychiatric hospitals, live long, even if they don't prosper?

What about the criminally insane? Just how human are they, in the biblical sense? Will they all be born again?

What of the paraplegics who also suffer from diabetes. Just how much effort should they put into prolonging their physical lives? We are back to pills. Pills of all colours and description. Pink pills and blue pills and yellow pills and... All to sustain this precious gift.

Chemicals are definitely a blessing. Right?

I think that the Moslems have it right, at least for men. They kill off a few infidels, die in the process and soon wallow in the arms of a few dozen virgins in paradise. Seventy-two, Steve tells me. I wonder what happens if they are gay? Seventy-two virgin boys? And what of women martyrs? My God, surely not seventy-two.... As a counter argument I must admit that when I was a virgin I suffered from quite undeniable stupidity. About almost everything. Not that I am doing so well even now. Had I been a man and found me in paradise, I wouldn't have touched me with a barge pole.

"Come in, Sister." I could recognize Sister Angelica by her knock. It was gentle, polite, but would not be ignored. I could do it in my own time, but I had to answer.

"May I?" she asked.

She followed her big smile into our room and shut the door quietly behind her. "How's the Colonel?" she looked at my husband with undisguised compassion. One could not fail to love her for that. Whatever her past peccadilloes, Sister Angelica was goodness incarnate.

"Did you have a chance to speak to Father Mulligan?" she asked hopefully.

I shuffled uncomfortably. I was sure Sister Angelica was asking me about Father Mulligan's well-being, whereas when I had got him cornered one day on the balcony, I talked about what was of interest to me, not what might have been troubling him.

"Sort of," I replied feeling a bit guilty. I still had no idea what exactly the Sister wanted me to say to the poor man. I couldn't convert him or anything. Surely, faith comes from within, not without. It is the way we see the world. With spiritual eyes, we discern only beauty. With physical eyes we see its advancing decadence. Like our bodies. Heaven and hell are, in my opinion, states of mind, mostly of our own making. Admittedly others have influence on us, but the art is to have our personal worldview so firmly entrenched in our psyche that no one can take it away from us.

The Sister waited. She reverted to her favourite hobby of examining the tips of her shoes peeking out from under her habit. She certainly got my vote for angelic patience.

"I asked him about the Pale Horse," I said at last.

At this Sister Angelica looked up. "Not the Apocalypse of Saint John?" she asked aghast.

Apocalypse or Revelation. A rose by any other name. "The very same," I confirmed feeling a little uncomfortable.

"But why?" Sister Angelica asked. "Wouldn't that make things...."

"...even worse?" I finished for her. "It didn't seem so at the time."

Sister Angelica took a step forward. Her eyes grew larger. I suspected that I would have to tell her the whole story. I took a deep breath.

"What actually happened," I started resignedly, "was that I'd just returned from Steven's, looked in on Dad, and found him in never-never land. When the children left, I decided to read my Bible on the balcony. It was a nice day and I wanted to squeeze as much sunshine from it as I could. It so happened that only the chair next to Father Mulligan was unoccupied. It seemed as though people were afraid to sit next to him. Perhaps his past was catching up to him. More and more people knew who he once was. He smiled as usual, but almost rolled his eyes when he saw what book I brought with me.

" 'You don't mind, do you?'

"I have no idea why I'd asked him that. Perhaps he thought that I was saying something about the practice that only priests read the Bible and we, the mere mortal, were supposed to wait until their learned interpretation is given us.

"His usual pallor moved rapidly toward red. At last, the old priest finally had some colour in his face. But I desperately tried to say something that would be less aggressive.

" 'As a matter or fact,' I said with as warm a smile as I could put on at a moment's notice, 'I rather hoped that you might be able to help me with a little part of it.'

"Father Mulligan looked partially mollified.

"'I have problems getting my reins on the pale horse,' I finished my question rather proud of my turn of phrase.

" 'Then you are a very lucky lady,' Father Mulligan replied."

Throughout my tirade Sister Angelica hadn't moved an inch. "There," I took another deep breath. "Now you know the whole story."

Sister Angelica gasped. "He said that to you?"

"No less. You are a very lucky lady, he said. As a matter of fact, he as much as looked me straight in the eye."

I pointed to the nearest armchair. Sister Angelica took three tiny steps and deposited the stern-most three inches of her gluteus *maximus* on its edge. I imagine the correct grammar would be to say *glutei maximi*, but you know what I mean. That's as elegant as I can make it when talking about a nun's rear quarters.

"So what happened, Mrs. Kordos?"

"Why, nothing. We had a very nice chat," I assured her.

"I don't suppose you would care to share it with me?" her eyes descended to her toes.

I was toying with her. I knew full well that she was dying of curiosity. To her credit I must add that I was very sure that her concern for the old priest was genuine.

"I found him very helpful. He was very well versed in the Apocalypse. In fact, he appeared to have made a special study of it."

She kept both still and silent, but she was beginning to steal glances at me.

"He told me that the same rider, the same ego, the same self, rides any or all of the four horses. But unless you are a circus performer, Mrs. Kordos, he said, you'll find it next to impossible to ride more than one steed at a time."

By now Sister Angelica had lost all interest in the tips of her shoes. For my part, I looked at the notes I'd made after pinning the old priest down to pick his brain.

"We make a conscious selection of the horse we ride, and we bear the consequences, he'd said. And by the way, according to Father Mulligan we bear the consequences regardless how cold and unfeeling or irrational, emotional or instinctive behaviour we exhibit."

"Not very forgiving," Sister murmured.

"Perhaps not to himself," I agreed. "It's rather like the law of Karma," I added remembering my son's views. Sister Angelica ignored my last remark.

"Did he say anything else?" she asked.

"Well," I glanced again at my notes. "He talked about the cosmic laws. Something about ignorance being no excuse for breaking them. It seems that there is some sort of equivalent of the law of cause and effect in the Christian apologetics. Somehow I'd never heard about it."

"As you sow so you shall reap; as you do unto others...." Sister Angelica mused.

She was right, of course. This was as clear as you can get. How come I'd missed it for so many years? I wondered what else I missed on my personal journey. Also, I gained new respect for the quiet nun so hungry for knowledge. How she must have suffered at the Convent laundry. She had a keen, perceptive mind.

"Of course. How stupid of me," I confessed.

"Please don't say things like that, Mrs. Kordos. We all regard you as a font of knowledge," Sister Angelica affirmed.

"Really, Sister. Let us be serious. You know ten times more about the bible than I do," I countered.

"The bible is a font of spiritual knowledge. It is quite another story to know how to apply it to everyday life, Mrs. Kordos."

"Thank you, my gracious Sister," I gave up eating humble pie. I wanted to tell her the rest of what Father Mulligan had to say.

The Sister seemed abashed at her own statement. Her eyes returned to her toes.

"Father Mulligan also explained to me some other aspects of the Apocalypse. He said that according to Saint John, we react to external stimuli in four principal ways. We can treat them as exclusively physical phenomena. When we do that, we ride a pale horse. He said that this is a very abortive modus operandi."

"The Bible is a textbook of spiritual knowledge," Sister Angelica put in again.

"That's what he said too." I looked up at her. "Can you tell me why the priests never seem to teach that from the pulpit? It is always do this and do that, but not why...."

"Do you think many would understand it if they did?"

She surprised me. Her last question was at odds with her almost-overt humility.

"Well, someone would have to explain it to us," I said defensively.

"I don't mean you, Mrs. Kordos. I don't mean the people who search. I mean the rest...."

"You mean the billion others?"

She said nothing. It was an unfair question. I knew from my own life that until some months ago, yes, just a few months, I'd never questioned the black and white fundamentalist doctrine that priests promulgated from the ambo. I realize now that Steve had become painfully aware of this some time ago. Perhaps others would understand, but surely, if they were really interested, then . . . then the doors would be open to them. It was evident that there was more to clergy than meets the eye. There was also that rather unpleasant admonition about casting pearls before the swine.

I was also thinking about Sister Angelica's assertion that the Bible was a book of spiritual knowledge. The way she said it, it implied that anything remotely physical was used only as an illustration. A person identifying with her physical body, i.e. riding a pale horse, is compared to Death itself and her state of mind – to Hell. I already knew that elsewhere in the Bible people who were not spiritually awakened were compared to the dead.

The pale horse was a biblical oxymoron. The dead don't ride horses.

And then it struck me. If life is such a blessing, then there has to be more to life than meets the eye. Or our ears. Or any of our senses. Or even our stomachs.

***

The Red Horse

"....and power was given him that sat thereon
to take peace from the earth,
and that they should kill one anther:
and there was given unto him a great sword."

The Revelation
of Saint John the Divine

7

The Institute

From outside, the Institute of the Immaculate Heart of Mary looks clean, almost elegant, worthy of its name. For my taste, the white brick cladding gives it a little too much of a hygienic appearance but considering the obsession the Sisters have on that score, it seems apt. The main building is recessed from the street by some forty feet, enough for a beautifully kept lawn and some pines and firs to set it apart from the humdrum of the street traffic. A fully-grown hedge of cedars, cropped to a regular, slightly pyramidal contour protects the edge of the property. At the main entrance flowerbeds are always well watered and trimmed to perfection. At the other end, the parking lot and our inner garden are secured from outsiders by metal gates, which opens automatically only by the mass of an approaching car, but remains stubbornly closed when the residents attempt to pull them open. Quite clever.

The rear garden, the place where most residents spend an hour or two during the summer months, is inviting. We congregate on a large wooden deck with built-in wooden and movable white plastic chairs, all around a wonderful ancient maple, which dominates the immediate area. This haven is surrounded by a lawn, which separates it from the cars parked in a single long row along the outer perimeter.

It's nice. Or as nice as one can make it with such limited space.

These days I find it a little tiring to go for long walks outside; Steven and Annette and I toss a tennis ball around. I can catch it reasonably well, even though I've never excelled in any sport. Not even in horseback riding that my husband insisted I try.

With Bart, and sometimes one of my granddaughters, I still go outside. On the street, I mean. There are two tiny parks within an uneasy walking distance. Once, they seemed quite close. I have no heart to tell him that my legs hurt for days afterwards. Perhaps it's meant to be. After all, I know the dictum about using or losing. Thanks to Bart, I can probably walk just a little longer. I often wonder how much we should fight the natural progression of aging. At all costs? Or should one just age gracefully, as they say. God knows, there is little grace in ageing.

How time flies....

I counted them. Fifty-seven to the right, forty-four to the left, then another thirty-two straight up or along the smooth terrazzo flooring to the right, towards the west end. I could walk those corridors blindfolded and never miss a step nor take a wrong turn. Of course, there aren't many turns to start with. In the beginning I counted the floor tiles. Some years ago all the floor tiles were replaced with terrazzo and I had nothing to count.

The years have mounted up on the invisible matrix of time. All any of us notice is the gradual deterioration of our joints, energy and acumen.

I glanced at the terrazzo beneath my slippers. Sameness. Everywhere sameness. Isn't life supposed to be change? Variety?

"Easier to maintain," one of the white, flowing habits told me. "To keep in good condition," she said. When I didn't say a word she added: "More hygienic."

Who needs a hygienic floor, I wondered? I never eat off the floor, never even touched it. I couldn't bend that low even if I wanted to. As long as it looks clean, that's enough for me. "What I can't see doesn't hurt me," I murmured but the white habit was gone. As I was saying, they just flowed from one place to another like white sheets carried by the wind. Only, there was no wind.

Again, I looked at the floor.

A good, insipid, yellowish-grey, nondescript pattern that's more hygienic. Rather like the cheeks of most of the residents. Yellowish-grey, although, in case of the cheeks, a little less hygienic. Less germ-free.

"Germs are dangerous when your immune system begins winding down," the same Sister insisted at some other time.

Until then they are just peaches and cream, I murmured. Actually, it was just a thought. I didn't want to engage in an argument on logic. I would soon hear what a gift life was.

Sister Cecilia was big on germs. When you're nearing the Gate, it doesn't really matter any more. They, the Sisters, thought otherwise. Well, you had to start somewhere with this tiresome hygiene. Why not the floor? At least they've left the carpet in our room alone.

The corridors run at right angles, forming the letter Tee. About half way along the base of the Tee, the corridor splits into two halves, with an unaccountable waste of space, but allowing the more mentally aware residents to cross the landing of the escape stair at the far end, and thus substantially extend their walking distance. The space between the two parallel corridors is windowless, assigned to storage areas and some shower cubicles that no one uses. I presume the showers are too far down the corridors for most residents. No one wants to walk that far. Except for me. I make my early-morning ablutions daily, before breakfast. Before going to Mass. They had to clean up one of the shower compartments just for me. Steven saw to that. He couldn't imagine starting a day without a shower. By now, nor can I.

My favourite promenade is the east-west corridor, with the procession of kings greeting me along its length. I nod to my favourite ones, those who left a mark on our history. They seem to like it. They grant me benevolent smiles of majestic approval. At least I'm spending my last days in good company.

The corridor runs from a window at one end to a decent-sized terrace overlooking the main street at the other. The terrace was fully roofed over, affording, even on hot and humid and even rainy summer days, a dry outdoor space for the residents. I used to call it a balcony, but it's large enough to be qualified as a terrace. That was where I'd once pinned down Father Mulligan with questions about the Pale Horse. Then we reverted to 'Good morning, Father,' and reciprocative smiles. Father Mulligan was a very unapproachable man.

I like going there, on that terrace, except when some nurses use it to smoke – an activity strictly forbidden indoors. Yet even on the terrace the smoke lingers on a windless day.

"Look at those people . . . still smoking . . . imagine that," Jan said out loud as he always did, unaware that others may not be as deaf as he is. "Imagine that," he repeated, evidently proud of having extinguished his pipe. He still kept it, fully loaded, but hadn't lit it for over a year. Just puffing for the sake of it seemed to satisfy him.

"It's like smelling Cognac without actually drinking it," he'd explained it to me some time ago. "You don't get a headache the next morning, and you still enjoy it."

To me it just smelled.

It must be a 'man' thing. Maybe he imagines he looks macho with a pipe. Not that many men would admit it, but there is a bit of macho in every man. Including my Jan.

"Enjoy it," I would tell him.

God knows he doesn't have much to enjoy anymore. Basically, like my elder son, I'm a hedonist. And anyway, by how many years was he likely to cut down his longevity at the age of ninety-eight? Apart from Alzheimer's, he's as fit as a fiddle. A slightly bent fiddle, especially around the finger joints, but still . . . for his age?

I wonder how fit I'll be in my upper nineties? I have problems enough at eighty-eight keeping up with my commitments. Oh, yes. I still visit Steve and Annette, still contribute articles to the monthly magazine, still keep a keen eye on Dad. Not that I don't trust the nursing staff, but there is no substitute for a mother's eye. Or a wife's of sixty years. No one knows him as I do. No one ever would.

The other end of the corridor terminates on a window. The view might have been reasonably interesting if it hadn't been for the thick Hydro-Quebec cables, which brutally crisscross the view, framed by the rectangular panes. Even at the elevation of the third floor, the cables cut the sky separating it from the green of the tree crowns that peek over the adjoining duplexes.

"Beggars can't be choosers," I told Dad when he was still able to make sense of my trite remarks.

He shrugged. What he meant was "I didn't choose to stay here." Poor Dad. By the fifth year – at least I think it was the fifth year, all years are exactly alike – it was much too late to move out. Even if he improved. It goes without saying that I've grown much too old to look after him alone. On one occasion I had to pick him up when he'd lost his balance and fell on the floor in our powder room. I pressed the nurse's emergency button. By the time she arrived, I had him up. It took me fifteen minutes and my muscles ached for two days after.

During the early days, Dad had up to three bad days per week. The rest of the time, we walked the corridor. On worse days, I'd push him in a wheelchair. During the first three years, we must have travelled this inverse Milky Way close to ten thousand times.

Eight times a day, for three hundred days a year. The rest of the time we walked outdoors.

Now, we hardly go outdoors at all. Not together.

Actually, the rest of the time Jan used to plot how to escape from the Institute. Not that he was badly treated. But it gave him something to do. Until he broke his hip.

For all of us, Dad's mishap, provided a new experience. Everyday Steven would come down, pick me up, and drive me to the Good Samaritan Hospital. We would spend up to two hours, just being there. When Dad became more aware of his surroundings, less lethargic from all the medications they pumped into him, we would talk.

Not that he heard much.

The hip operation nearly killed him. I felt a little guilty for not praying for his speedy recovery. For a man as active as he'd always been, his condition must have been verging on hell. For some inexplicable reason, he never complained. Perhaps he wasn't aware just how incapacitated he'd become. Perhaps his mind had retreated to some merciful realm where one is not aware of one's physical condition. Emotionally he seemed content. Coming out of his drug induced reveries, he'd smiled at me, at Steve, at Annette, and on weekends, at Bart. He recognized every one of us, which was more than he did some months before.

L'homme cet inconnu, wrote a Frenchman whose name I cannot recall. Carrell? Dr. Alexis Carrell? Didn't he pick up a Nobel Prize for something? I used to remember so much more.... But he was right, the Frenchman, I mean, in the sentiment expressed by the title of his book. No matter how much we analyze our human traits, in the end we remain strangers to each other. Man remains the unknown. Sometimes we meet, on a desert island, in an endless ocean of wandering souls. We discover whatever unites us. Whatever we can share. Then, with the next gust of wind, our meagre sails billow and we seem to drift apart, each retreating into the safety of our inner sanctuary. Perhaps that is what souls do. Perhaps we are just a body of emotions disparate, lonesome, yearning for companionship. It's a vast universe.

I think what we all really search for is happiness.

We are bundles of emotions begging to be recognized. For what we really are. Sometimes we succeed. We find a mirror. A mirror am I to those who know me.... We discover ourselves in someone else's eyes. For a while. Then that special someone moves away, escapes, or dies, or succumbs to Alzheimer's.

My form of escape is quite different. I escape into my dreams. Both those during my sleep and those when I just sit back, waiting for Dad to wake up. My mind drifts further and further back. Time wise. One afternoon, during what I thought was a short nap, I found myself in Schönflisse, a hectarage my father had owned in East Prussia, just after the First World War. It must have been around 1915, yet the images I saw in my mind were as fresh as though I'd visited them only yesterday. Only the lake seemed huge, the waves gigantic, the pines on the horizon as well as those nearby, twice as tall. I know, I'd visited them just once around 1930, and they all were much smaller. But not then. When I was seven or eight, they were all huge. The whole world was huge in those days.

The wind blew from the west. It bent the crowns of the ancient oaks in a regular pattern of arcs . . . bowing to someone hidden deep inside the forest. Two geese were flying hard to take cover. I heard them before I saw them. A single deer looked at me – enormous pools of such liquid beauty – then walked slowly away. It would be safe once it reached the undergrowth. Who would want to hurt it? The wind was not allowed on the forest floor. It only played with the crowns. To and fro . . . ffffssssff . . . it whistled high up above, so high.

It was still humming when I came to. The air conditioner. I wonder why we, Jan and I, haven't followed in my father's footsteps. Or his father's father for that matter. We've always been rustic folk. Not that we were unsophisticated; we just loved the countryside. I suppose once we would have been referred to as the gentry like our parents had been. People with large tracts of land administered for the sheer pleasure of it.

The wind kept blowing....

The waves swelled ever higher. One duckling was scooped up in the air and deposited onto another crest further east. Then another. It didn't seem to mind. It dove down, probably seeking safety under water. I wouldn't know.

The wind blew....

And then I remembered. Jan wanted to study agriculture, but he'd been dissuaded from leaving the regiment by his commanding officer, who foretold a great future for Dad in the armed forces. The commanding officer continued to rise to the Commander-in-Chief of the Second Corps. He'd become a Three Star General. Jan was eventually promoted to Colonel. Jan had an unpleasant habit of telling it like it is. Not a good trait if you want to rise to the top. Steve is exactly the same.

The wind blew . . . only the ducklings were gone . . . and only the wind remained...

My children would inherit the wind.

People of my generation who left Europe when already past middle-age had few souvenirs to leave their children. No buildings, farms, or art collections. All that was long gone. The latter had been transported west in late 1939 and what was left had gone east in early 1945. The paintings probably still give pleasure to someone. Somewhere. It doesn't seem to matter anymore.

I didn't have anything to give my children. Then Steve had an idea. He wanted my memories. It started with little poems I remembered, little songs with funny lyrics, from my youth. Funny how things from youth catch up with you. I had forgotten them for some fifty years, and, suddenly, here they were again, for the taking. Actually, for the taping.

For my first birthday at the Institute, some four or five (I can't be sure how many) years ago, he gave me a tiny portable tape recorder with a dozen little tapes I could replace with ease. We tried it out and, on the third attempt, I got it right. Of course, when you're just talking, the words come out without the benefit of a good editor leaving his literary mark. It is easier to record your memories when you don't have to write them down.

"No matter, Mama," Steve said. "I'm no literary giant. What I want is a souvenir from both of you. It is too late for Dad. I don't want to miss you also. You can talk. Think that I shall always be there to listen."

He did more than listen. He transcribed many of them on his computer.

"That could be embarrassing at times," I suggested.

"Well, in such a case, there is always the erase button."

We both laughed.

Now, after five years, I keep the recording machine going even when I'm alone. I've even allowed myself to think aloud many a time, imagining that I'm talking to him. I think that's what he wants. To hear my thoughts.

I often wonder what makes us remember things. I am fairly sure that memories are not a function of our mind. Or if they are, then at least the motivating factor, the trigger to bring them back, is emotions. When I am moved by some old song, moved emotionally, then I remember it instantly. When I just try to think analytically, then they elude me. The more I concentrate, the further they seem to retreat. Only when I relax and . . . and start to feel the song, or a poem, or something special that moved me, they come to me. The petals of the book of life unfold, like an enormous lotus flower when touched by rays of the morning sun. At other times, it seems to roll back the scroll, and there, behind the ripples of recurrent present, once again, the memories lay as fresh as they were the day on which they left an indelible mark on me. It's all emotion.

Perhaps it has something to do with love. I loved that poem, or that song.... and here they are. Time shrinks, contracts, to reveal them.

We are a complex emotional machine, which functions independently of our mind. And it's powerful. It stimulates the rest of us. In a way, it makes me get up from bed in the morning. It makes me look in on Dad. It makes me take a cab to go and see Steve and Annette. It makes me notice the autumn colours.

It also has something to do with beauty. Beauty is also beyond time. It lives in the present.

It's a blessing.

I've just turned ninety and Jan one hundred. ONE HUNDRED! He received telegrams from the Pope, the Queen of England, the Prime Minister of Canada, the Premier of Quebec and the Mayor of Montreal. Not bad for a poor emigrant. Of course I didn't tell him that such telegrams are 'standard' issue for all the centenarians who could be bothered to request them. Still, for the moment it seemed quite festive.

On the afternoon of Jan's birthday Raphael took a good hour to deck him up in the best (and the only) suit of his we brought with us. The rest of the time it was easier to dress Dad in loose trousers, a shirt and a sweater. Always a sweater. Even in summer his hands remained stone cold. Something to do with his circulation.

A half-hour before the appointed time Dad looked at his, virtually, old self. Old as in past glory not as a man who'd just turned one hundred. If it wasn't for the wheelchair, he could have gotten away with ninety, perhaps less.

The meeting room downstairs was filled to the brim. Steven and Bart thought that the word must have spread that there would be telegrams from his Holiness and such like. I knew better. The word had spread indeed, but it had more to do with the two enormous birthday cakes the ladies had provided. The elderly have one joy in life. Sweets. If Holy Communion wafers were sweet, the whole Institute would attend Mass daily. Anything sweet was good. Cakes, ice cream, puddings, desserts, you name it. Birthday cakes were on the very top of the list. A centenarian cake was the *crème de crème* of the thick whipped cream atop the tiers.

The telegrams were all read by *la Directrice* of the Institute. Each was followed by polite clapping, and a little shuffling intended to express annoyance at the unnecessary delay. Finally the cake was cut. People who heretofore had great problems moving even a few yards to do anything at all, suddenly approached the counter, breaking shuffling records of long standing.

The cakes were a resounding success.

The day after the celebration, I went to see *la Directrice.* I wanted to thank her and make one tiny suggestion. I suggested that in the future, the cakes be cut first and the telegrams read after. With such a tiny adjustment we could make one hundred and eighty-six residents much happier. And the telegrams would be none the worse for it.

She agreed.

PS. Dad fell asleep after the second helping. It was his right. He'd just embarked on his second century.

Periodically, the Institute takes some of us on an excursion. Our private bus can accommodate up to twenty-six residents. Most of us cannot travel, of course. Like Jan. The lucky ones go up north, or to the Eastern Townships. I like the trips because they stir the memories of the countryside. I always manage to sit by the window and inhale every field, every tree, every brook or river we cross. At the destination, there is usually a picnic, or a meal served at some generous Polish private house. They really go out of their way to be kind to us.

"Do have another helping of pierogi," the lady of the house would insist. "Or another pork chop...." she would push the plate in front of my nose as if to entice me with its smell.

"No, really, Mrs...."

There was no convincing them that I came for the trees, and the flowers and the smell of freshly cut grass. Not for the chops, no matter how delicious they smelled.

When I get lucky, I wander off, quietly, into the adjacent forest. What if I got lost? Father was well looked after, and Steve and Bart would look in on him. He might even recognize them. And I could die in the forest. Like lame animals do. With the doleful-eyed deer. And chipmunks. And . . . I really have no idea what animals die in the Laurentian forests. But I'm sure they are all beautiful. Not like aged humans. A veterinary doctor once told me that in nature we seldom find fresh corpses. Or any corpses. Just occasional bones. Clean, well preserved. Without burial. Without any holy ground.

The members of the First Nations only worship the grounds of the dead. The grounds where their forefathers were buried. Moses had been told otherwise. "Take off your shoes, a Voice told him. You are standing on holy ground." Why holy? No one died there, did they? I thought it would be nice to die in nature's embrace. To lie down on the soft forest floor, with the smell of pine needles, drift off to sleep and wake up in heaven. We could wave good-bye from up there. If anyone wanted to look that high up. But people worship bodies, dead or alive. That is why we kiss the ring on the Holy Father's finger.

"Bits of skin, or something," Steve called them. "We love carcasses of dead saints and kings and heroes," he said.

Steven was like that. He'd say what he thought no matter whose sensibilities he might hurt.

"It's the truth, Mama," was his argument. "People deserve to hear the truth!" He insisted.

"Your truth?" I remember asking.

"Just how many truths are there, Mother?" Mother meant that he was getting riled. I decided not to give in.

"You told me that three elements are needed for the truth to be announced, remember?"

He remained silent, his expression just a little pompous.

"And just what might they be?"

"You said that in order to say anything we must make sure that it is true, that it is kind and that it is necessary. Remember?

"Paul Twitchell said that," he admitted, his tone no longer dogmatic. "Perhaps some people can't handle the truth." He sounded retreat.

"They might, son, if it was kind and necessary".

I played with a piece of asparagus on the edge of my plate.

Perhaps he was right, I thought. Perhaps we don't care about the emotions. Just bodies. Surely, the emotions keep us alive and when we die, they don't remain in our bones. I am sure they drift over some beautiful fields, or valleys and hills, they soar over forests and swoop down over rivers and lakes.

"Do have another pork chop, Mrs. Kordos?"

"Perhaps some more juice? Or coffee?"

Why don't I stuff myself like everybody else, I wonder just for a minute. And then I drift into the forest again. My own, private forest. Like that frightened deer in Schönflisse. So many years ago. I would be safe there. Once I reached the undergrowth.

When I got back from that trip, Dad was still asleep. I wonder if he knew I'd been away. I am always afraid that if I am away for too long he might wake up and feel stranded. Alone. Was it just in my mind? Perhaps inside, at some deep level of perception he would want me to go out and enjoy myself. To have another pork chop. He couldn't eat them anymore. His false teeth were not a good fit. I've had them changed and adjusted a few times but he always made me understand that they were uncomfortable. He used to love apples. The last time he bit one, his upper denture remained firmly embedded in the apple. Now he prefers eating purees. No more pork chops. No more apples.

"He slept the entire time, Mrs. Kordos."

It was Raphael. The Archangel. He'd put his head in the door just to assure me. I didn't even hear him knock. I must be getting old myself. Not quite with it, I believe they say.

I raised the blanket over Dad's labouring chest. He also suffered from emphysema. Perhaps not really suffered. Just had problems breathing. He wouldn't be able to run fast. Or a marathon. His lungs wouldn't support him. Just as well, I thought. Just as well.

I remember the first time Dad kissed me. He was a second lieutenant then. We just got back from the Regimental Ball. He showed me a ring, and said some things that seemed important at the time. Then he kissed me. We were married three months later. We still are. Funny, how time flies.

***

8

Alzheimer's

I've lost all sensation of time. It's simply bloating insidiously to fill the empty spaces. There's breakfast, lunch and dinner. The rest is time. It's salted with minutia of meaningless activities. Sometimes with just sleep. Dull, dreamless, uninspiring sleep. A sort of absence. Abnegation. A denial. Unless one of my sons comes. Unless someone drops in not just to ask me how I feel, how things are, how Jan and I are coping. Nurses do that. And sisters. And an occasional physician.

"Thanks for asking," I tell them without bothering to give any substantial answer.

What can I tell them? Monday differs from Tuesday by its proximity to the next visit from one of my boys. The rest is... I don't really know what the rest is. Perhaps old people lose their short term memories because there is nothing to remember. Nothing at all.

I'm not alone. Nor's Dad. They estimate that there are eighteen million Alzheimer's sufferers worldwide. They figure the number will nearly double by 2025. By 2025 there will be twice as many people looking after their husbands or wives.

We've never talked about Alzheimer's. I read a lot about it, listen to the radio, watch TV, but we never talk about Alzheimer's. It's a sort of public secret. It's not good talking about the inevitable. It impinges on your concept of free will. Shakespeare said that not in stars but in ourselves we are underlings. Well, we are also underlings in Alzheimer's.

But we just don't talk about it. What is there to say?

Only fools wallow in their own misery. I prefer to listen to my boys. I don't care what they tell me. It is like living in a prison and being told what is happening in the outside world. My Sunday visits at Steve's are my parole outings.

Perhaps I'm just getting a little depressed. I've used up so much energy trying to cheer up others, there is little life force left for myself. Maybe that's what's happened to Father Mulligan. My own mind's been gravitating more and more often to suicide. Not now. I wouldn't dream of leaving Dad alone. He has enough problems. But after him? When I'm no longer needed in this world. Not needed by anyone. Not in the whole wide world. What am I meant to do then?

Dad was ninety-three, then ninety-eight, and then, suddenly he turned a hundred. How time flies in this jet age. Only yesterday we used to go for walks, together, hand in hand. He always held me by my elbow. The old-fashioned way.

"Where shall we go today?" he would ask.

It did not really matter. He'd forgotten where we'd gone yesterday.

"How about...." I would answer.

He would be pleased. He would pull me with the renewed vigour of one ready to conquer new territories. New horizons. That was the disease's saving grace. You were not aware how dull life had become. You were hardly aware of anything any more.

But that was then. These days, Dad doesn't get up much. For five maybe six hours each day, Raphael lifts him bodily out of his bed and places him gently into the wheelchair. Then he ties his safety jacket behind his back, around the chair, to make sure Dad doesn't fall out.

Imagining myself tied to a wheelchair. Suicide would be nice.

We shuffle together, up and down, along the speckled terrazzo. The Bed of Ganges. That's what the Hindus call the Milky Way. Minute pebbles on and on and on. Polished to shiny smoothness. There are no more floor tiles to count, and spots, the pebbles, there are just too many. Too many dark, burned-out dwarf stars. Cinders of an age gone by, long past their main-sequence. How appropriate. Like us. Well past our main-sequence. On a nice day we visit the balcony. We still did a lot of things together. Non-things. Non-activities. Like watching TV. Or I read to him from a book. I don't think he hears much. It doesn't really matter. His eyes follow me whenever I move around the room. Sometimes I feel like a prisoner. I only leave the room when he falls asleep.

What if we are not biological structures? What if we don't invite any superior beings to enter our bodies, use us, then discard us when we become of no further use to them? What if we are not our bodies, emotions, our minds, our personalities? What if we are not that which we appear to be...?

Then... what are we?

Perhaps we are just dreamers. One day we shall wake up and all this will be gone. Dad's so relaxed, seemingly, so happy. He'll wake up soon, well before me. I wonder if he, in his virtually permanent dream-state, could tell me things I don't know. Dear Jan....

What if we are from another galaxy? What if *we* are aliens from a different reality – superior spiritual beings, who enter the ineptly named temples of clay for reasons of our own? What if it is *we* who create the biological constructs to further *our* own ends?

Questions. Are we allowed to question who we are? What would my spiritual director have to say about my mental meandering? More questions.

"You must have faith," he would tell me, authority palpable in the tone of his voice.

"Have faith in what?" I want to ask.

There's no point. There have been so very few 'points' in my life lately. I live for my husband . . . till death do us part. What if death brings us together, instead? If we die together? It would take some planning....

Iago had a name for it. *La vechia fe dell ciel!* The ancient lie of heaven. Iago followed his realization with a devilish laughter. What the devil is a devil anyway? Or an angel, for that matter? Shakespeare and Verdi and Arrigo Boito, who did Shakespeare great justice with his libretto to Verdi's Otello, had a great deal more to say about that than my confessor. All I can do is ask questions. I have plenty of time.

"Father, what is a devil? An angel? Heaven? Immortality? God?"

"Father, are we really created unto the image and likeness of God? Does God also have Alzheimer's? Arthritis? Rheumatism? Dementia? Diabetes? Is God ever incontinent? Well, Father? Is He? Is He?"

The walls of my room are not only dull. They are also silent.

Say we create our own bodies....

Of course, we use the equipment which nature placed at our disposal. The chemicals, the sperm, the egg, a willing womb – whatever is available. In fact, we've become so involved with our ongoing creative process that we've begun to identify with the process itself. We terminate and replace thousands of cells each day. Hundreds of thousands. We rebuild many worn parts. We construct a superb immune system to fight off other bacterial and viral biological forms threatening the well-being of our creation. I read somewhere that we generate six trillion electrochemical reactions per second in our bodies. Don't tell me that our bodies do that on their own. Just by accident? We maintain a careful balance between the mental and the emotional energy currents flowing within our body.

Our body. Our very own body. The body we've built in our image and likeness.

You might say . . . we've gotten lost in our creative act. Sometimes we lose the distinction between the creator and the created. Rather like a Method actor identifying with the role she is playing to the exclusion of her own identity.

A reasonable option?

Jan coughed. Saliva must have wandered into his windpipe. I approached the foot of his bed and cranked up the top portion another notch. Just half a turn. He chortled once or twice more, and his breathing returned to normal. I decided it was time for my daily constitutional. I had to keep in shape if I were to be of any use to Dad. What else was there? More questions.

I put on my coat, took the elevator down and was soon out on the street.

It was autumn again. Funny how seasons come and go, in circles. Is this what we do? I don't mean our bodies, but we, the real we. The *we* that creates our bodies. The I within every one of us. The I AM. Do we also go around in circles?

The colours were as beautiful as ever. We see them every year and every year they enchant us. Perhaps Shakespeare was wrong. Perhaps it is not music but colours that are the food of love? Perhaps we need beauty, we feed on it. It reminds us who we really are.

I quickened my pace. If I am to maintain my condition I have to make an effort. A condition of a healthy eighty-eight, eighty-nine, ninety-year-old. I wish it didn't always take such an effort to do something good. It takes no effort to eat like a pig, drink beer, to laze around, to watch TV, to smoke cigarettes, to yammer gossip nineteen to a dozen. But it takes an effort to do something good. It seems unfair. Shouldn't good be effortless?

I sit down on a bench. It's a tiny park but it serves my purpose. It is my private escape. This time of the year my feet walked on a multihued carpet of gold and red. What a magnificent gift nature lays before us every autumn. Aren't we lucky? I mustn't sit long, I need the exercise. I must maintain my bodies. I created them – all three. The physical, the emotional and the mental. The spiritual takes care of itself. The others are my responsibility.

I created my bodies....

What now of suicide?

It all seemed very lucid and clear. The body was not alive before I finally entered it, nor will it be alive after I leave it. Is this suicide? Not if I define life as *my* presence. Not if *I am life*. Hadn't somebody said that? I am life? We, the aliens or souls, do not die. We enter our creation, our house, our transient state of consciousness, we work from within, then we move on. If we are spiritual beings experimenting with different biological structures, we enliven them even as gasoline enlivens the engine of an automobile. Yet a car needs a driver, a *conscious* presence. And this is what we are. The Conscious Presence. I am a conscious presence.

I am.

We enjoy the car while we drive it, but... there are other engines to test. When we build a new vehicle, we often take our toolbox with us: our minds and emotions. We have built those up over the ages. They help us along.

We, aliens, keep learning.

Dad was just waking when I got back. Soon Raphael would come round and help Dad up into the wheelchair. I wonder if I would even be thinking of suicide if Dad hadn't succumbed to Alzheimer's. Was this why he got it? Was he the scapegoat? God wouldn't be that cruel. Aren't God and good synonymous? Then why will thirty-four million people around the world get Alzheimer's by 2025?

When Raphael arrived I decided to ask him.

"There are Universal Laws," he said. It sounded as though he'd capitalized the U and the L. Some big laws, I thought.

What Raphael said next really struck a cord. Somehow, it really meant something.

"We, the Spirit, Soul, are above the Law, but as we become incarnate, we must obey our own rules of material existence. We are Life, Consciousness, and we are also Beauty. The latter is a concomitant of harmony and order. If our creation is to function, certain rules must prevail. For those among us who lost track of who or what we are, a word of caution: *every single murder is suicide*. At the elemental ground of being, we are all One. The killer must restore the balance by being the victim. This is the Law of Karma."

I was feeling very sleepy.

"...you should never consider yourself the cause of action, nor be attached to inaction. That way you do not inherit any karma."

Somehow I knew he was talking about Jan. I knew Jan felt himself responsible for all his actions. Always. Had that been his mistake?

I shook my head. "Could you repeat that, more slowly?" I asked.

"Repeat what, Mrs. Kordos?"

I scrutinized his face. He seemed completely concentrated on the task in his hands. He was helping Dad get comfortable in the wheelchair. His gentle smile gave nothing away.

"Didn't you just tell me...."

"I'm afraid I really must go, Mrs. Kordos," he cut me off.

He'd never done that before. Already at the door, he looked again at Jan, as though searching for confirmation. It was in that moment that I got it. My husband was a military officer. He'd fought in three wars. He'd fought for his country. We praise such men. We build them monuments, statues. Hang medals and crosses on their brave chests. But... but they accumulate karma.

Dad was paying back his debt in the only way he knew how. He was restoring the balance. He was subject to the Universal Law.

I don't like these thoughts. He had been awarded the very highest military honours. He'd risen through the ranks – the hard way – all the way to the Commander-in-Chief of his Regiment. He'd placed his life on the line dozens of times. He'd fought so that others might be free.

And he'd accumulated karma.

I don't think I like the Universal Laws at all. They are not fair. I must reread the Bhagavad Gita. I've only read it once, and not very carefully.

But what if we are immortal, if we don't die.

Then maybe those of us who kill must experience the agony of physical, emotional and mental wrongful death. According to Raphael – even if he wanted to pretend it wasn't him talking – every killing is also a partial suicide. That's a tough Law.

My dear Steven, as you read this one day, you'll see that we must continue. We must continue learning. We can save ourselves future heartaches by respecting others' creation today. The creation of other aliens, such as we are. Creation like human bodies. Or animals. Or trees and flowers. Nothing on earth is eternal. Everything has been, and continues to be created by someone.

By an alien. Such as you and I.

It's much too late for Dad and me. Not for you, my son. Remember, not for you and Annette. And don't forget to tell Bart.

"There are no coincidences. Everything has its purpose. Every cause results in an effect. And so on."

There was an echo of Raphael in his tone. What I like most about Steven is that he doesn't ask about my well-being, or Dad's for that matter, but plunges into a discussion as though continuing the one from last Sunday. Regardless of what we'd talked about at the time. It makes me suspect that he thinks of us quite often. Not that he would ever admit it.

After his opening statement, he brought out two glasses, filled them a little too high with Sherry and sprawled his considerable bulk out on the armchair. I still had no idea why he raised the question of coincidences. Or was it purpose? Probably something to do with karma.

"I brought you a book, Mama. You might enjoy it."

I looked at the beautiful illustrations while we chatted. For some reason, Steve looked uncomfortable. He kept swinging his legs, crossing his knees from one side to the other.

"Mother, I really don't want to upset your beliefs, but..."

With Steve there was always a but. I knew he didn't want to upset my set of beliefs but his Catholicism, if any, was unorthodox to say the least.

"....I would say that I am an ardent Christian rather than a Catholic."

There was a time when I thought the two were synonymous. I said so. He grinned. I asked him what he meant by that grin.

"When Catholics hunger for Truth, they turn to a priest, Mother. When a Christian needs to sate his or her thirst, he or she turns to the Bible."

Soon after that Steve left to let me read.

Had I ever met a Catholic who'd read the whole Bible? Of course, those who had weren't likely to hang a shingle on their forehead attesting to the fact. Maybe Steve did have a point. Catholicism has become a social rather than religious phenomenon. It made you feel part of a pack. An assembly. Or a herd – as in sheep. You felt strength in numbers. The Bible had nothing to do with that. If dealt with the individual.

The book he gave me was called *Reflections on the Light.* I liked the title. Usually, it is the light that is reflected, here, there was a touch of mystery. The reflections were on the light. Of course, Christ had once said, I am the Light. Perhaps the book was about a different sort of light altogether.

The book turned out to be a collection of thoughts and ideas, attributed to Jalal-ud-Din Rumi, a Sufi. Sufis, as far as I know, were Moslem Mystics. I decided to give the book a fair chance and opened it at random.

I am where My servant thinks of Me.
Every servant has an image of Me;
whatever image my servant forms of Me, here I will be.

I was fairly amazed. Steven lent me his book about Rumi a week after I had a discussion with myself about the Universal Laws. Or with Raphael, if you must. I recall I'd asked a dozen inane questions for which, I felt sure, there were no answers. Not that I'd given up asking. It was just that I was losing hope that I would ever find any answers.

I was determined to ask questions until some light would help me accept, with equanimity, my present condition, or release me from having to subject myself to the slow, degrading process to which my husband was already being subjected. If he had a reason for suffering, then what was my obligation? And here, thanks to Steven, I seemed to have found the empowerment I'd been searching for. It was almost as if not God created us, but we who created our God. I wouldn't dare to pose such an assumption to Father Mulligan, and there was nobody else. Perhaps Sister Angelica, but I didn't want to upset the mental equilibrium that I thought, at the time, she had found. I read on from Steve's book.

I am the servant of My servant's image of Me.

Be careful then, My servants, and purify, attune, and expand your thoughts about Me.

For they are My House.

Whatever Jalal-ud-Din Rumi had in mind, it took me by surprise. It was comforting and upsetting at the same time. It empowered me to create an image of my God according to my own needs, at the same time it denied me the stereotypical Father figure who looked after us regardless of how ignorant we might be. Perhaps even more so, if we really were stupid. Or obedient.

I wondered how much easier it must be to control stupid people. People of unquestioning obedience. People who do not ask embarrassing questions. Or any questions.

"Pray Father, bless me for I have sinned. I asked questions."

"How many times, my daughter?"

"Lately, most of the time, Father?"

"Do you promise not to do it again?"

"I don't know if I can. I could try, I suppose...."

"Say three Hail Marys and sin no more."

"Yes, thank you, Father. What is it that you don't want me to do again?"

"Go in peace my child."

Of course, the next step would be to engage Raphael in a conversation. This time, I would watch his lips. It they moved, I would pay attention. Whatever or whoever he was, he stirred in me the desire to learn. To get to know myself. And, in the process, to learn to know my husband. Not his body, his emotions, nor even his mind. But to get to know that aspect of him that I would meet, one day, in a halo of light. After all, are we not all destined to convert our bodies into light? Einstein already told us how to do it. Well, almost. He left the details to us.

Yet I recall from my daily reading of the Bible that there were not supposed to be any secrets. After the priest told me again last Sunday that I must have faith, thus discouraging the use of my mind, I actually took the trouble to write out the assurances that we can continue to search for answers without committing a sin. A sentiment certainly neither espoused nor stated by the Padre. The Church seemed to be imbued with Mysteries. Here's what I found.

Matthew 10:26: ...there is nothing covered that shall not be revealed; and hid, that shall not be known.

Mark 4:22: For there is nothing hid which shall not be manifested; neither was any thing kept secret, but that it should come abroad.

Luke 12:2: For there is nothing covered, that shall not be revealed; neither hid, that shall not be known.

Luke 8:17: For nothing is secret, that shall not be made manifest; neither any thing hid, that shall not be known and come abroad.

Enough? There is more. But quantity is not under discussion.

I wrote all my references out on a piece of paper and kept them tucked inside my Bible in case I ever had a chance to discuss the Mysteries with anyone. Like Father Mulligan, for instance. I know that if I hadn't, I would be too lazy to get up and get it. When you're my age, it is time you began to know yourself.

There were so many of them. The purported biblical secrets, I mean. I had been brought up on mysteries. The mystery of the Holy Trinity, the mystery of the Virgin Birth, the mystery of the Incarnation, the mystery of Transubstantiation, the mystery of Immaculate Conception, Transfiguration, Ascension, Assumption, Resurrection, the mystery of the Original Sin, the mystery of Papal Infallibility, the mystery of the Seven Sacraments. Whatever I couldn't understand, whatever was a question of *faith* was a mystery.

***

9

Father Mulligan

About two months before Jan's hundredth birthday I was pushing his wheelchair along the corridor when, quite inadvertently, we bumped into Father Mulligan. Such collisions aren't rare, no matter how careful one is. Not that there was any real harm.

Father Mulligan stepped aside as fast as a man his age can move, and opened his mouth. The moment he saw me, his tightened lips relaxed, an embarrassed smile wiped all anger from his eyes.

"I am sorry, Mrs. Kordos," he murmured, stepping out of the way.

I apologized in turn and went on pushing the wheelchair along the corridor. Seconds later, Dad reached over his shoulder and touched my arm. Thinking he wanted something, I stopped and took a step forward to face him. These last few years, we only communicated by looking at each other. And then I saw it. There was great pain in my husband's eyes. He swung the armchair around and looked behind him, to where we had our collision. His crooked finger pointed towards Father Mulligan. He didn't say anything, but I understood the message. He was telling me that the man we'd run into was suffering. It was at that moment that I decided to try harder to fulfill the promise I'd made to Sister Angelica.

That same day a chance presented itself.

"I hope I didn't hurt you, Father," I said sitting next to him. Actually I sat on the next-but-one chair on the terrace. As usual I brought my Bible with me. Just in case I needed moral support. I felt a little like a TV evangelist who without wielding his Bible seems completely lost, if not powerless.

Father Mulligan smiled. He was doing that more often lately, although the smile didn't carry much merriment. It was almost a professional smile, the sort that is sincere but placed on one's countenance by an act of will.

"Not at all, Mrs. Kordos. They made us of stern stuff, in my days."

I think he was referring to a number of women who wailed in agony whenever anyone touched them. I rather thought they did that only to attract attention. When you are really lonely, any attention is good attention. No matter how misbegotten. Anyway, I agreed with him, though I doubted the resistance to pain had much to do with the date of manufacture stamped on our foreheads. Father Mulligan's thoughts were anchored in the past, probably in the years when he felt more alive.

"In those days we were often moved from parish to parish. Sometimes twice in the same year. The War had decimated us. We had to make up for the lack of priests."

His words came in a quiet, distant tone, his eyes searching the far horizon. A horizon as empty of special features as our life here. Just distant. Even as he and I still were. How forsaken he must be feeling if he's choosing to share his memories with me. After all, having spent almost ten years on the same floor, in the same building, we were still strangers. Perhaps, for not much longer.

"They always expected more from us. I was only twenty-three when I finished the Seminarium of Saint Benedict. There had been seventeen of us, and there were forty-two parishes waiting to be served. We were moved like sheep, to areas with the greatest need...."

"What happened to the older priests?" I asked.

"They were where we are now. They were not only older, they were old. The problem was that there were no replacements. Young men no longer felt the call to serve. If they did, they joined the Peace Corps, or some charitable organization in Africa or South America. It was more romantic, I suppose."

That made sense. I had always wanted to travel, when young. Then I didn't – now, I did. Or at least in my later life. In my day, young ladies didn't travel much. Their husbands went abroad on business, or as Jan, for international championships, while we, dutiful wives, stayed behind looking after home, children and the staff. Someone had to give dispositions, make plans for future guests, bridge parties, plan the carnival season . . . there were so many items on the social calendar that seem, today, so very irrelevant.

And then, years later, the boys left for Canada. There was little point in staying in England. We sold our house. For the first time since before the War, we felt relatively rich. We flew to Paris, then Rome, Madrid.... It was like our second honeymoon. Or was it our third? The second was when we met in Italy in '46, after Steve and I had escaped from Poland.

And there was more. We decided to join our boys in Montreal. Within a year of arriving in North America we crossed Canada in a Pullman bus, all the way to Vancouver, Victoria, where I put my bare foot in the Pacific while Jan held my arm so as to keep my balance. On that one trip I covered more miles than in the remainder of my life!

On our return we touched on Chicago with its museums, its imposing buildings – the Sears, the John Hancock, with a drive in a horse-drawn carriage along the shore of Lake Michigan admiring the never-ending array of luxury yachts anchored along its length, for miles and miles....

A year later came the Guggenheim, Carnegie Hall, the tickets the boys got for us for the Lincoln Center – Aida, Celeste Aida with Pavarotti... The New York skyscrapers . . . they really did scrape the sky . . . the stroll after dinner along Fifth avenue....

And now? And now that too is in our past. But not the memories. The memories remain fresh, palpable, euphoric...

We are all swayed by the winds of change. Some more so than others. Father Mulligan evidently thought that his early years swayed him too much. Foxes have holes, and the birds of the air have nests.... St. Matthew said: The Son of man hath nowhere to lay his head. Father Mulligan had not chosen the easiest of paths.

"They always expected us to be something special. The parishioners, I mean. They would ignore the teaching we gave them, but they expected us to always be shining examples. One can grow tired, of being an example, Mrs. Kordos. There were moments when I wanted to sin. I, a priest, wanted to be sinful, Mrs. Kordos. What do you think of that?"

I don't think he expected an answer.

"They could sin, confess their shortcomings, and leave to start sinning again. On and on... the same sins every week, every month, every year.... I could recite what any one of my parishioners would say at the confessional before they opened their mouths. But *we* were supposed to be good. Not to sin at all. Was that fair?"

"Do you think those people were evil?" I didn't know what to say.

"What is evil, Mrs. Kordos? 'Why callest thou me good? There is none good but one, that is, God'. If the Master said that, could I say any less? And if He wasn't good, then how can I call anyone evil?"

I've often wondered how the Church could recognize Jesus as God, when He, Himself, had rejected the comparison. Perhaps He shouldn't have been allowed to think for himself either.

"People do not understand the teaching, Mrs. Kordos," Father Mulligan resumed after a moment of silence. "Sometimes I'm not so sure I do either." He looked up at me. "If the purpose of religion is to create bliss, then I have failed miserably. Not only in others, but in myself. I seem to have denied myself all the gifts from heaven that could make life worthwhile. Which, I often wonder, are our heritage to enjoy."

There seemed little I could add to that statement.

There is one other thing I recall from that 'traffic' accident. The way my husband had reacted, I knew with utter confidence that Alzheimer's is a disease of the brain, not of the mind. That we, the human species, are more than our bodies, no matter how deteriorated those bodies might become. That beneath the sheath of our skin and bones there resides a consciousness which obeys its own laws, which abides in its own timeframe, which is virtually independent of the biological robot it has created. I knew I would have to review these findings at a later date. Right now I was so full of joy, so confident of my discovery that analytical thinking could be swayed so much by my emotions.

After I took Dad back to our room, I took a little walk on my own. I went to our Chapel and sat there, alone, just being grateful. To Whom or to What, I didn't know. But it didn't matter. I felt, nevertheless, that I was in the right place to share my moment of bliss – with the fresh carnations, the orchids, and the little red light shimmering at the altar.

I spent a half hour just being happy.

Yesterday, for the first time in five years Father Mulligan talked to me without being prompted. Once again we met on the terrace, the one which I'd referred to as the balcony. He sat almost next to me, leaving only one empty chair between us. For a while he kept silent while I read more Rumi. I think what pushed him over the brink of shyness was the fact that we were the only two people on the terrace. Everyone else was taking an afternoon nap. Since turning one hundred, Jan seldom came up for air. He ate, he slept and he defecated. Mostly into his bed. Thank God they'd invented those extra large diapers for adults. Otherwise, we wouldn't be able to breathe in our room.

Father Mulligan glanced at my book. I noticed his interest and showed him the cover.

"I've never read Rumi," he volunteered.

"You missed a great deal," I returned. I was really beginning to think so.

"Yes, Mrs. Kordos. I've missed a great deal."

In that moment I knew that Father Mulligan's comment had nothing to do with the book I was reading, nor with any other book. For a moment I held my breath, then, remembering Sister Angelica's request, relaxed.

I closed the book, put it on the empty chair between us, and waited. I was sure that if he wanted to share anything with me, my prompting would only discourage him.

"I never wanted to be anything else," he said after a while. "Since I was a little boy, I've served the Holy Mass. I would get up early, and run to the church, and then run to school. I'd only just make it in time. If it was a Solemn Mass, the teacher would keep me in school after hours, for being late."

"You never told her why you were late?" I assumed it had been a 'she'. I was a teacher myself before I got married.

"I offered the injustice to Christ for my sins," he said. It sounded as though he was in confession.

"Surely, by doing so you were perpetuating..." I bit my tongue.

"...a lie? I didn't know it then. A boy of eight or nine doesn't think in such complex terms. I was glad there was something I had to offer," he said. A serious expression, which usually froze his face into a mask of complacent tolerance, began to relax. From the corner of my eye I could see the beginning of a smile.

"Boys are such innocents," I tried to make up for my previous observation.

"Yes, they are. At least, I was. That was a great many years ago, Mrs. Kordos. There was a time when we were all innocents," he said wistfully as if his future, or past, erased all his youthful attributes.

"We are told not to judge others, Father Mulligan. Don't you think the same should apply to ourselves?"

He looked over at me, drilling me with his eyes.

"What made you say that, Mrs. Kordos?"

"Those who try to be kind to others sometimes do not extend the same kindness to themselves."

I felt very uneasy. I expected Father Mulligan to get up at any moment and tell me that he didn't need an old woman to teach him about Christian Ethics. For quite a while, he remained silent. Perhaps I'd touched on some hidden scar. It was still evident to anyone over ninety, that the man was not a happy man. That he had demons eating at him from within. A funny comparison, I thought. A priest eaten by demons. And yet...

"I've always been so busy, Mrs. Kordos, trying to do the right thing, I don't think I've ever given the matter much thought." he said at last.

It sounded as though I'd guessed the problem. Priests, as indeed the whole Catholic Church, tended to externalize their God. The Father, the Son, the Holy Ghost, are all so perfect, so unattainable, that no matter how much we attempt to please any one of them, we are bound to fail. I remember hearing someone asking: what do you give a man who has everything? By definition, there is no answer. Father Mulligan had spent his whole life attempting to give something to God. Something that God did not have?

"We are all so busy, at times," I tried to console him.

"At times is all right, Mrs. Kordos. When you are busy all the time, you tend to forget why you became so busy in the first place."

Father Mulligan was getting the message. I hoped it wasn't too late to make up for lost time. There's a saying from the gospel of St. John. 'Ask and ye shall receive that your joy may be full'. There was so little joy in us. I would certainly not presume to quote the Bible to Father Mulligan. First, I was sure he knew it a lot better than I. Second, it isn't what we read, it is what we *notice* when we read. There are passages in the New and Old Testament that I hadn't noticed at all, on my first or second reading. Now, finally I had time. I didn't read it to learn, only to notice. It paid dividends. When you want to learn, you are really searching for confirmation of what you already believe. You seek reinforcement. Reassurance. When you shed that desire, you begin to notice things you'd never seen before.

"You are a very kind lady," Father Mulligan murmured. He began inching to the edge of his chair in order to get up. "May I speak to you again, sometime?"

I was flabbergasted. The silent one wanted to speak to little *moi*? I gave him my best smile. I thought that, at long last, Sister Angelica would be pleased with me.

"I shall always be glad to learn from you, Father Mulligan," I replied looking him in the eyes.

For the second time Father Mulligan graced me with a smile. This time, I actually saw his teeth. Quite regular, probably false. Then he waved his head from side to side like a bubblehead doll, sighed, waved his head again and ambled towards the terrace door. He used an aluminium walker but I suspected that if he really wanted to, he could walk without one. His old age was a function of his mind, not his body.

"You talked to Father Mulligan on the terrace," Sister Angelica said, putting her head in the door. I beckoned her in.

"There are spies everywhere," I commented dryly.

"Oh, Mrs. Kordos. I couldn't help it. I was just passing...."

"You will have to stay after school," I said thinking of poor Father Mulligan.

Sister Angelica smiled. "Gladly," she said, a meek expression on her face. She then whipped round her right hand, till now hidden behind her back. "I brought you this," she said.

She held out the most unusual exotic flower I'd ever seen. "It's from Brazil," she said. "I thought you would like it."

It was a single flower. It had a white centre surrounded by an explosion of red that turned towards brown on its outer edges. It was not only beautiful but utterly unique.

"It's called an Orthophytum. It is from Pico das Almas."

"Where on earth did you find such a beauty?" I was really taken by the flower and by Sister Angelica's kindness.

"I visited the family of one of our residents. We do that sometimes, especially when they fail to visit their kin here. They live close to the Botanical Gardens. I couldn't resist dropping in. All those flowers, and I was so close.... The man working there gave it to me."

"How? Why?"

"He asked me where I was from. Without thinking I told him I was from Brazil. He said that he'd never met anyone from Brazil. He thought I might like it. The flower I mean."

There you are. Sister Angelica was like that. She had to share her joy with me. She was still standing at the door. I got up to put it in some water. I had a vase just made for a single . . . Orthophytum?

"Is there another name for it?"

"I don't know, Mrs. Kordos. I've never seen one in my life!"

"You what?"

"The man told me they only grow on the highest peeks in Bahia. I am from the lowlands. Do you mind?"

Sister had remained standing at the door. I knew she was dying to find out what had happened between Father Mulligan and me. I waved her further inside.

"We just chatted," I said at last. It was unfair to keep her in suspense any longer, especially after such a beautiful gift. She immediately took a step forward. Her eyes seemed brighter than usual. Unfortunately, I didn't have much to add. I pointed to a chair. She remained standing.

"We talked about happiness, and kindness . . . about such things. Quite impersonal." This last one wasn't quite true. But I could hardly tell the Sister that I was trying to show the old man the error of his ways. That would be too presumptuous for words. And it wouldn't be true. Frankly, I was just fishing.

And then it struck me. Why should a plump, short, retired priest, with an evident chip on his shoulder, be of such interest to a joyful, carefree, ever-smiling nun?

"Was he all right?" she asked, her eyes riveted to her shoes.

"I'm not sure what you mean, Sister Angelica. But he was polite, sensitive to my ideas. We really exchanged just a few words. Why the sudden interest?"

"I took some time off. I haven't been here for a few days."

I waited. Sister Angelica's private life was her own.

"I flew to New York. My son sent me a ticket and Mother Superior gave me permission to go and see him."

This explained why she hadn't been here for a week but not why she was so worried about Father Mulligan. It would be easier to talk to her if only she cared to look me in the eye.

"Sit down, Sister, and tell me about your son." I thought changing the subject might loosen her tongue.

"He's just like Francis," she said after a while.

"Like son, like father," I put in my two-pence worth.

"No, no, Mrs. Kordos. He. Father Mulligan."

"Father Mulligan reminds you of your late husband?"

"Not physically, so much, although they were both on the short side, and rather liked their food. Oh, dear, I shouldn't have said they both *liked* . . . Father Mulligan still does. I think that's what killed him. I mean my husband. He liked food too much. It was my fault. I just couldn't refuse him anything. He'd been so kind to me. He...."

The rest of her confession was lost in a flood of tears. I waited, rising only to offer Sister Angelica my box of Kleenex. It didn't last long. Still catching her breath, she smiled. "I've always been such a baby," she said at last. Her eyes looked more bashful than filled with sorrow. They reminded me of that deer at the lake of my youth. Funny how that deer keeps coming back to me. I wonder if that means something. Perhaps I too am afraid of something and don't even know it.

"Really, Sister...."

"But it *was* my fault," the Sister repeated stubbornly.

I learned long ago not to argue with people who were having an emotional outburst. No logical argument appealed to them, and it often served to enervate them still further.

"So how else does Father Mulligan remind you of Father Francis?" I asked instead. That worked. Sister Angelica sat up and her eyes finally met mine.

"They were both priests, both retired from active duty, both loved food . . . I already said that. They were both on the plump side, both carried some sort of load of guilt they didn't know how to cope with. They are both sad, at times. Quite often. They both don't talk so much. They just sit and read and think...."

Somehow the 'they' of the past, became 'they' of the present tense. Was there more to Sister Angelica's interest than met the eye? Or did she also carry some sort of guilt on her narrow shoulders that weighed her down. Perhaps her smile was little more than a mask deigned to hide her inner turmoil, or God forbid, suffering.

"It's all my fault," she repeated out of the blue.

"Just what is it that you are blaming yourself for so much, Sister?"

She didn't look up from her toes. Whatever ate at her innards remained inside. I decided not to push. I knew she would come out with it in her own good time. When she was ready.

"They were so cold, you know, Mrs. Kordos," she whispered.

"Cold, Sister?"

"Her fingers. Mother Superior told me that when they'd saved Father Mulligan from Mrs. Merryweather, all he would say was that they were so cold."

"What was so cold, Sister?" I pursued gently. She wasn't making much sense.

"Her fingers, Mrs. Kordos. Mrs. Merryweather had such cold fingers."

The next moment Sister Angelica got up from her armchair, ran over to me and, crouching at my side, put both her hands on my forearm. It was a gentle, hesitant touch. "You don't think I have cold fingers, do you Mrs. Kordos?" And then, without waiting for an answer she got to her feet and ran out of my room.

For some strange reason I kept thinking of Mrs. Merryweather's cold fingers. Revenge is a dish best served cold, I remembered. Poor Father Mulligan. Was it she, the vengeful widow, that had awakened such thoughts of fulfillment? Or lack of it? I would swear that Father Mulligan was a virgin. I suspected that because, more often than not, the expectations are so much greater than the fulfillment. In all walks of life. And, by reading between the lines, Father Mulligan still harboured great expectations.

I couldn't help wondering if I was right. The next few weeks would show whether or not the good Father thought his fulfillment would meet his expectations. No matter what the 'Teaching' said. We'll just have to wait and see.

For a while I sat watching Dad. How come we never had such problems? Sixty or was it now sixty-six years of marriage, and we were as close to each other as ever. Even though quite deaf, by now in both ears, Jan seemed to understand whatever I said to him. Never understood anyone else. They would raise their voice at him, practically shouting, as if that was to have any effect. Deaf people don't hear better when you shout at them. What you must do is communicate with them at a different level. It is the smile, the expression, a gentle touch. But more than anything, Dad became very sensitive to people's feelings. He reacted to the mood people were in.

He returned some people's smiles and not others. I suppose that some smiles must have been honest, or joyful, and others a grimace painted like makeup on a rag doll. Somehow he always knew. I could even tell the disposition of any help, cleaners, laundry people, or domestics who brought us food, just by watching Dad. His facial expression would tell me what sort of disposition those people were really in.

He didn't say anything, but I just knew. I suspected that he could still talk, he just chose not to. Yet, in some ways, he told me so much.

Raphael was the exception. He didn't have to smile at all for Dad to cooperate with him. Whatever it was. Unlike with others. When others tried to 'handle' him, to change his sheets or whatever, Dad was capable of exhibiting amazing strength, as if he drew on sources other than just physical. On occasion it took two men and a nurse to do the job Raphael did easily, indeed easier, on his own.

Incongruously, I recalled how Jan had reacted to Father Mulligan. The man who seems to have lost himself while looking after others.

***

10

Sister Angelica

"In a way, Mrs. Kordos, our life, together, really began in Rio. Before that we had been ostracized, looked upon as people who did not deserve to be among decent folk. Certainly not among God-abiding parishioners. The paradox of it was that once Francis got his dispensation from his priestly duties, his parish remained unattended. For years."

Sister looked up from her shoes, searching my face for understanding. As usual she was sitting on the very edge of the chair, in grave danger of slipping to the floor.

As for her story, I could picture the situation. A lot of simple folk suddenly learn that their reverent priest is a father of not one but two children. A shock by any standards. I tried to place myself in such a situation, way back when we were in Poland. A Catholic country, through and through, which regarded its priests as something halfway to God, or at least to heaven. Priests held the keys to the Kingdom, and without them we would have been lost. Or at least the simple folk would have been. I hated to admit that there had been a time when I might have been among those lost sheep.

"You actually told them that?"

"What, that we had children?"

"Well . . . yes."

"No, Mrs. Kordos. We never said anything. We just didn't hide the fact. There would be little point. When I first got pregnant, Frank announced from the pulpit that he intended to step down as the parish priest. He told them that he was awaiting official release from his duties."

"So you can stop riding a bicycle...."

"I beg your pardon, Mrs.... oh, I see. Well, yes and no. You remain a priest, only, there are some functions that you are not allowed to perform. A bit like the Eastern Orthodox clergy. Their priests marry and Rome recognizes such contracts. It's a bit complex. Of course, he could no longer say Mass. But, should there be, for instance, the need of Extreme Unction, Frank could and did administer it even after he'd left the parish."

Sister Angelica had taken to dropping in on all her days off to see me. I rather think that she needed me more than I needed her. I mean that she really had no one to talk to. She certainly couldn't discuss her past with a priest or the other nuns. It would be highly unseemly. Her past weighed heavily on her conscience. I still hadn't learned why, however.

"So he no longer wore a cassock, Sister?"

"No. He became a regular guy. It was all wonderful except that both he and I became not only unemployed but unemployable. Not many people offered jobs to defrocked priests or wayward nuns. After all we lived in a deeply Catholic country wherein, apparently, only the Church was empowered to forgive and forget. Well, forgive anyway. I don't think anyone ever forgot.... Frank could have joined some other denomination but, for some reason, he remained a Catholic."

"You mean he could have become a Pentecostal or...."

"That sort of thing. Not that there is anything wrong with people searching God by different paths. Only, well, the Church, the Roman Church, was within his blood. After so many years...."

"In spite of getting such a raw deal?"

"He didn't think it was raw. He would not have accepted a stipend from the Church had he not earned it. He was a very honest man."

Then it struck me that Sister Angelica kept referring to him in past tense. Had they divorced after all this? And how come the

Sister had turned full circle? Her husband left the Church while she'd returned to it. Something didn't jibe. All the same, I didn't want to prod her mind, let alone her heart. Even now, I could see a mass of emotions in her face desperately trying to get out. She must have kept those memories bottled up within her for years. Her eyes alternated between reflections of great joy, and of utter misery. I began to wonder which would win in the end.

"So how did you cope....?"

"Rio is a big and popular place. He enlisted at the *Unversidade Federal do Rio de Janeiro*. That's a State University, where there are no fees. He began to study psychology. I kept the four of us going by selling doughnuts on the streets. Mostly to tourists."

"Doughnuts?" I asked incredulously.

"All I needed was an ordinary kitchen stove, some dough, some sugar and something to spice them with. Jam or marmalade or honey. All the ingredients were cheap in Rio. I had no overhead and Frank could study at home and look after the children at the same time."

"And you sold them on the streets...?"

I still couldn't picture Sister Angelica in her flowing robes and a flamboyant wimple selling anything on the streets of Rio or anywhere else. Not that her wimple was flamboyant. For some reason I must have been thinking of the flying monkeys. And come to think of it I have no real idea what the streets of Rio are like.

"Each time I had a trayful, still warm from the oven, I would run downstairs to the nearest beach, La Copacabana, and within fifteen minutes my tray would be empty. Then I would repeat the exercise until there were no more people on the beach. It was quite easy really."

A very pretty girl, in her middle twenties, with plenty of suntan, rosy cheeks from bending over the oven, and a gorgeous smile. That must have made a difference.

"It was quite easy...." she repeated, evidently her emotions taking her to the Copacabana along the shores of Rio de Janeiro.

How happy she must have been. After being cooped up in a convent laundry for seven years, here she was, a young mother of two children, proud of her educated husband, and the opportunity to look after them by her own efforts. I recalled my own life between 1939 and 1945. I too had looked after quite a bunch of people. It never felt like a hardship. For weeks on end I may have been physically exhausted, but the knowledge of how indispensable I was had given me all the energy I needed. Nevertheless, I looked at Sister Angelica with new respect. I realized that, in some ways, we had something in common. Perhaps she'd sensed that herself. Perhaps that was why she was here.

"I told Father Mulligan about Francis," she said to me, her face, her eyes even her posture pressed against the doorframe showing both shame and pride. As disparate emotions as you can get.

"Come in Sister," I said pointing to the chair. This was serious.

"I really just dropped by. I just had to tell you, Mrs. Kordos. I just thought...."

"Sit down, Sister."

Steven had brought me another bottle of Bristol Cream and as it was already past four p.m., I didn't feel guilty about getting out two glasses. If not Sister Angelica, then I certainly was going to need a little fortifier. I poured out two glasses and handed her one. By then the Sister had given up. She was sitting meekly, obediently, her previous bravado evaporated.

"Chin-chin," I said raising my glass. She raised hers but merely touched the rim to her lips.

"Do you think I shouldn't have, Mrs. Kordos?"

"Why not? It is good to take his mind off his own iniquity."

"His what?" She practically rose before she thought better of it. "Why did you say that, Mrs...."

"It's a private joke between us. Farther Mulligan and me," I lied to cover my Freudian slip.

"Oh...."

"Tell me, Sister. Did he find your story interesting?"

"What I really told him was that fifty percent of priests in Brazil leave the Church. Then I asked him if he thought that was true. Then . . . one thing led to another. We walked back together from the chapel to the elevator. I sort of mentioned that clergy in Brazil found different paths to God. That he is not alone."

"And how did he take that?"

"He said nothing." Her face turned sad. "I saw him sitting at the back of our Chapel, as though he was afraid to sit closer to the altar. When I passed him, he smiled. He'd never done that before." The last sentence she said slowly, her tone filled with wonderment.

"Did he actually tell you that he'd lost faith?" I asked trying to read her face.

"As a matter of fact, I am sure he hasn't. What I am sure of is that he's lost the Roman Catholic Church's definition of faith. A little like most, or at least a great many priests in Brazil."

"And how did you come to this conclusion?"

I couldn't imagine Father Mulligan confiding such intimate details of his inner life to anyone, let alone another person of the cloth. Male or female. When he'd talked to me, at least I stood on neutral ground. I did not represent any particular order or set of rules.

"Mrs. Kordos. All you have to do is look at him. The man is completely lost. Lost people search for God much harder than those who've already found Him."

I got her message. Whatever Father Mulligan was or wasn't, he was certainly lost. He appeared to have rejected the old ways, which did not bring him satisfaction. Or, to be more precise, they did not bring him peace. It seems that inner peace is what we crave most of all. More than success, money, fame or beauty. If you are truly satisfied, you are truly happy. No matter what.

"He is not a happy man," I murmured.

"But it was more than that, Mrs. Kordos. He reminds me so much of my husband. I don't mean just physically. His eyes are clouded in the same, slightly suspicious way, as if someone was, or had been, trying to get the better of him. As if for years he'd been exploited under false pretences. I know this is a lot to read just by looking into someone's eyes, but I'd seen that look in Frank for many years. There was that same hurt. That same unrequited hunger...."

I recalled my own conversation with Father Mulligan. Sister Angelica's perceptions confirmed my own. Father Mulligan hadn't lost his faith. He just hadn't discovered God at the end of it. This did not deny God's existence; it questioned the Church, the old priest's path. For the umpteenth time I had evidence that there may well be just one God, but that there were as many roads leading to Him as there are people in the world. And, what was quite depressing was that, for as long as we travel somebody else's path, we are unlikely to find what we are looking for.

"What should I do, Mrs. Kordos?" Sister Angelica sounded crestfallen.

"Try the Sherry."

She smiled and did.

"I don't think you should do anything, Sister. I think what should happen is that you allow That which he searches for to use you for Its own ends."

I don't think I'd ever constructed a more complex, twisted nonsensical sentence in my life. What was more, when talking, one cannot introduce capital letters that might, at least in part, clarify the message. I was about to simplify my pompous pronouncement when Sister Angelica looked up at me, joy flooding her eyes.

"But of course, Mrs. Kordos. That is what I always do. Always!"

The next moment she was gone without telling me what it was exactly that she'd told Father Mulligan about Father Francis. No matter, Sister Angelica was happy again. Happy that That had used her for Its own purpose. That was enough for now.

There is often little rationality to human behaviour. We are, on occasion, a bundle of emotions that insist, through some power of their own, to be released, to be given free rein. I wonder what would have happened if Sister Angelica permitted her emotions to run free. Apparently Father Francis was a forerunner of Father Mulligan, until Sister Angelica took him under her angelic wings. Probably a sedentary lifestyle, disregard of a healthy diet, tendency towards expecting too much of himself, even the search for God everywhere except within his own heart, seemed to characterize both men. In the case of Francis, he appeared to rely on emotional needs rather than on intuitive logic. In this respect, Father Mulligan was still an unknown quantity. When people are fuelled by emotions, men and women forget the physical or mental constrains which would normally control their behaviour. They seduce each other, never once thinking of the possible dangers of such a sexual union. They ignore not only the possibility of incurable diseases but also the probability of progeny. But more than that, they don't seem aware of the emotional storm that such a physical union often entails.

Sister Angelica had learned about this the hard way. By the time the plumpish, brooding, and apparently shortish Father Francis became a happy, outgoing, energetic Frank, she was pregnant. It was all emotional.

At the Sister's next visit, I learned how Father Francis, or rather Frank, had died.

"It came suddenly, Mrs. Kordos. He was already a respected scholar, he got his doctorate from the University, and then, within six years, he just died. In his own bed. At night. He fell asleep and never woke up."

Her words came out in short gasps, as though she'd just discovered her husband's body.

"We were just entering the good life. We'd paid off our apartment and moved to a better one, closer to the beach. We could even see the ocean from our balcony. 'It's as good as it gets', he told me. He was so happy. He said that we would always have all we need. Money for the education of our children, and a car, and a good place to live, and lots of food."

She looked up at me, her eyes filled with guilt.

"That's what killed him, Mrs. Kordos. It was all my fault. I had no heart to refuse him anything."

"Refuse what, Sister?"

"Bacon, Mrs. Kordos. He loved bacon. He had it with eggs, on a sandwich, chopped over his potatoes, sprinkled over his soup. He loved bacon."

A strange predilection, I thought. I felt no attraction for the hindquarter of a pig at all. Fried, chopped or sprinkled.

"I once tried to hold it back from him, and he just went out and ate at the trattoria. Eggs and bacon, but mostly bacon. He sneaked in there, on occasion, for *spaghetti a la carbonada* . . . a little Italian restaurant around the corner. A little too close to us. He had no other weakness, Mrs. Kordos. He didn't smoke, hardly ever took a drink. Only bacon...."

"He was a good man," I tried to console her. It would be highly inappropriate to smile, although I couldn't help finding the situation a trifle comical. A plump man getting plumper on the plumpness of pigs.

"He died from a heart attack. And I killed him."

"You are hard on yourself, Sister. He was a grown man. We are all responsible for our own actions."

"But I cooked for him. I loved him very much, Mrs. Kordos. And he loved bacon."

A *ménage au trois*, I thought grimly.

"And now Father Mulligan is getting fat," Sister Angelica said inconsequentially.

Sister Angelica was in great danger of adding two and two and ending up with an impossible answer. I wished she would keep her qualms about her husband and those about Father Mulligan well apart.

"Surely, Sister, you are not blaming yourself for that also?" It was meant to be a joke. She didn't laugh.

"I have experience that could help him, Mrs. Kordos. Shouldn't I do my best to help him?"

I wondered, not for the first time, if Sister Angelica had some guilt that she was attempting to allay with the aid of Father Mulligan. My suspicions were soon confirmed.

"I can do for him what I didn't succeed in doing for my Frank," she murmured.

"You want to keep Father Mulligan away from bacon?" I asked incredulously. We were venturing into the realm of emotions where logic had no place. I suspected that Sister Angelica was determined to placate her own shortcomings rather than Father Mulligan's. He may have been plump, but most men who do not exercise are. No matter what age. But he was far from obese. And I never observed him asking for extra bacon.

"He looks so sad." She changed tack again. "I wish...."

There was a knock on my door. I called out for the person to come in, but nothing happened. Sister Angelica seemed to have shrivelled into the armchair, for the first time sitting deeper as though seeking its protection. I got up and walked to the door.

Father Mulligan was standing, in the middle of the corridor, seemingly embarrassed at having approached my castle.

"Come in, Father," I stepped out of the way.

"Oh, no, Mrs. Kordos. I only came to return your Bible. You left it on the chair on the terrace."

I stepped back, looked to my bedside table, before answering. Indeed, my Bible was missing.

"You're right, Father. I must have forgotten...."

The door remained ajar, not wide enough to let Father see inside. As I pulled it wider, Father Mulligan took another step backwards.

"Won't you join us, Father? We have one armchair left."

I walked back and removed the pillows from the remaining armchair. As I turned again, the balding pate of the shy priest just crossed the threshold. The rest of his rotund body followed it, very slowly. Then he saw Sister Angelica. He froze. Whatever he saw was more than I could imagine, but he went pale, then bright red, then pale again. He handed me the Bible, turned and, without a single word was out of the door before I could stop him. I wondered what on earth was going on.

"What just happened?" I asked no one in particular. I forgot the good Sister was still cringing in the armchair. "Do you mind telling me what is going on?" I was going to add 'between you two', but decided to let her explain.

"Why, nothing, Mrs. Kordos. Nothing at all," she assured me. Her voice was surprisingly normal.

And the next moment she smiled, slipped from the embrace of the armchair and tiptoed to the door. "I really must go, Mrs. Kordos. Thank you very much for the Sherry," she added already facing the door.

Today, of all days, I hadn't offered her any Bristol Cream. I was waiting for Steven to bring me another bottle. What was going on with her?

The next moment Sister Angelica opened the door, peeked outside, left and right, and then was gone. Sister Angelica was either hiding or running from something.

The week after, Father Mulligan suffered a nervous breakdown. At least, so I've been told. I wouldn't see him again for at least a month.

***

11

The Messenger

There was nothing particularly significant about Mrs. Kowal's death. She slipped away in her sleep, as quietly as anyone would wish for. Don't we all hope to die in our sleep? Like Woody Allen said, "I am not afraid of death, I just don't want to be there when it happens."

As usual, we all met at the Requiem Mass in our Chapel. There was no need to book or reserve a Requiem Mass. Twice a week the visiting priest donned a black chasuble, and included the names of all the recently dearly departed in the appropriate place.

"Quaesumus, Domine, ut animae famuli tui (or *famulae tuae*)...

Here the priest mentions the recently departed such as Stanisław or Franciszek, or Jósef, or in this case Wanda Kowal and Zygmunt somebody, a name I didn't catch.

"*...cujus depositionis diem tertium...* ...sometimes the fifth or even thirtieth day... *....commemoramus, Sanctorum atque electorum tuorum largiri digneris consortium: et rorem misericordiae tuae perennem infudas. Per Domimum...."*

Basically the priest commits the souls of the people mentioned to the Lord and asks Him to join these souls with the society of saints and the chosen ones and to sprinkle them, continuously, with the dew of His compassion. Seriously: sprinkle them, that's the official translation. Apparently it also rains in heaven…

Quite poetic, if you can understand it. Most don't.

Not that I can be sure if my little Missal, which I bought in England in 1954, is still valid. It offers Latin and Polish versions of the Mass, side by side. I read both, probably out of boredom. I must have attended hundreds of such Masses over the years. Don't forget, I am ninety and my turn to be inserted by the priest in the appropriate place must be close at hand. After the Vatican introduced the Holy Mass in various languages, I'd put my Missal away. Recently I found it. The edges worn, stiffening, yellowing towards the outer edges… still, after years of neglect, I could use it again. I liked that. Somehow it made me feel younger. It reached back to the days when I didn't question a single word inside it. My Missal was entitled:

MSZAŁ NIEDZELNY I ŚWIĄTECZNY

A Missal for Sundays and Holidays (of obligation). I cherished my old Missal. So many memories... so much faith.

I was glad that the Mass was being said, once again, in Latin. Seven years ago, when Jan and I first came to the Institute, it was celebrated only in Polish. Then there were a number of Ukrainians who kept asking to have the Mass celebrated, at least occasionally, in Ukrainian. The fact that they weren't Catholic was apparently besides the point. How could they be if they didn't understand much of what was going on? As time went on, more and more Polish people found it difficult to understand the liturgy in their native tongue. They were emigrants of forty and fifty years. Some longer. They asked if the Mass could be said in French, the official language of Quebec. To that other voices joined in demanding both official languages be treated equally. French *and* English. A week later, for the first time since the pope had granted the permission for each people to say Mass in their own language, the Mass had been said, once again, in Latin. Just like in the good old days.

The ignorant remained the ignorant, and the . . . actually, no one understood Latin. Not even the Sisters. I wonder if all the priests do.

But getting back to the late Mrs. Kowal who died in her sleep. I expressed my sentiments as to how lucky she'd been to die so propitiously. Raphael who at the time was wheeling Jan into our room sounded surprised.

"What a pity," he remarked quietly. He might have thought that I hadn't heard him. I had and wouldn't let that go.

"Why would you say such a thing? She wasn't scared. Isn't that worth something?"

"It certainly is, Mrs. Kordos."

I waited for more and nothing came. I went on the attack.

"I wish you wouldn't make cryptic remarks which do not make sense to me and then leave me in the dark."

"We are all in the dark, Mrs. Kordos. That is why crossing the Gate in full consciousness is so important."

"The Gate?" I asked looking up at him. I was surprised. I'd never heard anyone use the term 'Gate' before. I wondered what made Raphael choose this particular word. Surely, he wasn't reading my thoughts?

"Each time we enter a new room, we go through a door. When we enter a greater expanse of reality, I prefer to call it a gate. To me it symbolizes a radical change of consciousness."

"Are we talking about the same thing? I was talking about Mrs. Kowal dying in her sleep."

"Indeed, Mrs. Kordos. She's crossed over to a reality she couldn't possibly imagine. And, unfortunately, at least for a while, she'll feel completely disoriented. Even lost. I was too late...." he added, regret in his voice.

I didn't know where to start my questions. In a single sentence he'd managed to cram in enough enigmatic ideas to last me a week. Maybe a lifetime, what was left of it. Until I met Raphael, I always regarded myself as normal. Now I find that that is not necessarily anything to be proud of. Normal people seem content to live in the dark. I now know that I was. Had been. Now, I'm just beginning to perceive a spark. A glimmer. But there are still too many unknowns. How could I have left it so late?

"Could you tell me more?" I asked. My voice must have been quite plaintive because I got a broad smile from the big man.

"Of course, Mrs. Kordos. We usually regard death as the end of life. Well, life has neither beginning nor end. Life is... life is energy, a force that brings about change. In physics we would call it kinetic or potential energy, or that which produces or arises from motion. It relies on juxtaposition of opposites. Remove the opposites and you have stasis. Stasis with infinite potential."

This was a nurse's help talking, using words I'd hardly ever heard before. Who was this man? Just then, for no reason I could imagine, I remembered Steve telling me about a phrase from the Bhagavad Gita. It rang fresh in my mind: *Anyone who, at the end of life, quits his body remembering Me, attains immediately to My nature...* A tough job for anyone asleep at the time. And what exactly was *My* nature? There was more but I couldn't quite recall it. It was something about reaching the next life in the condition in which we left the present one. In Mrs. Kowal's case she would be asleep. I wonder what shock she might have on waking up.

"You could say that life is change," Raphael continued, all the time tending to Dad's needs. He seemed in no way distracted by his mundane activity. His strong yet ostensibly gentle hands pulled the pullover over Jan's listless arms, adjusted my husband's ascot and made sure he was comfortable. He did all this quite automatically, yet, seemingly, with infinite care. "Without us, without you and me, Mrs. Kordos, without the rest of us, life would be no more than a potential. Like Soul."

"You mean Soul with a capital S," I said knowingly, remembering Steven's theories.

"If you like. Soul and life are attributes of the Infinite."

"Not of God?"

"God is such an overused expression that it's lost, at least for me, all meaning. There are no two people alive who think of God in the same terms. What do you think God is, Mrs. Kordos?"

I was about to unfold the smattering of my knowledge acquired from the Bible, the Bhagavad Gita and one or two treatises of mystics I'd read when I realized, to my considerable dismay, that all those concepts were other people's ideas. Not necessarily mine. Furthermore, in my terms of reference, God was never a What but a Who.

He must have read my thoughts. "We still repeat ancient concepts created by wise men for ancient people to get a handle on the image of God. I prefer the image that Rumi gave us, or even more that of Saint John of the Cross."

Just then Rumi's poem stood before my eyes… *I am the servant of My servant's image of Me...* Was he implying that God is whatever we imagine Him to be? A reflection of our thoughts? Our concepts? And then those words I still didn't quite understand, Something about purifying my thoughts….

"*…and expand your thoughts about M*e." I heard Raphael's voice. "*For they are My House*."

"My house?"

"My house is my consciousness. This is where we abide. He and I. Together, as we expand our consciousness…" Raphael continued working. "People always externalize divinity. They search for God afar. In heaven, I suppose. Rumi places Him within us."

Steve talked about that. I liked the idea, though I still didn't make it my own. It was still Rumi's image that I liked. Not quite the same.

"So what of heaven?" I had to ask.

"According to Rumi it lies beyond the doing right and doing wrong. It is the source of all, Mrs. Kordos."

This was all getting a bit too much for me. Those concepts were definitely not Catholic. If Rumi was right then it would have been us who created both heaven and… I shook my head.

"And Saint John?" I attempted to change the subject. I thought Rumi was still too deep for my way of thinking. The Catholic faith was black and white. It was distinct, based on clearly defined duality of good and evil. Rumi removed barriers, even those between heaven and earth.

"In his Apocryphal Acts John said *A lamp am I to you that perceive me – a mirror am I to you that know me*."

To me it smacked of blasphemy. Saint John's Acts? Was Saint John a Catholic saint? I don't recall my priest ever teaching us such a thing. On the other hand, I don't recall a great many things these days. I looked at my husband. Usually oblivious, he seemed to be listening. Was that possible?

Even while Raphael was changing Dad's diaper, he never changed the tone of his words. The work he did was carried out by his body, his hands, with instruction issued by the cerebellum or some other automotive brain function. His mind was elsewhere. I wondered where Raphael dwelled . . . where his consciousness abided. It was as though there were two men present, a physical entity working with the sick and the aged and a quite different being who seemed to be visiting his body for some reasons of its own. The man was an enigma.

...a mirror am I to you that know me.

His last quotation was no less enigmatic. Who was the 'I' speaking the phrase? Was it John? Surely not. Was it his image of God? Did he see the light or did he face the mirror when he wrote the Apocryphal Acts.

Why am I so ignorant?

I closed my eyes to try and make sense of Raphael's words. A lamp am I to you that perceive me. This implied looking as 'I' from outside. With a mirror, the position didn't change but the reflection offered . . . offered what? The image of me? What else? *I am the servant of My servant's image of Me....* Once again I recall Rumi's words. Had the two men met? There was also that thing about our thoughts being His house. That's right. *Your thoughts about Me are My House.* A house is where we all dwell. A place from which we go in and out. We are warned to be careful, and to purify and attune and expand our thoughts about Him.

Him? God? Or that which we observe in the mirror.

I decided to ask him. I opened my eyes and my mouth to speak simultaneously. I looked around. Dad was sleeping happily, and Raphael was nowhere to be seen. Surely, I hadn't imagined it all. Again. I did speak to him. He was here and he . . . he changed Jan's diaper... Didn't he? Does it really matter? Does it really matter who or what stimulated my thoughts? The important thing was that, for reasons I could not as yet comprehend, I was purifying, attuning and expanding my thoughts about Him. Perhaps I was just getting ready go follow Mrs. Kowal on her last journey. Through the Gate.

It's been a few days since that strange conversation with Raphael and I've begun asking various people what they think of Raphael. There are as many stories, as many opinions, as people I ask. Everyone is greatly aware of his presence; everyone has a very strong opinion.

"Raphael? He's a tower of strength. He can lift a man up with one hand. I saw him do it. I was helping him, slipped and he held Mr. Jakub up with just one hand. He must be a weightlifter or something." The nurse was quite adamant that Raphael should easily win the Mr. Universe title.

"Oh, he's so kind, Mrs. Kordos. I was sick once and he came to visit me every single day. Every night, actually, after work. What a kind man he is." This was one of the nurses.

This sounded more like Raphael. I bet the nurse had forgotten that at night her door was locked, she was in bed, fast asleep and she just dreamt he was there. Perhaps the man had the power to induce dreams in people? I prefer this supposition than imagining him walking through walls. That would be strictly illegal. And could be embarrassing at times.

"He's so gentle, Mrs. Kordos. He may not be very strong but he will try and try until he succeeds. He is always there to help you."

"Not very strong? He looks so big. Are you sure?"

"Oh, he's big enough. But when I work with him he makes me feel I am twice as strong as he is. I've been sick a long time, Mrs. Kordos. Now, he's shown me how strong I really am. There is nothing I cannot do, now. Nothing!" Another nurse was as happy as though she'd won an Olympic medal.

It figures, I thought.

"I don't know, Mrs. Kordos. Each time I look for him, he's somewhere else. Doesn't matter what time I need him. He must be the laziest man alive."

This was Mother Superior. She liked to boss people. She could never locate Raphael to boss him. I only just managed to hide my simper. There is no way Mother Superior would find Raphael against his will.

"He is everywhere, Mrs. Kordos." Sister Angelica's tone of voice was quite resolute. And then she began to sound both hesitant and confused. "You know, Mrs. Kordos, whenever someone dies, anyone . . . on any floor . . . he is always there. By the time anyone else gets to the room, he is already leaving. And . . . and when we get there, the poor soul's face seems relaxed in a gentle smile. It seems as though they saw...."

"...an angel?" I offered quietly.

"What was that, Mrs. Kordos?" The Sister was lost in her own imagery. "Well, anyway. People seem to die happy when he's around."

Sister Angelica walked towards the door. Even as she opened it, I heard her musing half aloud, "I wonder how he does it...."

So do I.

Raphael's Gate has something to do with transcendence. Transcendence of what, exactly. Of the way we regard reality? Or ideas?

I wondered if I would eventually benefit from his ministrations. And if so, how? After all that has been said about him, to me he represented something quite different. It wasn't his abilities I drew on, but rather his knowledge. Or knowingness, as Steve called it. The sort of knowledge that comes from within.

Now that I realize how many very different effects he had on people, I'm reminded of a saying attributed to the great Thomas Aquinas. "What ever is received," he'd said, "is received according to the nature of the recipient." It seems that we all see or experience reality, each in his or her peculiar way. Some see just the physical manifestations, some emotional, some mental. Or it could be that we do see them all, but we only pay attention to some, to those most important to us at the time.

Could it be that we see only what we want to see? Or only whatever we need? Perhaps the two are really overlapping. One thing is certain. Only that which we experience in our consciousness counts. All else is peripheral. And that is true of the consciousness itself. I am my consciousness. 'I am' is what really counts. The subconscious is what I was, the unconscious – what I could be. But only in consciousness do I have my being. And 'I am' lives only in the Present. And yet the concept of time comes into it all, somehow. I wonder what Raphael, the Messenger, would have to say about it.

"Our concepts change, Mrs. Kordos," I remember his words. "Concepts have a limited shelf-life."

At the time, I didn't quite understand him. We are all conversant with the concept of shelf-life. It simply defines the length of time that stored items remain usable. Our foodstuffs spoil within days, weeks at best. Our furniture wears out in a few years. Our cars, utensils, items of everyday use, have even shorter spans of usefulness.

"Even our bodies deteriorate with time," I muttered to myself. Whatever happened to my cornflower blue eyes?

But concepts? Ideas? Perhaps they metamorphose?

Mozart's music is as fresh today as it was on the day the young messenger transferred it to paper. The ideas of Socrates ring true today, thanks to Plato whose own message has survived over two millennia. But the longest shelf-life, surely, belongs to the Messages of the Great Avatars. The Vedas are so old we've lost track of the messengers who brought them to us. Other great envoys negated their own egos to become pure instruments for the transference of ideas from the Infinite Source to our unwilling ears. Are we unwilling? And yet, many an envoy died young, castigated, rejected by his or her own people. All for the sake of the Message.

The next time I hear real music, I shall listen for the celestial overtones. The Music of the Spheres. And when I listen to a humble speaker, I shall not question his worldly credentials, lest I miss his Message. He knows he is but an instrument. A postman delivering an immortal Message. If we listen hard, we just might extend even our own existence. By attrition – a sort of rubbing off.

By the power within the Message.

But most of all, we must try to hear the message before it becomes perverted. Rather than listening to 'updated' philosophies of spiritual Messages, twisted beyond recognition, we must try to get as close as we can to the Source. The Original. Some of It still lingers within the yellow pages of old manuscripts, but mostly the Source is within us. To hear It, we must become very still – and learn to listen.

I heard Raphael's smile. I didn't see it – I heard it. It was like a beautiful melody.

We, if we only realize it, are all the true keepers of the enduring Message.

Deep within.

If we could only realize it.

Jan tried to turn on his side. He had no strength. He hardly ate lately, just took some liquid. Even his diapers didn't seem to smell anymore. Like babies don't when still feeding at mother's breast. A full cycle. Round and round we go.

What sort of messenger was he, I wondered. Strange that I would think of my husband in the past tense. He is still here, and, at the same time, he isn't. I think he is moving in and out of the Gate, just making sure he will know the way when the time comes. He must know the way pretty well by now. What else could explain the smile on his face when he sleeps? God knows there is nothing here, in the here and now, that he has to smile about. Perhaps it's only his physical body that sleeps. Perhaps....

I am ninety years old and there are still so many unknowns.

Jan was a messenger of goodness, and honesty, and sacrifice. So many times he laid his life on the line, to protect or save others. He wife, his children, his colleagues, his country. Total strangers. What a rich life he led. What a dismal ending.

I turned him on his left side. I was surprised how easy it was. Often it took two nurses to turn him and even together they had problems lifting him. I did it on my own. Perhaps emotions have power of their own. Perhaps they have something to do with faith, as in moving mountains. Or they are like a rider on a red horse, to whom was given great power. Power to take peace from the earth. That they should kill one another.

Like Arjuna, the great master archer of the immortal Mahabharata, Jan was a warrior. He did his duty. Always.

Now he lay motionless, unaware of his surroundings. I dampened a sponge and massaged his parched lips. He didn't wake up. Where was his consciousness? Why is he punished so for doing what Sri Krishna demanded of him? Was it that Christ's message was so very different? Was the message of love so much more important?

***

12

Blessing

Steve and Annette were on holidays in Florida. They stayed with friends, called daily, but it didn't help. Bart dropped in on Saturdays but, well, it wasn't enough either. I felt really alone. Alone and tired. On the day I told Steve that Dad had been hooked up to an IV, he and Annette packed their bags and came home. They drove for twenty-six hours, non-stop, all the way to Montreal. Without stopping for rest or food.

The day after they got back, they came to see us. The nurses had just removed Jan's IV. The vein they'd been using had collapsed. Too feeble blood pressure, I suppose. And they couldn't find another suitable one to use. Father was in death throes. At last. He was nearing the Gate.

The last week of his life, Jan had spent on the IV. They use the intravenous feeding when the patient, for he no longer was just a resident, cannot ingest any food by means provided by nature. When they can no longer swallow. Or digest with any degree of efficiency. The peristaltic movement no longer functions. The last stage begins when your arms are too weak to feed yourself. For a while you are force-fed, often against your will, then hooked up to a tube that continues to introduce nutrients, medications and other body-sustaining concoctions directly into your cardiovascular system.

"Why do you do that, Sister?"

"Life is a gift of...."

"...of God. Why do you do that, Sister?"

"We cannot terminate life that is a gift...."

"Why do you remove from my husband the last vestiges of free will that is a God-given gift?"

"Mrs. Kordos. I really...."

There followed the usual claptrap about pseudo morals, pseudo ethics, pseudo logic. The Sisters, as most Catholics, are deeply brainwashed to detract any and all dignity from a dying person. No matter how much you want to die, no matter how much nature cooperates with them in this endeavour, you will not be allowed to die. Perhaps this good-natured torture to which the Catholics, indeed all Christians, subject others is meant as punishment for our sins. Apparently Christ's death on the Cross was all for naught.

"I wish you would stop torturing my husband," I whispered, but she didn't listen. "Please . . . please," I recall whispering.

I might as well have been talking to a stone. She must have put my ravings to old age, to dementia. How convenient, I thought. What an easy way to absolve your own conscience. Ignore the will of God, who surely made it obvious that He wants to remove His Presence from my husband's body, ignore nature, which for the last year or two had given him the same hints. Ignore the suffering, discomfort, indignity of force-feeding, prolonged incontinence... and most of all, ignore the last vestige of that ancient illusion of free will.

A God-given gift removed by the evil of ignorance.

The blessing of death protracted. Withheld. Heartlessly, callously, without mercy. May God have mercy on those who had none for my husband.

With a practiced hand the nurse finds the vein, stabs my husband's arm, inserts the needle, bandages the arm to make sure the needle doesn't fall out, and leaves, presumably with the feeling of a job well done.

My husband, an international sportsman, a Colonel of the Polish Army, a father of adult children, a man whose age alone should command respect – was helpless. Emasculated. He had to succumb to the pagan ritual of perfidy and crime and sadistic punishment administered by an angel in white floating robes and a ishment administered by an angel in white floating robes and a pure-white wimple. An angel who never stopped smiling as she fulfilled her misbegotten sense of duty. A fiend.

May God have mercy on her.

But the torturers would not have their way for long.

Within eight days, having punctured both of my husband's arms into a red and blue, living, trembling sieve, they couldn't find a vein large enough to insert their instrument of torment. God knows, they tried. Not even the Nazis ever sank so low. Not even Genghis Khan tortured the old and feeble. Not even....

For the first time in fifty years I cried. I managed to survive the World War, endless air raids by the Germans, the Russians, many nocturnal visits from the Gestapo, a number of arrests, and now I knew that when my time came, they would subject me to the same agony. And that, in the name of a God who died of the Cross, so that I wouldn't have to.

Any wonder that Father Mulligan had lost his faith?

"You don't have to be here, Mrs. Kordos," Raphael said a week earlier, a day before they'd put Jan on the IV. Somehow he knew what was coming. "There is nothing you can do any more," he whispered.

I didn't believe him. A wife's place is at her husband's side. Especially in days of trial. Of course, I hardly knew what was coming.

"I shall look after him for you," I heard him say. Only I did not understand him. I thought he would feed him and change him, as he always did. Or nearly always. I knew that Jan no longer recognized me. The last week he was in a state of half-sleep, half trance. His eyes didn't focus.

"I must be here," I assured him. "It is my job," I insisted.

I dare say I'd refused to accept that my husband had already lost all awareness of my presence. That wherever he was, I couldn't go. And vice versa. You can't accept things like that, not after sixty-seven years. And, no matter what I'd read, what I'd heard from Raphael, from my son Steve, from my own parents, I still pretended that my husband was still there. That any moment he would open his eyes, smile at me, and call me Mimi.

I glanced at him, now and then.

I still thought that we, human beings, are the body that contains our mind, our emotions, our mind and life-force. I still believed that the semi-embalmed, semi-alive, half-corpse lying on that bed was my husband.

"He is happy, Mrs. Kordos," I heard Raphael's whisper. "As you should be. He's no longer aware as we are aware...."

Words. They were just words. I wish he would stop talking like that.

For an instant I saw a strange light. I spun round to face my husband. I could have sworn that he smiled at me. I could have sworn.... Jan was resting in his comatose state as he had the last day or two. I wanted to talk to Raphael. I looked around. There was no one in the room but my husband and me. And then I understood. I was there alone.

Jan Kazimir Kordos, my husband for sixty-seven years, highly decorated Colonel of the Polish Cavalry, the Knight of the Virtuti Militari Cross – the highest the Polish army had to offer – received his final blessing on December 23rd at 12:27 a.m., in the dead of night.

I'd spent the last two hours talking to him. We just sat next to each other, our hands touching, our hearts locked in a peculiar happiness that neither of us could explain. Not for a moment did I think that I was losing him. If anything, he was leaving, just for a while, for the briefest of trips.

"I'll wait for you, Mimi. I always have," he added. We both thought of the five years during which the Second World War had kept us apart. I always thought that it had been I who had waited for him. He is old. He must have forgotten. And then I realized that he too must have been waiting. It's amazing how in all those years I'd never once thought of it from his side. How selfish we are sometimes.

"I know you will wait," I said. "You always have." This time I meant it. There was little more I could have said. He looked so happy. I wouldn't take that feeling away from him. He really must have thought that we would be apart for the briefest of moments. If only he could have been right.

We were both happy.

I wondered how few people realize that death is the final blessing. Not calamity, not castigation, but Blessing. The moment of liberation from the condition into which we have conducted ourselves through our irrefutable ignorance. We say we do our best, but our best is simply not good enough. Ignorance of the Universal Laws is no excuse for breaking them. So often we simply don't know that we are veering from the straight and narrow.

I called the nurses and they came and tended to the body. When they were finished, Raphael waited and asked me if I'd be alright by myself. I told him that I'd be fine, that I just needed to rest. He nodded and helped me to bed.

It was so quiet without Jan but eventually I fell asleep, somehow.

I spent the night before the funeral at Steven's. He and Annette didn't think that I should be alone. We did a lot of talking, mostly reminiscing about what might have been, and dreaming what still might be. We wondered if Dad was happy in his condition. I think that the fact that we lose contact with the physical world does not necessarily mean that we miss it. After all, the reality at the Institute, in the physical sense, was nothing to brag about. It was whatever we managed to create within our own, private little worlds.

I don't remember much of the funeral. Except that it was very cold. All I could think of was that wind was biting into my face. It distracted me. Wasn't I supposed to think about the ashes? About a little square box being lowered into a pre-prepared hole in the ground? God it was cold. Or was it just me? Bart gave me the details later. I think I already told you about that. I wanted to get back but we ended at Bart's for a small wake. Just us and the priest. I drank some vodka. It warmed me up. At least, I think it did.

The next few days are a blur. I think I went back to the Institute. I mean that Steve drove me back. I had to get back to normal. A week later, or it could have been two weeks, I went back to stay with Steve again. Just for a day or two. Just for a little while. I was free now. Jan wouldn't have minded.

I'm so glad Jan's gone. He'd suffered so. A man of action confined to a bed. Not anymore.

Steven and Annette thought that now that Dad is gone, I didn't have to remain in the Institute. After all, he was the main reason I moved there. I didn't want to talk about it but they insisted. It just wasn't important. Nothing was.

"Mother, please try. It's been three weeks…" there was a plea in Annette's voice. A touch of desperation.

Of course, since moving to the Institute I'd lost a lot of my own independence, also my dexterity, and I no longer had the same energy at my disposal. I'd also gotten lazy. Our room was cleaned, even the beds were made if I didn't do them myself. Our shopping was done for us, by Steve, Bart or the nurses. Our food was prepared and brought to us, to our room, and even served spoon by spoon to Dad. I wonder when my time will come to be spoon-fed.

Dad isn't spoon-fed anymore.

And I visited my children, mostly Annette and Steve – Bart was just too far away – it was no longer by bus or the metro. In Westmount we did not have a car. Too old to drive, I suppose. Since moving to the Institute, I took a cab and later, with my taste buds and pallet titillated, they drove me back. Dear children. They are a blessing. Yes. I've gotten very lazy. Spoiled you might say.

It's so nice to be spoiled.

We don't notice just how active we are maintaining our daily routine until we attempt to return to it after a long break. Like after a long illness. Or a Sabbatical. We all seem to do a great many things automatically in order to have an acceptable standard of living. You have to be young to try and improve it.

There is another thing. Whatever is done for us, in no time we learn to take it for granted. Not only that, but should anything that we consider, justly or not, to be our entitlement, we instantly raise Cain to retrieve our privileges. I suppose the elderly get spoiled at about the same rate as children. In many ways, an Institute such as mine precipitates this process. They do it all to make us happy. Instead, they make us dependent. Those who brought their happiness with them, kept it. Others...?

You must learn to count your blessings. Jan did. Always. I'd never heard him complain. Never.

Happiness comes from within. Like love and kindness and compassion and faith. It cannot be served on a tray no matter how lovingly the staff looks after your needs. That's right. Not even Raphael can do that. Except, perhaps, at the Gate?

I don't know when I wrote all this down. Must have been over a time. Whatever time meant in those days. My mind was still drifting to Jan. How long does it take to unravel a lifetime? Each morning I would get out of bed and glance around wondering where he got to. He's all right now.

Some weeks have passed. January sun was beginning to cast a little warmth, the days grew perceptibly longer. The last few days, weeks, had passed in a haze of an altered reality. I'll recount the events, past and present, as accurately as I can, though their order might have been different, perhaps confused, particularly with regards to chronology. There may be some contradictions. If the facts differ, the emotions that underline them remain true. I am sure that throughout that time I'd acted in a perfectly rational manner. My children may have thought otherwise. There were hints. No matter.

The eve of Jan's death was also the eve of Jesus' birth. They must have met on the way. On the way to and from their earthly abode. I bet little Jesus waved to Jan as they passed each other.

On the 24th of December, Christmas Eve, Bart dropped in during the day, Steve and Annette at ten at night, after the *Wigilia* they'd spent with friends. *Wigilia*, is a traditional meal many European nations have to celebrate Christ's forthcoming birth. At the Institute it is always celebrated on the 23rd, to enable more staff to be with their families. It is a joyful time. Children love it. We all do.

It is such a happy time....

When Steve dropped in, to share a moment with us, I was already in bed. Or I must have imagined that I was. I must have gotten out again after Steve left, to sit with Jan. I must have…

Memories are such fragile things. They come, linger and dissolve into the ethers. At least mine do. Faster and faster. We often remember what we choose to. Whatever makes us most happy. It's all to do with our emotions. With our emotional body. A body of light that always burns with such joy.

Jan died smiling. First time in a number of weeks. His lips had been too dry to smile.

When he finally died, they called Steve from the Institute, and he called Bart. At least I think that was how it happened. Does it really matter? Bart came to say goodbye to Dad. He was too late of course. Bartholomew is always so correct. He knew Dad was gone but he came anyway. Steve is different. He tends more to the living. Then, he loses all interest.

"He's not there, Mama," he whispered to me pointing at the coffin at the funeral Mass.

"*Ja wiem*," I whispered back. "I know".

Oh dear, I'm ahead of myself again. This was a whole week later. The funeral I mean. Or was it the burial? Time is playing tricks on me.

We both felt Dad's presence all around us. He was no longer sick. The Alzheimer's was gone. So were all his aches and pains. And incontinence.

It was such a happy time.

Dad's ashes were buried at the Cemetery reserved for Polish people. *Cmentarz Zasłużonych*. The Cemetery of the Worthy. Of the Deserving. Of those who'd earned the privilege. All the ashes buried there were born in Poland. Funny how time flies. It seemed only like yesterday. It was one hundred years.

Steve said that Bart organized it all. Bart is so good at such things. I mean, at organizing. Except for his concept of time. He's always late. But not today. That day. He was punctual for father's funeral. He must have known Dad would have liked it. He and Dad were very close. Still are, in a way?

Some days later, Steve and Annette offered me a choice of my own apartment in close proximity to theirs, or even to buy a new house with an in-law suite, for my use only. They knew that I had always been independent, and preferred my own place, if at all possible. They assured me that they could well afforded it, and it meant that I would have privacy of my own space, while being able to share some of my meals with them. Somehow, it all sounded so abstract, as if we were discussing someone else.

"You would be happy, Mama. You'd be perfectly free to do what you want," Annette assured me. "You would come and go as you wished."

"I come and go as I wish now, my dear, no one ties me down."

The moment I'd said this an image of Jan tied down to his bed, his armchair or wheelchair flashed vividly before my eyes. I was about to say 'not yet', but thought better of it. "If I stay at the Institute," I told her instead, "I can be of use. To someone. Sometime. Here... " I left the question hanging.

I really wanted to be alone. Just with my memories.

It wasn't quite fair to Annette. Of course, she'd said, she would find me something to do while I stayed close by. Like feeding their cats when they went on holidays. Only they were already organized for such contingencies. And the rest of the time she would rack her brain to find me something to do to make me happy. To keep my mind occupied and happy.

Where does it say that we must be happy? And then I remembered Sister Angelica with her angelic smile, Father Mulligan with the distant, lonely eyes, Mrs. Merryweather who was still bent on vengeance. No. Happiness was definitely better than virtually anything else. Better than money or fame or power. The only problem was that some misguided people thought they needed this unholy trio to achieve happiness.

I am sure Jan is happy. Now.

"But Mama, we could...." Annette tried valiantly. She made up some stories – not too convincing. She knew I was right. "You could stay with us a lot...."

"You have your life to lead, darling. Don't ever let anyone interfere with your happiness." My mind was made up.

Under no circumstances would I agree to live with them, in their own home. Back in Poland, my mother had spent her last years with us. There were no nursing homes in those days. Family was expected to look after one's elders. Their living ancestors, the grandmas and grandpas. Now, we, the elders, had no excuse to impose let alone impinge on our children's lives. We were even given a government pension to remain financially independent.

Things really have changed.

Of course now I would be alone. Is that also a blessing?

I firmly believe that moving in with them would be by far the best way to lose their love. Absence may or may not make the heart grow fonder, but excessive proximity most certainly did breed contempt. Like familiarity. Unavoidable at close quarters. And imposing oneself on someone else, with all one's quirks and idiosyncrasies, particularly those of old age, would be as far as one could push familiarity without actually declaring your children to be your servants.

I would rather count my blessings.

In my mind, implied in my assertion of independence, was the sentiment that if I'd accepted their offer I would be a burden to them, while here, at the Institute, I could still be of some use. I could, for instance, keep writing and editing articles for our local monthly magazine. But mostly, I would just continue to cheer people up. For some reason the residents seemed to have decided that by being at the Institute they were obliged to maintain grave faces, consistent with people who were standing at the precipice of life and death. Mostly death.

At the Gates of Mortality.

Of Immortality?

It would certainly help if they thought of them as the Gates of Immortality, but I found that the predominantly Catholic residents did not suffer from such flights of fancy. Some residents actually gave an impression of not worrying too much about their future. Actually Jan was like that. He never seemed to have worried. He just accepted life as it was, one day at a time. Dear Jan. I still feel his presence.

"What are you scribbling there, Mimi?" he would have asked.

They, the residents, seemed resigned, as though watching a great gathering of the clouds, with the inevitable downpour approaching from which they were quite unable to hide, to stay dry. They seemed prepared to die in the deluge. They were like Noah only without an ark. Hardly the most joyful way of approaching the Gate. At least their placid resignation gave them a semblance of peace. But only a semblance. To paraphrase St. Paul, peace beyond human understanding remained beyond their understanding. The real thing seemed quite unattainable for them. I wondered whose fault it was. The Church's? The priests'? Their, so-called, 'spiritual guides'?

Are we not all responsible for our own happiness? I knew that I was. Mine and Jan's. And the boys' of course.

So some of those physical derelicts achieved a vague semblance of happiness born of acceptance. Like a cat that ate well, but also knew that he was unlikely to get any more. Others made up for its lack with vengeance. They worried. They complained. They demanded attention. They wanted more, more, more... Of what? What was of no concern? More food? They were always given too much. Entertainment? They didn't even attend all events that were offered to them. Excursions? The last two times the bus was half-empty. It had been years since Jan came with me. It was such fun when we went together.

More happiness....

Then there were those who looked positively scared witless. They attended all the Masses celebrated daily in our chapel, confessed their real but mostly imaginary sins as often as humanly possible, took the Holy Communion at every opportunity. Their emotions seemed shuttered at the thought of their miserable existence approaching final liberation. Their final blessing. I wondered why people who hardly practised their religion throughout their lives, suddenly became so ardent in their Catholicism. Why they became so passionately ultra religious.

"Just in case," Father Mulligan once told me. He was beginning to open up more and more, but he was also searching for happiness outside his own self. At least, that was my impression.

I imagine, the newborn religionists were just playing it safe. I was reminded of a story about the late W. C. Fields, an avowed atheist, thumbing through the bible on his deathbed. “What are you doing, Mister Fields?” he’d been asked. “Looking for loopholes,” he replied, renewing his thumbing with renewed vigour.

Mr. Fields was a very wise man.

It’s well past midnight. I’d better put the notebook away.

Good-night Jan. Sleep well. Sleep well my love.

***

The Black Horse

"....and he that sat on him
had a pair of balances in his hand."

The Revelation
of Saint John the Divine

13

The Institute

How time flies... A month ago I wouldn't have dreamed of taking an elevator to ride one floor down. Not that my knees haven't given me, on occasion, severe problems. Now and then one or the other has given way without any apparent reason. For some years now I've used a cane, and when negotiating a staircase I would reach out with my free hand for a handrail. So stabilized, I could climb Mount Everest, or at least to the second floor.

Today I made for the elevator. Having said goodbye to our old room on the third floor, I did not feel like performing feats of endurance. Since Jan left us, my resolve seemed to have crumbled, the strength that I needed to look after him no longer propped me up. In a way, I've lost my *raison d'être*. Throughout my life I had to look after someone. Children, my own mother, then Jan. And now? The motivation was missing.

The room I left behind was devoid of any sign of our presence. The boys already took out the carpet, the furniture, even the pictures on the wall. Only the window facing west displayed a familiar horizon – the treetops swaying gently in the wind against the blue sky. And, of course, there was a palpable absence. A void. There was no Jan. No Jan tied to his chair, or his bed, like a prisoner of the do-gooders who were determined to torture him until his very last breath. Well, he'd won. He is free now.

With a peculiar hollow in the pit of my stomach, I hobbled towards the elevator, towards my new room. One floor down. One step closer to the earth. To the grave.

How time flies....

The procession of kings stretched as far as the eye could see. If not longitudinally then at least into the past. Distant past. Not that my memory stretched that far anymore. Once I stepped out of the elevator, the length of the corridor, on my right, and all the way to my new room and beyond it, displayed monarchs of Polish history. I was surprised that the mostly bearded gentlemen adorned the walls in no particular chronological order. Kazimierz Wielki, known outside Poland as Casimir the Great, hung side by side with Bolesław I, Chrobry – the Brave, Władysław I, Łokietek – the Short, who evidently, in order to compensate for his stunted growth sported a particularly fierce moustache. Anyway, they rubbed shoulders with Bolesław Krzywousty – the Wrymouthed, Ladislaus Laskonogi – the Spindleshanks, and even the latest electoral kings of the 17th and 18th century, Augustus III, Stanislaus Augustus and John III, Sobieski, among them, seemed to swap yarns with the Jagieloński dynasty. I vaguely recalled I counted some forty kings in all. More than half of them adorned our walls. Some looked like well-to-do swashbuckling heroes. Others, like Ladislaus IV, resembled one of the Three, or really the Four Musketeers, the young D'Artagnan, still others gravitated towards the more portly Porthos or Aramis or Athos, from one of the earlier Hollywood films. A good-looking bunch of men.

All the portraits were simply but carefully framed in narrow wood frames, each with a tiny but neatly engraved plaque attesting to their historical importance. Their swords sheathed, their arms at rest, yet their eyes still seemed to dominate whoever dared to meet them. Even from behind the sheet of glass. They proved their worth.

A long and illustrious procession. Jan would have enjoyed their company.

My mind drifted to my old, so very old, schooldays, where, or when, the walls of our rather drab village school also flaunted some portraits of Polish nobles, past and present, probably in a vain attempt to etch their importance on our young minds. Apparently we, as all people, always needed heroes, paradigms, to whom we could look up to. Now, looking at the ancient kings, all decked out in flamboyant regalia, as the artist must have imagined them, I wondered why people have such need of gods. Greater and lesser gods, and in their palpable absence, at least kings and presidents, lords and masters, who would gaze gently, benevolently over our insignificant lives.

The procession stretched back a whole millennium, to the time when Mieszko I converted to Christianity in 966, thus paving the way for his son, Boleslaus the Brave to officially welcome Emperor Otto III, in the year 1000, in Gniezno, the first metropolis, an archbishopric, and the first capital of Poland. This single event put Poland on the map of Europe. Twenty-five years later, Boleslaus crowned himself the first King of Poland.

As I stood gazing at the portrait of the first Polish king's father, I couldn't help smiling. More than one thousand years ago Mieszko I introduced Christianity to Poland. And now, here and now, Father Mulligan sill couldn't find himself within the complexities of this new religion with its convoluted theology. Whatever happened to 'love one another'? Slowly, with unwitting deliberation, I walked towards the temporal space, which was to define the rest of my own future. No one knew for how long. For a moment I saw myself visiting the Polish kings for years to come. I saw myself in a wheelchair staring up at them with something akin to dread. Surely, the God of Mieszko would not be that unkind.

I dismissed the dismal image.

After all, they are all dead, I mused. Long dead. We all die. Sooner or later. Jan died.

I saw my reflection in the glass. How I wished it could be sooner.

How time flies.

Steve, Bart and their wives were waiting for me. The Bristol cream had been poured out, little *bell gueules* Annette called them, were all prepared. We chatted for a little while. They soon realized I was tired. Funny that. I was the only one who hadn't done any work with the move to my new address. It must have been all the emotions. The women left first. The men followed, merging quietly into the procession of kings. For the first time since World War II, I was alone.

I sat back. The room was about half the size of the previous one. Also, it faced east, not west as we did previously. Of course, there was no more *we*. Only *I* remained. I and my memories. Bart, with Steve's assistance, reinstalled my glorious carpet in our new room. My room.

I must learn to say I, not we – my, not our.

There was light snow outside, but *my* carpet still held all the colours of autumn. All thanks to Bart. It was he who, originally, gave it to us. To both of us. Each time I would enter my room, even now, the smaller one, I would derive pleasure just from looking at it. He is a good son, Bart is.

I had to be given a new room because the previous one was for two people. I had a choice of staying there, on the third floor, and sharing my space with a total stranger, or shrinking into my present quarters. I chose the latter. Old people do not make good companions. We snore too loud, we are not well organized, we complain a lot and, worst of all, sooner or later we become incontinent. I had a foretaste of the latter as I walked the corridor of my previous floor. No. Not when my Jan succumbed to the anguish of this ultimate distress. Those moments are completely erased from my memory. It was only when I strolled the corridors. Now and then, I had to quicken my step to get past the odour that filled the corridor directly opposite the open door of some rooms.

It wasn't nice.

And talking of not nice. My room was single but I had to share my powder room, the washbasin and the w.c., with my neighbour, a nice Ukrainian woman of some seventy-eight years of age. She's been a resident for a long time. No one seems to know for how long. I still don't even really know why she's here. She can walk, keeps her room clean and tidy, has dexterity in her fingers. Yet she's here. Maybe some people like the smell after all.

That's unfair. She ventilates our common toilet well after each use. She really is a good sort. Even if her Polish leaves a lot to be desired. For some reason, my husband, during the later years, always thought that wherever he is everyone must speak Polish. Here, in Canada. "Make Québec Polish," Steve said when Dad was around. It's a sort of spoof on the Québec pour les Québequois. Or

Québequoises, for that matter, that some extreme separatists advocate. Pour guys. They don't know that we live in a global village, a phrase coined by Marshall McLuhan some twenty years ago that went hand in hand with R. Buckminster Fuller's Operating Manual for the Spaceship Earth. All of us, not just the Québeqois. He'd have liked that.

Strange how my thoughts still gravitate towards Dad. What he liked, didn't like. It is three years since he died. Three winters, three Christmases, three summers, and autumns without him. He was one hundred, I was ninety then. For three years I didn't make any notes, write in my diary, record anything. I wasn't in the mood. Also, I think I had a series of minor strokes. There were days when I had no idea where I was, what I was doing there, in my room, at the Institute. The Sisters were very kind. Those moments didn't last, and, in time, my memories returned. Most of them. Sometimes they came back embroidered, with extra fringes, tasselled borders. Little enhancements. Perhaps we really remember only what we want to. Still, I need them. Memories are all I have. Even the tassels.

Except for the boys. And their wives, of course. I still visit Steve's most Sundays. His wife, Annette, is so kind. She always takes extra trouble.

I am still adjusting to my new life. No one to look after, no one to come back to. A man, or a woman, for that matter, is an island unto herself. If you don't like your own company, you'd better learn to like it. By the time you get to be my age, that may well be all you've got.

On the day I moved, I went for a walk with my sons' wives. By the time we got back, the carpet had been trimmed and installed, all the furniture had been moved, placed, the pictures were hanging on the walls, and the room was filled with fresh-cut flowers. I'll never forget. There were three bouquets, red, white and yellow. I recall wondering how they got them in the middle of winter. Imported, I suppose. As much as I loved them for it, I couldn't help wondering what happened to other people who didn't have two strapping lads, who could perform miracles in a little over a half-hour.

I think I've finally settled into my new daily routine.

Morning shower, breakfast in my room, the Holy Mass in the chapel, followed by either morning exercises or some 'cultural' event such as watching a selection of old Polish films. There seems to be as inexhaustible supply of them. Thank God for the gift of dementia. Most of us kept seeing them for 'the first time', again and again.

Old age in not as unkind as you might think.

Daily exercise consists of about twenty derelicts, such as myself, sitting in a circle, while a physiotherapist, with a voice to wake the dead, screams enunciating every syllable:

"Now you throw it to me, Miss-iss Dim-wit! Come on . . .THROW THE BALL!"

"Now you Mis-ter Szewc, throw it to me, NO, TO MEEE, Mis-ter Szewc. NO, NOT at Sis-ter Ce-cil-ia. TO MEEE MISTER SZEWC! MIS-TER SHEWC!!!"

Every syllable.

The man's name sounded like Mr. Sheftz, which is Polish for cobbler. He may have been a good shoe mender but he sure was a cobbler at throwing the ball which was large and light. And unwieldy. Perhaps that was the objective. To make us try harder.

I never remembered her name. The Physio screamed too loud and also she did all the talking. She did it out of kindness, of course. Not everyone enjoyed half-decent hearing. Half-decent was as good as you could hope for on the second floor. The third floor was worse. That was the Alzheimer's floor. That's where Jan and I used to be. Now, I belonged to the younger generation. Those under ninety-five. I came down, Jan went even higher.

Exercises were all conducted sitting down. I, like apparently all the other residents of the second floor, found it progressively more difficult to get around. I still walked on my own, with just my cane for company. But when it came to climbing the eight steps at Steve's condo, I needed the taxi driver's assistance. Going down was even worse. Steve held on to my right elbow, Annette to the other. It was a question of supporting my whole weight on just one leg at a time. Strength, like memory, is the first to go. I think we are designed to last so many years, and then, if we outstay our welcome, we are left on our own. By nature and, yes, by God. God says come – we say not yet. A while longer, we say. What does God know about such things? He's immortal. He has no concept of time. He may be omniscient but with Him it's all theory. To make sure God cannot take us against our will we stuff ourselves with pills, chemicals, support ourselves with walkers, propel ourselves in wheelchairs. And then we surround ourselves with staff who do everything for us. By then it's too late to listen to God's call. By then, we'd have lost all our reasoning power.

Time drags on. Apart from Sunday lunches at Steve and Annette's, I have to wait until spring to get out of the Institute. I seem to have lost a year somewhere. Maybe two? After spring came early summer and then came June 23rd, my name day. On that day, I discovered what a magnificent gift life really is. Steve and Annette picked me up, sharp at ten in the morning, to take me for a drive.

"Just to enjoy Mother Nature," Annette said. "For a few hours. Tell us when you feel tired, Mama. We'll take you right back." I loved looking at her. Real pretty. She was about my height, blondish-brown hair cut short, and hardly any makeup. Contrary to most women her age, fiftyish I guess by now, she retained the figure of a girl. She could have been my daughter.

"Cm'on, Mother?" I must have been staring at her.

Out for a day? You just wait. After waiting the whole winter....

Lately, my staying power was limited to about four hours. Half-hour to get to Steve's, three hours for lunch, coffee and dessert, and a half-hour to get back. Then, a quiet snooze till dinner. The life of Riley. Nice but hardly building any stamina. A good life. O.K. A blessing. A gift.

But not the gift I was about to receive.

As that day was my name's day, I suspected that something special might be in store for me. Back home, in Poland, only children celebrate birthdays. The rest of us get presents on the day of our patron saint. A Catholic tradition. The kids (Steve was only sixty-eight and Annette many years his junior) arrived at the Institute with a magnificent bouquet of roses and a bottle of Channel Number 5. My favourite. I was almost sorry to leave the roses behind – they were so beautiful – but Annette can be pretty persuasive. Woman-to-woman type talk.

"Think of the fresh air, Mama, of the rosy cheeks you'll get. You might even get some suntan...."

Now that, at ninety-three, pushing ninety-four, would make my day.

"I've borrowed a collapsible wheelchair, just in case," Steve assured me. I wasn't sure I wanted to go anywhere where I couldn't get to without a wheelchair. No matter. I went anyway.

Thirty minutes later we were crossing the US border. I had no passport, no papers whatever. I was ready to spend the night in jail.

"It's our Grandma. She wants to see the lake, just once more," Steve said, wiping an imaginary tear. The guard waved us through.

"Lake? What lake," I asked.

They both grinned. Fifteen minutes later the road reached and then ran along the waterfront. It wasn't a lake at all. It was a sea. Practically an ocean. We were driving alongside the most beautiful shore I'd ever seen. The shoreline of Lake Champlain. An expanse of water, mountains on the horizon, each crowned with a personal halo of purest white wool. The rest of the sky was azure. Like in Italy.

Life is a blessing after all. Sorry Sister, I whispered.

Fifteen minutes later we arrived at the marina. Of course, I didn't let on that for the last twenty minutes or so I'd already guessed where we were going. Some weeks ago Steven mentioned that he'd bought a boat. I expected some sort of a sailboat, but, there must have been something else also. For some reason, my adrenaline began pumping the moment I saw water. Shöenfliess, I thought, the lake of my youth . . . only a million times larger . . . as I said, an ocean....

So I was about to see their boat? In the days to come, I shall be able to imagine them sailing. During the winter months, I shall close my eyes and imagine the sail billowing across the waves, against the backdrop of snow-covered peaks. Perhaps I'll sit on the shore and watch them sail? So many possibilities. It was like being young again.

Steve pulled up right next to the pier. They managed to unload me, always a problem with my stupid legs. I just couldn't rely on my knees. Annette offered me her strong arm, such as professional sculptors develop after years of work. In the meantime, Steve unloaded the wheelchair and went to park the car on the other side of the road.

I loved the way the sun picked up the ripples on the water, bouncing off the crests with a glittering shimmer. I physically pulled Annette to stand closer. Wobbly or not, I was charging forward, hanging onto Annette's arm for dear life.

She pointed up ahead. Another thirty paces forward, then left turn, another...

I can't be sure. Something happened that pushed me or pulled me forward. It wasn't Annette. If anything she was calming me down. I was in a trance. I was walking on water – the floating docks moving with every step were really incidental. Water was on my left, my right and straight ahead. Yes, I was definitely walking on water.

I heard stomping, felt an extra wobble under my feet, and then Steve's voice came from behind me.

"I've put the chair back in the car. I can always get it later," he said.

Chair? What chair?

And then Annette stopped. We went past a dozen boats, all impressive, their tall masts swaying gently in the wind. On our right there was another dock, half the width of the one that brought us here. I looked up from the deck. I overheard Annette telling Steven that my eyes were shining. It must have been the sun.

"That's her, Mama," Annette said, pointing to a ship on her right. "That's our boat."

Ten more steps along the narrow strip of the finger dock and I grabbed a lifeline on the starboard side of the boat. A boat? It was a ship! Well, a yacht at least. It must have been forty feet long!

"She's enormous," I whispered my admiration.

"All of twenty-seven feet, Mama. Not much but she's all ours."

Steve went past me and unhooked a length of lifeline to gain access to the deck. I put one hand on an aluminium rail – the stern pulpit he called it. I stepped over the gunwale. It politely sunk a few inches to make the step lower. Annette jumped aboard, braced herself with her knees, and offered me both her hands. I grabbed them, pulled myself on board, took a long step down onto the cockpit seat, from there onto the cockpit floor. We did all this in total silence. I was vaguely aware of water lapping the sides of the yacht, of the birds flying overhead, of the twang of lines against the aluminium mast. But most of all, I heard distinct moments of silence.

"Welcome aboard the Moravia, Mama," Steve announced.

I didn't answer. I just sat there, not quite believing what had just happened. To clear the gunwale, to get down from the seat to the cockpit floor, I must have negotiated steps twice as high as anything I'd dared to scale these last ten, maybe twenty years. Somehow I did it. I did it smoothly, seemingly without any effort.

"Thank you, Captain," I replied after a while. I still wasn't sure any of this was really happening. If it hadn't been embarrassing, I would have pinched myself.

The three of us sat in the cockpit, I on the starboard seat, they on the port side, staring at each other. We all seemed amazed at what had just happened. I couldn't climb the normal risers leading up to their condo, yet here I was, walking the length of wobbly, moving docks, scaling the gunwale, descending the height of a chair onto the cockpit floor, all with explicit lack of concern. More – with boisterous nonchalance. I was now sitting in the cockpit, as if nothing out of the ordinary was happening.

"Would you care for a little sail, Mama?" This was Steve, or some other imaginary character in this tale of witchcraft and enchantment. I couldn't believe what was happening to me. Was any of this real?

I nodded. Apparently a few times as my throat seemed to be dry.

They'd noticed. Within five minutes lunch was laid out down in the cabin. Once again, this time without any assistance, I negotiated the four tall steps, down a ladder, into the cabin. I think we ate something, we drank something, we... I can't be sure. I know that I used their head. For the first time in my life I used a head on a boat! How's that for new memories!

It might have been another twenty minutes, time simply didn't matter, as Steve and Annette prepared the boat for cast off. Steve started the engine, and soon, slowly, ponderously, the yacht began to pull astern from the finger dock. It all seemed to take place in a calculated slow motion.

Moments later, Steven did something to the engine and the tiller, and the bow began to swing towards the open sea. Soon we cleared the stern of the last windward yacht, then the few boats anchored to buoys, and . . . we were alone. The engine throbbed evenly, softly, moving us ever further out.

I was sailing. For the first time in my life, at the age of ninety-three, I was sailing.

"What do you think?" This was Annette. She was looking up at Steven who stood at the tiller. Her head nodded at the mast. She was now sitting again, facing me, on the port side. There was sunshine in her eyes, too. Perhaps all people's eyes shine when they sail.

"I'd say not more than six or seven knots," Steve said looking at the telltales, little wisps of ribbon attached to the shrouds. "Why not?" he asked, a supercilious grin on his face.

"I'll get the main up first," Anne said.

I had no idea what they were talking about. Annette climbed on the top of the doghouse, loosened the halyard and soon a big triangular sail, the main, seemed to crawl up the mast. Next she came back into the cockpit, freed another thick rope, a sheet, I was told later, and the foresail, a Genoa, began to unfurl itself from the forestay.

And then it happened.

Without any warning, Steve cut the engine. The silence I heard was deafening. It was the same silence I'd heard when I'd first stepped on board only now it was continuous. It filled me from within, it enveloped me from without. I held my breath so as not to disturb it. This was a realm I'd never visited before. I didn't know existed. Perhaps I'd died already? Perhaps I'd skipped the tunnel of light and ended up in heaven....

I heard laughter. Steve and Annette were both staring at me. The joy in their eyes was palpable.

"How do you like it, Mama?"

How do I like it? I have no idea. I'd never experienced anything like this in my life. I'd never visited heaven. How was I supposed to compare it to anything?

"Would you like to take over?"

Take over what? I was still speechless, slightly breathless, certainly apart from the world I'd left behind.

Steve directed me to slide along the seat, backwards, towards the stern, and put my hand on the tiller.

"Push to turn left, pull to veer right. Aim for that mountain, that peak over there," he pointed straight ahead.

I put my hand on the tiller. Very gently I tried pushing and pulling. The boat responded to even minute commands. I was in charge. I was the skipper. I was scared stiff.

Steve and Annette stretched out on the seats, their heads propped up against the doghouse. They were both facing me. They didn't even bother to look where I was steering them. They were either crazy or knew something I didn't. I looked past them at the expanse of water. The waves were not more than six or nine inches. The breeze was gentle, caressing the water, my arms, my face. Yet it filled the sails with ease. I glanced behind me. The wake, after some preliminary wiggles, was now drawing a straight line, gradually merging with a thousand tiny ripples driven by the wind.

The silence continued.

That silence is, I feel, the single greatest thing about sailing. It must be what the universe was like before creation began. The universe that wasn't there. Just silence. And then God said, let there be light. And I was covered with sunlight. Warm, loving, glorious sunshine.

***

14

Dementia

Exit Alzheimer's, enter dementia. At least I don't have to spell it with a capital D, like something to be proud of. Dementia is much kinder than Alzheimer's. You still forget, you still have moments of profound disorientation, but at least you are aware that such things are happening to you. You can stop, take a break, and then try again. And again, if need be. I know. From experience. When you turn ninety-something, you know many things from experience even if you don't acquire many new ones. Except for the yacht. It made me feel so very young. I guess that is what being young really means. You do so many things for the first time. It's worth being reborn, just to have that feeling again. A feeling of breaching the unknown. Like Captain Kirk. Or my son sometimes.

But things are not so bad. The redeeming feature of dementia is that often you forget that you've done something before. You forget that you 'suffer' from dementia. The activity or the idea arrives at your consciousness dressed in new clothing, fresh, untouched by profound analysis.

"How did you enjoy our walk yesterday, Mother?"

We had a walk? Yesterday? Together? How utterly delightful!

"It was wonderful, dear. I loved it." At the same time I said it, I was hoping that there hadn't been any rain yesterday. Actually being a scatterbrain and suffering loss of immediate memory are not the same. Things aren't that bad yet. Not yet. The clouds are obscuring only the horizon but overhead it's still sunny. A moment later I remember our walk very well.

"I thought you might have. You looked so vibrant. And the sun was so beautiful."

Now that sounded very good. I knew I could look vibrant, but no one had told me that for . . . for some time. I just don't know how to go about it. It must have been the sun. I really feel a different person when the sun is out. Perhaps we all do.

This memory business is a little unnerving. By watching others, my co-residents, I know that my days are numbered. Soon, hopefully not too soon, I shall no longer remember what I had for breakfast. I hope I won't forget my children's names. People do. Lots of them. Angelica told me. When it happens, the kinfolk feel so sad. Some of them think you no longer care for them. You no longer love them. You do. You know who they are you just don't remember their names.

I decided to keep writing down my memories, or recording them on my little machine. Someone, somewhere, might find them useful. Perhaps my son, Steven, could use some of my thoughts for one of his novels. That's if he can decipher them. I scribble so. But I can still talk intelligibly. Or Bart could use them to tell his daughters about their grandmother. Stories about Grandma and Grandpa. From the days of yore. Oh, my, it all sounds so ancient....

I was born in 1908, in Poznań, the western part of Poland. If my math hasn't deserted me, yet, that makes me ninety-three now. I was the youngest daughter of six children. I had three brothers and two sisters. Father referred to my elder sister and myself as *myszy*, which is Polish for mice. That's right, those furry little things that flit around. I think that was because his hearing wasn't that good any more and we scooted on tiptoe around the house, appearing out of nowhere when least expected.

I remember once, there was a big party. Sis and I were too young to attend. We were introduced, we curtsied, and were sent to our room. We played there until we heard the last of our parents' guests leave. When our parents' bedroom door closed, we crept out of our hole, like mice, and tiptoed to the salon. The maid had been given permission to only clean up in the morning. The tables were in disarray, dirty plates, cutlery, and semi-voided wine and mead glasses all over the place. My sister, eleven already, older than me by a whole year, decided to try the Bacchanalian nectar. She found a clean glass, and then emptied the different contents from glasses scattered around until her glass was full. The mixture, my sister told me, turned out to be sweetish and not at all unpleasant. It must have been the mead, the honey-wine so popular in Poland in the olden days.

My sister emptied her glass, collected some more near-empties, downed those too, and, buoyed by her brave exploits, we quickly scurried to our room. I didn't touch the stuff. Frankly, I was afraid. My father had once given me a sip of vodka, and after a bout of coughing I decided never to touch the stuff again.

In our room, we undressed and, as was our custom, knelt at our beds for night prayers. The usual Our Fathers and Hail Marys sufficed to assure a good night's sleep.

And then it happened.

Still on her knees, my elder sister began to whimper, then snigger, giggle and finally laugh outright. I assumed she'd received a revelation from the Virgin Mary or some other saint. After all, one simply doesn't giggle on one's knees. Not while saying one's prayers.

"I can't . . . ha, ha, I can't . . ."

"You can't what, Sis?" By now I was getting seriously worried. "Sure you can," I tried to console her.

"I can't . . . I can't get up?"

"You what?" She was such a tease.

"Please Mimi, help me. I really ha, ha, ha..." Apparently I was Mimi already then.

For the next eighty years I remembered that this is what happens when you drink mead on an empty stomach. The alcohol, by some elusive means known only to professional drinkers, deposits itself directly in your legs, with a predisposition for the knees. After a good portion of mead, your knees simply will not lock, no matter how hard you try. The problem is exacerbated by the fact that the rest of you appears to remain in a reasonably sober state, with the possible exception for sniggers, giggles and outright laughter. For some reason, you find your inability to get up highly amusing. At least my dear sister did. Some eighty years ago. She is dead now, but this memory lives on with me. And now it will remain with my two sons.

With you?

There are so many memories. Most of them will soon be forgotten forever. As if they never happened. Steve says that only spiritual memories, what he calls universal memories, are likely to survive. The rest, he says, will be recycled. Like good compost.

I'm surprised by which memories have remained in my head. Like that story about the mead. It was neither traumatic, nor involved any great emotional upheaval. It wasn't even that important. But for some reason it had just found itself a nook in my brain, and had stayed there happily these many years.

"Don't worry, Mama," Steven assured me. "Your cerebellum comprises more than half of your brain's neurons, and they are still functioning quite well."

I am not sure how that little tidbit of information was supposed to cheer me up. Then I remembered. The cerebellum is the smaller part of the brain that controls the movement of muscles. Steve must have been thinking about our yacht trip. Indeed, my muscles had performed miracles. They seemed to have a memory of their own. Steve must be more concerned about my remaining dexterity than distant memories. About the present, not the past.

Anyway, talking of the past....

I was about ten years old then. My sister, eleven. She died at the end of the World War, just after I'd left Poland with Steven, *przez zieloną granicę*, illegally, or as the Poles call it 'through the green border'. Had she lived, she would have been ninety-four now. My father, had he lived, would be 145. As I mentioned, I was a late child. My mother was thirty-nine when she had me, which would make her now about 132. My brothers, all considerably older than I, would have added up to well over three centuries. Imagine that! Three centuries... What is time except a means of keeping memories apart?

But there is also the nature of time itself. She is a fickle lady....

Whenever Steve or Bart drop in, they have an abundance of events to tell me about. They, the events, seem to pile up on them, like a capricious avalanche affecting their lives. With me, it's so very different.

When you're young, events follow or heap up one upon another. They are kept apart by a number of minutes, hours at most. When you get to be my age, you count years between incidents worthy of note. Years or even decades. Time is so fluid. It seems inexorably connected to the reality of the experience.

Or perhaps, it all has to do with the cool, impersonal, calculating intellect, the Black Horse. I feel little emotion when I recount old events. What if we remembered with our hearts instead? What if we, whatever we are, rode the Red Horse, the stallion that suddenly sprouted glorious, spiritual wings? We would then be able to relive those snippets of the past with all the joys and sorrows, all the entanglements that seemed so important at the time.

It appears that whichever mode of being we accept, with our calculating intellect, we are no longer the masters of our bodies, as we once were. In the past, we and we alone decided whether we should live or die. Now? Now we have the loving Sisters to do it for us.

I tried hard to remember when I was I. When I could say I am, and mean it.

What if we are little more than reasonably intelligent animals, feeding, defecating, procreating, resting and, on occasion, having a bit of fun. After all, isn't this what most of us do during most of our waking hours? And then, for some unknown reason, something, a spirit, a soul, an alien, invades our consciousness, and we are yanked from the primary preoccupation of our ancestors to a sudden awareness of beauty, love, poetry, music, the many fine arts... Perhaps we even develop conscious awareness of whoever it was that chose us to manifest His presence in such a humble abode: *...unto us a child is born... and his name shall be called Wonderful, Counsellor, The mighty God, The everlasting Father, The Prince of Peace.*

It was a precious, magical moment.

Remember? I have such strange memories....

Suddenly we become aware of the endless universe, our imagination soars to distant stars, galaxies... We feel as gods, or at the very least, as the chosen ones of some benevolent, wondrous, magnanimous Entity. Could such an Alien, such a Being really find His, Her or Its expression through us? Would such a Being really share Its divine attributes with us – semi-intelligent animals? And later, much later, there even came those enigmatic moments when we could not tell apart Its will from our own. Those precious moments... memories that are timeless. Then, gradually, we perceived a whisper of an unspoken promise that perhaps, just perhaps, when this Alien stops providing our bodies with Its glorious attributes, It might, just might, take us with It on a journey we feel – even now – a journey back home....

Back home to see Jan, my mother, my father, my brothers.

Take me . . . please take me....

This became my most ardent prayer. I would visit the chapel, sit alone in a deserted pew, close my eyes and repeat my plea. Take me, please take me. Why won't you take me?

Lately I have moments when I imagine that most of my memories are awaiting me in the future. That my awareness of time has nothing to do with reality. With the True Reality.

There is nothing quite so romantic for a girl in her early twenties as an officer, in a smart uniform, sitting upon a white steed, rearing to go. The rider, his back as straight as the pines silhouetted behind him against the setting sun, takes a deep breath. The horse stomps a tattoo against the densely packed, green *parcours*, gathering speed to tackle the high obstacle. He must clear the three horizontal boles of white birch without bringing one down. Jan rises in his stirrups, leans forward to help his steed in its forward momentum. Then... he and the horse are airborne.

They fly.... fly....

I think that was the timeless instant when I fell in love with him. He was a second lieutenant then. Young . . . so young, so handsome, so very much a cavalry officer. So exquisitely elegant. My knight on a white horse. Yes. This really happened. It happened to me. And this has nothing to do with memories. This moment, this instant when he took off on that horse, when he became airborne, when he flew towards me, it did not happen in the past. I cherished this image in my heart, every day, even when I looked down at his body prostrated on the bed from which he would never get up. He wasn't there, not him....

I know he is still flying, on a white horse... *and a crown was given unto him: he went forth conquering and to conquer, for ever....*

These are my memories of the future, of the present that will never end. They are mine to keep, to re-experience at will, today and tomorrow. Like the young ones . . . fresh, unsoiled, every day....

People think that we, the elderly, the old, the senile, supposedly suffering from dementia... that we forget. It is true, yet it isn't. First of all, we don't suffer. Not really. We feel sorry for the people we meet who think that we must clutter our brains with mental junk. We still do, sometimes, but only when we really have to. So as not to hurt the people who visit us.

But it's really quite boring. Those bits and pieces of everyday life are really of no consequence. They don't last.

And secondly, we don't really forget. We just eliminate from our minds things of relatively little importance. It is like Steven once said, we only keep the memories that are universal. That are outside time, outside the temporal reality. The memories we keep will last forever. They will merge with the matrix of the universe, enhance it, make it more beautiful. And we shall be part of that matrix. Like Jan clearing those birch boles. Like Jan flying on the white steed....

We know that we sometimes want to include, in the universal memoir of our lives, things that are not worth it. We keep them, for as long as we can, until they become slowly covered with haze, a mist of yesteryear, only to retreat into the past. They too will enhance the universal matrix, but just the lower strata. The places people will visit, from time to time in their dreams, just to pay homage to little, transient moments of joy.

This we must all do. Joy is as close to magic as anything that was born in a cauldron of life and love. Joy is what keeps us going, what inspires us to treasure every moment while it lasts. Every moment of beauty, of stargazing, of gazing into a newborn baby's eyes. There, joy rules supreme. There is so much joy in the world waiting to be discovered. I must tell Father Mulligan about that. He seems to have problems with vision. None are so blind....

As you read this, you might think that my mind is wandering. That the disparate bits and pieces I write, or speak into my little machine, are the products of dementia. Or even of a demented mind. Well, my darling boys, do not worry. I allow my mind to wander, but only to sieve through the countless trillions of those fragments to find something worthy of your attention. Not all memories matter, even to you and me. Not even those we shared together. They have their place, they belong to there and then. But not now.

What really matters is the present. Even as I record my thoughts for you, I am very aware that I am progressing closer and closer to that fascinating mode of being where there is no more time. Where present rules supreme. Dementia is not punishment. It is a blessing. It is what gives you a foretaste of infinity. Of the eternal instant of being. Where neither past nor future matters. Nor ever will again.

I saw him dancing. Then, in a flash of joy, I was at his side. He took my hand, bowed clicking his heels together. There we were alone on the polished floor. We never noticed the tens or hundreds of people around us. We were truly alone. I – lost in his eyes, he – in mine. It was a tango. Tango *Milonga.* Such sweet rhythm. Designed for love, for lovers. For us.

Suddenly there were the others.

The band struck the first chords of mazurka. *Mazurek Dąbrowskiego.* It became the Polish national anthem. Jan always led the dance. I, at his side, my hand resting lightly on the top of his gloved hand. How light he was on his feet. I? I didn't dance at all. I floated on air, lifted by his presence. It seems like yesterday. Like with my knight on the white steed.

Marsz, marsz, Dąbrowski.... Thousands of pennons atop lances streaming in the gentle breeze, a forest of plume, of red and white cockade with brass Polish cross, moving rhythmically, riding in pairs, marching four abreast, a long, long line. Thousands?

What had been left of the old Dąbrowski and Kniaziewicz's Danube Legion in 1806? One infantry regiment and one cavalry regiment in the service of the Kingdom of Naples. Those veterans became the core of the New Polish Legion. Under Napoleon's decree of 1807, new recruits came largely from Poznań and Pomeranian regions. Poznań, years later, was the home of the 15th Polish Cavalry Regiment. My husband's pride and glory.

Perhaps we don't really have memories. Perhaps we invent them. Perhaps all this exists only in my head. In the memories I willed to be mine. When I am no more... will those memories survive? The Vistulan Legion, the Duchy of Warsaw fighting alongside the French in Napoleonic Wars. The Mickewicz's Legion formed in Rome in 1884. The Polish Legions in Hungary created by Józef Wysocki and Józef Bem. The Polish Legions also known as the 58th New York Infantry, fighting in the US Civil War, Polish Legion in World War I formed in 1914 in Galicia....

Why do we always fight?

There were other Legions, in other places, fighting for freedom....

Why is freedom so dear to us? Why was Jan strapped to his chair, his bed?

Marsz, marsz, Dąbrowski.... All the way from Italy. Polish-Italian legions – the Vistulan Legion. *Z ziemi Włoskiej do Polski...*

marching to Poland. The long-lost legions coming home to join us in our struggle for freedom.... *Legiony to straceńców nuta...* They were not all lost. They lived on in our hearts, our memories.

They live on today. For me.

I saw him in my dream today. We didn't do much. We just sat on a bench in Virginia Waters. The freshness of spring blooms, efflorescence, a kaleidoscope of flamboyant colour all around us. The land sloped down, gently, towards the water, long wisps of weeping willow reflected in the pristine surface. We didn't talk. It would be like talking to oneself. We've already told each other all we could possible say in one lifetime.

I leaned against his chest, my head on his shoulder. We sat like that for a very long time. Watching, not quite seeing, listening, hearing nothing.

The albino peacock was away, probably on a peacock hunt for juicy morsels. For whatever peacocks enjoy. The ducks, on the other hand, watched us intently. For once they too were silent. They liked to sit close to the little waterfall. As we did. Perhaps they too shared memories. Or, perhaps, they were making new ones.

***

15

Father Mulligan

Once again, the three of us were sitting in Steve's condo, munching delicious *saumon fumé*, washing it down with thimbles of *cytrynówka*, the *nalewka* my eldest reserved for special occasions. For me, every Sunday was a special occasion. I was with them. That was enough.

"Here's to Father Mulligan," Annette proposed.

I'd just finished telling them as much as I knew of the Merry-weather-Mulligan saga, with just enough of the Francis-Mulligan overtones to make it interesting. In spite of Annette's 'who would possibly want to know' pleas, I swore them to secrecy. According to Steve, it was all Mrs. Merryweather's fault.

"After all," he said raising his glass like a judicial gavel, "it had been she who'd awakened Kundalini," he declared looking triumphantly at Annette and me. I had no idea what he was talking about and I strongly suspect neither did Annette. This in no way deterred him from pursuing his line of thought.

"Kundalini, Mama and my dear wife, is the serpent-goddess. She sleeps in the *muladhara chakra*, corresponding to the pelvic or sacrococcygeal..."

"*Sacrebleu* what???"

Annette had to put up with this sort of language more often than I, and still she had little idea what Steven was talking about.

"...plexus of Western physiology, about two inches above the perineum."

"Which is...?" I prompted.

"...the lowest part of the trunk, between the genital organs and the rectum."

"*Bon appétit*," Annette put in lamely.

"I'm so glad we got that straight," I commented. I was never quite ready for Steven's explicit explanations. I often thought he made them up as he went along.

"She, the Kundalini, is the coiled one, Mama, like a snake with her tail in her mouth, thus closing the door of knowledge. She is the latent vital force in the body which, in Father Mulligan's case, has apparently remained asleep for many years."

"More salmon, Mama?"

I nodded. The way Annette served it was delicious, and so far away from the bland food we were served at the Institute as to make my mouth water.

"So what's all this to do with our Father Mulligan?"

"Well, sometimes, in answer to a compelling call, she uncoils herself. The Kundalini," he added when he noticed our eyes, Annette's and mine, glazing over. For myself, I was already sorry I'd asked.

"The Kundalini," I repeated out of sheer politeness.

"When roused," Steve continued undeterred, "she raises her head and pierces the other lotuses along the spine, until she reaches the *sahasrara chakra*." Steven looked triumphantly at both of us, ladies, frankly more preoccupied with the *saumon* than his exposé of Eastern philosophy.

"The *sahasara chakra*, ladies, is the 'thousand-petalled lotus'. It sits at the top of the brain!"

We both looked up questioningly.

"Didn't you say that Father Mulligan was in a coma? What else could induce such a condition when pre-empted by Mrs. Merrywater's frozen fingers?"

"Merryweather," I corrected. I let the cold fingers go. We were almost through with the salmon and I was about to dig into the *quiche lorraine*. God, how Annette spoiled me! When I was her age, I could only just get past boiling an egg.

"Mother, you are not listening," Steven protested. "Father Mulligan obviously suffered from catabolic . . . from a destructive metabolism. He was aging, bloating, sad, depressed, suspicious and that sort of thing. All signs of catabolism at its worst. Then, suddenly Kundalini was stimulated by external forces . . . ah, the icy fingers. There was a surge of static and catabolic energies, of the passive and active principles . . . a sort of reverse of the creative process. Instead of the descent of spirit into matter, Kundalini raised the gross to the subtle."

With that Steve raised his glass for the . . . actually I hadn't counted how many times, but if he was to drive me back to the Institute, I hoped it was the last.

"*Bon appétit*," Annette repeated, this time without attempting to change the subject. She'd escaped most of the lecture by busying herself with serving the *quiche*. It came with a beautiful tomato salad sprinkled with finely chopped marinated onions. Steven shrugged and poured the wine. Have I mentioned that they were spoiling me?

"So what exactly are you telling us, Steve?" I asked.

"Mother, something down below affected something up above. Work it out yourself." He sounded just a little exasperated.

"Nevertheless, how do you know all those things about Kun-dah-lee-nee?" I had to ask.

"I read it this morning," he confessed, looking away. "Surely, you don't think that I carry all that Sanskrit stuff in my head, do you?"

I didn't.

"And by the way, son, Father Mulligan is not in a coma. He's just had a little bit of a nervous breakdown."

Steve stared at Annette. "I must have overheard," she said meekly.

The *quiche lorraine* was excellent.

Perhaps it would have been better had Father Mulligan remained in a semi-dormant condition for the rest of his days. Alas, the jinni, or Kundalini, would not jump back into the bottle, or crawl back between his legs, for that matter. Into his perineum? It so happened that Sister Angelica had once seen symptoms of a very similar nature. There is something within a man's psyche that once stirred refuses to die down. If a man opposes it, dire consequences may result. The only way to repair the damage is to discharge the energy which Kundalini demands to be released. According to Steven, the Hindus knew this millennia ago. Judging by their numbers, they still do.

We were approaching the end of another wonderful Sunday outing. In five minutes they would take me up to my room and kiss me goodbye for another week. There were the daily phone calls, but it wasn't the same. Seeing is believing. When I saw them both, so happy, I believed that there was life outside the Institute. Real, normal, exciting life. Vicarious pleasure of life is better than no life at all. I wished the Sundays would never end.

"Apparently you're wrong, darling," I told Steve when he insisted that the only thing that would snap Father Mulligan out of his condition was a form of very advanced yoga. Sister Angelica had discovered an alternate method two decades ago.

"Or you know what..." he'd added with a touch of exasperation. "There is also the natural way, Mother," he smiled.

He only called me Mother and not Mama when he had something to say that he wasn't sure he ought to. I preferred not to ask for details. Nevertheless, I was hard pressed not to smile knowingly. I really had no wish to imagine Father Mulligan undergoing a natural therapy.

"Let sleeping Kundalinis lie," Annette whispered to me just as we parked at the Institute. I smiled my understanding. I only wished that were possible.

All was not lost. Within a month, perhaps a little longer, Father Mulligan was already showing all the requisite signs of life. Not that he'd been in anything approaching a coma to start with. He spent a few weeks reclining on his bed, rising only for one or two meals a day and an occasional trip to the washroom. He took, I knew from Sister Angelica, all his meals in his room. Apparently he was a reasonably good patient.

Yet all good things come to an end, as do most other things. On Wednesday afternoon I heard a very gentle knock on my door. This time, on my invitation, the door opened and Father Mulligan's head appeared in the crack.

"Good afternoon, Mrs. Kordos. I wonder if I might have a word."

I asked him to come in but he declined. It wasn't fitting, he explained to me later. I wasn't quite sure why. Because I no longer had my husband to protect me? I tried to picture Jan, some months ago, jumping up from his bed, tearing off his IV and drawing his sabre in my defence. Perhaps Father Mulligan's imagination was even more developed than mine.

I had no choice. As Father Mulligan hated witnesses to our trysts, I guessed that he would be waiting for me on the terrace. I put on my coat, late afternoons were getting quite chilly, and I sauntered towards the balcony. He was already in his usual chair, and rose on my arrival. I was appalled. A plump, not to say rotund man wore a new body on the same frame. Only it looked taller, slimmer, even more athletic, this latter hardly likely. This astounding metamorphosis took place within a month, maximum six weeks. Of illness?

There was something else that didn't tally, but I didn't spot it till later.

I left one chair empty and sat down in the next one. All propriety had been preserved. Even without Father Mulligan's invitation, I might have ended up on the terrace, if only for a short while. I felt a little freer outside. Even on the second floor.

"I've been talking to Sister Angelica," Father Mulligan started. He evidently wasn't comfortable with the subject.

"She is a wonderful woman," I said. A second later I realized my *faux pas*. I should have said nun, not woman. My slip did not go unnoticed.

"She is so much more than a nun," Father Mulligan confided, but there he stopped. I wondered why he'd really called me out on the balcony.

"I have been thinking a great deal about what you told me some time ago, Mrs. Kordos."

Until the breakdown, we had talked, on average, once a fortnight. I had no idea which chat he was referring to. I decided to wait.

"About doing good for others, and forgetting about oneself," he said at last.

"Father Mulligan! That was years ago! So many years...."

"Not for me. If we count time by the sequential events that define our lives, then it was no more than a week or two ago, Mrs. Kordos. You see, I don't know what to do, so . . . I do nothing." He twisted in his chair to face me. "All my life I have been told exactly what to do. There were rules. I passed on those rules to others. I never questioned them. Obedience is a prerequisite for priesthood. An absolute prerequisite. And now...." His hands slowly drifted away from each other, as if giving the world around him a protracted blessing. "And now, Mrs. Kordos, I don't know what to do."

I was about to suggest that he visit a priest, when I realized how absurd it would have sounded. Probably like vicious sarcasm. I had no intention of hurting the man, especially, as he was down already. I suddenly recalled the dozens of people who came to me asking for advice during the war. The Big War. Somehow I always knew how to help them. How to give them hope, a little more faith. A little more strength. This was peacetime and I was racking my brain for something to tell him.

"You mentioned Sister Angelica?" I asked. Frankly I was playing for time.

"You must talk to her, Mrs. Kordos." There was a plea in his voice.

It was my turn to twist in my chair. I took another look at the man. Apart from the apparent, indeed easily visible, loss of weight, Father Mulligan had never looked so good. I raised my eyebrows.

"She took away my walker," he nearly sobbed.

I looked beyond him and, indeed, the walker that always accompanied Father Mulligan, wherever he went, was conspicuously absent. I knew something was wrong initially but couldn't put my finger on it. People don't realize, but we train ourselves to recognize patterns. Not things as such, but their relation or lack of such to other things. Or it could have been all the *cytrynówka* not to mention the Merlot I had at Steven's.

"Why would she deprive you of the ability to move around?" I asked compassionately.

"As you can see, Mrs. Kordos, she hasn't. That woman has a knack for knowing the truth," he sighed the sigh of the long-sufferers. But there was a smidgen of admiration in the tone of his voice. "She is also starving me, Mrs. Kordos. Really."

I suspected that was at the core of his plea. Starvation diet. I was right.

"How can I be happy, kind to myself," he glanced at me sideways alluding to our earlier conversation, "if she withdraws the one thing that gives me pleasure, Mrs. Kordos?"

Poor man. The one thing he still liked . . . food. The autumn colours, the sunshine, the smiling nurses, the walks around the block to the tiny park at the back. The autumn asters exploding in great abundance all around the parking lot; the radio broadcasts of concerts from *Place des Arts*, the weekend plays on the Vermont and the New York Public TVs. Charlie Rose . . . I couldn't count them all. What he was missing, of course, was someone to share those things with.

And he didn't have *cytrynówka*.

"When I was talking about being kind to oneself I wasn't confined, exactly, to one hedonistic pleasure to . . . to, ah..."

"...to stuffing oneself like a pig for slaughter?" he offered.

I'd never heard anyone talking like that about himself. Let alone a priest. It came as a shock. I was about to say so, when I saw his face from the corner of my eye. I witnessed the biggest, brightest, most joyful smile that ever graced Father Mulligan's face.

"I'm taking myself much too seriously, Mrs. Kordos," he averred, nodding vigorously.

Whatever Sister Angelica had been doing with this extemporaneously smiling man must have been more than just looking after his diet.

"She also makes me walk, got me a book of exercises, makes me sit up straight . . . I am not a boy, Mrs. Kordos. I deserve some respect!"

Somehow this last plea sounded in direct contradiction to his previous statement about taking himself too seriously. The ex-plump man, not to mention his ex-morose disposition, was or were considerably mixed up. On the other hand, Sister Angelica's vivacity might have carried her away, particularly towards a man who imagined that looking solemn, walking slowly, with dignity, was what he was expected to do. Poor Father Mulligan, I thought. Once Sister Angelica gets through with him, he'll be young again. He'll be alive, will have nothing to complain about, he might even be happy.

Or else . . . she'll kill him.

"I'll talk to her, Father. Leave it with me."

We talked a little about this and that. He told me that, for the most part, he was quite unaware of having been sick.

"It was a little like going on holidays and coming back to a different parish. The place looked different somehow . . . although I couldn't put my finger on it," he mused aloud. "Then I realized that there were no parishioners."

"Perhaps you began seeing the world from a different point of view?"

"Perhaps. A few times I felt as if I'd just been born. As if I was looking at the world for the first time." Then he gave me one of his long, penetrating looks. "It appears that you are right again, Mrs. Kordos. The world hasn't changed at all. It is I . . . it is I who have changed my point of view."

I suspected that under Sister Angelica's influence, the good Father may have stopped being critical and began observing. It is amazing what we can see when we regard reality without feeling compelled to form an opinion about it. About what we see. I recalled a phrase Steven once read to me from the Gospel of Thomas, the Nag Hammadi Gnostic. "Become passers-by", he'd read. There were 114 logia, or sayings, attributed to Jesus, and this was the shortest one. That's why it stuck in my memory.

Become passers-by.

Father Mulligan was definitely not a passer-by. Not yet. All his life he'd been a messenger for other people. He carried out orders. He served, but not God, nor himself, only other people. His superiors. No wonder he felt lost, perhaps even bewildered.

I never took Steven very seriously, but he did have some interesting notions. I recall, some weeks ago, his giving us his understanding of Jesus' admonition.

"Pretend," he'd said, "that we are an immortal soul. It assumes a human form. Usually it spends a few years learning the skills of physical survival and then reverts to those aspects that are imperative for its advancement on the ladder of spiritual evolution. When the specific lesson assigned for that particular embodiment is learned, the soul sheds the body, which it had created for this specific purpose, and returns to its more permanent abode."

"We just die?" I mused. He went on undeterred.

"Not to the *ultimate* heaven," he said. "There is no such thing."

Oops, not very good news for someone who's over ninety. But I let him go on. After all, I could always ignore him later.

"Heaven is a state of consciousness and, as Jesus had never tired of repeating, it is within us. Not within our *physical* body," he stressed the word physical, "but within our state of consciousness which, if imbued with spiritual qualities, becomes integrated with our immortal Self, which constitutes our spiritual body."

Later, I checked some of the stuff he'd said in the Bible. To my amazement, he was right. Jesus did say that heaven was within us, not on some distant planet or in another universe.

"Furthermore," Steve had been on a roll, "there is no limit to the expansion of our consciousness. If soul develops new interests in matters which it '*can* take with it', then the duration between physical reincarnations lasts longer. According to some mystics, it can last up to the equivalent of a thousand or two of our earthly years. There, in that non-physical reality, our Self, or soul, continues to develop its heightened perception of Truth. It works on the seeds that have been planted on fertile soil, here, on earth."

"And if not?" I asked.

"And if a soul on its stopover within material reality has been only vaguely, if at all, interested in the matters of spirit, then its sojourn in Bardo is likely to be very short."

"Bardo?" He would come up with words that were completely meaningless.

Steve waved his hand dismissing my question. "It is a Buddhist concept. It defines the intermediate state between death and the next rebirth or another of the transitional states of experience."

Apparently my expression did not look satisfied.

"The word Bardo means . . . transition. While the transition refers to the period between successive reincarnations, the very word implies change."

"Thank you," I said, being a little the wiser. He never seemed to consider that not everybody spent as much of their time in books as he did. That's when he wasn't 'elaborating' wine, or *cytrynówka*, or any other of his 'spiritual' concoctions. He was definitely keen on the spiritual....

"Soul that has little to dwell on," he continued, "returns quickly to assume or construct another body and, hopefully, try harder."

Or not, I thought. Most people were determined to walk around in circles. I say this not as judgment only as an observation. As a passer-by.

"Nevertheless," Steve continued still further, "it seems that we are not urged to make our stay on earth either long or short, regardless of the duration of our sojourn in Bardo. It seems though that we are urged to recognize our sojourn on earth or within material reality, for what it is. A transient state of becoming. We are to watch and learn. Hence, be passers-by. We are also told not to get obsessively involved with "things that are Caesar's". Once we step on the spiritual path, they do not really concern us. We enjoy them, appreciate them, even rejoice in them, but . . . we do not lose sleep over them."

"We are in – but not *of* this world," I recalled another saying, only mine was from somewhere in the New Testament.

So it appears that here, on earth, we are to be passers-by. At least according to Thomas. According to the gospel that Bishop Inrenaeus so desperately tried to destroy. He almost succeeded. The Bishop was definitely not a passer-by.

Steve, on the other hand, seemed to be practicing what he preached. Actually, he never preached. He shared with me, and others, his acquired knowledge. We could take it or leave it, he'd always said. "It works for me," was as much as he would say.

"But don't you want people to agree with you?"

He smiled one of the sardonic smiles he reserved for just such occasions.

"I learned, in the past, that usually it's too late."

"For what, son?"

"Too late to agree with me. By the time I've succeeded in convincing someone about something that cannot really be proven, I've already changed my mind. The discussion was enough to raise my own awareness to a slightly different level."

I am sure it did. For some time now, a smile hadn't left his face. He must be doing something right, I thought. A little like Raphael. Only about fifty lifetimes younger.

***

16

Sister Angelica

"I couldn't let her do it, Mrs. Kordos. Not out of vengeance." That's all I heard before Sister Angelica burst into tears. I had no idea what brought on this crisis. Only two days ago the Sister seemed quite content with her lot in life.

"Sit down, Sister," was as much as I could say. I wondered if my customary glass of Bristol Cream was in order. She seemed quite broken up.

For a while we sat facing each other, each lost in our own thoughts. The glass of Sherry stood untouched by Sister Angelica's elbow, on a little table, next to a tiny vase with a single carnation. The table could be wheeled around, even cantilevered over my bed when I didn't feel well. Most of the time, it acted as a table for two glasses, a blue bottle of Bristol Cream and the tiny flower vase. Annette had gotten into the habit of doing that for me. Each time she came, invariably with Steven, no matter what other flowers arrived, there was that single carnation. Always red, always beautiful.

Finally Sister Angelica looked up from her sandals.

"I can't stop thinking about him, Mrs. Kordos," she whispered.

I have the same problem. No matter what I do, my mind wanders to Jan; I quicken my step to get back sooner to my room, to make sure that he's not alone for too long. Old habits take a long time to die. And being with Jan was the longest habit of my life.

"I know," I said absentmindedly. "I too have that problem."

Sister Angelica looked up with a start.

"You are thinking of him too, Mrs. Kordos?" I detected a hidden challenge in her voice.

I realized my error. I'd been so preoccupied with my own memories that I forgot that other people didn't share them.

"I am still thinking of my husband, Sister," I said, suspecting that Sister Angelica needed confirmation that I presented no threat to her own inner turmoil. I now guessed that her mind gravitated not to her husband but to a different object of fascination.

"I told you I killed my husband, Mrs. Kordos. I did so by taking care of his every wish. I was so afraid to lose him. I needed him for my children. I couldn't let them grow up without a father. When I was young, a little girl..."

I could guess the rest. The youngest of fourteen children, she'd hardly had the chance to experience an abundance of parental love. I was only the sixth child and even I often thought that I was short-changed in that department.

"... and Frank was never really happy," she interrupted herself. "Except...." her eyes drifted back to her shoes and stayed there.

"Except when, Sister Angelica...?"

The silence stretched. Slowly her eyes moved to the crystal glass in front of her. As though in a dream, her hand moved forward, in slow motion, her eyes staring right through the glass. When she finally picked up the sherry, she emptied it into her throat.

"Except when we were in bed, Mrs. Kordos," in a tone inviting contradiction.

I said nothing. It was hardly the right time to give Sister Angelica a lecture about sexual intimacy being principally a fulfillment, a confirmation of what was already firmly established between two people who loved each other. It may be different the first few times, a few months, even after a year or two, but later, after years of friendship, it was like icing on the cake. You didn't really need it, at least not so much as in the past, but it was awfully nice to have it.

"I know," the Sister added, still sounding defiant. "He told me so," she added even more sternly.

"I believe you, Sister," I put in gently. "I never doubted that you loved one another."

She was beginning to calm down. For some reason I detected a smidgen of guilt in her confession. Again, I was partially right.

"I shouldn't even be thinking like that," she murmured, confirming my suspicions.

Again, hardly surprising. After all, I was listening to a nun, who, with or without acquiescence, had seduced a priest. Of course, it might well be that the priest had seduced her . . . but if so, why the undertone of guilt?

"I don't know what to do, Mrs. Kordos."

I wasn't aware she had anything to do, other than her sisterly duties. And then I began to suspect that there was an emotional dichotomy developing in my frequent visitor. During the last few months, Sister Angelica had dropped in on me at least once a week, each time skirting the subject I recounted above. She'd reached a certain point in her, what can only be described as, confession, and then she'd leave, leaving me in the dark.

As time was what I had the most of, I didn't push her. I almost treated her visits as running instalments of a soap opera that I was privileged to watch, to the exclusion of all other viewers. There was something brewing in Sister Angelica's cauldron, and I was sure we were very close to tasting the magic concoction. Alas, I was wrong. Once again Sister Angelica's eyes descended to her feet. Abruptly she stood up and left.

"I really mustn't go on like this, Mrs. Kordos. You must be tired of my bellyaching...."

Talk, talk, keep talking . . . I would have liked to say, but it wouldn't be polite. I realized that she hadn't told me what she couldn't let herself do, to whom, and why. After all, that was the plea with which she'd entered my room. And now I shall never know... I almost felt sorry for myself. Only almost. The rest of my brain knew full well that the Sister would be back with another instalment of the unfolding saga.

Obviously poor Angelica was treating me as an escape from her self-induced anguish, whatever it might have developed into. I was glad I could provide a willing ear that gave her some succour. I never realized just how lonely people of the cloth could be. I imagined that they all suspected that whatever misfortunes had befallen them, they, the misfortunes, had been sent upon them by the Good Lord, to give them an opportunity to make up for their sins. They believed in a God that, apparently, punished them at every opportunity. Something to do with getting rid of, what my son Steven would call, karma, and, upon their demise, pave their road directly to heaven, without stopping for a few million years in purgatory. A complex, and in my opinion, a very misunderstood philosophy. Yet only such served to explain their apparent qualms. This applied to both Sister Angelica and Father Mulligan. And, according to the Sister, to her late husband, Father Francis. And that, by extension, to fully fifty percent of priests and nuns in Brazil. God only knew what happened to the sacerdotal ranks in the rest of the world.

I realized how lucky I was that my God was a God of love, of laughter, of beauty and had a superb sense of humour. True that on occasion He could be a little exacting, but we all are. On occasion. But most of the time my faith filled me with awe of beauty, of compassion and, yes, definitely with joy. And also, my God was the God of the living. I may have been attached to my memories, subject to the force of habits, but I was glad Jan was finally free, that he could ride the white stallion wherever he was, as much as he wanted. Death may have brought a sense of guilt to Sister Angelica; for me it was a great sense of relief. It was part of life.

I may have created an impression that I only spoke to two people at the Institute. Father Mulligan and Sister Angelica. And Raphael, of course, but he is in a class of his own. I assure you, however, it isn't so. I could write volumes about the others, other personal accounts that would bore the best among you. Most people need an ear, even Marc Anthony did, especially since so many of us are, *per force*, involved in burying our friends. We bury them and we praise them, even if during their lives they were consummate bores. Anyway, many other stories would have been fascinating, not because of their content, but because they represent the reality of every person recounting it.

We, the human species, have developed an amazing capacity to create mountains out of molehills. No matter how prosaic a particular life is, or appears to be to many of us, we, the travelers, manage to elevate our puny problems to Olympian heights. We contrive to introduce complexities into things that are not only simple but utterly banal. We even manage to extract personal suffering from causes that should only stimulate in us profound indifference or, at most, a sense of lackadaisical compassion. I'm not sure if compassion could ever be lackadaisical, but something very close to it. After all, the vast majority of those people were extremely listless.

We like drama, with overtones of tragedy.

At best, I observed typical lives aspiring to tragicomedies. At worst, to a prosaic farce. But not so to the people who shared their innermost feelings with me. To them, their personal dramas are earth shattering. Their earth. Their personal reality.

Two weeks later, Sister Angelica knocked on my door again. Also again, she seemed to be holding back her tears. Out came Bristol Cream, two glasses, and I sat back waiting to see what developed. Sometimes I wonder if I would have anything to recount if it weren't for the Sherry. Not that anyone drank to excess. But it did create an atmosphere of ease and confidentiality. Somehow more conducive to sharing than water or even tea.

"Aren't you going to tell me what happened?" Sister asked me after no more than thirty seconds of ponderous silence.

"What happened?" I asked dutifully.

She wasn't amused. I saw that she was under some particular sense of stress. I tried to make up for my frivolity.

"Relax, Sister. I am always here for you. You know that?"

Her face softened. She even managed a smile. A smile that, no more than a year or two ago, never used to leave her face. How sad, I thought, smiling my encouragement.

"I caught them again," she said hardly above a whisper.

"You caught who with whom?" I whispered back.

"Them," she was capable of an amazing theatrical whisper that would be heard on the gallery. We were in my tiny room. It sounded very dramatic.

When my face still remained blank, she added, "She's like the Merryweather woman. And, you know...."

And then she burst into tears.

Unless I was very mistaken, Mrs. Merryweather had barricaded herself in her room with Father Mulligan about five, maybe eight years ago. God, how time flies. She must be a hundred now. Ancient. What a plucky woman.

I tried to think back. Mrs. Merryweather had been barricading herself in her room, with suitable gentlemen, for the purpose of extracting vengeance on her late husband, who had been unfaithful to her, presumably while still alive.

So far, so good.

Now, with a little prompting from me, Sister Angelica confided to me that the very same Mrs. Merryweather hadn't confined her once-every-five-year sieges to poor Father Mulligan. She had designated him, it seems, a *pièce de résistance*, a *coup de grâce*, a feather in her hat. In the meantime, she continued to practice her art of vengeance on both, the second and the first floor residents. The third floor would have been easy prey, but hardly offering much satisfaction. They would offer no resistance. There would be no sense of victory. Of blood. She had been seen prowling the third floor corridors, now and then, but her face registered an unmistakable expression of disappointment, mixed with frustration. The men, apparently, not only offered no resistance, but also no life of their own. Fortunately or not, her progressive dementia enabled her to visit the same haunts, seemingly for the first time.

Even on the second and first floors, where at least some of the men showed signs of being libidinously alive, even if they didn't quite remember why, her conquests were invariably, at least for her, revelatory. In more ways than one. According to Sister Angelica, who under considerable prodding on my part, divulged the secrets about which, apparently, the whole Institute knew with the sole exception of yours truly, Mrs. Merryweather had no recollection whatever of having cornered the gentlemen in question on any previous occasion. Aah, the blessings of dementia, I thought. They say that the first time is the most unforgettable....

"In this respect, she's as lucky," Sister Angelica murmured, "as her prey. They too have little or no recollection of any conjugality with the vengeful widow."

I decided to steer the good Sister onto our subject matter.

"And, Sister Angelica, how does all this affect Father Mulligan?"

"For a number of years, not at all, Mrs. Kordos."

"She no longer found him, ah, a worthy opponent?"

"Oh, no, Mrs. Kordos. Father Mulligan..." she pulled herself short. "What I mean is that Father Mulligan took great steps to protect himself from any repetition of the previous fiasco."

"He had a lock installed on his door?"

"No, Mrs. Kordos. He told me he prayed for Mrs. Merryweather... but I didn't say it was Mrs. Merryweather, Mrs. Kordos. I said she was like Mrs. Merryweather."

I took a deep breath. Presumably she meant strong, determined and wouldn't take no for an answer. "You mean Father Mulligan has another . . . admirer?"

Sister Angelica wiped a tear forming at the outer corner of her eye.

"I don't think she loves him, Mrs. Kordos. I think she's only after his..."

"Spare me the details, Sister. I am sure Father Mulligan has a great deal to offer in all respects. But what is it, do you think, that women find so attractive in him?"

Plump – though less so than before. Pensive – hardly stimulating for a good conversation. Certainly intelligent – but that would hardly serve to quicken the blood in the arthritic veins of women usually over seventy. The way Sister Angelica sounded he was driving the ladies into uncontrollable palpitations. I really couldn't understand what it might be.

"It's the cloth, Mrs. Kordos."

Aah, yes. That I could understand. For simple folk, of the Catholic persuasion, most women regarded priests as direct descendants, or at the very least, close cousins of God. They wielded the power over life and death, if not in the here and now, then certainly in the yon and after. A single denial at a confessional could mean eternal damnation. On the other hand, I thought, surely that would also dissuade them. Unless playing with the eternal fire was their version of Russian roulette.

"When they know that a man was a priest, but that he no longer wears clerical clothing, some women regard this as an open invitation."

"You are not serious!" I exclaimed. I was sure that Sister Angelica was imagining things, perhaps she, herself, felt a certain weakness towards the retired priest who seemed to be so very alone. It could be her maternal instinct, I thought.

"I am afraid, I am. Mrs. Kordos. I really shouldn't use names, Mrs. Kordos. Anyway, the lady who cornered Father Mulligan was the fourth woman. Not the second. I didn't tell you about the others because I felt embarrassed."

"Embarrassed for the women?" I mused aloud.

"Oh, no, Mrs. Kordos. Embarrassed for Father Mulligan. He had done nothing, nothing Mrs. Kordos, to encourage those women. Nothing at all."

No doubt he hadn't. Whenever I spoke to him he seemed like a man as shy as he was retiring. I wondered how he defended himself against those passionate purveyors of the feminine charms. Some sort of female Don Juanitas? Or else, the Edenic serpents? This was not the area of my expertise.

"They are Jezebels, Mrs. Kordos. They are all Jezebels."

With all my reading, I was becoming very good at biblical references. Jezebel was the daughter of Ethbaal, the king of Zidonians, and wife of Ahab. Jezebel, the name meaning 'without habitation', worshipped Baal, a god quite popular at the time. Baal stood for master, possessor, lord, owner, husband and, on occasion, the fertility-god. Baal stood for just about anything that was useful, nice and, like Baal-hanan, he was even gracious. No wonder he was worshipped. For some reason, Jezebel came to represent a self-centred soul given to sensuality and material concerns. As far as I could see, such a description could apply to, say, ninety percent of women I've met. Not that men were any different. For women today, young women today I mean, sensuality is recognized as something eminently positive, indeed encouraged in all the soap operas. As for material concerns, isn't this why the same percentage of women get married? I may be cynical, but I defy anyone to prove me wrong.

Furthermore, all the women Sister Angelica failed to mention, did not, to the best of my knowledge, lead promiscuous lives, but worshipped a man of God, with, perhaps, a slightly uncontrollable dedication. Hardly Jezebels, I thought.

"Hardly Jezebels," I told Sister Angelica. "Perhaps they find Father Mulligan attractive?" I offered. After all, having retired from active duty, he was surely no longer bound by the exigencies of celibacy.

"Of course they find him attractive!" Sister Angelica practically exploded in Father Mulligan's defense. "Why, he's the best-looking man..."

"...on the second floor?" I asked.

Sister Angelica realized that her outburst was not very nunnish. Her eyes found their way to her shoes, yet even though she looked down, I could see her flushed cheeks. Sister Angelica, I decided, was in love with Father Mulligan.

"He is a very attractive man," I tried a different tack, slightly embarrassed at trying to loosen the Sister's tongue. As I mentioned before, we have too much time on our hands here. We must also find our own forms of entertainment. Alas, Sister Angelica did not rise to the bait.

"Attractive and kind," I tried again. "And lonely," I added for good measure.

Here I was, a woman of ninety-something, playing with gossip, trying to play matchmaker. Never in my life had I time or inclination to indulge in such feminine proclivity. I was always too busy. Shame on you Mimi, I told myself. And then I looked expectantly at Sister Angelica.

"Yes, Mrs. Kordos. He is very lonely. So very...."

"...lonely." We were not getting anywhere on this tack.

Since Steve and Annette had taken me sailing, my mind operated in nautical terms. Especially since, after that single occasion, we'd talked for the next ten Sundays of nothing else. What I mean is that I was still at sea.

"The Merryweatherites did not get through to him, did they? I mean figuratively, of course."

"Oh, no. Mrs. Kordos. He is a very pure man. You, of all people, know that, Mrs. Kordos?"

"Yes, Sister. I know that. And that is why, I think, you have absolutely nothing to worry about. Father Mulligan will always remain faithful to his own conscience."

For some reason this seemed to quiet her. I for one, give my conscience a fair amount of latitude, though, admittedly, not in matters of moral comportment. In this field, neither Jan nor I ever had to compromise. It was never even an effort. Our love was too strong. But in other matters, such as politics, social mores, the arts, and particularly TV, I never held my tongue to express my dismay. I had considerably more tolerance for people I knew personally. Father Mulligan, I knew, did not allow himself the same latitude in any field. He was constrained by years of moral discipline. He just didn't criticize others. He really was a good man.

I also enjoyed quite unbiased conscience when indulging my imagination. I began to build happy-ending stories about Sister Angelica and Father Mulligan. The Decameron's Boccaccio may have been the ultimate survivor, but I put my money on Father Mulligan. I was sure he would find his way out of his self-imposed shackles.

There. I told you we have too much time on our hands.

On the other hand, who could tell? Perhaps it wasn't my imagination. Perhaps in my old age I've acquired the gift of prophecy? If I were proven right, vindicated in my speculations, then it couldn't happen to two nicer people.

***

17

The Messenger

I've known him for ten years. I was eighty-three when I came to the Institute, I am ninety-three right now. *Le temps passe et coule,* as the French assure us so poignantly. Exactly ten years. In all this time, Raphael has never sat down in my presence. Nor anywhere else, as far as I could see. Didn't the man ever get tired?

"Tiredness is a state of mind, Mrs. Kordos."

"Isn't everything?" I countered. I was up to his clever little sayings.

He smiled. "Indeed, Mrs. Kordos. But I would rather call it a state of consciousness."

"There's a difference?"

"State of mind is a means, an active process through which creation takes place. Consciousness is our awareness of that process. It is still. It is an observer of that which the observed does."

Now that made it perfectly clear. It is quite remarkable how Raphael managed to confuse me without even trying. And he did so especially when he explained things. At least to me. Perhaps I am already retarded, or my reasoning capacity has been diminished by the onset of dementia. I know it's coming.

"Care to expand on that?" I pointed to a chair.

To my amazement, after ten years, the man-mountain lowered himself to one of the armchairs. To my joy he now looked considerably less imposing. He didn't dominate the space he was in, at least, not until he started talking again. He was still a head taller than I was when we were both sitting. He really was huge. I've never understood how a man that big could be so gentle.

"In the beginning, the observer and the observed are apart. Later, they become one. It is as it should be. You once mentioned the saying of John of the Cross, from the Apocrypha. About the lamp. It is all the same thing. It is the way of progress."

"I thought you were going to expound on the first chapter of Genesis," I quipped. "In the beginning..." I stopped when I saw his face.

They say that there are no coincidences. That everything happens at its particular time, that there is a particular order of things. You know? Like a time to be born and a time to die, a time to mourn and a time to dance, and all those other times in the Book of the Ecclesiastes.

Anyway, if it weren't so, Steve told me, the planets would fall into the sun, the sun into the galactic centre and the centres would smash into each other, and the whole place would be an unholy mess. I suppose he meant that there must be some order and harmony in the world.

Well, I wasn't out there, and nor was he. As far as I am concerned, the universe works because . . . well, because we're just lucky. After all, even Einstein wasn't sure. He wanted to know the thought of God, right? If we weren't lucky, then we wouldn't be here. On the other hand, looking at some of the residents here, that wouldn't be such a bad thing.

But then there is that book of Genesis, which attempts to put a different spin on it all. Just to get one over on Steve, I decided to reread the whole Bible, for a second time, starting with the first chapter of the Pentateuch. From end to end, and then we'll see who can come up with smart quotes.

I'm already at chapter four. At a chapter a day I will get through the first book of Moses, the Genesis, in forty-six days. The first time I read the Bible, I read it in Polish. This time, I borrowed the King James Version. I must say, I rather like it. So far. And now, coincidence or not, Raphael, who appears to know just about everything about everything, was talking to me about Genesis. And he did so sitting down!

"Ah, yes, in the beginning... That's quite a different story, Mrs. Kordos," he resumed, seemingly giving me time to settle down. "It has to do with creation, or to be more precise, with the creative method."

"I thought it had something to do with how God created the world," I put in smugly.

"In a way, it does. Although the real importance of the first chapter is to tell you and me how to create ourselves. How to act as gods."

"Are we talking about the same book?"

"The first chapter of Genesis. Moses found a judicious way to explain how the method works. Had he done so without employing the parable, the method would have been long destroyed by his successors."

"I thought only the New Testament employs parables?"

"It does, but they got the idea from the old prophets. It was a well-established teaching method of the early Hebrews," he smiled shyly as if giving something away.

"You sound as if you were there at the time," I smiled.

I thought that my quip was quite funny. For some reason he didn't laugh at all.

"Would you like me to tell you about Moses' creative method, Mrs. Kordos?"

"Would you like a glass of Sherry, Raphael?"

He smiled but declined. As I got up anyway, to help myself, I also reached out for my tiny recorder. I was going to get this fellow with all his accumulated knowledge. "You don't mind, do you?" He didn't. I left the bottle out on the table, with an extra glass, in case he changed his mind.

"The biblical model of creation is as valid today as it was some three and a half thousand years ago. It delineates the steps we all must take if we are to be both efficient and successful in our endeavours."

As he spoke I felt a great relaxation coming over me. It was as though I was about to fall asleep, yet I could swear I heard every single word. What was more, I felt that I would not need my recording machine. That I would remember every word, as though it were etched in the essence of my being. As though I were metabolizing Raphael's knowledge. Somehow, I was making it my own.

"*In the beginning God created the heaven and the earth,*" Raphael began to quote the first verse of the first chapter of Genesis from memory.

"Two important items of information are hidden in the very first verse. One, God is always at the beginning of everything, and two, in order for anything to become manifest, to happen, we need to initiate the concept of duality. In heaven, every idea is in its potential state. On earth, it is concretized. Thus, the two states of consciousness: the spiritual or heavenly and the non-spiritual or of the earth. Before anything at all can happen this concept must be accepted. It is imperative to remember that there is no duality in the spiritual realm; nor, by definition, is there any matter, or mass, as our scientists would say. To successfully convert a spiritual idea into concrete or material forms we must follow the instructions closely."

His face seemed to assume a sheen, as if the western sun touched his skin through my window. Only . . . my window faced east. Perhaps a reflection from a window pane of some building opposite?

"Once we understand that, we can get down to business," he said watching my face intently. I wondered if he wasn't making sure I hadn't dozed off. Then something moved me.

"*And the earth was without form, and void; and darkness was upon the face of the deep. And the spirit of God moved upon the waters.*" It wasn't Raphael quoting the second verse. I was. I knew it by heart. I didn't know I knew it by heart.

"Quite so," he nodded. "Obviously, the earth, namely matter, was without form; it was void, in other words, it wasn't there! It was only in *potential* form." He stressed the word potential. "It was an idea. The darkness always represents the absence of light, and light always stands for knowledge."

"Is the whole Bible so full of symbols?"

He nodded again. "As the Bible concerns itself exclusively with spiritual matters, the knowledge it refers to is divine knowledge."

It was my turn to nod, although I wasn't sure I understood what he meant by divine knowledge.

"The *face*," he pointed to his own, "symbolizes the power of recognition. At this stage in the creative process there is nothing to recognize. The *waters* symbolize the thought-stream. So we now have an idea, an incredible potential, symbolized by *the deep*," again the stress, "yet without any knowledge of what to do with it! The Spirit is attempting to spirit-*ualize* the thought-stream. The uncoordinated thoughts, the chaos, are the original building blocks of the universe, and thus of absolutely anything within the universe. They are what atoms were before they became atoms. They could be regarded as quanta of energy and information not yet organized into patterns."

I thought of the stem cells that have the potential of becoming any body-part we may need. For some reason Raphael looked at me as though I wasn't paying attention. I dropped the stem cells and concentrated on his words. I decided to make up for my meandering thoughts.

"*And God said. Let there be light; and there was light.*" I said, supplying the third verse.

"Light, as we already know, is the source of all knowledge. An illuminated person is a knowledgeable person. To put ideas into concrete forms we need knowledge."

Now *that* I could understand. I smiled my acceptance of his thesis. I think Raphael was pleased. He looked down at me with expectancy in his eyes.

"*And God called the light Day, and the darkness he called Night,*" I quickly quoted the next verse. Fifth, I think. Somehow I had them down pat in my declining memory.

"This is a fascinating piece of instruction." There was genuine pleasure on Raphael's face. "We recognize the day as time between sunrise and sunset. The Hebrew did the opposite. The Hebrew day *started at sunset*. I repeat. All knowledge recorded in the Bible is spiritual knowledge. It begins in our unconscious, in the darkness, and seeps into our minds while we are not consciously active. Thus knowledge begins at night. In order for an idea to take root, we must *not* try to think about it but... sleep! The greatest ideas anyone ever had did not take seed in the scientists' labs, but at night. We are reminded here about the true source of ideas, and the true developer of such. The observer and the observed, remember Mrs. Kordos? The nearest we get to participation at this stage of the creative process is through our unconscious."

Whenever I talked to Raphael, my ego invariably took a beating. It was time to take a sip of my Bristol Cream. Raphael waited until I'd put my glass down before resuming.

"*And God said, Let there be a firmament in the midst of the waters, and let it divide the waters from the waters.*"

"Verse six?" I offered. Raphael nodded.

"I love the King James version of the Bible. But when poetry and accuracy compete for attention, poetry always wins! After all, there is great diversity in creation, whereas poetry is beauty, and beauty is a divine attribute. The Hebrew word *raqia*, translated as firmament, in fact means *expanse* or *expansion*. What we are told here is that we must go through the process of sifting our thoughts into the relevant and the irrelevant. As the idea grows, develops, our attention must be placed on the thought process. We must separated them from each other. If we are to develop an idea, we cannot be scatterbrained. The great thinkers, inventors, artists, invariably demonstrated fantastic powers of concentration. The ancients knew that!"

He was right, of course. Steven had said the same thing. Not that Steve was an authority, but it was nice to hear.

"The following verse deals with the same subject. It is interesting in verse eight that *God called the firmament Heaven*." He italicized the words with his fingers. "It suggests that the process of expansion of ideas is still a divine process, i.e. it must take place before the idea enters our conscious mind. We love saying that *we* have a marvellous idea. But, in truth, if the idea is any good, it originated way above the 'we' or the 'I' concepts. Our egos take another beating..."

Now there was something I was getting good at. Beating up on my ego!

Pensively he offered verse nine. *"And God said, Let the waters under the heaven be gathered together unto one place, and let dry land appear."* If I were to read the Bible at this rate, I would be one hundred and fifty before I got through it.

"We made it." Raphael smiled as though he'd read my thoughts. "Finally the dry land. When we gather together our thoughts, symbolized by waters, *under* the heaven, i.e. in our conscious mind, a manifestation takes place."

I knew that word. Steven had mentioned Emmet Fox, who, he claimed, had been a superb exponent of the spiritual interpretation of the Bible. Only Emmet Fox referred to this manifestation as Demonstration. Demonstration of doing something right, I suppose.

"A demonstration..." I mused.

"If we follow the process accurately," now Raphael's voice was dreamy, "if we let God do His work, mostly while we sleep, if we are humble enough to let our thoughts be gathered at our unconscious level *before* we take active part in the process, we end up with a demonstration." And then his voice turned just a little sad. "We can hardly be expected to develop an original idea when, some say, we are, at present, using hardly five percent of our brain. Now, can we?"

I have no idea how long we just sat there, facing each other, like old friends who, having told each other all the latest news, are now just enjoying being together. Through a fog of memories, I heard Raphael telling me things that, for the last ninety-three years, had been a mystery. A mystery that my Church is so very fond of.

It seemed that at least one riddle had been unveiled for me. Not just the substance of the first chapter of Genesis, but the whole approach to understanding scriptures. I wondered if other ancient writings, the Bhagavad Gita, the Koran, the Tao Te Ching, the Vedas, the Upanishads... so many others, held as many mysteries that a wise man, a man like Raphael, could unravel or unfold before my myopic eyes. To see and to understand. I am so old and yet, if it hadn't been for Steve, I wouldn't have even heard about them, let alone attempt to understand them.

Am I too late?

"....the rest of the creative process described in Genesis shows us how not to rush an idea. How to keep checking, at every stage, if the idea is good," his voice reached me from afar. "This simply means that if we allow our ego to take over, we might channel the idea for our own ends, for our personal gain or advantage...."

Wasn't that what ideas were for? To take advantage of opportunities to score one over the opposition? Wasn't that the nature of the game....?

"...God, whatever we mean by this concept, is one. It, or He, is not concerned with our puny egos but with All. With the Whole." The words sounded capitalized. "As we grow in light, in divine knowledge, our interest begins to reflect that which can benefit the largest number..."

The largest number of people... Where had I heard this before? Then it came to me.

During the Montreal Expo, in 1967, I recall reading about R. Buckminster Fuller, who was the designer of the American pavilion. In 1927, at the age of 32, Fuller committed all his productivity potential only towards dealing with our planet as a whole. I made a note of one particular phrase of his. He wrote at the time:

> "This decision was not taken on a recklessly altruistic do-gooder basis, but in response to the fact that my Chronofile clearly demonstrated that in my first 32 years of life I had been positively effective in producing life-advantage wealth . . . only when I was doing so entirely for others and not for myself."

...not taken on a do-gooder basis. I wondered how many do-gooders have the same attitude, and how many rise to the top of international charitable organizations only to drive a Mercedes or even a Rolls Royce, when representing their do-goodnik ideals. Over the years, the press has had fun reporting their peccadilloes.

I opened my eyes, expecting to see Raphael's smiling face. I was alone. I reached out for my recorder. I must have forgotten to switch it on. I am quite sure that I had not imagined my little tryst with Raphael. With the strange messenger who came and went in his own peculiar way, who was everywhere and nowhere, yet who always left his indelible mark. A nurse's help. A man who did the most menial tasks, tending to the aged and infirm. Who helped those who were unable to help themselves.

What a strange man he was.

***

18

The Blessing

"Grant them long life," Father Donovan prayed loud enough for most of us to hear his steady droning. This was no '*vitam eternam*'. Not yet. This was the here and now. At the Institute. He must have thought that he was expressing the deep-seated desires of all present. Of the infirm, the incontinent, the senile, the derelicts that had been wheeled here, to the chapel, by the nuns, the nurses, and many by the residents still capable of performing a good deed for their neighbours.

"Just how long is long," I whispered to my neighbour who nodded in a wheelchair. I was answered by a bout of coughing.

"Can I help you?"

More coughing.

"Grant them long life," Father Donovan repeated.

In spite of my Sunday outings, I remained unconvinced about the beatitudes assigned to long life. I found walking progressively more painful. I also seemed to be losing my sense of balance. I'd fallen three times in the last few months. The last time, it took the nurses three hours to find me, on the floor, and pick me up. All right. It felt like three hours. But my elbow and my hip hurt me for a lot longer.

The candles at the altar burned with a steady flame, untroubled by the tiniest breeze. The windows were all shut, and most of the congregation was asleep. Like the candles, or nearly so, our lives burned untroubled by a single creative thought. The residents certainly wouldn't move sufficiently to make the candles waver in their reaching up, towards God in slim, imploring flames.

It was a small chapel. Just over twenty feet wide by about eighty from the doors to the altar. The floor looked clean, the usual polished terrazzo, the walls were plastered with depictions of the Stations of the Cross equally spaced along its lengths. The ceiling looked the shabbiest. The acoustic tiles were worse for wear. They were beginning to turn yellow, brown around the edges, with some tiles a bit askew.

Perhaps we were not meant to look at the ceiling. We were meant to pray, I suppose.

Instead, I couldn't stop wondering why the priest insisted on God granting us such a long life. Maybe if he tried to define life, he would understand us more. No matter, I liked being there, in the chapel. It was the only place where things were orderly. God was up, hell down, we, the people, were to the left and right and towards the rear. In front was the priest who knew all the answers. Or at least, he was good at pretending or relegating them to mysteries. Nevertheless, it was good to be there.

It was my chapel.

The priest turned to Latin and my thoughts drifted back to long life and its dubious blessings. In the past, we were exposed to the dangers that living entails. We picked up germs, tripped over icy patches, broke some ribs, developed pneumonia, and our problems were over. Then came the antibiotics. Then the anti-flu immunizations. Then the sterile conditions of the Institutes dedicated to the welfare of the very old. Now they or we, the infirm, the aged, the decrepit, could spend many happy years tied to a bed, or a wheelchair, relaxing in our own excrement in full knowledge that sooner or later, usually a bit later, someone would come, raise our legs, wipe our hind quarters, sponge-bathe us, and give us a new, long-lasting napkin. Specially designed for the aged.

In the meantime we would continue to count our blessings. I heard voices as I walked the corridors.

"Nurse, my arm hurts."

"Both my arms hurt."

"It's my stomach, nurse. I can't hold anything down."

"I can't empty my stomach, nurse. It's been four days."

"My eyes, ears, kidneys, both kidneys hurt, nurse. My livers..."

"You only have one liver, Mrs. Golonka."

"Well, it hurts anyway. It hurts on both sides."

"I'll give you a pill for that, Mrs. Golonka. Don't worry."

The pills were the real blessings of God. Pills of all colours. Blessed pills.

With pills you could spend ten, twenty years waiting to cross the Gate. The good sisters of the Immaculate Conception would see to that. The pain would be nominal. The pills would also dull your brain, your reflexes, your ability to make decisions, to think for yourself, but there would be relatively little pain. What a blessing!

"Life is a gift of God, Mrs. Golonka," I heard as I moved along the corridor. Now where have I heard that before? "Our job is to make sure you enjoy it as long as possible." I moved on.

Another door was open.

"Thank you sister... may I now have a clean napkin? And perhaps some more painkillers?"

"It is not time yet." I recognized Sister Cecilia's droning voice. She was a good sort, only well, she lived in a different reality. "You must learn to suffer for your sins, like the Good Lord did," she whispered, her voice filled with compassion.

"How very immaculate..." the old man passing me on the corridor remarked, but the sister was already gone. There were others who were in need of her assurance about the gift of God. They were nearly all ungrateful. All in need of being reminded. She was already in the next room, administering good cheer.

"Please, Lord, grant me patience," Sister Cecilia murmured piously, her eyes rolling momentarily towards the ceiling. Even from the corridor, the room smelled of copious excrement. The Sister knew patience was a divine virtue. What a pity so few of the elderly had any. They wanted pills, clean napkins, something to wet their parched throats, more pills. So very impatient....

Again, my mind drifted back to the good priest at the altar advocating long life. How important is life? And just how sacred is it? What are, or should be its qualities? Our spiritual leaders, in an effort to guide people who are at the stage of development that requires guidance, add such elements as dignity, equality, well-being, and an adequate level of financial security as prerequisites for good life. According to other authorities, steadfastly supported by the sacerdotal fraternity, we all have an inalienable right to employment, education, free medical care, pensions, a roof over our heads and enough to eat to make us at least reasonably unhealthy. All to enhance our life.

Most sacred life, of course. The Gift.

Presumably to make sure that we do not overindulge in this Edenic euphoria, the Holy Father, for instance, demands of us unquestioning obedience. He demands this obedience while insisting that presidents, dictators and disparate heads of other misguided faiths and political systems give us absolute freedom, so that we might obey him, the Holy Father, absolutely. A paradox? Not according to His Holiness. We are assured that all this is so as to improve the physical not to mention moral quality of our life. Perhaps. But before we accept the precepts of all the infallible paragons of virtue, there is a tiny little question that begs to be answered:

What is life?

I remember looking around the chapel. Wheelchairs, eyes devoid of any intelligent thought or feeling . . . waiting, waiting, waiting . . . for Godot?

What is life, I wondered?

The following Sunday I raised the question with Steven.

"Some claim that life begins at the moment of conception," I said after we finished the traditional salmon with vodka chaser, and waited to see what developed. In my mind's eye I saw a sperm winding its murky way toward an unsuspecting egg, making a tiny puncture and bingo, we had life.

"Others, Mama," Steven decided to join in my mental ramblings, "say that life is only manifest when the cranium appears in the outside world and the baby takes its first breath."

I talked to Father Mulligan about that. He told me that somewhere in the Old Testament the word *neshamah*, meaning breath, is translated as soul which would suggest that soul is synonymous with the first breath. Likewise the Greek *pneuma*, he'd said, meaning breath, is translated in the New Testament as Spirit. Could the first breath of a baby have something to do with the Spirit entering its body? Or is the Spirit omnipresent? Father Mulligan had refused to commit himself.

"Spirit in the sense of Consciousness. But life...?"

"But how did the baby get there?" I mused aloud. This was back at Steve's, between snacks.

"That's an easy one," Steve was warming up to the discussion. "There is a cell which divides into two cells, which divide into two cells each, which . . . rather like a single bacterium which in mere eight hours can merrily divide to produce one billion bacteria."

"In one day?" I must have looked and sounded incredulous.

"That's right, one billion," he grinned. "All in a day's work. Talk of life! Of course, according to some religious authorities this life doesn't matter. It is not sacred; it is not human."

Convenient.

A week later, this time over coffee and delicious Belgian chocolates, he read some of the notes he'd prepared for me after the last time we'd met. He was like that. Whatever I asked him, particularly from the realm of the reasonably esoteric or arcane, he would research and then treat me to his notes. He read them aloud.

"The baby eats, defecates, sleeps, crawls, walks, grows. It, the grown up baby, walks *on* and *in* its own offal. Then it no longer needs the security of diapers, he/she is trained now," he looked up from his page, "rather like my kitten – only it took a lot longer," he smiled. "Nevertheless it, the baby, does walk in its own biological waste. How? As it walks, every hour it sheds around 1.5 million dead skin flakes. We recognize them as dust on our floors. But not to worry. A veritable army of insatiable mites spend their entire existence eating up bits and pieces of our dead, dried-up pieces of skin."

"Epidermal delight," Annette put in. Steven offered her an appreciative grin.

"The more we shed, the more they eat... and multiply. Our loss is their gain. But although they save us from eventual drowning in the dead cells of our own bodies, their life is not sacred either. I suppose they are a little like domestic help in some illustrious residences of our social elite. Sub-human?"

You may have noticed that my older son had little regard for the trappings of 'illustrious residences' or their occupants.

I wondered if life is a biological infestation? Is there life in our organs, brain, heart, blood, cells? Are we impregnated with it? Are we alone imbued with this *sacred* cycle of life, which so diligently omits all other biological forms?

"Are we alone?" I asked, thinking of the blessings given us.

"Certainly not physically," Steve insisted. "We live in great togetherness."

"Not with other people. With them – we fight," Annette barged in remembering her pre-*Solidarność* days.

"True," Steven agreed. "But for the most part we live in relative harmony with some 100,000 billion microbes. For the more mathematically minded this figure looks like this: 100,000,000,000,000 or 10^{14}," he wrote it out on the napkin.

I, for one, was impressed even if the 10^{14} was quite meaningless to me.

"We are permanent hosts to this diminutive congregation," he continued glancing at his notes. "Diminutive in size, certainly not in numbers. Without them we would die. That is to say, our biological functions would cease. We are at the mercy of vermin. But they are not sacred either. And worse. We are also hosts to hosts of viruses – pieces of genetic material surrounded by protein. Lately the scientists have added 'preeons', pieces of protein which, contrary to bacteria, viruses and protozoa, do not even need DNA to divide and multiply."

He looked up but only to add more Amaretto to our glasses. We must, I thought, keep our vermin well pickled in case they decide to take over our bodies. Assuming they haven't already. But seriously, dark chocolate, black, bitter coffee and sweet Amaretto. Who needs to die to be in heaven?

"Do they all want to live?" Annette asked innocently.

"Never asked," Steven threw over his shoulder.

"Want is an expression of free will," I commented. "I don't think our guests have much choice in the matter."

Steve nodded and continued. "And then there are the parasites. They seem to attack the sacred human and the unholy animals alike. No preferential treatment is accorded. Parasites are responsible for more death than any other organism."

"Even more than humans?" Annette asked facetiously. Steve gave her a dirty look.

So, I wondered for the umpteenth time, what makes us, humans, so sacred? Or better still, what makes our biological existence so sacred?

I was back in my room, my legs up on a chair, the TV on but without sound. Judging from what Steve had said, we are a battlefield on which viruses, bacteria and our immune system are engaged in a fight to the death. Eat or be eaten. There is no mercy in this world of which we seem to be such an integral part. We – the sacred cows of religious powerhouses. To my knowledge, most religions acclaim us to be superior to whatever we come in contact with. Even if we can't even see it. Even if it kills us with the ease of a microscopic virus.

Is this really life? The Blessing?

Or is life something which has nothing to do with any of the above?

Is life not at all a biological infestation? At the biological level, we all eat, defecate, multiply, kill with no mercy. All of us, including the sacred cows. Perhaps more so. We, humans, kill even when we are not hungry. Just for fun. For sport.

I wish those looking after our moral and ethical welfare would stop worrying. That which truly is sacred, is also present in all other biological and non-biological manifestations. It is outlined above, then, if you are truly alive, you'll never die.

You probably wonder what any of this has to do with the story I'm sharing with you. How does it advance the story, as Steven would ask? Well, not much really. And frankly, there is no story to tell. Not anymore. All that happened in my life that is of any interest to anyone, has already taken place. Even Jan's hundredth birthday. Even his protracted death. Even the yacht sail on Lake Champlain. Nothing happens in my life. Not anymore. The action without has translated itself to a sort of meditative action within. My musings, my meandering thoughts that wander often without rhyme of rhythm, are all I have left to share. I am resigned to a vicarious life of dreams that other people might bring to life, of what might still happen to others.

Wouldn't it be fun if life for Sister Angelica and Father Mulligan began, once again, after sixty? It wouldn't be the first such event to take place among people I know. If ever long life could be a blessing, it would be so for those two.

Their lives had been, supposedly, fulfilling, but, in the beginning, Sister Angelica's blessing had been diluted by her feelings of guilt. Of this I am convinced. She felt guilty for having run away from her convent, for having seduced a parish priest, and then for having killed him by not being strong enough to deny him his beloved bacon. I sensed that she felt particularly unfulfilled in her duties on that last account. Had Francis still lived, her life would have been very different. She would never have become a nun again, presumably only doing so to make up for her transgressions. And, of course, I would never have met her.

Father Mulligan did his duties to the letter but, in a way, perfunctorily. He had given me the impression that he had become and remained a priest out of a sense of duty. Not love, not passion often referred to as a calling, but an obligation of a gentleman who keeps his word. A noble sentiment, but hardly satisfying. Not in the passion department.

Nevertheless, for the first time in my life, they were the two people to whom the avocation 'Grant them long life' appeared to belong. May they live long and prosper, as Mr. Spock would say. With accent on the word *prosper*. In love, in companionship, in having someone to share one's joy with. God knows Father Mulligan was in great need of joy. And, if my Decameronian dreams were to be fulfilled, then Sister Angelica was the right person to fulfil them. I'm sure it was her influence that had caused Father Mulligan to forsake his walking stick for a hat with a jaunty feather. He did look strangely rejuvenated. The only question was whether it was due to the Jezebels or to my dear Sister Angelica. I prayed the latter.

That left me with everybody else. With my co-travellers at the Institute. We are told in the Bible that Abraham had been rewarded with long life. His name in Hebrew means 'father of a multitude'. Indeed, he must have had a long life to sire such a multitude as the later prophets claimed. On the other hand, there is the symbolic meaning that claimed that multitude referred to an abundance of ideas. Perhaps you had to be extremely bright, in those days, to get away with such a large progeny. Anyway, he is said to have lived to a ripe old age of 175. Not bad in the absence of our modern medicine. Or . . . perhaps because of it?

But his relative longevity pales when compared with biblical accounts of Adam who lived 930 years, Seth 912, Enos 905, Cainan 910, Mahalaleel 895, and Jared 962 years, breaking all records. Think of the taxes you would have paid in Canada had you lived that long. On the other hand, if you retired at 65, you would collect a handy pension for almost nine-hundred years. Florida? Mexico? Or a nice house overlooking the Georgia Straight.

Hmmmm....

I strongly suspect that we are not meant to take the Bible literally. Come to think of it, didn't God shortchange Abraham a little?

There is one other possibility. The possibility that the concept of time has changed. That time, as a concept, should be more flexible. I waited for next Sunday for Steve to tackle that one.

"Well," he said taking a deep breath, "St. Thomas Aquinas proposed three types of time."

"Three times or time thrice or...?" Annette asked innocently.

"*Tempus* concerned the 'temporal' or earthly time," Steve said reaching over to his shelf for a book and then leafing through it. "It measured the duration of changes taking place on earth. The second type of time Aquinas called *aevum* or time affecting changes in or of mental processes," he swung round offering us his reference to check.

I shook my head. I would rather listen.

"It did not concern material changes but rather changes in mental states," Steve continued only occasionally glancing at the text. "It also applied to all that is incorporeal, to angels and to states of consciousness."

As both Annette and I had been drawn into his dissertation I noticed that the book he held open had vast numbers of lines highlighted with a yellow marker. I had no idea he read so much.

"The third type of time Aquinas called the *aeternitas*. It concerned the divine. While it was the domain of God, it also embraced our ability to experience infinity, or immortality, in a single instant. It is this third type of time which permits the present and infinity to be one."

This was all great fun but I was no closer to finding out how long the ancients really lived. I told Steve as much. He got up, picked up a book or two from his shelf (he had plenty of those, both, books and shelves), scanned a few pages, then settled in his armchair.

"You're not making this easy, Mama," he said.

"It's not me, son, it's the Bible," I defended myself. "It's all those multi-centenarians that bother me. The very thought of such a life keeps me awake."

"I don't believe you'll have to worry about being a multi-centenarian, Mother."

"But only the good die young?" Annette whispered. There was nothing wrong with my hearing. I gave her a dirty look. We both laughed.

"In science," Steven resumed glancing at more highlighted pages, "Aristotle and Newton measured time unambiguously as the duration between two events. They believed it was *absolute time*. Then, dear old Einstein destroyed the misconception that time is absolute. In Albert's theory of relativity he married the concept of time and space into a single idea of space-time. According to the physicist Stephen Hawking, the distinction between space and time disappears completely when using *imaginary time*; time measured using imaginary numbers. There is no difference between going forward or backward in imaginary time. We can also go in any direction in space. Are you following, Mama?"

"Can fish swim?" I gave him my best surprised look.

Of course I didn't follow, not all of it, but I knew he would jot down some notes for me over which I could pour later, at my leisure. I had lots of leisure. Steve smiled as though he'd taken me seriously. Nevertheless he started flipping pages in another of his books and went on.

"Other scientists took up the banner and came up with different definitions of time responding to different qualities or events of past, present and future. Another physicist, Frank Tipler, offers us an elaborate menu of different 'times'. He measures duration in terms of *proper time*, as measured by our clocks in the present astrophysical environment. Using this definition, time and space are measured in the same units, i.e. if time is measured in years then distance is measured in light years."

He glanced at Annette and me. There was no way either of us would admit that we had trouble absorbing it all. He was already sufficiently pigheaded. In the meantime, the ancients' longevity receded deeper and deeper into the murky past.

"He also computes in *conformal time*, which is measured in terms of a specific scale factor. We don't have to worry about that because, as far as I can understand, it is used only to calculate the behaviour of light rays." He dismissed the matter with a wave of his hand.

"Son…?" I tried to stop him. I didn't have a chance.

"Then there is the *entropic time*, which 'is a more physically significant time-scale than *proper time*'," he read out. "It is used to measure the amount of entropy that exists in the universe at a specific proper time. Next there is the *subjective time* defined as the time required to store irreversibly one bit of information. Rather as in the speed of computers. Finally the theoretical physicists use the *York time*, so called after the American physicist James York, which simplifies the mathematics of the field equations."

"Son, what does all this have to do with the time of the…."

He looked up a little sheepishly. "Quite a choice...?" he asked ignoring my unfinished question.

"It doesn't really answer my question," I managed to get in at last. It certainly raised about a thousand others, though.

"Well, Mother, once science broke down the rigidity of time, the universe became fluid, relative. So did we. We can no longer claim the privilege of age. Someone might ask us how old we are in conformal, subjective, entropic, *aevum,* biological or absolute time, to mention just a few." He spread his arms.

Frankly, I no longer believe there is such a thing as *real* time. It would probably be just somebody's vision of reality. Yours and mine might be different. Having already given up on Enos, Cainan, Mahalaleel and company I wanted, at least, to make sure I knew the answer to the question regarding my own age. So that we, the old ones, might enjoy the privileges accorded senior citizens because of our contribution to society. Not because we are old.

Alternatively, as Raphael would say, we might choose to live in the present.

Back in my room, I sat quietly, gazing idly at the puffy clouds drifting aimlessly toward the eastern horizon, or at least as far as the tall maples and oaks would allow them. There they disappeared as though having reached the very end of their life. For a time I was mulling over our conversation or, more accurately, Steve's monologue. It didn't help much.

So what could I tell our retired citizens packaged into time-defined residences? The Seniors' Residences? We could no longer regard ourselves as 'old' in terms of 'real' time. Not according to all that Steve had said. There was no such thing as Residences for the Old. All is relative. We simply don't know how old we are. We don't even know how to measure our age. Is there a way we might protect ourselves from the illusory wiles of tradition?

Perhaps.

Are we old because we've been around a long time, or do we *act old*, because it is expected of us?

I felt strongly that the Sisters should not, must not, be afraid to allow my friends and neighbours on the second floor of the Institute to participate in, what is normally referred to as *hardship*. They, the well-meaning Sisters, were protecting us all from the wiles of life until we no longer felt fully alive. Solving problems, particularly mental problems, is what sets us apart from other animals. Surely we have earned the privilege to face problems more complex than those allotted to the rest of the animal kingdom. Yet we were all treated like mental derelicts. Until problems are treated as challenges, until we learn to rejoice in the new, the unknown, we are no more than the dilapidating shadows of our own pasts. We created our subjective universes and now, in our 'old age', we watch entropy dissolve them.

I, for one, refuse to participate in such a scurrilous farce!

I recall the day after my trip to the US and the sail on Moravia. "It is my contention that old age is the most glorious age of all," I'd announced to anyone who would listen.

No one did.

In time, I forgot about it myself.

The following day I made a few new resolutions. Like on New Year's Eve. I forgot those also. I was tired. Perhaps old age is just a state of consciousness after all. Or is it just a state of resignation?

Next week we discussed life again. This time we were sitting outside, on the tiny terrace. Green table, green chairs, blended with the cedar hedge. A tiny crystal bowl of short-stemmed red roses contrasted with the tabletop. We were already having coffee when Annette returned to our subject of last week. She'd read that somewhere in India, among some casts, there is a custom that when a man assures a reasonably safe future for his wife and children, he is free to retire to pursue his spiritual life.

"He just retires into some sort of an ashram," she said. From her tone I gathered she did not consider the Indian custom to be very good for the 'reasonably well looked after' womenfolk.

"We, in the West, can surely offer the very same opportunity for both sexes, for men and for women," she insisted. "It is the time in our lives when we can apportion the majority of our time to the study of Self. We can finally do justice to the admonition: *Know Thyself*. I've never discovered any endeavour more fascinating. Apparently, nor has Socrates."

Annette . . . Socrates? She didn't strike me as the philosopher type. Perhaps Steve was beginning to affect her too.

Annette was growing up.

By the time Steve and Annette drove me back, I was, once again, in a blue mood. There had been no *cytrynówka* this time. I'd learned to rely on it to raise my spirits. Purely imaginary, of course. I drank a few thimbles-full.

My mood had to do with old age, again. Or was it with the concept of time? I sat looking for the clouds I'd watched last Sunday. They were all gone. Everything was the same only the sky was empty, void, like me. Like my heart, of late. Like the blessing. The story of my life. Lately.

I was tired. Of life.

What difference does it make whether you live long if your life is filled with misery? Alexander the Great, Jesus of Nazareth, Wolfgang Amadeus Mozart, Felix Mendelssohn, van Gogh all died before they reached forty. Can anyone of us claim that we achieved more by living longer then those few? Albert Einstein achieved his greatest insights when we was twenty-six. Which of us got smarter than he by living longer? Is length of life the measure of success? Some scientists tell us that we might attempt to measure the duration of our lives by the frequency and quality of our thought impulses. If we don't think much we might live a long time.

I wonder why? What for...?

There is now evidence that the human life span can be extended by genetic manipulation. Will it also enhance our will to overcome new, evermore challenging problems associated with critical overpopulation of the Spaceship Earth? If we live longer, shall we be smarter, or shall we only prolong our stay in the Florida doldrums, packed like sardines in multi-story condominiums with rationed water consumption?

I decided to seek my blessings elsewhere. Maybe even in the hereafter.

Like in reincarnation.

Another blessing?

***

The White Horse

"...he that sat on him had a bow;
and a crown was given unto him:
and he went forth conquering and to conquer."

The Revelation
of Saint John the Divine

19

The Institute

The kings were still all there. At least, I think they were. For a time, I'd stopped looking at them. I knew them by heart. And then, one day, I did notice a change. The kings had turned a little older, greyer, the glass a little less transparent. There were also different reflections in it. Not like before. I used to look them straight in the eye. Now, I no longer faced them. Somehow they seemed more inaccessible. More aloof.

I realized what had changed. I was looking up at them from a wheelchair.

There was something else. The order, or the chronological disorder, which I had already memorized years ago, had also changed. I wondered why someone would move the kings around just for the sake of it. Perhaps they had tried to correct their previous mistakes. I looked again. No. It wasn't that. Mieszko I still hung next to Bolesław Krzywousty. They ruled centuries apart. Only then did I realize that the order in which I'd memorized them was still there, only my recollection of it was missing. Like so many things. Memories are such fickle things. One day here, another day gone. Like wisps of gossamer carried by the gentlest breeze during Indian Summer. Like *babie lato* I remembered in the cornfields of Poland. In early autumn. Just transient, ephemeral.

Like memories.

Some people are lucky. They walk into an oncoming truck, miss their footing atop an icy flight of steps or just swallow some tainted rice, like Gautama Siddhartha. Like Buddha, who ate something that did not agree with him. Some tainted rice? A short time later, it was over and done with. One moment he was Gautama Siddhartha the next he was Buddha, the Enlightened One. Only he was no longer alive. As were all those other lucky people even if they did not get to be very enlightened. But they were smart enough to take their chances when they had them. Now they are all out of their bodies, gallivanting in the hereafter in brand new, probably astral or some other variety of sheaths. And they took all their memories with them. Still intact.

Unto Adam and to his wife did the Lord God make coats of skins....

Well, Lord God. Thanks, but no thanks. I don't need my skin anymore. Please Lord, won't you take it back? I'll make do with what's left over. Please Lord? You can even have my memories. Most of them. Including the gossamer carried by the wind....

Others are not so lucky.

Death creeps up on them in steps so small, they think it'll never reach them. It shuffles along, propped up on canes, hiding behind aluminium walkers, glides on silent, rubber-wheeled chairs, insinuates itself into our bones, our joints, slowly, insidiously, remaining all along quite invisible. Like a thief in the night.

There are signs, of course. The number and duration of our aches and pains increases, as does the number of pills we, or I, swallow, in an attempt to eliminate them. Sometimes the pills work – for a while. But that is not what destroys you. For as long as you are really determined to get on with your life, to contribute something, anything, to the well-being of the universe, you either get along pretty well, or you get lucky, like that first bunch of people. Those with the truck, the icy steps or an inopportune diet. Otherwise, you're in for the surprise of your life.

There is a saying: heroes die but once, cowards die a thousand deaths.

Am I a coward?

The Catholics have a habit of saying that suicide is against their principles. They are the very same people who for years smoked cigarettes, overate, got drunk as often as they could afford it, did not exercise their bodies properly, and didn't even overtax their brains with the tasks for which it has evolved over millions and millions of years. They wasted the boon of evolution. They long ago decided to indulge in a protracted suicide pact they'd signed early on with the devil.

The devil called Stupidity.

That is true of the majority of us. The vast majority.

Then there are those who lay claim to principles, their beliefs, and they do their best to be faithful to their acquired morality. They live a decent life, and although they do slip occasionally they do not make a determined practice of it. Not like smokers, for instance. Or having beer for breakfast. But this group is driven into a quite-unexpected danger. By remaining whole and hale longer than their friends and neighbours, they tend to reach the stage when they get a little lonely, they miss their established way of life, they try to slow down the very essence of life itself. They get set in their ways. They become tolerant but also complacent.

They reject the most fundamental tenet that defines life. Change.

They forget that challenge, the unknown, is what makes life worth living. They take off their crown for fear of it falling off. They dismount their white steeds, and no longer go forth conquering. Perhaps they are tired?

And this happens to those who, surely, deserve better. In all humility, I would like to count myself among them. I can honestly say that for the last ninety-five years or so, I've never abused the gift of life. At least, neither knowingly nor avoidably. And in consequence, I have been 'blessed' with long life.

I recall vividly how it happened. When I think I surrendered the crown and got off the horse.

One day I just felt tired. Exhausted – having done nothing. I no longer had Dad to look after. People ignored my attempts to cheer them up. Whatever I imagined was my mission in life, it seemed over. I no longer felt of use to anyone. In a way, I gave up. On living. On life itself.

"You can't do that, Mother," Steve insisted. "You can take an overdose of sleeping pills, but you cannot give up on life."

Now that sounded like oxymoronic nonsense. You can commit suicide but you cannot give up on life.

"Very funny," I snapped. I don't snap often. Certainly not at Steve. Or anyone close to me. I looked up to apologize and saw that his face was deadly serious.

"I thought you were such a good Catholic, Mama," he sighed.

"I try..." This was getting personal.

"I am not attacking your morals nor your commitment, Mama. I am questioning your *a priori* assumptions. Your knowledge, in a way."

I didn't reply. With my memory going at an alarming rate, I could hardly argue that my knowledge left a great deal to be desired. I also realized that he was trying to help.

"I would not question your belief system, Mama. To each his own. But as a Catholic it would seem to me that your choices are defined for you.

I nodded for him to continue.

"Well, Mama, there is that quaint story in Matthew, about blasphemy. Apparently all sorts of sins, including blasphemy, will be forgiven, with the sole exception of blasphemy against the Holy Ghost."

"So what's your point, son?" I was interested but I couldn't follow his reasoning.

"Well, to me…" he was searching for the right words, "to me, the Holy Ghost, or Spirit, is a synonym for life itself."

"And...?"

"It seems to me that you are free to get rid of your body, but you cannot deny Life acting through your body."

This was becoming complex.

"If I understand you, we are in charge of our physical envelopes, but for as long as we decide to keep them, we cannot refuse . . . refuse living?"

"Sort of."

I mulled that over in my mind. He did raise an interesting point. If he was right, then we would all stop killing time, and work it to death instead. Rather than do nothing, do something. Later I looked it up. *All manner of sin and blasphemy shall be forgiven unto men: but the blasphemy against the Holy Ghost shall not be forgiven unto man.* Well, Steve knew his bible. If he was right about Life being a synonym for the Holy Ghost, then I had a problem. According to Matthew, I was in danger of eternal fire. Perhaps if I wanted to opt out of my physical envelope, I should try and try again to use it to the maximum, until, with a bit of luck, I would, with my diminished reflexes, fall down some icy steps....

The alternative was to join all my inmates in a slow, lingering, protracted death. That's as close to eternal fire as I ever want to get. Not me, I told myself. I shall not spend years lying on my back, defecating into my oversized diaper, be pretty much force-fed three times a day and then, after a bout with an IV, give up my ghost.

Not me!

It was some hours after Steven left that Sister Cecilia came into my room and presented me with a fully adjustable, light-as-a-feather, wheeled walker. Last week I slipped and fell. I'd slipped and fallen half-dozen times, when we still lived in Westmount, and no one ever offered me a walker. Wheeled or otherwise.

"You really must be more careful, Mrs. Kordos. I think we should give up our cane and use the walker instead. It's much safer."

Safety was all-important at the Institute.

I never realized that the serpent can be dressed in white flowing robes crowned with an angelic wimple and a fresh, kind, smiling face. Well, he or she can – and was. I tried the walker to please the Sister. After all, I am sure she meant well and, I must say, I was also a bit curious. I'd seen lots of my neighbours shuffling along surrounded on three sides by their cherished walkers. They seemed happy enough. So, as I said, I tried it – just for fun. Just to see what it was like. Like smoking that first cigarette, just to see if you like it. The first puff of marijuana.

It was fun.

That same day I walked twice as far, twice as fast. It gave me extra confidence. I didn't have to rely on my sense of balance, the walker did it for me. I pushed it along effortlessly. I hardly used it at all. I certainly didn't lean on it. I didn't have to try so hard. A week later, I was leaning on it, but just a little. Really. In two weeks, I had to admit that walking without it didn't make any sense. I wouldn't dream of leaving my room without it. Within two months, the good Sister Cecilia convinced me that it would be even safer if I propelled myself around in a light, comfortable wheelchair.

"We can even get you one with a tiny electric motor, Mrs. Kordos. That would save a lot of your energy." Her face was a smiling effusion of concern for my welfare.

"Surely, Sister, I can still walk," I said out loud.

"Of course you can, but this is safer, Mrs. Kordos. Much safer. And much more comfortable. You'll see...."

She was persuasive.

In three more months I needed someone to push my chair. I could do so myself, a bit, but couldn't get very far. Certainly not enough to go outside. My legs and arms had gotten too weak. God, how quickly we lose strength! The adage 'use it or lose it' only comes really true when you're really old. As for the electric motor, thank God I never used it. At least for a month or two I used my own body to propel myself. I remained alive for another sixty days.

The next month, I officially became an invalid. At least so I overheard the Sister saying. Dear Sister Cecilia. She was actually smiling when she said it. Perhaps she always smiled. Perhaps she could have had the decency to stop smiling just for that one moment. For that announcement. I might be getting demented, or psychotic, but to me her tone sounded distinctly proud of her achievement.

"It's for her own good," she said.

Steven was right. I had sinned against the Holy Ghost. Against Life itself. It had not forgiven me.

I recall when Steven first saw me with my beloved walker.

"Mother, today the walker, tomorrow the wheelchair," he'd said.

I laughed. "Don't be silly, Steve. It will never happen to me. Never!"

Not long after I said that, I had my last visit to Steve and Annette's. Steve and I in the front seat, Annette and my folding wheelchair in the back. I was about to lose the remaining vestiges of my freedom. A funny thing happened on the way back to the Institute. For the first time in my life the police pulled me over. Not me, of course, only Steve. Apparently my son was speeding.

The officer swaggered up to our Honda Civic and Steve opened the window just enough to ask him, as innocently as he could, what was wrong.

"May I see your license and registration, sir?" the officer inquired. While he was examining the documents, for some reason I stated coughing. Something tickled the back of my throat and, for a little while, I couldn't stop.

The officer handed the documents back to Steve and leaned into the window.

"You'd better get the lady home," he said. I swear I could hear concern in his voice. "Only take it easy, sir. This is a fifty-kilometre-an-hour zone."

Steve thanked the traffic officer, and we slowly pulled away. "Thanks, Mother," he murmured. I suspect he was referring to my cough which at that very moment stopped. Neither of them believed me when I said that I hadn't faked it.

Honestly, I really hadn't.

I glanced at Annette who, to my vague annoyance, was sporting a lopsided smile. It wasn't like her. Usually she shows great concern for my welfare. Of course, I wasn't coughing anymore. Still…

"I'm sorry, Mama, it's just that it reminded me of a policeman in Gdańsk…"

"In Gdańsk? That must have been ages ago!"

"It was during the days when *Solidarność* was just getting off the ground, around 1980. We were driving to the Gdańsk shipyards with a delivery of money collected surreptitiously for the Solidarity purposes. They had no other financing, of course."

"So why did the cop stop you? Speeding?" Steve asked. Evidently the story was new to him too.

"In those days the *milicja*, our traffic police, didn't need an excuse to stop you. They were our lords and masters. Their power was virtually unlimited. Had he felt like it, we could have found ourselves in jail. On the top of it all, the shipyards were on strike. Illegal, of course. The strike that started it all…"

I remember the Gestapo of my days, a full thirty-four years earlier. Steve and I left Poland in 1946. Jan was already in England, liberated from his POW camp. Not much had changed in those intermediate years.

"There were five of us in the car, all packed into the *Maluch*, like sardines. I was holding the briefcase with the money…"

A *Maluch* means 'little one': a nickname for a tiny Fiat, smaller than the British Mini.

Annette was smiling. Evidently she was enjoying herself.

"For some reason," she continued, "on the spur of the moment, I decided to tell the *milicjant* the truth. I said that we were taking the money we collected for *Solidarność* to the *Stocznia*, the Shipyards. By the time I realized what I'd said it was too late. I felt sure that our goose was cooked." She grinned again, this time her smile was even broader.

"So what's so funny?" I asked.

"There must have been pride in my voice, I suppose…" Annette murmured.

"So?" Steve was not a patient fellow.

"Funny…" Annette paused. "Actually, the *milicjant* was. He put his head inside the car, looked us over and wagged his head like an oversized puppy. 'Gosh, you're lucky,' he said and waved us on. He really looked jealous."

It is quite amazing how quickly it can happen to you. Of course, being ninety-five helps. But at my age, I know that for the slightest concession one makes for one's laziness, the payment is inversely proportional. Whatever your disability, it progresses along an exponential curve. I must say that I was becoming a little discouraged. My husband never gave up on his intrinsic 'life-force'. Once, with his hip still in plaster and a brand new steel pin holding his thighbone together, he'd climbed over the high railing of his bed. He just wanted to take a little walk, he told me. To the bathroom. Admittedly, he had little choice – the railing could only be lowered from the outside of the bed. The nurses had left it up for the night to make sure he would not fall out and hurt himself. Again.

The next morning they tied him with straps to the bed. Then to the wheelchair.

"Safety first, Mrs. Kordos," they assured me. "Always safety first."

Why shouldn't we hurt ourselves? Thousands of sportsmen harm themselves every day. The world over. My husband fell off his horse a number of times. He broke many bones. He lived on. And if he hadn't, he would have been spared....

He lived on for another three years. If you can call that living.

And now I was rapidly sliding into the same pit of depravity. Rather than take my own life, rather than release it into the realm of freedom, I chose to remain a good Catholic. Perhaps that was the only sin against the Holy Ghost I had ever committed.

As you read on, you might well find a certain change in style. If I were a writer, I might call it a change in the 'literary' style. Not that I've joined the illustrious ranks of the literati. Far from it. Day by day, I feel my strength seeping away from me. I think just as well as I used to, at least I think I do, but somehow those same thoughts, concepts or even discussions do not seem to come out the way I thought they would. What I mean is that there is a barrier forming between my inner and my outer reality.

Steven insists that the whole affair, this book that you are presumably reading, is my own memoir. Well, in most ways it is. But for the last month or two I am sure he'll find it more and more necessary to edit my efforts to entertain you. As a matter of fact, that was never my purpose. What I really wanted to do was to put down sufficient information for Steve and Bart, and their wives, to do whatever was necessary to avoid ever ending up in such an Institute, waiting out the rest of their days. But most of all, I hope that my granddaughters, Anula and Krysia, will have some recollection of their grandma when she could still talk. Or write. They are such pretty girls.

"Do whatever is necessary," I told them. "But do *not* do it here."

At the same time, I was careful not to suggest that I am constantly suffering. Well, I am not. At least, not physically. There is an abundance of multi-hued pills that the kind nurses, kind Sisters and an occasional kind visiting doctor are only too glad to feed me, to keep me in relative comfort. For some time now, due to my progressive loss of teeth, they've been squashing the little analgesics into powder, mixing them with either apple puree or some other sweetish concoction and delivering them directly into my open mouth.

"Say aaaah, Mrs. Kordos!"

Like to a little child. The first few times it annoyed me. I wanted to tell them that I am not a child, that I can be asked to open my mouth in so many words. I suppose 'say aaah' is faster and easier. For them. Most things are designed to make things easier for the staff. Perhaps they are short of people? At any rate, lately, when I see or hear a nurse approaching I open my mouth and wait for the arrival of the spoon. They don't have to say anything.

And then, I usually manage to go back to sleep. Perhaps the pills help. I thought of accumulating those little pills and then swallowing them all at once. Now I can't. They're already squashed and mixed with puree. Had I succeeded, a few months earlier, before the squashing, it wouldn't have been suicide. Not really. It would just save so much of the nurses' time. They wouldn't have to visit me so often. Two, three times every day. At least.

"Just wait a few weeks, nurse, and then give me all my cute little pills at once. It will save you lots of time," I wanted to say to them.

We are always clever in hindsight.

Only I didn't say anything. We miss out on so many things, when we're old. So many little things. Of course, we can no longer do the big ones. Like feeding eleven people for four years during the war. So long ago. Last century. Last millennium! And now, when they, the little pills, are premixed with applesauce, it's too late. I would have to swallow an enormously large jar of apple puree to do justice to the powdered chemicals. I'd probably vomit just from the sheer quantity. I don't eat much, lately. At least, I try not to. Not that I haven't any appetite. The less I eat, the less often they'll have to change my diapers, I reason.

I still do reason.

I sleep a lot lately. Sleep is the single greatest friend of the old and infirm. It is like going on holidays. You forget, for a while, where you are. You imagine things. A beach . . . water lapping the rocks, spilling over the sand. Or a forest with crowns meeting together like in a huge Gothic cathedral. I always loved forests. Or even just sitting in the park watching the ducks diving for whatever ducks dive for . . . their cute tails sticking provocatively above the water. So many holidays. I used to remember my dreams. I could recount many of them, in detail. I even made some notes about them in order to later decipher their meaning.

My mind is wandering so....

At first I didn't like my wheelchair, now I do. Different parts of me ache. Not always the same. I've learnt to sleep in my chair as well as stretched out... I keep telling them that. I wish they wouldn't fuss.

Just put me in my chair and go away.

Don't fuss.

Don't take me down to the recreation room.

Don't take me to see any films.

Don't put me in company of other people. They are as deaf as I am. Sometimes worse.

Don't shout at me. I don't hear any better when you shout. Speak slowly, using short sentences. I am hard of hearing but not deaf. It's just that I find it harder to concentrate. Especially when asked stupid questions.

"How are we this morning, Mrs. Kordos?"

Is it morning? Already?

I could have slept all night, I could have slept all night, I've never slept before.... I feel like singing. I don't dance but I can sleep. I am getting pretty good at that. *I didn't know that it was so exciting....*

Don't feed me. Don't stuff me with tasteless goo you substitute for food.

Don't pretend that it's good for me.

"We must keep up our strength, Mrs. Kordos."

You go right ahead. Keep all the strength you need. You can have all of mine, what's left of it. I don't need it to sleep. If you must, then give me something to drink. My throat it parched. Why am I always thirsty?

Bart comes more often nowadays. Every Saturday. He's always smiling. He doesn't seem to change. Year after year... the same smile. Sometimes he brings his daughter. I think her name is Kate? No, Krysia. I am not very good with names. Even the names of people I see every day. Do names really matter? I recognize their faces. Most faces wish me well. Good face, bad face, boring face, shouting face. Babies recognize their mother's face. Mine did. I was the good face. The face that brought food. And love. Yes, I was definitely a good face.

Where was I?

Aaah, yes. Bart brings me flowers. I have more flowers in my tiny room that I ever had in my life. My husband was not very good at flowers. He gave me all the money he earned, never kept any for himself. He couldn't buy me flowers. Poor Jan. Penniless. He doesn't need any money anymore. Lucky, lucky Jan.

Steve and Annette drop in twice a week. They must or there wouldn't be so many flowers in my room. But, you already know that. They take me for a little spin in my wheelchair. On sunny days, in summer, around the block, or the car park, or, if it's raining, onto the covered terraces, along the corridors, up and down . . . up and down . . . up...

It's a shrinking universe.

The other day Steve pushed my wheelchair to the balcony, just to look outside at the falling leaves. It was autumn. There was a little sun. I asked if we could go outside. He pulled the door open. Just a crack. A gust of wind touched my face. I shrunk inwardly.

"Cold!" I said as loud as I could.

A cold gust. I might catch a cold, I thought. He pulled me away. Funny how the body reacts on its own. I didn't want to catch the death of cold. A minute later I wondered why. Why I didn't want to.... Two minutes later I forgot all about it. The memory came back later. In my room. I wrote it down, I think. Or maybe I taped it. Does it matter?

I'd lost another chance.

We say hello to the people we meet. Or I wave my arm. Just a little. My arms are getting quite heavy. But I manage a small wave. They seem to appreciate it, the effort, I suppose? They wave back and smile. Both the residents and the nurses. They are all nice people. If only they wouldn't keep feeding me. If only they left me alone....

When I was still better, Father Mulligan would drop in more often. As I got worse, he got better. Frankly I don't know what he's doing here. I mean in the Institute. We talk. Actually, he talks, I mostly listen. And then there is my dear, favourite Sister Angelica. I made some notes about both of them. I hope Steven can decipher them. My writing's gotten pretty bad. As has my recordings. Too many unfinished sentences.

Poor Steve.

"You'll have to spend hours pouring..." I forgot what I was about to say.

" ...over my meandering mind," he finishes for me. It is often like that, lately. I start a sentence; he finishes it for me. My mind wanders so.

"Leave that to me, Mama. You just jot down what notes you can. Or speak into the mike, only hold it a bit closer to your mouth...."

Things like that. Soon I'll stop altogether, only I can't tell him that. He thinks that making these notes keeps me . . . sane, I suppose?

But it's getting harder. I start with one thing, then go to another and, if lucky, I get back to the original subject. Not always. Sometimes whatever I say will remain a mystery. Forever. Like in the Catholic Church. Mysteries galore. I suppose, life itself is a mystery. We are born, we walk around for a little while, then we ride a wheelchair, and then we die. That's it. Only I don't know how to die.

I don't know how to die.

I suppose I am too weak, now. It must take strength to die. I had my chance. With the pills, and the slippery steps, and crossing the street....

I don't cross streets anymore.

I don't cross anything.

I just wait. For death to take me to my husband.

I just wait.

***

20

Dementia

People have it quite wrong. They equate memory loss with dementia. Nothing could be further from the truth. I looked it up. Dementia comes from Latin *dementia*, meaning madness, insanity, from *demens* (*-entis*) meaning mad, out of one's mind, or the impairment or loss of one's mental powers. There is also a psychiatric term *dementia praecox,* which refers to a psychosis or form of dementia, usually beginning in late adolescence, and is characterized by melancholia, withdrawal, hallucinations, and delusions.

I must have written this at least a year ago.

Now this latter version of dementia, the *praecox* one, probably applies to the vast majority of adolescents. They invariably go through a period of melancholy, or withdrawal from doing their duties and obligations, while simultaneously suffering from delusions of grandeur and other hallucinations. That is virtually what being a teenager is all about. Even Anula and Krysia my otherwise charming granddaughters seem, on occasion, to drift off into a realm of their own, where melancholy and unspecified illusions that they are the centre of the universe, seem to hold sway. And trust me, my granddaughters are gorgeous in all other respects.

But we, the elderly, all right – we the abysmally old, have long outgrown this adolescent phase. We no longer display symptoms of dementia. *Praecox* or any other. We just choose not to clutter our brains with useless pieces of information.

The last time 'my' doctor visited me, he told me that dementia is not a specific disease.

"It's a descriptive term for a collection of symptoms that can be caused by a number of disorders that affect the brain, Mrs. Kordos."

"A syndrome," I offered. "That would cover a large territory, Doctor?"

"And a great many people," he admitted.

Dr. Fenwick was not a psychiatrist, although the mop of grey hair would certainly qualify him to be an accomplished Freudian. Or a famed physicist, for that matter. But he was a reasonably old-fashioned physician who believed that you should treat the person and not the disease. I liked that.

"And just what are the symptoms?" I pushed, determined to know what on earth was happening to me and my memory.

"There is a whole list of them, Mrs. Kordos."

"Humour me, Doctor."

"Well, people with dementia suffer from agitation, delusions and hallucinations."

I already knew that. I didn't believe I had dementia.

"That's it?"

"They also experience personality changes and behavioural problems, such as those I mentioned before."

"Go on," I pushed. I wanted him to get to my memory bit. He must have read my thoughts.

"There is also memory loss, yet while it is a common symptom of dementia, memory loss by itself does not mean that a person suffers from dementia."

"So I am not mad, insane and deprived of mental power?"

"Who on earth would say such a thing, Mrs. Kordos?"

Actually, one of the nurses. When I didn't answer, Dr. Fenwick continued. "Doctors diagnose dementia only if two or more brain functions, such as memory *and* language skills, are significantly impaired without actual loss of consciousness, Mrs. Kordos. Believe me, you sound a lot more sane than a lot of people on the staff I meet here." He looked over his shoulder. The nurse, always in attendance when he was around, pretended not to hear.

He prescribed some pink pills for me, for my aching back and left.

So, I am sane. Medically speaking, of course. The fact that a number of things definitely demented me, drove me mad, had nothing to do with it. Like I have no idea why I am still alive. I could have asked Dr. Fenwick that, but he would have told me....

"If your heart remains as strong as it is now, Mrs. Kordos, you will live forever, ha, ha."

He'd told me that before. With and without the ha, ha.

I didn't mind his diagnosis, but his ha, has drove me mad. They demented me. That's right, they drove me daft. Also angry, distracted, infuriated, close to murderous. Why was I still alive? Isn't the purpose of life to leave the world at least a bit better than we found it? I did nothing to ameliorate the human lot. Or the inhuman lot. To improve the lot of anyone or anything. Why am I still alive?

I definitely am demented.

As for the symptoms the good doctor described, I knew they were coming. Two or more symptoms, at the same time. I did experience not only memory loss but, more and more often, I had considerable difficulty expressing myself. I would start a sentence and, half way through it, the thought would leave me. I felt it was still there, close-by, but just outside my reach.

It was tiring. It was about then that I began to speak less. I could still put down the thoughts which Steve would later arrange into a semblance of order and literary harmony, but that was because the thoughts that left me when I spoke tended to return when I no longer needed them. That is to say, when speaking. When writing things down, I would, of course, go back to unfinished subjects and add whatever was necessary.

Sometimes. Sometimes I would leave all that to Steve. He seems to have learned to read my mind. Almost, my memories.

But, I feel my time is coming when my universe will shrink still further. Even as a child expands his or her horizons, so mine are shrinking. I no longer walk, have problems with most food (virtually all my teeth are long missing), cannot get up on my own. I can't even move from my bed to my wheelchair. There are other things I would rather not write about. They are in direct opposition to the common definition of human dignity. In fact, by any definition.

I leak, literally, and can do nothing about stopping it. It is a most unnerving experience. The first time it happened, I was surprised. I even told my son about it. I felt that it was happening to someone else. That I was a bystander. An outside observer. Well, I wasn't. Sooner or later my son would leave and a nurse would come to change my diaper. That was the worst. The fact that the nurses were well used to performing this function, that by now at least half the people on my floor were incontinent, didn't make the ordeal any better. When they first tried to put the diaper on me I rebelled.

"Don't even think about it," I said. "Please...." But I knew I was unreasonable. They had to change all the bed sheets. All of them.

My universe is shrinking. I am reverting to being a baby. A diapered baby.

Why am I still alive?

There is one advantage to being incarcerated in an Institute such as this. If you take trouble to move around the corridors, you know, fairly exactly, what's coming. Most people cannot foretell their futures. We know, almost exactly. We know that, in so many months, years at best, we will be unable to walk, unable to get up from bed on our own. That once or twice a day our room will smell like a public washroom in a Third World country, in which a dozen people forgot to pull the chain. Or missed the hole in the floor altogether.

Why is it, I wondered a number of times, that the excrement of old people smells so much worse than it ever did when we were younger? Don't we digest properly? Are we missing some enzymes? After all, until we actually lose control of our peristaltic, digestive system, or, to be more precise, the control of our sphincter, the little room I share with my neighbour never smelled that bad. I know this is not a pleasant subject, but when you are exposed to it again and again as you walk or wheel yourself along the corridor, it begins to prey on your mind.

When I wrote this, I could still wheel *myself* along. On my own.

But that's not all.

As I wind my way in my chair along the gaseous corridors, I see people prostrated on their beds, seemingly for days at a time. Some are fully dressed but they never seem to get up. Some are constantly trying to attract attention. Guttural sounds escape their throats, something halfway between a wail and an agonized call for help. I tried to help one such woman, when I was still able to walk. The wreck of a human form on the bed looked at me as if I had come down from the moon. She had no idea what I wanted. Apparently, the wailing was the only sign of life she was capable of, and seemed to enjoy sharing it with others.

How long do I have, I wondered?

Then there is Mr. X, he's still alive so I'll keep his name out of it. He sits on his bed and spends the whole day putting on his shirt, then taking it off. If I went past his door six times, I would witness six changes of wardrobe, so to speak. He is always totally absorbed in his activity, quite unaware that his door, like most others, was wide open.

Whatever modesty our mothers or grandmothers instilled in us when we were little girls, is progressively shed. The same is true of boys, or rather of old men. I am sure this is not a question of not caring. They, *we*, are just not aware of the world around us. Not the world further away than say five or six feet.

Our universe is indeed shrinking.

Day by day, inexorably, constantly, irrevocably shrinking.

How long do I have?

And then, when the pills no longer help, caplets are inserted into your rectum. You lie on the side; they would fall out sitting up. One or two suppositories and then lie on the side, dear.

"It won't be long, dear," an angelic smile tells you. "Just relax, it won't be long...."

When I wrote this I knew that my days were numbered. I knew that it wouldn't be long before I was moved to one side to receive my medicine. I dread tomorrow. I dread waking up in the morning and finding myself in my own excrement. I dread being alive. I wish my dementia was more aggressive. More complete. I am no longer human; I don't need to be aware.

People die. Here, at the Institute of the Immaculate Heart of Mary, people die daily. Like Saint Paul only more permanently. Ten years ago I tried to look the other way. Somehow it reminded me, my husband and me, how close we were to the Gate. To that tunnel of light. The threshold into the unknown was closing in on us. Daily. That was some ten years ago. I could have taken a single step and I would have been saved. We still enjoyed life, then.

Within weeks, months at most, death became commonplace. Perhaps I didn't notice it then. It was further away. It affected other people. Them, not us.

"It is like being on the front line, Mimi," my husband had said. "You keep your head down and hope that it's not you." He actually laughed when he said that.

It was easy for him to say. He'd been on so many front lines. He fought the Germans, the Russians, then the Germans again. He always fought. He was the gentlest of men.

"Now you don't have to duck, Mimi," he would add when another body was wheeled by on an elevated stretcher. I often wondered what they did with all those bodies. I never asked.

Now I could ask, but I don't care anymore. I no longer think of myself as my body. I am just a visitor. A passer-by, as Thomas said in his gospel. Or as Jesus said according to Thomas. It doesn't really matter. They were both right. I observe the shrinking world around me, I make my notes, I say a few words into the recorder and I go back to sleep. Ain't we got fun?

Perhaps I am demented. Or just tired. So very, very tired.

Steve came to see me today. I called him Bart. Dementia? They are so different yet to me they are both the same. I don't mean in appearance. They are both part of me. I'm glad they visit me, yet I do not remember, from day to day, when was the last time I saw them. Either of them. Steve's wife, or Bart's daughters, I remember even less. He has two or them, I think. Surely, I love them all. Does it matter? Love is an act of giving. I have nothing left to give.

Except for my smile.

Just after Steve and Annette left, I had a memory flash. I saw all of us sitting at *Wigilja*, at Christmas dinner. Dad and I were sitting side by side. Steve and Annette, Bart, his wife and both daughters completed the table. For some reason we were all fairly young. There was a big Christmas tree in the corner of the room. Or was it outside?

We were happy.

And then I fell asleep again. I do that often these days.

What a lovely dream.

My neighbour died today. She was a nice old lady. Younger than I. It seems unfair. Why her and not me? Am I not ready? I've been ready for the last five years, since Jan died. I've been ready ever since. Ever since.

We never actually talked. The lady and I. Now, we never shall.

"Hello?"

"Hello." A polite smile.

That was about all. She kept to herself. Perhaps she had rich dreams to fall back on. I guess, I'll never know. Not now. Some people dream a lot better than others. This I do know. I am still learning.

I saw her through the open door on the way to the Chapel. She was still sleeping. Or so it seemed. On the way back, she wasn't there anymore. I wonder if it is as easy to get to heaven as it is to leave one's body. Now you see me, now you don't. Like magic. She didn't say goodbye. No time, I suppose. She must have been in a hurry. Perhaps someone was waiting?

I wondered where Raphael was at the time.

She didn't speak much to anybody. She was reserved, perhaps lost in her thoughts? She smiled shyly when I went past her door.

Now, no one smiles. Until the next in line is moved into her room. I hope he or she will be happy, whoever it is.

It is important to be happy. Next door is a good halfway station. Perhaps I should move there myself. Perhaps I... I wonder if it would help.

Why am I still alive?

It is Saturday and sunny. Bart should be here any moment. It's his day to visit me. By the time I open my eyes, he'll be here. I play that game, sometimes. Actually, I play it quite often. I pretend they are already here. Bart or Steven. Sometimes they really are.

At least I think I do. Play this game, I mean. I can't be sure of anything these days. People change things without my knowledge. Anyway, I close my eyes and will him to be there when I open them again. It works sometimes. Didn't I just say that? Steve will edit it out. Sometimes, no matter how hard I try, it doesn't work at all. Other times I wish for Bart to appear and Steve is there instead. Or Annette. Or the other way around. It keeps me busy.

Before I forget. Steven was named after my brother who died, murdered actually, in Katyń. Jan made some notes on Katyń. I've still got them. Steve read them, but I want to make sure that Bart does also. Bart is so much younger. My baby really. With a Ph.D.. Here they are.

In 1943 the German soldiers discovered a mass grave in the Katyń forest, near Smoleńsk in western Russia. The grave held the bodies of close to 5000 Polish army officers. Despite the evidence that the Kremlin was behind the massacre, Britain and the United States chose to look the other way. Winston Churchill opposed a call by the Polish government-in-exile for an investigation by the International Red Cross. In the Nuremberg war crime tribunal, Katyń was on the list of war crimes. Later it was dropped. They didn't want to embarrass the Soviets. In 1990 President Mikhail Gorbachev admitted Soviet involvement.

There is a lot more, but, well, it's too late now. Jan made those notes before Alzheimer's got him. It seems like so many years ago. Yet I can still see him at his desk, writing his notes, his memories. All I have to do is to close my eyes.

Thanks to Jan, my brother's name lives on. It was he who'd insisted that we call our first son Steven. Stefan, in Polish.

Bart is short for Bartholomew, the English version of the Polish name Bartłomiej. That was Jan's father's name. Bart the grandfather. At least I think I am right. It's so hard to remember anything anymore. Even the simplest things. Like what did I have for breakfast this morning?

"Good morning, Mrs. Kordos. Here's your breakfast," the nurse is all smiles.

Actually, that is rather funny. I haven't had any breakfast yet this morning.

I think I really am getting dementia. There is more than one symptom of my . . . of my dementia. I started making notes on this chapter three years ago. Just bits and pieces. I put these notes together from twenty little pieces of paper. I hope Steve can sort them out. I know I can't.

Just before Sister Cecilia gave me my walker, I fell down. In my room. Things got dark before my eyes and the next moment I was lying on the floor. Thank God for the carpet. I still had it then. I think what happened was that I had a tiny little stroke. For a moment or two my brain didn't get enough blood to keep going. Enough oxygen. Or maybe it got flooded . . . I really don't know. At any rate, from that moment on, I had three, or was it thirteen . . . such little occurrences. Each time I lose a chunk of my memory. Then, some of it comes back. The rest?

"The rest, Mama, becomes part of the matrix of the universe," Steven assured me. "Nothing ever disappears in the world. Nothing."

There is so little that is really worth remembering. There are my children. And my children's children. They are harder to remember. And my boy's wives. And the rest?

There is also Father Mulligan and Sister Angelica. And Raphael, of course. I wonder what happened to all the other people I knew. There had been so many, once.

Perhaps they've all died already. I really don't know.

Perhaps they were lucky.

Bye, now.

***

> [These were the last notes on this subject that I managed to decipher. Mother's writing has become quite illegible. For a while she seemed unaware of this and kept adding squiggles that later proved quite incomprehensible. Even to herself. But, now and then she would say something that I feel belongs, here. It might not be quite accurate, but it's the best I can do. I am Steven, by the way. Here's a sample.]

"*Osioł*" I said. This was my mother talking, meaning 'an ass' or 'a donkey'.

Under normal circumstances, Mama could never remain serious for longer than a minute or two. She often said vaguely inappropriate things with a straight face, just to see what reaction she would get. Well, after some seventy years mother was onto me. Only this time I hadn't said anything. "*Osioł*," she repeated. Her son, was evidently an ass.

I find it deeply satisfying that my mother assigned such a noble animal's name to me. After all, asses are known to be very smart. She repeated this '*osioł*' moniker now and then, without any apparent reason. I put it down to her 'condition'. After all, she couldn't say much anymore, nor express herself with clarity. Except for '*osioł*'.

Only later it came to me what in fact had happened.

Sometimes, seeing mother in the state she was in, must have invoked an expression on my face that was compassionate, or, at the very least, serious. It negated the omnipresent smile that mother bestowed on us. The only gift she still had left to give us. When I pulled that face, she called me an ass. I think what she really meant was that I was not to take life that seriously. That what happens to our bodies is not that important.

In recent months, mother's speech has become very quiet, hardly audible, her syllables slurring together into three or four rather incomprehensible words. Nevertheless, I decided to test my theory. As usual, I offered mother a drink that she drew with a bent straw from a cup I held close to her lips. She seemed to be thirsty quite often. Probably dehydrated.

As on some previous occasions, mother choked when swallowing the third or fourth sip of the liquid. Obviously my face must have shown concern for her. Remembering my intention of testing my theory, the compassionate expression on my face may have been slightly exaggerated. Mother swallowed hard, coughed once more, than looked me straight in the eye and said loud and clear, the single magic word: *"Osioł"*.

And that was that.

***

21

Father Mulligan

I must say that, ever since Father Mulligan lost weight, straightened his posture, and stopped looking as though he was being chased by a bunch of invisible demons, he became a very welcome visitor. I no longer had to find ways to cheer him up. He smiled easily, didn't confine himself to philosophical discussions, and, more than anything, allowed his innate sense of humour to come forth, like sunshine after decades of murky skies.

"Come in, Father, come in," I called out the moment I recognized his specific knock. It was a hardly audible triple knock, followed by a pause, and then by three more knocks applying greater force.

"May I?"

It being Tuesday, the day on which movies were shown downstairs in the hall, I knew it would be him. He would always wait for me to get back to my room, then, a few minutes later, I would hear his gentle knocking.

"And what did you think about today's showing?" was my usual opening.

"I didn't go today, Mrs. Kordos," he replied. "I had a book I couldn't put down."

I raised an eyebrow.

"Sit down, Father. A drop of Sherry, perhaps?"

"Well..."

From my wheelchair I find it difficult to reach down for the glasses which I keep on a low shelf in my bedside cupboard, and completely unable to get the Bristol Cream. But he knew where it was. On the upper shelf of the wardrobe, hidden behind the scarves and hats I would probably never use again. Throwing them out would be a little like dying. The Sherry wasn't really hidden, but for some reason I found it vaguely embarrassing to flaunt my cellar, even if it did consist of a single bottle.

I expected to use the opportunity and ask him about this business of life and death. One day I would really have to make up my mind, if I was for life or against it. It sounded a little like a discussion about abortion. The pro-lifers always assume that those who are for a woman's choice are opting out for murder of the 'unborn.' It sounds like a Hollywood B movie. The Unborn versus the Undead.

Like a perfect gentleman, Father Mulligan poured the Bristol Cream himself. I was quite sure that both, he and I, were just waiting for an excuse to wet our whistles.

"So what book's gotten to you this time, Father?" I asked leaving my suicidal ravings till later. I didn't want to scare him away.

"Actually, I've read it before. Now I am revisiting it. It is a book by Aldous Huxley. No, not the *Brave New World.* It has two novelettes under a single cover. They're entitled *Doors of Perception* and *Heaven and Hell.* I must say, I'm both riveted and disappointed."

I waited. Lately, Father Mulligan no longer needed prompting.

"In his *Doors of Perception* as well as in *Heaven and Hell*, Huxley not only surprised me, but, I regret to say, left me quite disappointed. Not by his personal experiments with mescaline and other drugs, but by his apparent desire to equate the artificial effects, or any effects for that matter, with Reality for which he, quite obviously, had been searching. It's the same error Castaneda quite blatantly committed later in his Don Juan series."

It seemed that Father Mulligan was well read. For a man who until a few years ago never had time for a novel, he was obviously catching up with a vengeance. For some reason and to my delight, he chose me to share his impressions with. I was quite flattered.

"Periodically we hear of other experimenters, such as Timothy Leary, whose LSD trips are known to have been very successful in leading absolutely nowhere." Father Mulligan smiled. "I find it quite fascinating that in spite of repeated failures to substitute synthetic results for the real thing, the new waves of misguided aspirants have never manifested in such numbers as in our present drug-laden generation. It seems that those who partake in this exercise are not really searching for a new reality, but rather endeavour to escape the reality of their lives, devoid of anything worthwhile. The euphoric states achieved by such means are eminently artificial and the antipodal hells are reputed to be very real."

Slowly Father Mulligan's eyes returned from some distant lands and found me sitting opposite him with a glass of Sherry in my hand.

"I am boring you, Mrs. Kordos."

"Not at all," I said. Really, he wasn't. Apart from my son, he was the only man, or woman for that matter, I'd met in recent years who had interests outside aches and pains, food, or making money. "As for the euphoric states," I said, "artificial or real, I understand that they invariably produce transient results?"

"You've read him?" His eyes lit up. He seemed as hungry for intelligent conversation as I was.

"Some time ago. Castaneda, I mean."

Father Mulligan again smiled a little wistfully. It was evident that he was still searching for his own taste of euphoria. He was much more balanced in his approach to life than he had been when I first met him, but there was still something missing.

"This misguided search for a different reality is all the more abortive since it misses both proven methods of widening one's horizons without sacrificing one's sanity," he said, searching my face for confirmation. I must say, I know nothing about drugs that induced any state other than a good night's sleep. I decided to nod my agreement and see what developed. Father Mulligan seemed satisfied.

"It is quite true that mescaline, carbon dioxide, LSD and other shamanic entheogens induce various *unearthly* experiences in our brains and sensory systems under the guise of *exploration of spiritual growth*." He stressed the words I've italicized. "I suggest," he continued, now sounding exited, "that the reason we keep looking is that all externally applied methods strive to empower man to the limits of his physical potential, rather than to free him from his inherent bodily limitations. As long as we see ourselves as men endowed with latent divine abilities, we are destined for a painful dead end. I am not aware of any examples to the contrary."

Nor was I, not that I could follow the whole line of his reasoning. But if he was right, then why bother, I mused? On the other hand, he did raise an interesting point.

"Then why travel a road which leads nowhere?" I put in just to show him that I was paying attention.

When Father Mulligan nodded with an unusual degree of agitation, I decided it was definitely time for another glass of Bristol Cream. He'd hardly touched his own glass, whereas mine had been empty for some time.

"Meister Eckhart or Thomas Morton on the other hand would tell us not to dwell on our limited material potential but to expand our horizons through *devotion* and *contemplation*." He looked at me triumphantly.

"Rumi would probably agree with you."

Father Mulligan rose to his feet. "Then you agree, Mrs. Kordos!" He sounded as though he'd finally found a soulmate.

A chime announced lunch time. Actually it was a cuckoo clock, but chime sounds so much more elegant. Father Mulligan glanced at his watch and looked apologetic.

"I've taken all your time with my rambling, Mrs. Kordos. Please forgive me..."

And he left without another word. My own questions would have to wait for another day. Or had he told me something I should think about. Contemplation. Could that be where I would find my answers?

Neither method relied on the expansion of our physical potential, but rather on sublimating our physical nature to our true or real state of being. When your body is becoming as decrepit as mine, this is a very vital difference.

Raphael confirmed my suspicions that same afternoon.

"The supposition in no way denies living life to the full," he told me, "but merely transfers our consciousness from sensual to spiritual. This is accomplished by, as a Moslem would say, submitting to the Highest. The question which separates the two methods lies in where we place this Highest. Those who have the need to adore, to serve, place divinity squarely outside their own being and serve what they believe will, one day, assure them of heaven in whatever form."

"And the second? The contemplative method?" I asked.

Raphael smiled with the appearance of deep satisfaction. It was quite evident that, like Father Mulligan, he had come to the same conclusions.

"The contemplative method, Mrs. Kordos, assumes that the ubiquity of the Divine is so prevalent, so uncompromising, that it already exists in Its full Majesty *within* our being. All we must do is to *realize* this fact. This system is not an intellectual pursuit. It is not a philosophy to be argued back and forth until some common ground is achieved. Every practitioner of the contemplative method will reach his or her own realization at a different time, in a different way, to a different degree."

For some reason I found this assurance deeply satisfying. I nodded to confirm my agreement. I also recalled Steven saying that every man is Buddha, just waiting to be awakened.

"The reality the aspirant is seeking, Mrs. Kordos," Raphael continued keeping his eyes on mine as though he was about to say something very important, "is one wherein all effects, all conjuring tricks, have been left behind. Wherein we no longer have any need, good or bad, yet partake in all of them as observers. By sacrificing the personal traits of our individuality, we become truly *individual* or *indivisible*, in fact indistinguishable from the Whole, from the Universal. We partake in all that was, is, or could ever be."

I took a deep breath. Raphael leaned forward in his chair.

"There is one other major difference which separates the two methods, Mrs. Kordos. The devotional method implies or threatens constant escape towards some elusive ethereal state, an eventual heaven, to be achieved on liberation from the present material reality. The contemplative method does not suffer from such preconditions. Heaven is already here, everywhere, indestructible, waiting to be admitted into our awareness."

I wonder if Father Mulligan has also reached the same conclusions. I hope he has. It seems to me that he's earned it.

I tried to imagine a state of mind in which heaven was already here. Is this what Raphael had already achieved? It seemed that Father Mulligan, after years of priesthood, faithful to the dictates of the Church, had, at long last, taken steps to free himself from all the preconceived ideas.

In my experience, most religious leaders assure you that, if you behave yourself, you might get to go to heaven. There, you shed all worries, forsake all ills, rise above all evil, all pain and suffering. You also presumably terminate all effort, give up strife and striving, content yourself with just being. Like gods. Eternal, unchanging, unfeeling, indifferent. Being integral to That which is All Knowing, I think I would lose all interest in discovery. Being above and beyond human emotions or intellect, I would neither feel nor think. Being integral to Love Itself, I would no longer merely love someone. Having all, I would desire nothing... basking in the Eternal Light of Eternal Intelligence, devoid of personality, of friends or enemies, ever unconcerned. I would have reached the desireless state of Being.

Forever.

I thought about it again.

I could spend eternity in a state of Being, relishing my immortality. I would perhaps retain a vague awareness of my individuality, of an individuality I once had, perhaps enjoyed, but mostly I would be immersed within the Ocean from which I once emerged. I would enjoy the inexplicable Bliss of Being. Isn't that what heaven is all about? About having one's Being in abundant Bliss.

On and on... and on... Forever.

For Eternity.

Eternity is a very, very long time...

Are you sure this is what you want, Mrs. Kordos? Well, is it?

I heard the question so distinctly that I looked behind me. I was alone.

If God is so happy just Being, why did He create man? Or better still – the world? Or even more so, why did God create the evolutionary process, which led, under His omniscient guidance, to an entity which, or who, eventually, could experience self-awareness, in a mode of being?

Or is it the mode of Becoming?

Self-awareness in the mode of Becoming.

It seems that if we are in one such mode then we, locked into the state of continuous becoming, can offer but this mode to our Creator. *A mirror am I to those who know me.* Self awareness.... It seems that in heaven God IS. On earth, and surely God is omnipresent, God shares in our mode of Becoming. We, humans, offer this mode, at least for six days out of seven. Some, who wish or can, may attempt to take Sunday or Saturday off to merge into a state of being, but the rest of the time we are busy becoming.

What's the alternative – eternal stasis?

Father Mulligan came by again. After he'd poured some more sherry we started talking about heaven. Well, I started talking about heaven and he followed.

"I can see it now, Father. I see myself sitting outside my expensive condominium, beside my pool of lukewarm water, basking in the penumbra of the Royal palms . . . forever sipping my tall, cool Bloody-Mary, Manhattan or Martini, and never being in danger of developing cirrhosis of the liver. Perhaps this heavenly indulgence will finally give due credit to the contention that the liver is the seat of emotions and desire."

I glance at him to assess the effect my lunatic musings are having on his sanity. To my amazement, he was still there, in his chair, seemingly enjoying himself.

"Furthermore," I ploughed ahead, "in this heaven everyone is very important. Since we're all clad in equally flowing robes (swimming trunks and costumes), no one will be able to tell how we made our living in the down-under. In the here-in-before. In fact, we all look pretty much alike. Regardless of how we gorge ourselves, we display divine figures, full heads of hair, and equally as divine suntans. Skin cancer will be abolished, as will all other diseases. Nobody will be able to tell if we came from Europe, the USA or Australia. There will be no Afro-Americans, Euro-Canadians, Sino-Europeans or Euro-Australians. English will be the spoken language, although some will speak Spanish while the menus will be, of course, served in French (some will also speak it – rather badly). It will be just like home. An enormous retirement home. And we'll all enjoy getting bored together. In style."

Father Mulligan had always displayed a surreptitious sense of humour, but I wondered if this time I'd gone too far.

"Others, Mrs. Kordos, imagine heaven quite differently," he said unabashed.

I raised my eyebrow not quite sure if I was about to receive a theological lecture.

"Some think, Mrs. Kordos, that if they blow themselves to kingdom come while murdering some innocent people who disagree with their demands, they will take the elevator directly to paradise where they will be instantly surrounded by seventy-two beautiful concubines, or women. At any rate – virgins."

This last he said very softly. I preferred not to comment.

"Then there are those," Father Mulligan continued, "who'd rather recline on a puffed-up, fluffy cloud, surrounded by ever-smiling, perhaps also seventy-two angels, strumming their golden harps. I strongly suspect the angels would be attired in Mozartesque regalia, and be conducted by the immaculately tailed, fiddling Tarzan, known hereinbefore as André Rieu. They would play on and on and on. For ever and ever."

"Brrrrr....!" I shrugged involuntarily. Not that I didn't enjoy André Rieu. Now and again. But forever?

"Given seventy-two harpists, with or without André, versus seventy-two beautiful concubines.... We all sleep with our choices," he finished, his eyes drifting to presumably a different heaven altogether.

Father Mulligan was warming up to the idea of analyzing our future eternal abode.

"And then we have the serious people," he cleared his throat as he must have done for decades standing on the ambo every Sunday. His voice assumed an oratorical, droning sound.

"Ye shall spend your eternity at the feet of your chosen deity (catalogue available at the gate), basking in His glory, rejoicing with the (above-mentioned) angels; peeking down, way down, (only most innocuous of smirks are allowed) at the poor unfortunates who still didn't even make it to the antechamber of the heavenly palace." (Had he enough breath in his lungs, I felt the sentence would have continued forever). "Here ye shall luxuriate in lavish and eternal peace, serenity, and peace. And serenity. But mostly peace," he concluded. He took a sip of Bristol Cream before resuming his sermon. "Our joy will in no way be tempered by our knowledge (we shall be fairly omniscient) that our aunt and uncle, possibly also that second cousin (she was a bitch), are frying dead (though seemingly alive) on the sharp prongs of the glowing spits wielded by the long-tailed and horned (if not horny) devils."

I'd never head Father Mulligan in such a mood. His language had changed diametrically. His vocabulary had expanded, although he may have picked it up hearing all those confessions. Nevertheless, his sense of humour had risen exponentially. Something must have happened since I last saw him. I wondered if Sister Angelica had had something to do with it.

"Anyone for Florida?" I asked weakly. I found my alternative less exhausting.

"For reasons of my own," Father Mulligan said ignoring my interruption, "I refuse to list the possible alternatives of hells. Gehenna, Hades, the Valley of Hinnom, Tartarus, are just some of the attractive-if-unseen locations, of which we also have a ready supply. The most prominent and popular of them all is the make-it-yourself hell. I am an expert on the latter, Mrs. Kordos. Surprisingly, some of these locations do *not* sound as bad as having to put up with seventy-two wives, day in and day out (alternatively night in, night out) or, alternatively once more, to put it mildly – to getting bored stiff."

Father Mulligan smiled, rose, bowed deeply and left. He was becoming a very different man. Correction. He has become a very different man. I was left alone with both, the comical and the more serious speculations.

Is there a heaven?

That rather depends on the definition. If the question suggests that there is a place we *go* to after we're dead and buried, I doubt it. I am deeply convinced that heaven is for the living, not for the dead. According to my Bible, heaven is a state of consciousness. It is that, the awareness of which, we develop, over the years, perhaps over countless reincarnations. This same reference assures us that God resides in this elusive state, and since God is in heaven and heaven is within us....

A wondrous proposition.

To me, heaven is a state of being, in which I shall forever have the opportunity to learn, to improve, to reach out further and further, without ever being in danger of reaching the end. It is also an inexhaustible source, which continues to supply the allurements and the challenges for my journey. It is a destination yet also a beacon in the endless ocean. It is infinite. I find infinity the most fascinating of concepts. For me it embodies eternity, unbounded intelligence or knowledge, eternal pursuit of the elusive. It means being forever beckoned, tempted, fascinated, enchanted. For me heaven is also a condition in which I can share my joy with others, share my findings, discoveries, conquests. Also forever.

Once again, that's a really long time.

And my heaven embodies one other attribute. It is a state of consciousness wherein the greatest power is the power of love. In fact, there is none other. There is just one other thing. Heaven is a state in which people like Father Mulligan do not have to spend countless years before finding happiness. Happiness, in heaven, is free. Available to everyone. Always.

***

22

Sister Angelica

She stood at the door, smiling, but no longer studying her shoes. She looked up, the sparkle in her eyes was particularly noticeable. Something must have happened. Something good. Sister Angelica always smiled, but her eyes? Well, today they were something else.

"Come in, Sister. You'll have to get the Sherry yourself, I'm afraid. I can't reach the shelf from my wheelchair anymore."

"Oh, Mrs. Kordos! I didn't come for that, really," she looked shocked.

"Pity. I reckon I'll just have to remain sober." I made a suitably sad face.

That did it. She pulled the sliding doors of my wardrobe open and found the Sherry on the upper shelf. She also got the glasses from the bottom shelf in my bedside table. Later, I hope she would wash them. I'm so very uncoordinated these days. Have been for a while now.

Soon she was facing me across my sliding-rolling table tray. I could roll it towards me and slide it up and down over my knees, while still in my wheelchair. The glasses glistened with my favourite nectar. It's been weeks since I dipped my whistle.

"Cheers, Sister!" I couldn't wait to raise my glass. Unfortunately the very first sip made me cough. Apparently my 'drinking' days were soon to be over.

The Sister sat opposite, a glass in her hand, yet she did not follow my example. She seemed to be fidgeting, not quite knowing how to begin. Whatever it was she had to tell me, it seemed to leave her confused. Two or three times she opened her mouth, took a deep breath, only to let it out in a slow, hesitant exhalation. Sister Angelica had a problem.

"It's been nice, lately," I offered a marvellous observation considering it was raining outside.

"Not really, Mrs. Kordos." Sister Angelica pointed to the window with her glass.

"Wouldn't you rather drink it?" I asked.

"Oh," was the good Sister's next contribution to our stimulating conversation.

The next moment she stood up, sat down again, and looked at me as though daring me to contradict her.

"He's a very fine man, Mrs. Kordos."

I nodded in agreement. I was beginning to suspect what it was all about.

"I said I'd think about it," she said. "After all, it would be a bit unorthodox."

I nodded again.

"Don't you think, Mrs. Kordos?"

"I'm not very good at it, lately," I confessed. "Especially when having no idea what you are talking about".

Sister Angelica's eyes found her shoes again. Actually they were sandals today. Only just peeking out from below her habit. They seemed to hold a particular fascination for her. I decided to help.

"You told me that he is a good man. You also said that you have to think about whatever the good man presumably asked you to do. How am I doing so far?"

"He really is. And he hasn't been active for six years now. It's not as if he was still a real priest, is it Mrs. Kordos?"

In spite of my suspicions I still found it difficult to accept what Sister Angelica was telling me. For crying out loud! Twice in a lifetime?

"His name is Francis, Mrs. Kordos. Did you know that?"

"Of course, Sister, you've told me many a time." I must have been wrong all along. How could I accuse her of...

She looked up at me. Then she shook her head. "Oh, no, Mrs. Kordos. Not Frank. Father Mulligan's first name is Francis. Just like . . . don't you think that's an omen?"

I didn't think The Sisters of the Immaculate Heart of Mary cared about omens. Good or bad. Still, we're all human. When in doubt we look for confirmation wherever we can find it.

"Shouldn't you tell me all about it, Sister?"

She took a sip and in that moment, for the first time since she'd come in, she relaxed. She leaned back in her chair and smiled. She seemed far, far away.

"He always did his duty. He never once thought of himself. He tended to other people's needs, day and night. He didn't have a home of his own. He was like...." She looked up at me. "He deserves better, Mrs. Kordos, than waiting for another Jezebel, another Mrs. Merryweather to disturb his peace."

Her eyes drifted back to her sandals. Her cheeks were rosy, she looked shy, uncertain of herself. She looked like a seventeen-year-old about to go out on her first date. I didn't dare to say anything.

"You know I told him about Frank and me. And what Frank was before we were married?"

I nodded. As far as I remembered, she'd told him that years ago, but it could have been yesterday. My memory was playing unholy tricks on me lately. The recent became the past, the past as vivid as the glass in front of me. I took another tiny sip. This time I didn't cough.

"We talked daily," she said, her voice coming to me from far away. "He told me about his parents, he'd lost them when he was young, Mrs. Kordos. All his life he was all alone. Can you imagine? All his life . . . then he told me about his seminary days, later his parishes, his moving all over the place . . . we would sit out on the terrace till dark . . . just talking. He thinks Brazil is beautiful.

Not that he's ever been there. But he thinks..." I didn't interrupt her. She obviously needed to let it all out.

"And then, only last week he told me that his name is also Francis. Just like . . . you know. It was as if he'd saved it for last. Strange that I'd never heard his first name. I could have looked it up, in the files. I never did. I just never thought about it. I suppose, I didn't dare. Now you see, Mrs. Kordos? It was just meant to be!"

So doubtless it was. There are people who hold that everything on earth happens on purpose. That there are no coincidences.

"You and he . . . you decided to make a man...."

Sister Angelica jumped to her feet. "Mrs. Kordos! How can you! I wouldn't do that to Father Mulligan! Not in a million years!" The last two phrases were supported by exclamation marks.

"I'm sorry. I thought that after Mrs. Merryweather and the other...." I never imagined that making a man of a man was such a crime.

"I am not Merryweather nor any other Jezebel, Mrs. Kordos. Really I am not." There were tears in her eyes.

I've really put my foot in it, I thought. I had no idea how to apologize.

"He asked me to marry him, Mrs. Kordos. Can you imagine? It would be like Francis coming alive again. And my sister in Cordoba asked me to go and see her. There is a house there, all empty, after my parents died and my brothers moved out to Sao Paulo. There was no work in Cordoba. And Francis, I mean Father Mulligan, and I both have federal pensions. From Canada, I mean. We're both over sixty, you know. We would be very comfortable there. It's so nice in Cordoba. And so pretty. And the climate is kind for our old bones. You can see flowers the whole year round. It's just standing empty...."

The sequence of her story was getting a bit mixed up. I waited till she calmed down. Finally, her eyes drifted again to her sandals.

"I am sure that the two of you will be very happy together in Cordoba, Sister, or should I say Mrs. Mulligan," I said very quietly.

At that she looked up. The old sparkle returned to her eyes.

"You think I should accept then?"

I was sure she'd already done so. Surely she didn't expect me to decide for her whether or not she ought to marry a retired priest.

"There is usually a precondition to such a relationship, Sister."

I suddenly found addressing her as 'Sister' distinctly out of place. Should I call her Angelica? I was old enough to allow myself such a familiarity. Nuns usually took on a name of a patron saint when entering the vows. I wonder what her real name is.

"You are talking about love, Mrs. Kordos?" Her eyes gave me her answer even as she posed the question. I think she loved Francis Mulligan as himself and also as the reincarnation of her late husband. A sort of second chance at happiness, both getting and giving.

"What is you name?" I asked instead.

"Bernadette," she said, her eyes descending to her toes again. "Like the girl who saw Our Lady."

I knew the story of Lourdes. Among the old Polish emigrants, when families still produced a dozen or more children, such fairly holier-than-thou or at least fanciful names were popular. I've known Mary-Magdalenas, Eleonoras or Florencias among my prewar maids alone. I suppose when you have a dozen children you must take steps to tell them apart.

"That's a beautiful name, Bernadette," I said.

"Francis liked it," she said.

"And does Francis like it also?"

She laughed. For the first time, since she'd come in, she looked truly relaxed.

"Then the only question remains, does he love you?" I murmured.

"Thank you, Mrs. Kordos," Angelica-Bernadette said. She seemed satisfied with my contribution to her dilemma. If ever there was one. "Thank you very much," she repeated. "You make everything so simple. Simple and right. Francis, I mean Father Mul . . . Francis said that you are a very wise woman. A righteous one, he called you. I know he thinks very highly of you."

With that she got up, and started cleaning up. The glasses were washed, dried and returned to the shelves in my bedside table. The bottle, which seemed to be lasting a lot longer than a few years ago, found its way back to the wardrobe. I wished I could reach for it myself when I was alone.

"Thank you again, Mrs. Kordos. We shall come in to say goodbye," she added and ran out like a maiden in love. It's good to be a maiden when you're over sixty, I thought. It's good to see people not just loving, but being in love. In a vicarious way, I too felt young. Well . . . younger. For a few moments the wheelchair, the lack of physical strength, the strange kind of loneliness when you not only have no one, but have nothing to share, left me. I wished them well. For a while I will see them, in my mind's eye as a couple such as Jan and I were. Seemingly, not so long ago. I still talk to him. And he answers with a smile. Always with a smile.

It is good to be together.

I'm glad I kept my recorder running when Sister Angelica, when Bernadette, last came to see me. I would never have remembered our whole discussion. Steve is taking care of the transcript. He types it out, brings it to me for comments, then polishes it so that others can make head and tail of it. Not all things I record make too much sense. Sometimes they are just snippets of conversations, when I forget to switch my machine off. Sometimes I record a thought or two, and then forget what I was trying to record. There are days when I have better recall. Perhaps not days, but hours. Usually in the morning. Just after I get back from the Holy Mass. Then, soon after, I fall asleep again. In my wheelchair. Time flies when you're asleep. And I visit such wonderful places. Often Jan is there. Like in Virginia waters. It's always replete with flowers. Funny how my dreams are so full of flowers. Like my room, thanks to my boys. Yes, like my room.

I tried to re-examine my discussion with Bernadette.

I find the whole business of priesthood and marriage very confusing. From what I've heard, a man can have a dozen children, yes, with the same woman and, should the Church decide that his marriage had some legalistic aspect omitted, he is free to leave his wife, his progeny and, if he so chooses, marry another woman, in church, or, better still, he can become a priest.

So far so good, or bad, depending whether you're the father or one of the children. Not to mention the wife.

But what really made my gall rise up was that, apparently, if a priest has children, he can leave them with impunity, recite a quick 'sorry for I have sinned', and go back to being a priest. But what he cannot do is to say 'sorry, I'm not a very good priest', marry the mother of his children, in church, and live happily or otherwise, ever after. In other words, once a priest always a priest, regardless of his acquired responsibilities.

I wonder how Father Mulligan will get past this little hurdle. There's that quiet triple knock on my door. Once we were settled I asked him about marriage.

"Well, Mrs. Kordos," he said, "this marriage business never lays easy on the Church's shoulders. The Holy Church didn't always regard conjugal relations between a man and a woman as sinful. In fact, until the twelfth century, virtually all priests were married. It was as natural for them as nature had ordered."

I nodded knowingly. I'd read a little on the subject. "Until the Second Lateran Council?" I offered.

"Yes. After that Council, even those already married had to separate from their wives. Since people indulging in sex had been declared unclean, they could hardly celebrate the Eucharist."

In a strange, twisted way that made sense. What didn't make sense was the initial premise. Were it true, the human race had been forced to either live in sin, or die. Maybe that was why most Christian denominations bashed it into our head that we are all sinners. I said as much. Father Mulligan smiled.

"It was mostly a question of inheritance. The Church didn't want the domains of its priesthood to be dissipated on the progeny."

"So money, not sex, lied at the root of all evil after all," I said before I remembered that I was speaking to a priest.

"In a way," he said but didn't comment any further. "Anyway, Mrs. Kordos, the priests continued to get married, on the quiet, so to speak, knowing the reasons behind the prohibition. Obviously, they didn't take it so seriously. The prohibition, I mean, which was more a question of custom than any dogmatic pronouncement."

"So the priest can still marry?" I must have sounded incredulous.

"They still do, in Eastern Orthodox Church. Anyway, the Church enforced celibacy by insisting that only a priest that was already celibate could grant the sacrament of marriage. What was more, there had to be at least two witnesses. This latter regulation was only enforced from around the sixteenth century. Quite recently, by Church standards. Anyway, the 'on the quiet' days were over," he said sadly.

Light was beginning to dawn on me. As Sister Angelica had said, in Brazil she was already known as a married woman, or presently as a widow. As for Father Mulligan, well, no one knew him from Adam. All he had to say was that he had never been married, and defy anyone to prove otherwise. He could be married in any church with impunity.

At last I realized what freedom from religion really meant.

"But why marry in a church at all, Father?" I asked.

"Oh, that's not for me, Mrs. Kordos. That's for Bernadette. She never had a proper ceremony. Apparently, women like that sort of thing."

Father Mulligan would make an excellent husband.

They came dressed for impending departure. He wore a Harris Tweed jacket, grey flannel trousers and an open necked shirt. He seemed a little uncomfortable, as if trying to make sure that no one could recognize him. But he most certainly didn't show his years. I'd met him some fifteen years ago and he must have been in his middle sixties then. Now he must be past eighty. But his posture, the clear look in his eyes, belied his years. I remembered that when my husband was eighty, he had twenty years still before him, ten of which were in perfect health.

"Come in, Father..." I beckoned.

"Francis," he corrected. "Please call me Francis."

Sister Angelica, or rather Bernadette, was right behind him. In spite of Francis's evidently successful dieting, she remained slim enough to hide behind his back. She peeked over his left shoulder, her eyes wide, her smile as broad as a full moon on a clear night.

"Hello?" she said, waving her arm. "It's me," she added, making sure that I recognized her.

She was a picture to behold.

Her eyes not just sparkling but shining like a young girl in love. She was holding onto Father Mulligan's, to Francis's elbow, for dear life. She seemed determined not to let it go. Ever. But what distinguished her from her previous appearance most of all was the most delicate rosy-pink rouge that she'd applied to her still relatively full lips. And those no longer just smiled. They beamed as if to show off her regular, sparkling teeth. In fact, all of her seemed sparkling, jaunty, almost frivolous as though she was playing hooky from school. That, or after a few good flutes of contiguously sparkling Champagne.

"It is us," she explained when I just sat back taking in the picture before me.

"I suppose you'd better come in," I said at last, unwilling to lose the image framed by the doorway. "Yes, do come in. Make yourselves at home." I still had two armchairs, now redundant but, on occasion, useful for visitors. And this was certainly an occasion.

"You are the first official visit we are paying, Mrs. Kordos."

With that her other arm, the one not congenitally attached to Francis's elbow, swung round, and an enormous bouquet of red roses appeared from nowhere. "Roses stand for passion," Bernadette whispered to me confidentially. "He bought them himself."

Without waiting for permission, Bernadette found the largest vase and put them in water. They really looked magnificent. There must have been two dozen of them. They completely dominated my small room. I could even smell their aroma from six feet away. She then pulled the two armchairs together and pulled Francis next to her. Both her arms returned to his elbow. She did all this with the efficiency of a good trained nurse. Francis, I decided, was a very lucky man.

"Shouldn't it be I who presents you with roses, my dear," I asked, tears welling in my eyes.

"No, no, Mrs. Kordos. It is you who brought us together," Francis announced. "Without your encouragement I would never have freed myself from the fetters I'd worn for . . . I'd worn practically all my life." The ex-padre sounded as though he meant it.

"So you blame me for all this?" I asked trying to look hurt.

They both laughed.

"Definitely!" they spoke in unison.

"That's why we both love you, Mrs. Kordos. In fact, we have only one regret...." I looked up. "We shall have our wedding in Brazil. And you will miss our vows."

"My thoughts will be with you. You can count on that. But, may I ask, why Brazil?" I forgot that she'd already explained it all to me.

For the first time since they came in, Bernadette's lips formed a pout. "I never had a wedding. Before, Mrs. Kordos, we couldn't quite make it, well, to make it very formal. You know, with the bishop and the pope giving us little problems.... But now it's different. Francis is already retired, and anyway, no one has ever heard of him in Curitiba."

"Nor in the whole of Brazil." Francis put in. "And until then, we shall...."

"...live in sin?" I put on my most severe expression.

"Yes, Mrs. Kordos! Isn't it lovely?" She was overjoyed to be acting like a young, naughty girl. Francis looked a little abashed.

"What I meant to say was, Mrs. Kordos, that until then we shall..."

"You don't love me anymore," the pout on Bernadette grew more pronounced.

"Of course, I love you, darling," he was quick to assure her. He was evidently not used to women's wiles.

"You don't want to live in sin with me."

"But we are..." He turned towards me with exasperation. "Are women always like this, Mrs. Kordos?" His eyes were wide yet the look of abject adoration hadn't left them.

"And worse," I assured him. "At heart, we are all Jezebels," I said with a straight face.

"You mean that I shall never be bored again?" He did his best to look aghast.

"Don't you dare even think about it," Bernadette tugged on his elbow. Francis didn't seem to mind at all. He glanced at her, as though to make sure that he wasn't dreaming. In spite of his age, he looked a little bewildered.

"I cannot quite believe that this is happening to me, Mrs. Kordos."

"They say that all things come to him who waits patiently. I never really gave much credence to such saying. I shall revise my view from now on," I assured him.

"Do you realize, Mrs. Kordos, that I have gained my freedom by gaining a wife?"

"Usually it's the other way round," I mused. "At least that's what most men say."

"If you ever meet any of them, tell them that they couldn't be more wrong...." Again he glanced at her beaming face.

This went on for an hour. Towards the end, I felt quite sleepy. They must have withdrawn soon after, as I woke up stretched out on my bed. For a moment I thought that I'd dreamt the whole affair. The whole visit. And then my eyes fell on the enormous bouquet. The roses brought the two smiling faces back to me. And frankly, they never left me. They are as close to me as any members of my own family.

A month later I received a picture postcard, followed by a letter. The postcard I propped up on my bedside table. It was a photo of a village church in Curitiba. A small, whitewashed building, surrounded by a sea of bougainvillea. Red and white. Like in Canada. Or Poland. There was a scribble in the margin with one word. It said HERE. I guessed the rest.

The letter was full of happy thoughts, a description of their flight, their arrival in Rio, then Curitiba and finally of the wedding. Then there were the photographs. There were forty-three people present, the majority of Bernadette's family, and most of them under twenty. Quite a few looked well under ten.

I was about to discard the envelope when I noticed the return address. It was spelled out in large, block letters, probably making sure that I wouldn't make the mistake I was about to commit. The back flap of the envelope said:

MR. & MRS. FRANCIS MULLIGAN.

Mr. & Mrs. had been underlined. I looked back at the photos of the children playing around Francis's knees. He seemed in seventh heaven. Maybe even higher.

Father Mulligan had inherited a family. How lucky can a man get?

***

23

Messenger

[In late 1999, under piles of family photographs and correspondence, I found stacks of tapes and notes entitled simply *The Messenger*. I have no idea when mother made them, but there is some evidence that mother had been trying to arrange her ideas in a semblance of order over a period of time. Some of them dated back at least two years. Others seem more recent, since the subject matter deals, for the most part, with mother's deeper understanding of reality, and therefore, I feel, that chronologically they belong here, close to the end of her story. I offer them in the present tense, in which they had been written. As I cannot be sure if Raphael's words are real or illusory, I show them in italic].

Sincerely, Steve Kordos

"The practice of the Presence of the Omnipresence of Good was taught by Emmet Fox, Mary Baker Eddy, and a great many other mystics," I announced as Raphael smiled his understanding. I'd already read some of Emmet Fox's books. Steve had lent them to me.

For once Raphael sat in my armchair. Usually he stood by the door, like a sentinel to protect me from whatever lay outside. He nodded, as though having read my thoughts.

"And before them the same had been taught by Krishna, Moses, and of course Jesus Christ who said I and my Father are one," Raphael said in a relaxed tone as though discussing the weather. He always talked like that. *"There is no greater presence than being one with the object of one's contemplation. Thus wherever Jesus was, his Source was. Moses was told to take off his shoes, a symbol of treading on holy ground. That's because wherever he was, there God is too. A conditional definition, subject to the raised consciousness or realization. We could say that if you don't believe in it then it isn't so."*

"But surely, God is omnipresent regardless of whether we believe in Him or not."

"Omnipresent yes. But not in denial of our free will. Omnipresence is, strangely enough, not a spatial definition. It deals with consciousness which is a divine attribute."

"So if we do not recognize the Truth then we cannot benefit from it?"

"Oh, we still benefit from it. After all, the good and the bad are coexistent in our consciousness, or, as Matthew put it, the rain falls on the good and the bad alike. But what we cannot do is benefit from it fully. We cannot achieve a higher level of happiness which Paul described as peace beyond human understanding."

The next moment Raphael got up, bowed, and left without another word. Something or someone must have called him. I heard, the next day, that about that time a man died on the third floor. He must have been needed.

> [I'm sure some of the above does not sound like mother talking but I no longer have the benefit of her meticulous scrutiny. Below is a fragment of her later life that I jotted down on one of my visits. It seems to belong here].

Mother was already in bed, where she spends most of her time. Twice a day, the nurses, two at a time, with the assistance of a hoist anchored to the ceiling, lift her, and slowly transfer mother to her wheelchair. I'm not quite sure what for. After all, we can seldom take her anywhere. She sits still, sleeps and dreams whenever I come.

Recently her chair-hours have been reduced to about two, twice daily. Also recently, she's given me to understand that she's begun having visions. To see and hear things. Luckily, her dementia did not manifest itself in attacks of raving madness, but in, often pleasant hallucinations. I strongly suspect that those visions must have persisted already for quite some time. At least as far back as some of the fragments I am offering in this chapter. Perhaps even Raphael himself at times was a creation of her dementia, as implied by the next fragment.

And now, through half-closed eyes I can see Raphael, his tall figure silhouetted against the doorframe. Perhaps he wasn't really there, I couldn't be sure of anything anymore. But I am sure I heard his voice. And, for some reason, I was deeply aware of a certain transcendental peace, even as he spoke.

"I and my Father are one," I heard him say. It was unmistakably Raphael's voice. Perhaps I only heard what I wanted to hear. Don't we all create our reality?

He sounded as though he was about to continue our discussion from yesterday. Or was it last week . . . month? Even as I became aware of his presence I felt that I was about to discover something new.

"Sometimes, in the affairs of man, a wondrous event occurs. The universal and the particular merge. It is the most miraculous event to manifest itself in the consciousness of mankind. It never lasts. It comes and goes like a comet. Prodigious, spectacular, surprising, wonderful, awing, phenomenal, shedding light, intangible yet real. To our forefathers – supernatural. Yet the event is so short, so ephemeral, that in spite of its transcendental glory many people fail to notice it. And those who do notice, do so only

after the fact. Like being aware of sunshine only after it hides itself behind a transient cloud."

Pity, I thought. I hope I can experience every ray. My hands are always so cold these days. And then I notice that the sun is streaming through the window. How could this be? It was raining this morning. Wasn't it?

"Perhaps the event is beyond the understanding of even the greatest minds. The Whole expresses Itself through one of Its parts. The two become one – qualitatively the same, quantitatively the part remaining insignificant. The message having been delivered, the messenger fades into oblivion. What remains is our hunger, our inexplicable longing for his divine attributes, his superhuman powers, knowing naught about his real personality."

Do divine messengers have personalities? I often think that they are the message. Will Raphael disappear after I stop hearing him? Do others hear him even as I do right now? And just how shall I convey his words to Steve?

"Tribal heroes, such as the emperor Huang Ti, Moses, or the Aztec Tezcatlipoca, commit their boons to a single race. Not so the universal heroes. Mohammed, Jesus in his later years, Buddha, others lost in the mists of antiquity, brought their message for the entire world."

> [I don't know where else to put the above paragraph. The thoughts below appear to be a continuation of the sentiments expressed above.]

Yet none of the heroes are greater than their Master, I recalled from somewhere. A part cannot be greater than the Whole. Yet, it seems that for some people, and only for a fleeting instant, the two can merge. A particular becomes fully aware of the Universal. The rest of us seem destined to sate our hunger through the diversity of Its expression. The diversity of creation. Except for the sun. Sometimes I can feel it even on a rainy day. My mind began wandering again.

Raphael continued to respond to my thoughts.

"If one could experience the totality of the universe, simultaneously, one would see the Face of God." His voice seemed to come from within my own mind. *"It stands to reason that this cannot be accomplished with the physical senses."*

"What then?" I asked. "Are we destined to tread water forever?"

A smile filled my room. Or was it that enigmatic sunshine again? I felt its rays on my face, caressing....

I began answering my own questions. That which is universal we call Whole, or Holy. And that which is holiest of all we call God. With our minds we can only experience parts of the universe, whereas the realization of God reaches beyond the mind. I must have read that somewhere. Or maybe Steve told me? He reads so much. I think he does so just to be able to answer some of my questions. Funny that. A son teaching his own mother.

> [I think I know where this came from. Some time ago, on one of our visits, I quoted Krishnamurti: To go beyond the mind there must be a cessation of the self. It is only then that That which we all worship, seek, comes into being. And when that happens, the Universal merges with the particular. I suppose that is when the Father and I become one. Later mother continues seemingly with Raphael's voice…]

"The prophets assert that to reach this state of consciousness we must keep still."

I knew that. We must still our mind. Still the subliminal chatter.

[And then she explains…]

This was that disembodied voice with Raphael's smile talking. I was now facing the window; he must have come up behind me.

"We must not think but know. We must still our minds and reach a condition of absolute silence. When King David says be still and know that I am God, he is talking about the stillness of the mind."

There. I told you I knew that. Am I talking to myself?

It sounded as though King David was right there, with me. Didn't he die thousands of years ago? Or do some people never die? Do they suspend their act of living until needed by someone, somewhere? And particularly sometime . . . like now.

"This condition of stillness, of silence, is a precarious mode. Any form of resistance destroys this state".

Yet, it is possible, I heard within me. "It is the heritage of mankind," I said. "Then why do we find it so difficult to achieve?"

"Because we create gods in our own image. We take our human attributes, increase them many fold and call the creation of our minds 'god'. An anthropomorphic god. We find those puny, variegated images in countless churches and temples the world over."

"...where thousands make millions by exploiting millions," I thought and the next instant I was ashamed of my criticism. Why must I always be so judgmental, I wondered? I turned my attention to Raphael. Was he still here?

"Yet in order to achieve the state of unity with the Infinite, with the Whole, the first thing we must do is to shed all material attributes. We must cease to be that which we are, which we have become, and reverse the direction of our perceptions. Instead of looking out, we must look in."

Apparently what we really search is not plastered on canonical walls. I was beginning to understand where Raphael was going. That for which we search is omnipresent. Thus – it is also within us.

I felt a smile enveloping me. Again, it had the warmth of sunshine. How lucky I felt in that moment.

[Judging by the quality of handwriting, the next paragraph must belong to a much later period].

Raphael is definitely everywhere. I must have created him. I do so when I need him. As when I dreamed about love as an act of giving. *"I don't help people, Mrs. Kordos, I help myself. I cannot differentiate between you and me. We are one. That's what Good is. One."*

"Don't you mean God?"

"What's the difference? Unless we recognize God as the Omnipresent Good, then our faith is for naught. All the prophets, the avatars, the great teachers, the mystics would have wasted their time."

"So it's all just a question of faith?"

"Not at all, Mrs. Kordos. Faith is expressed through our actions, throughout our lives. There is no point whatever shouting at the top of our voices that we believe in the omnipresent good if our actions deny this very premise."

"So Paul was right?"

And then I woke up. Raphael was nowhere to be seen, but his smile lingered behind. Like that of the Cheshire cat. Exactly like that.

> [The following explains some of my problems in my attempts to transcribe even mother's earlier notes. I continue to show words that I feel she attributes to the imaginary figure of Raphael in italic].

I began making notes ten years ago. Maybe more. Then I got them all mixed up. Times and notes. I wrote them on loose pieces of papers, little fragments of memory suspended in time. I've left them for Steve to sort out. The way things are, by the time Steve finds time to work on them, I shall be a blithering idiot. Or, at best, incapable of an intelligent conversation.

I found some notes I'd made two, three years ago. Maybe even before that. I stuck them in one of my books. I asked Steve to read them to me. I must have gotten them from some Krishna people. I think they called themselves members of the Society for Krishna Consciousness. I wish I'd made a note of that.

In the relative world the knower is different from the known, but in the Absolute Truth both the knower and the known are one and the same.

I suspect that most of us are firmly anchored in the relative world! The Swami continued:

In the relative world the knower is the living spirit or superior energy, whereas the known is inert matter or inferior energy. Before we can enter the bridal chamber, the duality of the material world must be erased from our consciousness. Once we recognize ourselves for what we really are, we begin our return journey – back to our source.

It is amazing how many of us insist on identifying with the inert matter, with the swirling atoms that combine to form our bodies. We insist that we are what we eat. Einstein's assurances regarding the interchangeability of matter and energy does not seem to spur us on. At best, we identify with our minds (the Cartesian 'I think, therefore I am'), without realizing that the mind relies heavily on the subconscious, which in turn is preoccupied with the preservation and maintenance of the biological constructs we occupy.

Raphael explained that to me some time ago. According to him, we do not have to be imprisoned, life after life, in this cycle of ignorance. Raphael says that all it takes is a *conscious* decision. We must decide, as an act of our will, that we shall identify with the spiritual energy which, after all, is the life within us; that we are not inert dust, nor even transient animals endowed with the ability to think. We must decide that we are 'superior energy'.

That we are spirit.

"It's up to us," Raphael had said. *"In a way, we are all unwitting expressions of the universal. So are the stars and galaxies over our heads. So is the dust under our feet. All these react to the indomitable laws. The universal is holy. It is the Whole. We, humans, however, are endowed with free will – a divine gift which we fail to exercise. To do so, a diametric change must take place in our consciousness. Regardless of the promulgation of countless religions, we are what we believe we are. Nothing less, and nothing more. Behind us millions of years of reactive evolution. Ahead lie limitless possibilities. Our destiny...."*

We must discard our free will by an act of our free will.

Funny that.

....for an instant, hovering within an infinite procession of sequential fragments of divine present, we might become a unit of consciousness through which the Whole finds Its expression. The

universal and the particular shall blend into a singularity. Perhaps to shed light, beauty or joy on just one other being. Like a smile or a ray of sunshine. These precious moments are known to artists. True artists – those who sublimate their egos sufficiently to allow their soul to communicate directly with the Source. With the field of infinite potential. Until we earn this privilege, we must continue to gather experience. Perhaps Aristotle was hinting at this, eventual union, when he wrote: 'experience is knowledge of particulars, art of universals.'

If we are to become artists, let us gather experience.

Why didn't someone tell me this fifty or sixty years ago?

"We are all artists, Mrs. Kordos, every one of us."

This time Raphael was standing just behind me. I felt him more than heard him. I held up my recording machine and repeated the words I heard.

"A mother creates when she brings a new channel into the world we live in. A new vessel though which the Universal might, just might manifest itself."

"So we are not all created unto the image and likeness?" I interrupted.

"We are created for that purpose, but most of us choose not to be. We think we know better..."

"We can deny God!?"

"Most of us do it all the time. The religions call it sinning. What it really means is that we set ourselves apart from our source. From the Field, Mrs. Kordos. The potential is still there."

"So we really do have free will?"

"We are gods, Mrs. Kordos. And there shall be no other gods before us."

"Thou shall have no other gods before me?"

"For thou shall worship no other god: for the Lord, whose name is Jealous, is a jealous God."

I knew all that. I read it very recently. In the Book, the Bible.

"Just who is this Lord?" I asked. I felt strangely elated.

"I AM," I heard the answer. *"I AM THAT I AM."*

I am the Lord? This was too much.

[Apparently mother had had those visions even longer than I'd suspected].

This must have happened some years ago. At the time I heard it, it made sense to me. You need a good brain to absorb some of this stuff. Like a concert violinist needs a Stradivarius. You need an instrument; mine was already out of tune.

"All knowledge already exists," Raphael said at some other time.

How can it? Don't we constantly make new discoveries?

"That which has not yet been materialized exists as a potential state of consciousness. Creativity is limited to bringing out to the conscious awareness that which heretofore has been hidden within."

I really did understand some of his words.

The awareness of this fact enabled Mozart to write down complete compositions, sonatas, concertos and symphonies, without the need to make a single correction on his manuscripts. He saw or heard them complete, whole. All he had to do was to 'bring them out', dispose the notes neatly on music-paper, and hope that performers would do them justice. Great sculptors have been known to say that the work of art is already extant within the stone, within the slab of marble. They just have to remove the redundant pieces of material. The poets hear, or rather feel, the poems before they write them down. It is not the process of writing . . . it is the art of listening.

It is self-evident that this attitude demands a great deal of humility. We are not really the creators although we partake in a creative act. We are instruments through which creative activity manifests itself in our physical, mental and emotional environments. At best, we are co-creators, though only in a very limited sense.

"Creation of the world is finished. Complete. All we can hope for is to become aware of its wholeness. To do so we must learn to be silent, then – to see and to listen. To observe."

There is so much noise in the world. I now understand why the old go deaf. It is a blessing. We need to in order to hear the inner voice. We slowly merge into the silence of the universe. The divine silence. Only then we learn to truly listen.

How difficult it is to open ourselves to fleeting, spiritual ideas that germinate in our unconscious. I am now sure that I created the persona of Raphael to feed me those fragments of understanding. I don't mean that Raphael is not clever, nor that he is not a very, very good man. But the messenger who visits me has supernatural powers. If he also exists within Raphael, then so much the better. Perhaps we can both enjoy his wisdom. The wisdom of the Messenger.

I know that I've learned a great deal from him.

"We must submit to the thought-streams which flood our awareness. In their own time they gel into fragments of mental images. The catalyst for this process is emotion. It is that which gets us involved, which inspires desire, which instills commitment. When ideas mature into concrete thought-structures, like Mozart's compositions, they are ready to become manifest in the material universe. That which is beholden in the eye of the artist is whole. To translate this wholeness into material forms, verbal, visual or audible, some of the purity must be sacrificed. Perfection is not a quality of the physical world. The process is often painful, like any birth. This final act is more that of sharing than of creation. That which becomes tangible, detectable to our physical senses, is but a shadow of our thoughts. Remember, the ideas were complete before we brought them out into the open. A true artist is not really interested in the end product. When a piece of music, a poem, a painting, a sculpture materializes in the physical universe, the authentic artist's work is long finished. He loses interest. History is profuse with masters who delegated this final phase to their pupils."

"Isn't this a rather bleak concept of the creative process? Doesn't the idea that the ultimate diminution of the ideal rob it of its magic? Of its happy accidents and the discovery of new ideas and concepts through creation?" I found myself rebelling against Raphael's postulates.

"We do not create, Mrs. Kordos. We are the instruments through which the creative process manifests itself. At this highest

level we merge with the process itself. The Hindus call this state Nirvana, or Bliss."

***

I put down the sheets of paper and looked at mother with a mixture of surprise and admiration. They were also about the Messenger, but an earlier version. Not the deep stuff you read above. I was in the habit of reviewing my notes with her whenever I had an opportunity. The contents invariably come to me as a surprise.

"This is what you wrote, Mama?"

She smiled.

Her fingers... she couldn't write anymore. I asked, "Did I really write this?"

She cleared her throat but nothing came out. Apparently I was already on my own.

"Yes, Mama?"

Now I know that Raphael must have stood at her elbow. She would never have been able to write such....

"Just how did you know?" I still couldn't believe it. "It's in your handwriting, Mama. No one scribbles as badly as you do!"

She heard me. There was that smile.

"I brought you a little excerpt from the Secret Garden, by Shabistari, a Sufi mystic, Mama. Would you like to hear it?"

She nodded, though I doubted she would hear well enough to appreciate the poetry. No matter. I read slowly, not even looking at the piece of paper.

In an instant, rise from time and space
Set the world aside and become a world within yourself

There was more.

I watched her eyes. She seemed to absorb the words, even as I read them. For a moment a thought crossed my mind that perhaps, just perhaps, I too could be a messenger. In small measure. Just for her. Then, with equal certainty I realized that we all are. Sometimes. And the next moment her eyes grew misty, as though all thought had left her. As I closed my eyes, I felt a great joining, deep inside me; a great stirring. Like something strange and wondrous coming alive. I must have read her thoughts. I heard them inside my head. “It won’t be long now,” she said. “It won’t be long now…”

***

24

Blessing

There were no more floor tiles to count. As of last month, five years after father's death, mother sat in the wheelchair, while I pushed her slowly along the procession of kings. That was what she called it, when she was still capable of speech. We moved slowly, to fill the time, I suppose. Even now, as we left her room, she raised one hand an inch above the armrest and whispered *król. Król* means king in Polish. She remembered. Annette walked ahead, attracting mother's attention. With nothing to look at, she tended to doze off. Or else my Annette pushed the chair, while I walked beside the wheelchair, holding on to mother's hand. She liked that. Sometimes her grip was surprisingly strong, considering she lacked strength to feed herself. To raise a cup of coffee to her lips.

Old age is cruel. On all of us. Young and old, although in quite different ways.

Sometimes, when sunny, we would take her down in the elevator to the car park. There was a sizable lawn, some footpaths, and a few flowerbeds. Annette and I would stop at each and every flower, point it out, extract a smile from mother's lips and then go on. It was a different kind of smile. Her eyes seemed to be asking, "How could I not smile? You are trying so hard to make me happy." Really. She seemed to be saying those very words with her eyes.

Funny that. There was no need to extract smiles from her lips when she slept. It was always there. It lingered on for minutes after she woke up.

"The gladioli, Mama, aren't they pretty?"

"Yes," she'd reply in a voice slightly above a whisper. Her throat seemed to have been drying up by the week. If a car was just being parked close by, I wouldn't hear her voice at all.

"What, Mama? Please try to speak up..."

"I am speaking up..."

"Look at that Clematis, Mama." It climbed over the trestle gate to the wooden platform we would often visit. "Look, the Trumpet Honeysuckle . . . the Sweet Peas...." Earlier in the spring we might point out Forsythia, closer to autumn, those Asters.... Look Mama...."

She looked. She smiled at the flowers. All of them. Sometimes she would point out one that we missed. This made us smile in turn. It became a game. A silent game of find your flower.

There was little conversation. The best we could hope for was to have mother join us, mostly me, in humming an old song from fifty or sixty years ago. Her recollection of those days seemed far better than what happened yesterday. Or that same morning, for that matter. They called it dementia. She understood me better when I crouched besides her chair than when I was standing up. She liked it when I was little. My grey beard didn't seem to matter. When I crouched down, I was again her little boy, I suppose? Her first born.

Until two years ago, every Sunday mother would take a cab to our place. The table was always laid out as though for a long awaited VIP. It was *the* lunch of the week. We would have everything ready so that we could both spend all our time in her presence. As though they were precious moments. As though there weren't many of them left.

Then, after coffee and a chat, we would all three drive back to the Institute, take her up to her room, help her with her coat, shoes, sit her down in her armchair, give her a sip of some juice a kind nurse would have left out for her. Later, we would leave her with her happy dreams.

Then, one day, she met us with a walker. Some weeks later the Sunday lunches were over. For some reason she convinced herself that she'd lost the ability to walk. Altogether. Not even from her wheelchair to her bed. The doctor said that such things were common. He gave no medical reason for it.

"It happens," he said, an understanding smile never leaving his face. I was beginning to find those complaisant smiles a bit annoying. "To all of us," he added, "sooner or later. Your mother is ninety-seven years old," he said.

Now there was a surprise.

"But her heart is still strong," the doctor said in an obvious attempt at cheering us up. "Very strong."

It did not cheer us up. Mother was always active. Or as the good doctor would say, very active. We both knew, Annette and I, that she would not be as happy in a wheelchair. A week later mother explained it to us.

"I don't want to live any more," she said in a steady voice. Steadier than she'd spoken for a while.

She repeated this same sentiment each time we came to see her. Twice a week. Initially, she would also ask, "Why am I still alive?" There was no anguish in her voice, just curiosity. God, for mother, was the personification not only of goodness and compassion, but of logic. She wanted to understand His thoughts. Like Einstein.

"Things always happen the way they should," she averred frequently.

And now, for some time now, she could not understand why God was keeping her alive.

"I don't think God has a great deal to do with it, Mama," I tried to free her from her mindset. "We are given free will. We make our choices."

"But I am a Catholic, Steve." She rasped, her throat dry again. "We don't make our choices. We are told what to do."

Again, there was neither complaint nor attack in the tone of her voice. Just acceptance. Or, what is not as good, total submission. Apparently not to the will of God, only to the teaching of the Church. "We are told what to do..." she repeated again, seemingly listening to her own voice. What had happened to all the discussions we'd had?

In the past, she often assured me that there were very wise men who spent their lifetime trying to determine what is good for us. No, not physicians, but the elders of the Church. The pope, the cardinals, bishops, priests. Such people.

"And who told them what to do, Mama?"

She only smiled. The expression on her face implied that I was still young, that one day I would understand. I'm still waiting.

And then something changed. She stopped asking about life. The anger that both Annette and I detected towards the end of her inquiries about her lot in life, ceased. Evaporated. She was no longer angry. She no longer asked us anything. We continued to come to see her regularly twice a week. On weekends and once during the week. Invariably, we would find her sleeping. I often wondered if we were doing her any favours by waking her up with our presence. She seemed content, when asleep. There was an unearthly peace on her face. That enigmatic smile. Also, when she came to, for a while there was a great distance between us, as though she was coming back from a place far, far away.

She stopped complaining about anything.

No more aches and pains. No 'why am I still alive' questions. No mention of her incontinence. No comments about the noise in the corridors. No comments about anything. She seemed strangely content. Not just resigned but definitely content. Whatever was eating at her, whatever had caused her previous anger, dissatisfaction, rebellion . . . was all gone.

As far as the world we lived in was concerned, my mother had already left it. In a manner of speaking, my mother had already died.

Sometimes she emerged to visit us.

I'll never forget her smile. Imagine. Being tied up in a wheelchair for two hours, then fed slop, everything was puréed, then put to bed for a few hours, then two hours up again, dinner, and back to bed. Three times a day her diapers were changed. Sometimes more often. There was seldom if ever any bad smell in her room. Perhaps that was why she refused most of the food. She didn't want to offend our sensibilities. She hardly ate at all.

And in spite of all this, she smiled. The smile filled her eyes, spread her lips to expose three remaining teeth. Yellow teeth, almost brown. There was no way to clean them. Yet her face displayed an open, sincere, appreciative smile of contentment.

This was, at least to me, the greatest mystery.

We visited mother this morning. For the half-hour that we were there, her smile again illuminated her room, the corridors where we wheeled her, the main hall where twenty or so sad faces resignedly waited for lunch. Actually, three of the faces did greet us, mother, Annette and me, with an expectant grin; as though hoping for something to happen that would dispel their misery.

Not really surprising. There are people there, who, during the last ten years hadn't been blessed with a single visitor. The husbands, or wives, or children were all either dead or too far away to visit. Some had emigrated all the way to Vancouver, some had even settled in the United States. I often wondered why people had children. Is it for the joy of those first few years when the innocence is bursting out from their round, sparkling eyes? Those first few years when one can actually hold them close and cuddle those bundles of joy and innocence that boggles the mind? Those few years before the daily tantrums begin, followed by cigarettes, kegs of beer, parties with pot and the years of nights of worry while waiting for the teenage daughter to come back at night?

"Of course I trust you, darling. Of course I do."

How often had I heard that? Somehow it did not make the waiting any shorter. Or easier. "Of course we trust you, dear." Then why do we wait up, sometimes till the early hours?

I heard people say that they were blessed with children. Our little blessings, they said. I never thought of myself as being my mother's blessing. Rather an occasional hardship. A cause for apprehension, disquiet, concern . . . when waiting for my fever to drop, for my breathing to return to normal, the colour to return to my cheeks. A strange blessing indeed.

No, definitely I would never consider myself a blessing. Nor any other children I've known. Of any age. We are always causes for concern. If lucky, of occasional pride, and then concern again. And again....

Sure some of us visit our parents when they are unable to visit us. But that hardly seems like much to pay back for the years and years of room and board, and laundry and oodles and oodles of love. No. I have been blessed with parents – not they with me. A different story altogether.

And now this long saga of being blessed with such wonderful parents is coming to an end.

I spoke to Sister Mary today. We talked about resuscitation, IV and other methods of extending life. The Sister was quite understanding. We agreed that we would not submit mother to the indignity of extending the hardship of her present condition.

Mother was semi-conscious today. She reacted with a glazed look, yes, with a smile even though it seemed as vague as her eyes. Perhaps she didn't really want to come back from the reality where she'd been spending most of her time lately.

She sleeps more and more. The staff wakes her up only for meals. The meals she hardly eats.

I suspect that her dream reality is more tangible for her, more genuine and authentic, than the here and now we all share. She goes in and out of the parallel universes. She escapes into a different realm altogether. I recall a verse from Revelations. "Him that overcometh will I make a pillar in the temple of my God, and he shall go no more out...."

Him or her, I presume. My mother is still going in and out of that strange reality from which she invariably emerges with a smile. A distant smile. A day will come, soon, when she shall go no more out. She'll remain enveloped in that smile that shines through even to our valley of tears. Until then, she'll continue to sleep. More and more. Longer and longer. Can anyone blame her?

The whole Institute is falling asleep. Perhaps this is the greatest if not the only blessing of the old. Sleep. The land of dreams, of actuality where all things are possible, where they can go in and out at will. From wherever they are.

"And now you will go and I shall sleep," she whispered, often, within ten or fifteen minutes of our arrival.

"I'm so sleepy..." she would whisper as often.

Perhaps mother dreams she's at the Institute. Am I a man dreaming I'm a butterfly or a butterfly dreaming I'm a man? Perhaps she's a butterfly that dreams that she's a woman. Perhaps she comes back just to say hello to me, to Annette, Bart, his daughters, his wife? Just to give us her smile. A gift from beyond.

Perhaps mother stopped asking questions because of her hearing. It got really bad. Even with an 'ear-mic' she doesn't hear much. I think it's also a question of concentration. She might even hear, but not understand. Not absorb, metabolize.

Yet immediately before this present state, she admitted to me that she'd asked questions she'd never asked in her lengthy lifetime before. I wonder why people leave *those* questions till the very end. And who, amongst us, is competent to answer them? Perhaps Father Mulligan, but he, mother had said, is also a searcher. Shouldn't we all be? All the time?

I found, not just with mother, that the closer one is to the Gate, the more one is unsure of one's direction. Would that be true if one were to ask the way, the directions, much, much sooner? Oh, mother is blessed with a deep-rooted faith. Surely, that is a great blessing. But, it seems to me, that even faith is not a substitute for knowledge. A knowledge that comes after some twenty or thirty years of daily contemplation. Descartes claims that he thinks, and therefor he is. *Cogito ergo sum.* I disagree. I know, and therefore I am. I do not stop being when I stop thinking. Not if I know who I am.

I found this among her notes. As usual, her thoughts had been written on a number of small bits of paper, as if she'd been unsure just how long the flow would be coming. Also, the ideas were put down in a shaky hand, with some words overlapping, others slurring into long, compound words, such as Germans like to do. I've done my best to reflect her thoughts. I don't know when mother wrote them but they go a long way to explain her smile. Her constant smile.

I'm suspended in the vastness of space at the cross axes of the universe. My mind envelops me on all sides. I am a sphere yet the sphere is not me. The sphere, the universe pulsates. It reacts to pleasure and pain. I watch it as it reacts with the world. With temporal reality. Often it is fascinating. But it does not affect me. Not really. I know it is not me. It is what I used to interact with. It gives me pleasure and pain, unless I reject them both. But it does not bring happiness. That comes only from within.

I am protected from the outer fringes of the universe by a luminous haze. These are my emotions. They change colour. They oscillate like reflections of flowers in the ripple of a mountain lake at sunset. The colours are set against the purest blue. Sometimes they become quite red, almost crimson, then they dissipate, and are gradually replaced by other hues. Beautiful blues, and greens and yellows. A little like Aurora Borealis, only all around me. Now and then I see golden shades reflected in the outer shell of my mind. These are wonderful moments. Pure gold, sparkling in the intensity of my happiness. A sun of my own.

When am I happiest?

When I sleep. I withdraw within. Nothing is impossible in my sleep. I cross galaxies, I enter the fiery hearts of stars, I perform miracles, untrammelled by my mind. There is no sense of logic to curb my freedom.

How do I know? How do I know that I am asleep?

I don't. Not really.

There is sleep of the dead and there is sleep of the living. Most people are not alive yet, not fully awake. Some are dormant to the point of indifference. Others are just beginning to awaken. I meet some of them. There they grow in numbers further out. Closer to the perimeter of my mind. It is only when I am fully awake that I can also be fully aware of my dreams. And that only happens when my body is asleep. Conscious, uninhibited, unrestricted dreams. Beyond my mind. On the other side of the sphere. Why do you think a baby's eyes shine so when they awaken? They, in their dreams, they were fully awake.

I don't understand most of this.

Perhaps mother doesn't know whether she is still alive. It doesn't seem to matter that much. Perhaps she just oscillates between the universes, realities, realms of happiness of which we can only dream but cannot imagine....

"Say hello to Dad," she asked the other day in a whisper. "Tell him I am coming."

I thought she was already there.

She sounded as though Dad and we still lived together. She was about to join us. We are not what we seem to be. I think that our true selves remain beyond the horizon, at the end of a glorious rainbow, beyond the sphere of our mind, beyond the wondrous tunnel of light, waiting for our fragmented consciousness to return to our true and only reality. To become whole, again. But, in truth, we never really leave that realm. It is our home.

Watching her face, it is evident to me, to Annette, that we are not our body but rather a state of consciousness. We are states of consciousness that, if we're lucky, manifest down here, below, as a happy, disarming smile. That alone is our blessing. A moment of joy. When mother finally chooses to go out no more, I'll miss that smile most of all.

*****

Epilogue

After almost three years of suspended animation, on December 12th, at the age of ninety-nine, mother died in her sleep. I was wrong about her smile. I still see it, behind my closed eyelids, whenever I think of her. It is by far her most lasting gift.

Acknowledgment

I would be remiss were I not to thank Bryn Symonds and Madeleine Witthoeft for their diligent editing, each in his and her inimitable way. I am indebted to my many friends for their meticulous proof-reading with particular thanks going to Adam Goldman, who took great pains to perfect my manuscript. As always my gratitude to my wife, Bozena Happach, who put up with being a grass widow for weeks on end, and then offered me her inspired insights.

Sincerely,

Stan I.S. Law

INHOUSEPRESS, CANADA
http://www.inhousepress.ca

932452013-Gate.pdf

CPSIA information can be obtained at www.ICGtesting.com
Printed in the USA
LVOW10s0231050316

477880LV00023B/313/P

9 780978 026707